MW00849472

A SKETCH OF THE FADING SUN

A Sketch
of the
Fading Sun

Stories by
Wan-suh Park

Edited and Translated by
Hyun-Jae Yee Sallee

Introduction by
He-ran Park

White Pine Press • Buffalo, New York

WHITE PINE PRESS
P.O. Box 236, Bufalo, New York 14201

Copyright ©1999by Wan-suh Park
Translation copyright ©1999 by Hyun-jae Yee Sallee
Introduction copyright ©1999 by He-ran Park

All rights reserved. This work, or portions thereof,
may not be reproduced in any form without permission.

This is a work of fiction. Names, characters, places,
and incidents are either the product of the author's imagination
or are used fictitiously, and any resemblance to actual persons,
living or dead, events, or locales is entirely coincidental.

Publication of this book was made possible, in part,
by grants from the National Endowment for the Arts
the New York State Council on the Arts,
and the Korean Cultural Foundation.

Book design: Elaine LaMattina

Printed and bound in the United States of America

1   3   5   7   9   10   8   6   4   2

Library of Congress Cataloging-in-Publication Data

Park, Wan-suh, 1931—
A sketch of the fading sun / stories by Wan-suh Park ;
edited and translated by Hyun-jae Yee Sallee ; introduction by He-ran Park.
p.cm — (Dispatches series ; 4)
ISBN 1-877727- 93-8 (alk. paper)
I. Title   II. Series   III. Sallee, Hyun-jae Yee.
PL992.62.W34S54 1999
895.7'3421—dc21   99-045700
CIP

Contents

INTRODUCTION

THE EMERGENCE OF WOMEN FROM AN ARCHAIC ROLE

Although it is a cliche to say that life is a continuing saga of the relationship between man and woman, a vast number of literary works have been written dealing with man-woman relationships. Notwithstanding, there has rarely been much written that has grasped, much less challenged, the relationship between man and woman as being one of oppression. As Wan-suh Park notes in the epilogue of her work, *The Beginning of the Day Alive*, it would be safe to say that most writing considered as literature beautifies this oppressive relationship between the two genders.

Park feels that not only the oppressor but the oppressed are disguised in the relationship between the genders by "a mask of beautiful and familiar public morals." This mask has been passed from one generation of women to another until it has become almost a woman's flesh. Consequently, her mask can never be taken off and thrown away without her shedding blood. Park, who shudders at the violent nature of men, as depicted in literature, uses the cruel phrase "blood shedding," and implies that it is impossible to solve this repressive relationship through "understanding and compromise."

Writers, both men and women, who make a self-claim of throwing themselves into the liberation of mankind, often lean toward treating the problems of women as secondary. This stems from ignorance, based on the misunderstanding that women's problems are somewhat different from those of humanity or society as a whole. Those few writers who have tasted commercial success by superficially writing of women's problems want only to depict women's lives as those of human beings, assuming the attitude that the difference between man and woman is innate and unalterable. These writers amicably advise feminists, who assert that society regards woman as "woman" and not as a human being, that it would be well for them to discard this hyper-persecution complex.

Park continuously questions what causes our society to put a noose around women. In spite of our changing times, this attitude seems incapable of being changed. She points out that this is a male-dominant mentality which has evolved within the culture of a patriarchal system.

Korea's highly developed economic status, which has been accomplished during the past thirty years, has made it inevitable that women be included in the work force. Subsequently, without actually being noticed, women's participation in society has changed in an atmosphere where this participation has been accepted as a natural flow. As it stepped into the '80s, the legal system's discrimination against women appeared on the surface to be nearly extinct. However, if you look carefully, you can easily observe that the total landscape of discrimination against women has changed very little.

Along with rapid capitalization, the authoritative political culture, which has been firmly maintained, has only deepened our search for the meaning of life as decent human beings. However, this culture has failed to present a new model. Accordingly, the delineation of life in Korean literature has ruled us, not leaving us alone to reshape our own lives. In a land where authoritarianism and materialism reign, what man would truly enjoy the lifestyle of a decent human being? By the same token, to survive as a woman in this landscape is deemed to be excruciatingly painful. In order to sustain men's inhumane lives, the inhuman life of women is necessarily even more stringently demanded. Hasn't the theory of our patriarchal system pressed women to "look after" and "comfort" men at all times?

Upon the change in the world, no matter how the level of a woman's education may have been raised and her economic muscle strengthened, a woman is prohibited as yet from being emotionally independent. This inequality in the relationship between a man and a woman is not only nature's providence, but also an order system that enables a society to function properly and is deemed to be the most beautiful virtue in the entire human relationship. Therefore, those who have challenged this inequality have not always escaped punishment. Since the growth of a human being is a process of adapting to a socially controlled value system, in order for a woman to grow, she must actually restrain herself. This is a self-contradiction—her growth as a woman translates into her refusal to grow as a human being!

Women's resistance, however, has continued as tenaciously as the history of the patriarchal system. Since their resistance was not organized but formulated only on personal dimensions, it could not of necessity develop into a challenge to culture itself. Although this challenge has been attempted every now and then in literary works, it could not reach beyond the frame of personal, existential angst. This is because our writers as a whole have simply not been mature enough to penetrate the structure of our enormous and complicated culture and discover the patriarchal system which serves as its infrastructure,

Only recently have women understood their problems as part of the general vision of human freedom and united themselves to establish a new direction in their efforts to solve these problems. It wasn't until the latter part of the 70's that these efforts evolved into a new, distinct social movement. Its ultimate goal was to create and produce a change of both system and culture in the humanization of women, democratization of society, and rejection of the patriarchal system which suppresses human nature. In other words, this women's movement was freed from the frame (tradition) of the movement which would merely improve women's position. Instead, it pointed to equal freedom.

It was at this opportune point in time that Park's works, which dealt with the lives of highly-educated, middle-class housewives who were solving their problems from the viewpoint of women's freedom, emerged. What historically profound meaning do these works have when viewed in relationship to the Korean women's movement? None of Park's women characters have ever experienced participation in the women's movement. Park herself has never experienced such participation. Park has stated that she has never regarded herself as a feminist writer and therefore has never intentionally written a story to fall in that category:

> In any event, I have not even once felt an urge consciously to engage in feminist literature. I think feminist literature can be born by itself, without a deliberate attempt, in the process of making good literature. If it is genuinely good literature, in my opinion, it must be regarded as feminist literature. I declare that women's position has been ruled by a cunning and clever system. As opposed to the viewpoint of men, who have been living in the position of oppressing women, the women themselves can see most clearly the contradiction in every class and walk of life in our society.

Women in Park's works resist the fixed idea of a society which demands for a man-woman relationship to be one of control/obedience. If home is a true nest, these women believe that a sense of harmony should be formed in the family, regardless of what type of relationship the man and woman find mutually satisfactory.

Nevertheless, every husband in Park's works regards his wife only as a possession, refusing to recognize her emotional independence. Take for instance In-chul Chung in *Beginning of the Day Alive*. He considers his wife's economic capability and even her own time as his possessions. For instance, he is not at all sorry for being late when he has agreed to meet his wife at an appointed time.

> He loved to be masculine. He nearly worshipped this aspect of himself. This "masculinity" which he worships also encompasses a dim memory of his appointment with his wife. Even if he remembered it clearly, the result would have been the same. Just as in every other aspect of his possessive relationship with his wife, it seemed obvious to him what he had, and that what belonged to his wife belonged to him as well. Thus his wife's time belonged to him. The fact that his wife's time belonged to her and her alone, he did not consciously recognize.

According to one of the heroines, marriage is a "humiliating relationship" as a "woman gives all and receives back only one percent."

From the beginning, due to a fear that women might conspire to revolt, which stems from the nature of a relationship which lacks symmetry, men exercise a strong power of control, which they term "masculinity." The belief that a "one-to-one equality" between a man and a woman simply does not exist has been used to justify man's violence; and this belief has been handed down from generation to generation.

The relationship which distinguishes the oppressor from the oppressed is the same relationship which exists between husband and wife. At this stage, it is "destiny" for a woman to become the oppressed and the man the oppressor. Within a marriage, the relationship between a man and his wife depends solely upon the woman's ability to display a high degree of "womanliness," which she does in order to maintain a harmonious marriage. Her capability in this realm is considered a virtue (a.k.a. mask) that society demands from a woman.

In the power struggle between a man and his wife, who is dominated, Park tries to depict the reality of this same pattern of patriarchal power even when the wife enjoys economic independence. In a capitalistic society, where money is the most powerful essence, these capable women make a great financial contribution to their respective households. Yet, just because of their economic power, these women are in reality oppressed. Park tells with complete candor how the cunning patriarchal system rules.

It is inevitable for a woman to work due to economic hardship, and it is even considered commendable to do so since it is deemed to be "wife's help." Working outside the home to help her husband is a necessary action and can even be regarded as virtuous. By the same token, if her purpose for working is not solely to earn money, but also to pursue her personal desire to better herself, then she cannot be forgiven since it is interpreted as a challenge to her husband. A woman cannot cross over the perimeter of a set range of qualities of "womanliness." This subtle rule implies that she must work only for one purpose: to help her husband. In the life sketches which appear in

Park's works, she portrays with great versatility middle-class women workers who are saturated with this notion.

In any event, it is a big mistake for anyone to think that men refuse to accept women's ability to make money or even to accept the money itself. In some stories, Park depicts husbands as thus being both the product and the prisoners of capitalism. These men consider it ugly for a woman to covet work, yet money possessed by a woman greatly enhances her "spark" of "womanliness."

> Essentially unbearable to her was an insult to her job, which she considered a worse insult than an insult to her as a human being. She loved and respected her job. A job provides not only a strong sense of independence but also a root of self-respect for a woman. It was a matter of values, whether this was recognized or not.
>
> "Beloved, Are You Still"

It is an even a greater humiliation for a woman to have her job insulted than for her to be physically abused or sexually humiliated. From this kind of woman, we, the readers, anticipate as reality the possibility of emergence from her traditional role.

The sexual relationship, getting away from the perimeter of purely animal instincts, enters into a dimension of power. A woman's body is not a weapon, but a man's body is a weapon in that relationship. However, the world indulges in portraying women as persons who, in making deals, use their bodies as a weapon. Park tells us that ultimately the principle of man's role as active and a woman's as passive applies and is expressed even in the sexual relationship between a man and wife. Park's view on this common saying is that a woman's body in any case is nothing but a last yearning plea for a partner's mercy. Not only that, but in her writings it is men who reveal their bodies.

A "mask" which a woman recognizes as imposed on her, or a "shell" whose true color she recognizes does not necessarily motivate her to take it off or emerge to prove that she is alive. Through her characters, Park speaks for those who are afraid of changes in their lives. For instance, Kyung-sook, one of her characters, holds an impressive position. No matter how vain had been her married life in reality or how cruel her oppression had been in the past, she comes to the conclusion that her married life is better than nothing at all. Thus she returns home. She cannot bear the thought of not being a wife.

> The only place which still held a trace of her, which still held the rewards of her life, the place where she had lived and the only place in the whole wide world where she was indispensable was her home."
>
> "A Standing Woman "

In spite of unbearable personal humiliation in marriage, in reality those women who are incapable of supporting themselves after a divorce have no choice but to stay in that oppressive marriage. However, one of Park's characters comes to a reality check after twenty years of marriage. Chung-hee admits that her twenty years of married life with her husband have been "mercilessly destroyed and cunningly concealed." Whether she so desires or not, her life with her husband is trying to arise from the ashes of marriage right in front of her eyes. (From *The Beginning of the Day Alive*) A woman who dared not look into her husband's eyes begins to reveal freely her inner self. Thus she throws away the mask of womanliness, which she has been wearing thus far and expresses herself without any reservations.

> "Look here, I am not afraid of being unattractive to you anymore...I don't regard a man as my destiny any longer. Like work or children, a man is only part of my destiny. That's that!"
>
> "The Beginning of the Day Alive"

Chung-hee decides that the one and only way for her to prove she is alive is to dissolve her marriage with her husband and become independent. Thus she embarks on the bloody task of "peeling off" the mask.

Park depicts, nearly in despair, the structure of the patriarchal system encompassing our lives and the effect of its obstinate root. By describing this reality, Park drives her readers into a pit of despair. As for providing any insight into a solution of women's problems (in other words, a possibility of women's liberation), she shows instead an extreme pessimism. The choice of two women in her stories, divorce, Park leaves hanging under a big question mark. Can divorce truly be a first step in solving women's problems?

Nevertheless, Park has succeeded in writing about women who penetrated the deepest roots of the structure of women's oppression. This fact alone indicates her suggestion for the future of women's liberation. Unlike stereotypical women, women portrayed in Park's works are not the helpless ones who lament not being able to free themselves from the tight grip of fate. Park's women are not passive ones who end up contributing, out of a sense of self-abandonment and self-ruin, to this deep-seated social structure, thus helping to maintain our present patriarchal structure. These women are independent and free-willed, able to grow and expand themselves through maladjustment to society, not by adjusting to society unconditionally. Therefore, Park has already suggested the future path of women's liberation by depicting women who could assert proudly and decisively, "I am."

Ms. Park stands at our center as the author most capable of supporting the body of women's liberation, which has just been born.

—He-ran Park
Instructor in Women's Studies
Ewha Women's University
Seoul, Korea

TRANSLATOR'S NOTE

As is generally true of any birth, the birth of this anthology was indeed difficult. From its inception, I have crossed countless bumpy stretches of a steep and winding road. I had to wrestle with the many facets and levels of Ms. Park's plots, but her engrossing tales must be told. Readers will be rewarded not only by the entertainment value of Ms. Park's writing, but by close and emotionally-deep glimpses into Korean history and culture.

The various selections in this anthology have been carefully chosen by the Daesan Foundation and the author. Five stories were chosen, each portraying the world as it appears to members of a varied group of beholders, from the eyes of a child to those of a shrewd physician. The stories encompass life as it has progressed from pre-modern into contemporary Korean society. Ms. Park's keen eyes and sharp mind combine with her use of words to enable us to see, hear, and feel the pain, joy, defeats, and triumphs of these ordinary people, the backbone of society. I have tried to deliver her message as eloquently as possible so that English-speaking readers who cannot read Korean might feel and taste the familiar emotions and flavors that life constantly throws at us all, even though we experience them on opposite sides of the globe.

I cannot find adequate words to express my gratitude and appreciation to those who helped bring this anthology to light. I would like to thank Marion Peterson, my long-time friend, for her tireless editing and re-editing; Dr. Yumi Chun for her seemingly impossible task of comparing my translation to the original and straightening out my lapses; Professor Judith Hemschemeyer and my husband, Rawleigh Sallee, for their keen critique. Without their emotional support and encouragement, I may easily have become too discouraged to continue during the wintry hours of this project.

I am grateful to the Daesan Foundation for making this anthology a reality. Without its financial support, it would have been impossible to carry out this task. I am also gratified by the genuine interest and continued support of Korean literature shown by Dennis Maloney, editor/publisher of the White Pine Press.

May we all celebrate life and everything in it!

—Hyun-jae Yee Sallee

During Three Days of Autumn

1. Three Days Before

Only three days left.

Outside the window, fall beckons. Each day the sun peers more boldly and deeply through the south window. The velvet armchair by the window, once boasting a rich hunter green fabric, has faded to a soft ashen gray. Brushed in a certain direction, the gray fabric becomes mustard green. The chair has had a useless existence. It has been standing in the same spot for more than three decades now, doing nothing but changing colors as the sun embraced it. From the beginning, the chair has been abandoned, bereft of purpose.

The Korean War still ravaged the country in the spring of '53. Rumors of a cease-fire brought a stirring of life in Seoul. Although the city's population swelled considerably as each day went by, it was too early for the government to return to the capital city. Twenty-seven years old and single, I bravely came to the city alone to open an office, and I searched like a hawk for an ideal location.

I was more than qualified for my line of work. The only possible obstacle to my success was my girlish looks. Right before the war raped our nation, I graduated from the Women's Medical School. During the war, I took care of wounded soldiers who were transferred to its affiliated hospital. As a refugee during the war, I worked for a woman doctor who was my senior in my medical school days. She and her husband opened a joint practice and enjoyed thriving success before he was drafted as a military doctor. Left alone, she became swamped with the heavy workload, and that's when I came to her rescue. Back then, the professional physicians' system was not established as rigidly as it is now. Based on my colorful and sweeping experience as a doctor during the war, I was confident I had all the qualifications required to open my own office. I was not concerned about what kind of medicine I should practice since it was entirely my own decision.

Since the government had not yet returned to Seoul, office space was readily available in the heart of the city. However, I adopted a wait-and-see strategy, postulating that the value of real estate would skyrocket upon the imminent return of the government. Furthermore, I presumed that renowned specialty doctors with shining degrees would occupy those locations which would be considered "gold mines." I decided it would be best for me to deliberately avoid these hot spots.

I resolved to open my office in a less sophisticated residential area in the outskirts of Seoul, and I shopped around to locate an appropriate and adequate place. Finally, I found a dream location where I am renting my current office—the floor above Kyungsung Store. Back then, over thirty years ago, this area was the official gate to the east of Seoul. Once you crossed the railroad tracks, you stepped on the ground of Yangjoo, a county where the foul odor of fuel stifled your nostrils.

The sign on the Kyungsung Store, written in Chinese characters, was reminiscent of an earlier time. Kyungsung was the name they used for the capital city during the Yi Dynasty. The store sold farm equipment and implements to the locals. Betraying its literal meaning, *capital city*, the overall impression of the Kyungsung Store was extremely rustic and provincial, a tapestry of the surrounding landscape. Nevertheless, the name of the store, although the store itself was so countrified, gave reassurance to the people of Yangjoo who left home at the crack of dawn with their oxen-pulled or horse-harnessed carts for the early morning market to trade firewood. The name, Kyungsung Store, brought them a sense of relief. They were actually out of Yangjoo town and now entering the city of Seoul.

The old man at the real estate office in the neighborhood informed me that the second floor of the Kyungsung Store was available. He took me there to show me around the place, and I noticed the sign for Kyungsung Photo Studio upstairs. I was told that the photographer who had rented the place was missing during the war, and since then the studio had been unoccupied. Every useful item had been stolen, and it had become a messy playground for urchins in the neighborhood.

The door and the partition between the studio and the living quarters were detached and lay where they had fallen on the floor. The black curtain once used in the dark room was shredded into pieces and transformed into rags. The door leading to the stairs was no longer there. Moreover, every single window was broken. In the midst of this forlorn scene of disarray, I found a luxurious velvet armchair. The chair gave the impression of an effeminate prince brought from his kingdom as a hostage to a strong, violent country. The chair looked strange, yet noble.

Later I realized that the velvet chair was too extravagant for any setting, even a setting not in such shambles. In fact, it was a thorn in the eyes of the beholder. I didn't think it would find an ideal place for its worth. The chair was not made for a person to sit down and rest, nor did it complement the other furniture. The sole purpose for its existence undoubtedly had been to serve as a prop in a professional photograph. When you see an old-fashioned studio photograph, you see one person sitting in a chair while another stands by it. When it happens to be a portrait, it is quite common to see one standing stiffly, resting a hand lightly on the back of the chair. To celebrate a precious son's hundredth day since his birth, the comfortable and good-looking chair might have been used to take a picture of the naked baby boy, cradled alone by the chair. The velvet chair, therefore, might have been especially ordered for this purpose. Its wooden back was impressively high and was decorated with a hand-carved Phoenix. Each arm rest boasted a hand-carved, twisted dragon. The chair was unreasonably lavish, particularly in the midst of the chaotic empty room, and the sight of all this threw me into an utter sense of bewilderment.

The old man from the neighborhood real estate agency seemed to interpret my silence as a sign of approval for the place. He trumpeted his confidence that he could negotiate with the owner on the monthly rent and try to persuade him to compensate me for the expense of repairing and redecorating the office. He declared optimistically that he'd make sure I'd be the winner when the talk was over between the owner and himself, and he then went downstairs. Old Man Whang was and still is the owner of the Kyungsung Store. Left all alone upstairs, I was gripped with the intense curiosity of a little girl whose heart pounds with desire to try on her mother's clothes while she is alone in the house. In a similar mood, I sat gingerly on that velvet chair. Even then, the chair was placed by the window, facing the south.

Across the main thoroughfare, the old Agricultural High School had been transformed into an army base for American military personnel. The landscape of the current neighborhood had changed to high rise apartment complexes. An experimental laboratory extended to the vast assembly ground where countless Quonset huts were erected, reminiscent of mushrooms. An American MP in a helmet guarded the front gate of the school.

I had been enveloped in a strange sensation when I first stepped into this neighborhood. I had seen some degree of potential here in spite of the unavoidable impression that the entire area was a slum. Poverty hovered over the town, but, although I couldn't immediately put my finger on it, something else didn't feel right. More than poverty plagued the area. It was contaminated with a peculiar air of whorishness. Soon after, I found an answer: the American military base.

Shaking my head to dispel such an undesirable thought, I sprang out of the velvet chair and stood up straight. I felt as though I were locked up. I didn't know what to do with myself. I could only pace the floor back and forth. The floor creaked as if it were screaming.

Unwittingly I began to gather up the crumpled photos that were scattered around the floor. I saw a picture of a school girl with short blunt hair. She supported her chin with two hands, her expression serious. A handsome, one-year-old baby boy's birthday picture caught my eye. I also saw a picture of a gracefully aged elderly couple sitting side by side, leaving some space between them. Their children must have expressed their filial regard for their parents by having the photograph taken. Stamp-sized identification photos displayed various faces, yet I felt a unifying element in all of them, as in pictures taken at different times and from different angles yet all of the same stone face.

Naturally, I recognized *none* of those faces. Strangely, however, I felt a compelling closeness to these people in the different pictures, understanding that we had shared a single strong stroke of fate: the Korean War. The war was a commonly-shared experience to every person on the peninsula. As we went through this trauma in our national history, what kind of wrenching adjustments had each made to pacify the hand of Fate, I wondered.

I shook my head emphatically again as if I wanted to dust off something swiftly from my body, and I resumed picking up those pictures on the floor. Then I picked up an erotic picture of a naked man and woman in a grotesque, twisted position. Immediately I tore it into pieces with my trembling hands; stepping backwards, I sank into the velvet chair. However, I could not suppress the surge of emotions that sprang from my body as I shredded the picture. I lived again a sordid act of fate in my own life. I remembered all too well his stifling odor. As if it were a broom, the bushy hair on his chest swept my face whenever he moved. His limbs, long and strong like a rope, crushed me as I felt an excruciating pain when he invaded and pierced my vagina.

Just like right after I was raped, I felt the meaning of everything in life becoming obscure. I sank into a deep sense of self-loss. It was then that the old realtor reappeared, all smiles. Why in the world is that old man grinning? I was still remembering my past.

"You don't need to open your mouth. Just do as I say. Okay? We are about to have a doctor's office in our neighborhood. I am not going to do anything to harm you. Okay?" the realtor said, putting his nicotine smelling mouth close to my ear.

At the end of each sentence the old man repeated "okay" in a dialect which did not sound offensive. In fact, it was pleasing to my ears like a cute saying. Old Man Whang, the owner of the Kyungsung Store, joined us soon after. The realtor presented a contract. I offered my purse to him to use as clipboard so that he could do his paperwork comfortably. As Old Man Whang read through the contract, the realtor took my side and urged the owner to reduce the amount of the deposit. He even insisted on lowering the monthly rent to a rock bottom amount, justifying himself by finding every possible fault with the studio. Old Man Whang was either taciturn or held in check by deep-seated emotion. He was blunt and abrupt in his manners, yet he seemed involuntarily swayed by the realtor's tactics.

Thus the negotiation ended, without any complication, in my favor. Old Man Whang agreed wholeheartedly to restore the windows, and door, and even to provide a partition. The realtor filled the empty space on the contract with the agreed conditions and terms in his sesame-seed-size handwriting. Old Man Whang and I read it without much scrutiny and presented our stamps to seal the document.

Only after the contract was complete and the commission was paid, did Old Man Whang ask me what kind of specialty I was going to practice. Before I had a chance to answer, the realtor, who was used to being a spokesperson for me, volunteered an answer.

"She'll have a general practice. Didn't you say so, ma'am?" the old man said.

"No. I am going to practice gynecology," I said as I jumped out of the velvet chair. It was not an impromptu decision by any means. In fact, the nightmare I was driven to recall from the pornographic picture that had caught my eyes and the hint of a hovering brothel which I had seen in the neighborhood helped me to reach this final decision. Only a woman who is carrying an unwanted baby in her womb can fathom the magnitude of this agony. Pain of any other disease or illness can engender sympathy but the pain of carrying an unwanted baby can cause others only to mock and blame. If it is the dream of medicine to liberate people from disease, it would be my dream to free women from this lonely misery which is far worse than disease itself.

"In case she goes out of business and has to leave town, I suggest you put a statement in writing to avoid an argument concerning the repair costs. Why don't you write down—something like the owner is not responsible..." Old Man Whang said as he cast a hasty side glance at me. I could glimpse a streak of contempt on his face as he made this new suggestion to the realtor.

"Look here, my friend. How can you say something like that instead of wishing her a thriving business? Please don't be offended, ma'am. As you can see, ma'am, he has no tact with words whatsoever. He has a good heart, ma'am, and please try to understand, *okay?*" the realtor said.

"You know darn well, Uncle, about the people in our town. Don't you remember it's a simple matter for any woman to bring a baby into the world in our town? Why in the world would a decent woman, who does not wish retribution from the three goddesses of childbirth, visit a gynecologist? It's disgusting...." Old Man Whang said.

"Oh, man! You used to be so quiet and reserved when you needed to voice your opinion. Why must you now spit out rude remarks so readily? Didn't I tell you that she would open a family practice? It would be a serious problem for you if you decided to change your profession and go into a fabric business, giving up selling hoes or scythes. All she learned, mind you, is to cure people's illnesses. Are you worried that she is going to tend only those with female problems? I will buy you a drink with my commission. How about it?" the realtor said.

The realtor took Old Man Whang downstairs, nearly pushing him on his way down. As I reflected their ignorant but common perception of gynecology, I smiled sadly.

Preparation for opening my office progressed speedily. As he promised, Old Man Whang hired a carpenter and had him make and install a door, a new partition, and windows. In the meantime, I hired a painter who painted the office inside and out, and a sign shop man who hung the sign which read "Eastside Medical Clinic." I hung below it a smaller sign, "Specialty—Gynecology." At that time, used office furniture—a desk, chairs, a sofa — could be purchased very inexpensively in Seoul.

Crossing the Han River a couple of times, I could buy most of the basic medical equipment I needed. As I examined the glistening metal instruments—vaginal speculum, flexible and versatile forceps, curettes, Hegar sizes #1 to #15, and a long teaspoon-like dilator—I found my cold heart being calmed by these cold metals. Although I did not feel fully competent using these medical instruments, I was enshrouded with a peculiar sense of comfort, as though I had encountered an inevitable fate.

I also bought an examination table with stirrups which was made specifically for examining women so that their vagina could be seen as easily as their face. To most people, the examination table is nothing but a convenient piece of medical equipment, which is designed in a most scientific way to aid the practitioner. However, once a woman lies on it, she finds that it is an unbearably degrading tool of torment. I gritted my teeth as I was forced to recall my own undeserved persecution.

Every detail was complete for the opening. The photo studio was completely transformed into a doctor's office. Nevertheless, one remnant of the studio still lingered, and it was an eyesore, detracting from the decor of my new office: the velvet chair. When Old Man Whang cleaned the studio, he had put the chair aside; when the carpenter worked on the room, he did the same. And when the painter did the painting, rather than using it to stand on he covered it with a dropcloth to protect it from spilled paint. I knew the chair was absolutely useless, and yet I couldn't bring myself to give it to someone else or throw it out. Meanwhile, I neglected the chair, leaving it in the same spot by the south window where I'd first found it.

Even after all the preparations for opening the office were complete, no patients came, as Old Man Whang had foreseen. However, I wasn't that nervous about it. The velvet chair seemed foreign in a doctor's office. I was forced to feel that I wasn't quite ready to open my practice.

One day I came home from downtown after buying a few essential kitchen utensils and found someone waiting for me. The person was sitting in the velvet chair by the south window. He was not a patient, but Father. He was wearing a white cotton *durumaki* [traditional Korean robe for men] and shiny leather shoes with pointed-toes. He had a long beard and was fine looking. He was sitting comfortably in the chair, and somehow he made that useless chair impress me with its sudden elegance. At that moment, I congratulated myself on not giving it up. Nonetheless, I wasn't thrilled to see Father.

"How did you find me?" I asked.

"I dropped in the hospital where you used to work in Eri and was told of your whereabouts."

"You may rest assured that I'll be in tip-top shape no matter where I might be. Why must you insist on looking for me, especially when your health is so poor?"

To be honest, I knew nothing about the condition of Father's health. My older brothers used to urge me, the baby of the family, to get married before

Father passed away. They would make me feel guilty by reminding me that Father would not live forever. They entreated me not to cause more heartache for Father and to get married while he was still alive. I'd listened to these pleas until my ears hurt. Judging from my brothers' words, I vaguely thought Father would not live very long. Furthermore, since I'm the youngest and we lost Mother when I was a child, I'd always had a premonition that I might become an orphan. In any event, Father had never expressed to me personally that he would like to see me get married before he died. He was the last person who would interfere with his child's destiny by using himself as an excuse.

"Your office is in an excellent location." As usual, Father approved of the business upon which I'd already embarked.

"Hardly. It's in the slum area," I said, feigning innocence as I hid my inner thoughts.

"Don't you know that slums have more sick people? Please don't expect to make a fortune from your hard-learned medical training. Since olden times, the art of medicine has been called the art of healing. With that in mind, practice it with good intentions," Father said.

I had to clench my teeth to suppress bursting into laughter. No one could suspect my secret past, future, and the wrenching pain that was billowing in my heart.

Father indicated that he would leave soon. I asked him to wait a moment. I had no idea how Father interpreted my gesture; he asked me not to fret about fixing anything for him since he had no desire to eat. But I didn't detain Father to offer him something to eat. I simply did not want to see him get up from the velvet chair in which he sat so comfortably. At that moment, I could understand people's desire to have their parents' or children's picture taken in it. Although I didn't have Father's picture taken then, the vivid image of him sitting in that velvet chair with his meaningful gaze and tired yet dignified features has remained profoundly imprinted on my heart.

Father sat around a little while longer before he bashfully gave me the gift he'd brought. As he was leaving, he told me he was on his way to see my oldest brother and his family in Taejon. That was the last time I saw Father alive.

The gift that Father gave me on his visit was a framed copy of the Hippocratic Oath. I accepted it with a greedy, hearty laughter which had been suppressed while Father was preaching this and that from the velvet chair about the art of medicine and the art of healing. I didn't hang it. It became another object that I couldn't bring myself to throw out, yet which proved to be useless; from that day on, it remained in the store room.

During the past thirty years, my office has been completely renovated five or six times, although I never changed locations. I've also had the office cleaned thoroughly twice a year. Considering all these drastic changes over the years, the velvet chair should have been removed long ago. Except for the time Father sat in the chair, it has proved to be useless and has been an offensive sight. It's failed to complement other furnishings, sticking out like a sore thumb. Whenever my office went through renovations or spring cleaning, the chair was mistreated. However, I'd protect it, placing it under my wings, as it were, and then return it to its former domain. If I discarded the chair, I was afraid that I'd be obliged to hang up the Hippocratic Oath on the wall. Perhaps that was the reason I couldn't do away with the chair.

Ironically, my very first patient was Old Man Whang's daughter. Old Man Whang had been living all alone. From the north window of my office, I could look down and get a full view of the main living quarters of the Kyungsung Store. I'd seen Old Man Whang washing clothes or rice in the middle of the front courtyard of his shabby, inverted L-shaped house with its tiled roof. Judging from the makeup of the soy bean jar terrace, wooden floor, and kitchen, I could easily detect that Old Man Whang had once enjoyed a full family life. I was told that his wife had been killed by a bomb during the war while on her way to get food from her folks in the countryside; his two sons were dragged to the North; his aged mother died from illness, and his only daughter had fled alone and had not yet returned.

I hadn't the foggiest idea when his daughter returned. Old Man Whang came to me for my service in the dead of night. He was violently trembling in extreme distress. I wouldn't go down with him in my nightgown although the distance was very short. While I hurriedly dressed, he became so fidgety and jittery that he couldn't stand still. He kept sitting down and getting up and opened and closed the door repeatedly.

"Ma'am, I urge you to hurry up. Please hurry. She's seriously ill. I can't imagine what kind of ailment she has. Her stomach is so swollen. She complains of some kind of pain. I can't pinpoint what's bothering her. I'm afraid that something awful will happen to her. Are you sure that you can take care of any problem, as you said before? If someone finds out that an unmarried girl went to see the gynecologist, it would be a disgrace.... That bitch! Leaving her father all by himself while she fled south to save her own neck. I tell you she has a big stomach. Anyway, now she's returned home with this formidable illness. Ma'am, I'll surely die too if I lose one more child. Ma'am, is it really true that you can cure every disease? Is it, ma'am? What if someone finds out that a virgin went to see a gynecologist? Nonetheless, she's taken a serious turn. Ma'am, please save this poor creature. I won't live if I see another death." His voice trembled as he tried to explain the situation. His gibberish was non-stop.

Emotionally, Old Man Whang clung to me as in a daze, yet he showed his disdain for gynecologists as if he were holding onto a rope smeared with dung. I was tempted by this opportunity to mock his ridiculous ideas. Although Old Man Whang's daughter was my first patient, I remained calm and confident. I finished getting dressed and even put on a doctor's white gown. I also sanitized my hands. Every necessary instrument to deliver a premature baby was all ready in the bag. Old Man Whang took my bag in his shaky hands and ran down the flight of stairs. I could hear heart-wrenching cries, reminiscent of a beast being strangled, from the main living quarters.

In an inner room, I saw a girl in her bloomers violently compressing her already-tight lips. She glared at me as she clutched the waist of her bloomers. Her face was matted with perspiration-drenched strands of hair, and her bulging eyes appeared to be so intensely full of acute pain and loneliness that they didn't look like the eyes of a human. I had no idea when her water had broken; her bloomers were soaked through.

I pushed Old Man Whang to the head of the bed while I went to the other end and pulled down her bloomers. My mouth was so dry that I couldn't utter a word. The girl's hands, which could no longer hold onto the bloomers, waved frantically in the air. She reached toward the legs of her father who had been standing still, like an idol along the road. The girl's wide-open vagina was like an over-ripe chestnut ready to burst.

Old Man Whang let out an incomprehensible scream as he plopped down. His daughter clutched onto his waist and gritted her teeth; she then roared like a wild beast. The head of the baby had emerged. Amazingly under these circumstances, it opened its eyes easily. It was not a fetus any longer but a baby. Momentarily shocked by wonder that filled every fiber of my body, I gave her a stern order to push once more with the next contraction. My own voice sounded fresh and undaunted, as if I were hearing a stranger's voice for the first time.

At the same time the woman roared once again, and I managed to pull the baby out. Just like a midwife of long experience, I took care of the afterbirth with competence and speed. Not that it was a textbook delivery, but I congratulated myself for an excellent performance in delivering the baby without a hint of aid from any previous knowledge or experience. It was as if another force were controlling me. Old Man Whang's daughter had a baby boy.

After I returned to my place, I slept like a log until morning. I opened the window and sang as I fixed my breakfast. Then Old Man Whang came up to see me. He had transformed overnight into a shabby old man beyond recognition. His eyes were downcast and his shoulders drooping.

"How are the mother and baby?" I asked.

"I have no face to look at you, ma'am," Old Man Whang said.

"Do you understand now why women need a gynecologist?"

"Gynecologist? What have I done to be punished so severely?"

"Punished? You have a grandson! What a wonderful boy he is! Did you know that he opened his eyes and looked up at me when his face was only halfway out? He is a great warrior type. You just wait and see." I jabbered with unjustified bursting excitement. Old Man Whang lifted his eyes. They were lackluster and hollow, reminiscent of an entrance to a cave.

"What am I going to do with this dishonor? Ma'am, she said she has no idea who the father of the baby is. I tried desperately to get something out of her. I told her I don't care whether he is a pock-marked man or if his nose is twisted. I told her I would give her a lavish wedding regardless. She only kept crying, saying that what I said was irrelevant. You know what she said? She bombarded me with the news that she was raped. Raped...by a scum whose name she doesn't know...."

Old Man Whang was shaking with fury and dejection. However, I suddenly sensed a hint of lust in the dismay he was expressing. I was so disgusted that I thought I was going to vomit. I frowned deeply. Every man is capable of raping a woman. It's more important for me to know that a man is able to be a rapist than to know his full name.

"Why in the name of heaven did this kind of shame come upon me? To my completely ruined house? Why was a wretched daughter left behind? I can't say how much dishonor she has brought to this already destroyed family..."

I didn't know about his great and impressive family background, but the only thing that mattered to him was upholding his family's invisible name, which he claimed had now been stained. He was absolutely ignorant of his daughter's experience in a living hell during the period of her unwanted pregnancy.

"Ma'am, please help us," Old Man Whang pleaded. A touch of feigned servility on his grief-stricken face made him look even more repulsive.

"I'm sorry, but I have no talent for putting a baby back into his mama's womb," I told him, regretting that I couldn't think of something worse to say.

"Ma'am, even I know that much. That's not what I meant..." He slurred the end of his sentence, and his face lit up. This spark was out of place on a man as stupidly honest and unassuming as a farmer and watching him made me uneasy. I didn't want to miss the reason behind this change, so I didn't take my eyes off him. Old Man Whang turned his head away as though my stare blinded him and stood rubbing his hands.

"That's not what I meant...Ma'am, if you'll just pretend you know nothing about the whole thing...I'll trust you entirely, ma'am. I thought about killing the newborn baby by putting it upside down but couldn't do it after seeing its face."

"Uncle, why don't you please tell me first what you're talking about?"

"Yes, indeed, I'll tell you. My wretched daughter knows she's brought shame to herself, and fortunately she's seen no one since she returned home last night. So I want to let you know that I'll pretend my wretched daughter hasn't returned and that I wish to adopt the baby as my son."

"As your son, Uncle?" I was speechless at his unexpected words.

"Yes. Don't you think that it can be done by my creating a great commotion over a foundling foster child? Meanwhile, my daughter will hide in a back room until she is well and can appear. People will think she's just returned from her refugee life, and then I'll come up with some excuse as to why."

"Did your daughter agree?"

"How dare that miserable girl agree or disagree now? The fact that I saved both the mother's and her son's life was terribly kind of me."

"Nonetheless, it's your daughter's baby."

"What if she is my daughter, and the boy is my grandson?" Old Man Whang challenged me like an elementary school student who insisted that his answer was the right one. Then he became servile again; he didn't know what to do with himself, rubbing his hands as if he had remembered something. Was it my place to try and stop his impromptu yet flawless scheme? I fell into a subdued mood as I asked myself this question.

"I think it's an excellent idea to save your daughter from being disgraced if she only will agree with you," I said. I ended up agreeing with him.

"Do you really believe that I came up with this scheme in order to avoid dishonor? Now that a child had been born into a family whose sons had been taken, my family may well be compared to a formerly bare tree that now has flowers. If I tell people the news of a baby being left at my threshold, I bet you all lips both in our town and every neighborhood in the vicinity will make a fuss, expecting a celebration to be observed. My daughter herself, I'm sure, will regard her son as her brother and her brother as her son and raise the infant for several years with tender loving care. In the meantime, if her hand is asked in marriage by a good man, she'll marry him and no one will ever find out about the history of the baby."

Old Man Whang was obsessed with turning the event of the previous night's nightmare into an amazing fortune, solely depending on his wit. His face began to flush, and it was suffused by something that looked like an acute sense of pleasure, a sign that he was enjoying this play of fate, sparkling suddenly like a fish scale reflecting sunlight.

"If you, ma'am, could only ignore..." Although he said it as he cast his eyes downward, I knew they were no longer the holes of despair that I witnessed before. I also felt that he might strangle me if I failed to go along with him. Men are capable of doing anything and everything in order to fulfill their own desires. Old Man Whang appeared to be wicked yet he was far from being a brutal man. I harbored this sentiment about him as I half-heartedly promised him that I'd seal my lips about this matter concerning his daughter. It would indeed be best for his daughter, for the baby, and for Old Man Whang himself. I might even be jealous of his blessing so cleverly and cleanly transformed from misfortune.

The moment I agreed, Old Man Whang bowed his head countless times and searched through his pocket and took out a bundle of money.

"How can I possibly measure and repay you by monetary means for saving two lives last night? In time, I'll show you my gratefulness and pay you back in full. Please take this for now as a token of my appreciation."

Old Man Whang went down the stairs as fast as if he were running away. After he was gone, I counted the money. The amount was at least three times more than the normal delivery fee set by official regulation. He must have included a "hush" portion in that amount. Once again, I was enveloped with a sense of unexplainable jealousy. I spat on the money as the International Market merchants did on their first earning each day. Old Man Whang's money was my first fee from a patient. It certainly was a generous sum; however, I had no desire to deliver a baby again. From the start, I had been depending only on the air of XXX-rated adult entertainment that hovered over the neighborhood; consequently, I hadn't set up a delivery table in my clinic. My intention was to make money from only illicit unions resulting from the adult entertainment business.

The premonition which I'd felt when I first set foot in the neighborhood was correct. My business took off after a couple of prostitutes, whose customers were American GIs, began to visit my office; I had to perform several abortions a day and eventually became a veteran in that field. If all of those babies whom I forced to be unborn had lived, would we have had to build another large elementary school for them? Or would we have had to make a small town for them? Rarely do I submerge myself in this sea of idle emotion. If there was a single nagging sentiment which still lingered within me, it was the velvet chair that I failed to move from the south window. As the chair got older gracefully with time, it became even more an eyesore in the clinic; it didn't blend in with the decor. Every nurse who came and went in my office pressed me hard to discard the chair. Generally, I allowed my nurse to run the office for me; despite this, I couldn't bring myself to remove the chair.

If I threw that chair out, I'd feel compelled to hang the framed Oath of Hippocrates on the wall. To be totally honest, I had no heart to get rid of the chair. If I went ahead and discarded the chair, then I might no longer be able to picture my fine-looking father lounging in it, wearing shiny, pointed leather shoes and a white cotton *durumaki*. The only master of the chair was Father. The reason that I couldn't throw the chair out was the same reason that I couldn't easily erase the sad face of Father. My affection for my now deceased father was deep, and I would rather he be gazing at me as a true physician than at someone who had been transformed into a medical technician with an illicit connection with prostitutes.

Nearly thirty years went by during which I performed the same work in the same office above the hardware store. During those years, a great change came to the neighborhood. It was not the outskirts of the city any longer; rather it had become a community located near the heart of the city and it had been a long time since the last of the prostitutes who had entertained the American GIs disappeared. Nevertheless, the enveloping air of the brothel, which had magnetized me from the start, lingered for a good while even after the GI's girls left town.

Even after the government returned to Seoul, the Agricultural High School remained as an army base for American military personnel for two or three more years. After the high school has been restored to its former status, another large American army base was established near our town. As a result, the booming adult entertainment business in our neighborhood continued, and even after the army base was considerably down-sized, the roots of prostitution were not easily dug out. Our neighborhood had been transformed into a cheap red-light district, street after street. Due to a recent crackdown in the residential area, most of the business scattered elsewhere. However, I still have some loyal customers who travel long distances to visit my office. Also, the norm for married couples is to have only two children, without regard for the sex of the child, and it is safe to say that there is no housewife in this neighborhood who hasn't needed my service at one time or another.

The Agricultural High School later sold its lot to a construction company and moved to the outskirts of the town. Its site has since been transformed into an apartment complex. However, much to my dismay, for some strange reason not even one single new customer came to my office from that densely populated new district. My faithful customers, for better or for worse, came from the dilapidated, old neighborhood located behind the Kyungsung Store. I was widely known as a cheap and reliable doctor among respected women in that old neighborhood and among keepers of brothels in every nook and cranny throughout the city, who were incapable of shaking off the habit of making a living off prostitutes.

My popularity was further supported by the general belief among my patients that I hadn't made any serious mistakes during my career. It was natural for a poor woman who needed my service frequently to realize that it would be more practical to visit a place known for low fees and confidentiality than patronizing a doctor with an arrogant university degree, equipped with intimidating, extravagant facilities. Actually, there is a slight difference between my reputation of not having erred and the facts. I take care of the consequences of any mistake speedily, pertinently, and discreetly so no one finds out about it. Fortunately, my method of handling mistakets has resulted in no further complications. Such was the difference.

Three callused areas, like knots, were seated deeply in my hand, where I held forceps and curettes. They were reminders of the lives I destroyed; lives which might have populated a decent-sized town with their numbers. Although I was so accustomed to the work that I could perform it with my eyes closed, mistakes were made frequently. Many times I made the most dreadful mistake of rupturing the uterus. The crux of the problem was my over-confidence that I could do my work with my eyes closed. In fact, performing a curettage did not require one's eyes. Even a renowned doctor cannot see with naked eyes the mysterious interior where life has been conceived. The only eyes needed are those attached to the end of either the Hegar or other curette. However, in order for the curette's eyes to keep alert, the doctor who is holding it must have her whole soul concentrated every second on the task. When the doctor's whole soul isn't in the task, she won't be successful.

Just like picking a well-ripened Chinese lantern plant and unwittingly making a hole with a match, the sensation that something is amiss at the tip of the Hegar brings the consequences of lost attention home. It's a different story when one's attention is undivided; however, when it comes back after a lapse, every fiber of being feels momentarily like an alien object. When this feeling of heartless touch returns to me, I feel like my entire soul is filled with hatred. That's it! I did my work with hatred. In order not to make mistakes, I had to have this hatred brewing within me at all times. I hated the women who lay flat on their backs exposing their odorous private parts as if their faces were in front of mine, and I hated the unwanted lives that were taking shape inside the womb. Feeling this hatred was the only way I could instantly recover from any mistake I made. As my whole soul returned to the task at hand and controlled me completely, I was able to cope with any situation coolly, swiftly, and accurately.

My demeanor didn't change a bit from the viewpoint of the disinterested beholder. The color of my face was unchanged; the more mistakes I made, the calmer I became. I'd finish up the abortion flawlessly and give the patient antibiotics and muscle contraction shots. Then I'd make the patient rest and observe her progress. I had plenty of evasive words to say: "It was a difficult operation due to the severe retroflextion of your uterus, causing acute pain." Like a fully-ripe Chinese lantern plant, the uterus could rupture; however, the uterus is quite different from a Chinese lantern plant. The uterus has a self-healing ability. To this date, no ruptured uterus under my care has ever developed into peritonitis or something fearful; consequently, after every operation the uterus was as healthy as before the surgery.

I did, however, have an Achilles heel: I became gravely ill with exhaustion after performing an abortion. Whenever I fell ill, I would find myself detaching, as if I'd never be able to resume this work. But, by and by I'd soothe my psyche again. I planned to work until I reached the age of fifty-five, a number having no significance to me. Without realizing it, I'd probably borrowed the idea from the retirement age set for people who work for either the government or the bank.

At last the time came when, within three days, I'd be fifty-five years old. Coincidentally, my birthday was the day that the Kyungsung Store was slated to be demolished according to the city plan. Since I'd dutifully saved the money that I'd earned during the past years, I could afford to live an easy and bountiful retirement, traveling at leisure overseas. I had no terms to complete like a government worker nor a contract with anyone that I would work until I was fifty-five. Nonetheless, I hadn't the slightest intention of working after fifty-five. I had already bought a handsome house with a spacious yard in a quiet residential district and finished decorating the interior. Besides that, I had considerable rent fees coming from real estate I own, and I'd submitted the final premium for impressive retirement insurance. The only thing left for me was to receive money from the insurance company each year. I also had stocks and bonds. The only task I had to undertake from then on was not to make money, but to spend it all before I died.

In spite of all this, however, I found myself being overly anxious and jittery about the fact that there are only three days left before I washed my hands of my profession. There was one last thing that I wanted to do before I retired: *deliver* a baby. The first customer I had when I opened my office was a pregnant woman. Since then, for one reason or another, I'd never delivered a single live baby. Because I had consciously avoided delivering a baby, I'd been known only as a doctor expert in performing abortions. For the first few years of my practice, I had several inquiries about the matter of delivering babies; I invariably referred them to a nearby obstetrician, and the inquiries lessened gradually until they stopped. There was, therefore, no real possibility of having an unsolicited visit by a pregnant woman whose baby would be born in my hands.

For the past two months or so, I've been counting down—sixty days, fifty, ten, nine, eight days...to three days now, and I've been waiting for it anxiously. The more I think of how impossible it seems for me to deliver a baby, the more I go stone crazy, wanting to have this experience. As I flash back, compared to what I am now, I was an extremely inexperienced novice when, in a moment of bewilderment, I delivered a baby for my very first customer. Nevertheless, I think of myself as a person, who during that time, could barely guess the destination of her life no matter how hard she might try; a person who lived always for tomorrow; a person who lived in an impeccable completeness; a person who succeeded in idealizing herself. As if being crept up on by senility, the passing of time has altered my memory.

Only three days left. Only three days...

Only three days left to fulfill the fervent wish, which took hold of me the very moment I saw Maan-deuk's wife in her last month of pregnancy.

Maan-deuk is Old Man Whang's grandson; he is the first and last baby I was responsible for bringing into this world. On the day he begged me to turn my head about his daughter, Old Man Whang spread a rumor all over the neighborhood that the baby had been left at the gate of his house. At first, people were just curious about the baby, and everyone called him "the baby who was brought on a piggyback ride" since no name was given to him. As time went by, however, after serious discussion, the people in the neighborhood advised Old Man Whang that it would be a good idea for him to adopt the baby as his son. The baby could then inherit the family name. Although Old Man Whang had that same plan from the beginning, he acted as if he were yielding reluctantly and with great difficulty when he named the baby "Maan-deuk," which means "one had a child in one's old age." Old Man Whang begged everyone to never again to utter the phrase "the baby who was brought on a piggyback ride."

A month after "the baby who was brought on a piggyback ride" came into his life, Old Man Whang's daughter returned home as well. Although she could not attempt to nurse the baby, she raised her brother with her utmost love and care and received high praise from everyone. When he turned five years old, she had reached the age when she was considered a spinster. An opportune time arrived when a childless widower became available. Old Man Whang married his daughter off in a hurry, and now she leads a peaceful life with two children—a boy and girl. The plan that Old Man Whang dreamed has been fully realized. *What was my role in this scenario?* At the time thinking about this made me contemplate moving my office elsewhere, but my business prospered more and more each day, so I remained where I was.

Old Man Whang, stubborn, suspicious, and so stingy that his nick name is "Skinflint Old Man Whang," was becoming an eccentric old man while Maan-deuk was growing up as a tall, good looking young man, a big spender living in the fast lane. During all those years, people came and went in the neighborhood, and it was surmised by newcomers that Old Man Whang had raised Maan-deuk as his only son all by himself after his wife's death from childbirth complications caused by her advanced age. No one raised any suspicions concerning this generally accepted version of Old Man Whang's life.

Perhaps only I knew everything about the family. From my viewpoint, the conflict between love and hate which Old Man Whang had felt for Maan-deuk was severe. He should have corrected his son's habits of picking at food, gobbling snacks between meals, speaking rudely, and so on. But Old Man Whang could not discipline him and merely became a "yes" father. However, on the infrequent occasions that his son brought home a paper with a perfect score, Old Man Whang used to lift a switch, insisting that his son confess from whose paper he had copied. He even falsely accused his son of changing the grades on his report card to better ones. As a result, his son ran away from home for a few days Upon learning of this, Old Man Whang's daughter came to his house and secretly wept bitter tears before returning to her home.

I had the feeling that Old Man Whang tormented himself about accepting the fact that Maan-deuk was not only borne of his daughter, but also of a rapist. The man who had once been healthy and generous was now a highly-suspicious, miserable, and melancholy old man. That misfortunes become blessings were not, after all, universally true. I, once jealous of him, now felt sorry for him.

Although Old Man Whang's daughter dared not disclose that she was Maan-deuk's birth mother, she assumed more than the role of a sister, expressing her love for him by secretly providing him with plenty of spending money. Because of her indulgence, he developed the habit of spending freely and compulsively. Upon being discharged from the military and finding a new job, his spending habits escalated. He preferred talking about his company's annual export revenues rather than his own salary. As if he were a high-ranking company official rather than an entry-level clerk, Maan-deuk was elated over the company's profits and tried to justify his grandiose spending habits based on his company's prosperity.

Old Man Whang was contemptuous of his son's attitude and kept his distance from him as if he were a thief. He assumed a miserly role, pinching every penny, refusing to spend money on food and clothes, as if he were ignorant of the demands of a human body, fattening only his money pouch, desperately hanging onto it. The sign of affection in his eyes when he gazed at Maan-deuk had already diminished. When he looked at his son, he no longer saw the blood of his daughter in him, but only the blood of the scum bag who had raped her.

However, Old Man Whang's prejudice did not end with Maan-deuk only. If his son bragged about his company's exports as valued at tens of thousands of dollars, he would snort that the amount of the company's loans must be more than double that amount. Instead of subscribing to his own newspaper, Old Man Whang intercepted my copy and combed through it; consequently, he was very knowledgeable. He was more perceptive about the amount of foreign debt than about the value of exports and had more insight into the reasons people live in a wretched human condition than into the reasons some lead easy and comfortable lifestyles. He was quicker to know negative news than the positive. It wasn't just Maan-deuk with whom Old Man Whang found fault. He could see only the dark side of everything in life as he became an eccentric, lonely old man.

It was natural for Maan-deuk to move out of his house as soon as he proved to be self-sufficient. No one could measure whether his absence affected Old Man Whang in any significant way. His countenance had already changed into that of a most unhappy man who could not become any worse off than he already was.

Two months ago, Maan-deuk returned home, bringing a girl who was in full pregnancy. Old Man Whang neither welcomed them nor ran them out. The only thing he inquired about was whether or not they had been actually united in a wedding ceremony.

"Father, how could we possibly get married without your presence even though you consider me to be a pitifully undutiful child? I'd be truly heart broken if you treated me like a hopeless bum. Yes, indeed I'd be so sad," Maan-deuk said sarcastically.

Old Man Whang's heart must have still been palpitating from the shock when his own daughter had shown up unexpectedly and given birth and, as if he were under a spell, he was determined to have the couple get married as soon as possible. He showed absolutely no concern for the family background of his future daughter in law. Her age, her past—he asked about none of this. He rented a shabby wedding hall on the second floor of a supermarket near the bus terminal and made her wear a sordid wedding dress.

Although Maan-deuk tried desperately to proceed with his own plan for a lavish wedding at a hotel in the heart of downtown in the presence of relatives and friends from both sides of each family after the baby was born, he could not outdo Old Man Whang's high-handedness. Instead, except for a few neighbors who knew the true situation well, the hall was empty and cold. Although she was wearing the largest dress available, she could not even zip it up all the way and a safety pin had to be applied temporarily. She was an embarrassing sight with her slip exposed and her waistline blossoming under the dress. The wedding was more of a farce than Old Man Whang could have hoped. Despite this, however, the loquacious, buoyant Maan-deuk joked that this wedding ceremony was only a preview to the formal marriage ceremony which would soon follow and asked a handful of attending guests to look forward to the main event.

"Look at that senseless fellow. If you open your big mouth, you must have something to back it up. On the other hand, if you do have unlimited funds, you should keep your mouth shut. I tell you, boy, you have both—a big mouth and wasteful hands. You don't even realize that you have brought shame on yourself...tsk, tsk, my family is on its way to ruin."

Judging from the way he talked, it seemed to me that Old Man Whang promoted the wedding with only one intention—to disgrace his son. At any rate, it was an odd event for me to watch. Every guest cackled and talked in whispers. The moment I saw that bride's seemingly bursting stomach, which made it look as if the snap fastening the waist of her gown would surely break, I was engulfed with the desire to deliver her baby with my own hands. My heart suddenly pounded fiercely. Even after I returned home, I could not escape from this desire. I felt in my heart an urgent thirst to see once more a baby's virginal and translucent face, wide-eyed and gazing at the world even before he was completely out of his mother's womb.

I'd now practiced my specialty for nearly thirty years; despite this, I believed that Old Man Whang would emphatically nod his approval if I asked him to do me this trifling favor. I'd be more than happy to render my service free of charge as a token of my appreciation for a long-time landlord, or to give him a considerable discount, knowing what a penny-pincher he was. However, Old Man Whang flatly rejected my request to deliver Maan-deuk's baby.

"I beg of you to stop talking nonsense," he rudely remarked. "Do you really believe that I'd willingly leave my first grandson in the hands of a human butcher?"

After speaking these harsh words, he punctuated his remarks with an expression of such disdain that I felt as if he were sprinkling salt in my open wounds.

During my long career in this neighborhood, I had experiences with a pimp, who accompanied prostitutes who came to me for treatment of sexually transmitted diseases. Rather than addressing me as "ma'am," he would tap me on my shoulder and say "hey" or "you," as if I were one of his partners. I didn't blame him for having this attitude, which stemmed from our taciturn understanding that we both made our living by dealing with girls who sell their bodies. Accordingly, I didn't allow myself to be offended by his lack of respect for me as a doctor but tried to acquiesce. I took him with a grain of salt. However, the phrase Old Man Whang used to describe me — "human butcher"— made my heart bleed as if a nail had pierced it.

Only three days after the wedding, Maan-deuk's wife gave an easy birth to a son at the obstetric ward at the university hospital. In spite of the heart-breaking humiliation I felt, I went to see the baby as soon as they returned home. Remarkably, the baby looked strikingly similar to the very first baby I delivered. I had no idea who delivered the baby, but I was consumed by a fierce jealousy toward that obstetrician. At the same time, I was overpowered by a yearning to deliver a baby. This yearning persisted despite the discouragement I experienced after Old Man Whang's demeaning remark. Maan-deuk's baby was not the only one. I'd make sure that I delivered a baby before retiring. My heart was filled with a burning desire to touch a newborn babe during his virginal, translucent, and vociferous crying.

After that, the countdown began. Sixty days remained until my retirement. Surely I'd encounter a woman in her ninth month of pregnancy in these sixty days. Alas, the days had come and gone—60, 50, 10, 9 days—and then only three days were left.

On the day when only three days were left, I performed three D&Cs and treated two people with venereal disease. That was it. I went downstairs. Although the Kyungsung Store, which used to sell agricultural tools, was converted into a grocery store, its original sign was still intact. However, in accordance with the government regulations, the Chinese characters it bore had been changed to Korean ones during the period of control which forbade the use of Chinese. On the sign, "Seoul Grocery" written in Korean, I felt the spirit of Maan-deuk's touch; the letters made me laugh spontaneously.

"Give me a yogurt drink."

Old Man Whang, who had been reading a newspaper, cast a quick glance at me and took out a big bottle of yogurt from a refrigerator and gave it to me. I wasn't that crazy about this drink; but I bought it and drank it down anyway, as if I were paying a toll for the convenience of going through the store to get to the inside of his house. I could trace the course of a vein in the old man's neck, and his whiskers were as white as frost columns. As I watched him, I choked with sorrow and thought that Old Man Whang had aged considerably in recent days. Despite our differences, my feelings for him were deep. I had mixed emotions—both affection and hate—which had developed during the thirty years we had involuntarily spent under the same roof. Old Man Whang, whose eyes were still glued to the newspaper, mumbled, "It's the end of the world, the end of the world." Every day was the end of the world to him. In Maan-deuk, he saw only the creepy rapist, not his daughter; he was more aware of imports than exports, more interested in increased debt than in noticing signs of a better life for all of us. I concluded that he was solely obsessed with the dark, hidden side of every person and thing.

In any event, it was true that Old Man Whang still had a strong backbone. He was hard to approach compared to his imprudent neighbors because of his unique ability to discern matters clearly even before they were fully came to light. Just because I was more familiar with the private parts of a woman than her face didn't mean that I knew more about women than did others. By the same token, just because his ability was wonderfully sharper than others to see the dark side of world affairs, how could anyone claim that he knew world affairs any better? As I developed this preposterous theory, I tried to feel sympathy toward him as a kindred spirit, as in the old adage, "Misery loves company."

"Has the baby grown a lot?" I asked, hinting that I was going inside to see the baby as I turned in the direction of the living quarters.

Maan-deuk's wife was quick to laugh. She giggled when she bragged about her baby, when she criticized her husband, and when she revealed that she fretted over her father-in-law. Perhaps that's why the baby loved to laugh, too. After he focused his eyes fairly well, the baby's mouth hung open widely. Although I came to see him with extravagant hopes of pacifying my irrational desire to deliver a baby, my visit caused me to be even more determined to do so. If I washed my hands completely of my profession without having fulfilled my dream, I felt I'd never be able to get away from my woeful condition until the day I died. However, only three days remained. Only three days.

2. Two Days Before

It was a dreadful dream. I was writhing desperately to wake up from a dream in which the calluses on my fingers had progressed to be cancerous, spreading into every corner of my skin with alarming speed. Then I seemed to hear a distant roar of croaking frogs in the mid-summer night.

It was the croaking of a frog I had heard, too, as I fought desperately to free myself from the alien odor of the Westerner, from his hairy chest, from his limbs as long and sturdy as ropes, and from the weight of his rock-solid body as he attacked me from various angles. The frogs, indifferent to this human's war, sounded so peaceful that it made me realize I was only dreaming of being raped as I drifted between states of sleep and wakefulness.

Unlike the time when I actually was raped, I awakened gradually from my dream to the sound of frogs croaking, separating dream and reality. To reassure myself that it was merely a dream, I first felt the calluses on my fingers, then put my hand inside my nightgown and rubbed my chest, stomach, and thighs. The aged, slackened skin of a plump woman who had never given birth and had now reached fifty-five years of age, felt as soft to the touch as a piece of silken thread; I felt not a bumpy spot anywhere. It must have been a dream. These damned calluses, they will disappear completely in a few months after I wash my hands of this job. Despite this, I was in ill humor. The calluses which had mutated to cancer and spread all over my body in my dream, may not only be on my hands. I may have calluses in my heart. At this preposterous thought, my heart became heavy. I opened the bedroom window, prompted by an old habit. The distant sound of frog's croaking became loud, abruptly surging into my room as if a microphone had been installed to enhance them.

I heard the cries of Christians gathered for a worship service at dawn in a recently formed church. These church-goers wailed in this fashion every day. Whenever I heard them, I felt within me the urge to wail loudly, too. But, alas, I felt unable to shed even one tear. It was still early dawn. The neighborhood behind the Kyungsung Store was framed by the dark blue night sky.

Only two days were left. Only two days... As I became more wakeful, the first thing that came to my mind was that I had only two days left before moving. More importantly, the possibility of delivering a living baby was now reduced to two days.

My living quarters and the dual-purpose room that was used for examining and operating on patients were at opposite sides of the south facing window where the velvet chair was situated. From the living room or the operating room, I could see the inverted-L-shaped roofs of the houses which stood in the topsy-turvy, cramped, dilapidated neighborhood. No one who had ears and lips dared contradict the saying, popular then, "the brilliant progress of Seoul." For one reason or another, however, this neighborhood, where my regular customers had lived and departed and where I'd received newcomers, had remained nearly the same as the first day I opened my office thirty years ago.

The houses in my neighbor were neither traditionally Korean in style nor of the modern Western style, but shoddy, cheaply built houses with tiled roofs constructed during the final chapter of Japanese colonization when raw materials were in terribly short supply. They were cramped, squalid, and aged, with no appeal to potential home buyers. On top of that, from the road where two- or three-storied stores, including Kyungsung Store, were located row after row, even within the past ten years the ditch had been open and sordid, though later it had been improved. The character of the neighborhood was gradually going down, approaching the same level as the ditch. The place was seemingly sinking in a stagnant pool. Each summer brought a flood. Since each house covered an area less than 30 pyung, it was impossible to obtain a permit either to demolish or to renovate a house. Once they had the financial means to do so, people moved away from this neighborhood as soon as possible. Therefore, one could now purchase several houses and knock them down to build a new one, but who would appreciate such a luxurious house in this slum? Definitely there is not a person firmly attached to this worthless area who would actually do such a foolish thing, considering the odds against the neighborhood. Given this was the current situation, the cheers about better living conditions heard from every corner of the world were not echoed reality of this neighborhood. Nevertheless, hearing such rumors was better than hearing nothing at all.

ÂSuperficialy, everyone seemed to live better. Everyone is capable of imitating what he sees and hears. Maan-deuk's wasteful spending and trusting his company's export figures more than his own salary is an example. The residents live well without real substance, like dancers shaking their hips merrily whenever they hear drum beats in the air. First of all, the housewife's underwear and her private parts have become as clean as those of prostitutes; judging from this fact alone, anybody can see that people in general have come to a better way of life.

I know it's insulting to a virtuous woman to compare her private parts to those of a prostitute. I'm merely making a statement judging strictly from outer appearances. Common sense dictates that a prostitute's private parts are dirty while those of a virtuous woman are clean; however, according to my own observation, it is the opposite. Some prostitutes' private parts are nearly as clean as the innocent face of an idiot. The more a woman believes her private parts are pure, the more she's unaware of their filth. This metaphor can be compared to a living room considered to be the cleanest place in any household.

After nearly all the prostitutes vanished from this neighborhood, the most striking change was the emergence of seven new churches which came into existence in this not-so-large area. The town hall is always crammed with people who come to take care of their business, and one always has to wait in line due to this concentrated population. When I settled here, not one church was here. But now, once a church finds an appropriate site, its construction begins immediately. Consequently, they have increased in numbers every year, soaring into the sky. Church is the only place one finds evidence of a truly booming business in this neighborhood. Each of the seven churches is a different denomination with distinct beliefs, despite their same faith in Jesus Christ. Although it seems these Christians migrate from church to church from time to time, no church appears to be suffering from a lack of members.

The newest church, whose denomination I did not know, had a flock of believers who gathered there every morning to cry out and sing hymns praising their holy God. They clapped their hands joyfully and sang in exhilarating voices at the end of the service. It must be the pattern of the denomination's worship service. Their non-Christian neighbors might not have appreciated their enthusiasm, but judging from the ever heightening cries during the dawn service, which changes from day to day, it was clear that the power of the church in the members' lives had strengthened.

More than half the members were women, some of them my regular customers. *What are they praying for in their sobbing? Why in the world does this steadfast wailing arise every single day?* When they came to see me, pregnant with unwanted babies, I could see clearly the despair on theirs faces. I knew that many felt like they wanted to die on the spot. However, upon learning about the low risks associated with a D&C, their countenance would lighten immediately, becoming peaceful. Assured of a safe and prompt termination of the pregnancy, they'd change instantly, a light and carefree expression on their faces. My ability to rid them of their agony without a trace to remind them of the incident was simply miraculous to them. It's only possible for a person who is filled with pent-up hatred to feel for a woman suffering this kind of pain. I, once in their shoes, was the principal architect of the liberation of these women from their painful shackles.

Nonetheless, every single day these same women wailed bitterly, disturbing my early morning sleep. *Is there any sin that can make them cry like that? Even God cannot be as magnificent as I am. I can pick up an embryo with tweezers and show it to a woman.* However, the churches were growing by leaps and bounds.

One day I asked one of my regular customers, a housewife, why she went from one church to another. My intention was not to embarrass her, but instead to learn from her, in my humble way, a little bit about each denomination and the differences between them. She informed me that she went to her previous church hoping to be cured of her chronic rheumatism, solely based on its reputation for healing. She told me that her current church is also known for its power to bring good luck, and the reason she had transferred her membership was to help her husband's business prosper. *If this is the case, what kind of promise is offered by church, which is a Mecca for these women wailing each dawn?*

God, Father, even though these women say hundreds of times over and over again that they believe in You, do not trust their words, God, Father. They are seeking for God, Father, with their lips, but I know well what their pussy is after and what it has done for men. I felt an air of arrogance toward the One whom these women sought in lamentation. This wailing at dawn was responsible for raising the thought in me that I might have accumulated a lump of wailing that has finally become rock solid, residing in a secret chamber of my heart.

As the veil of darkness lifted slowly at daybreak, the first sight that emerged from across the horizon was of steeples of churches. Since every house was still cloaked in milky darkness, the entire view through the window seemed like a densely foggy sea; in this light, the steeples of the churches appeared suddenly like the masts of a sinking ship. The sound of lamentation became like bickering among passengers on that ship as they desperately tried to climb up the masts to save themselves. No one was yet seen at the top of the masts for they were too busy quarreling with one another. Whether or not anyone reached the top, the result was the same: the ship was destined to sink.

As the face of blackness paled, the rooftops were more discernible, and I could almost make out the image of a person at the top of a mast. Alas, it was a cross, not a human figure and the mirage of a sinking ship faded to reality.

Only two days were left. Dawn on those last two days was destined to break with rapid speed.

The first patient I saw during the last two days was a prostitute named Wha-young who came to receive treatment for a sexually-transmitted disease. Although the owners of the whorehouses did not live in the vicinity any longer, not infrequently they sent their prostitutes to my office for treatment.

Today, Madame Jun, the owner of the whorehouse, accompanied one of her girls. Madame Jun had aged a lot, too. Unlike Old Man Whang, the aging of Madame Jun was accentuated not only by her forlorn looks, but also by the naked truth of fading with age, making me feel sorry and embarrassed, as though I were experiencing this also. My words, however, did not reflect my inner feelings.

"Oh, my word! What wind has brought you here personally? Goodness, you must be desperately needing more girls! That girl Wha-young must be the main source of American dollars for your business," I spat out curtly, sticking my face into the waiting room after readying the girl on the examination table.

"No. Do you really believe I accompanied her here out of curiosity to find out what's troubling that bitch's private parts? Ma'am, I was told that you will keep your business open only until tomorrow."

"Yes. Are you sorry?"

"Yes, I am. You don't think I have a heart made of stone or wood like yours, do you, ma'am? I am sorry and envious, too. When can I give up this damned business of mine and live an easy life?"

Madame Jun expelled a deep sigh as she smoked a cigarette. The maroon fingernail polish on her plump hands looked dirty and pitiful.

"For crying out loud! What are you bellyaching for? What happened to all that money?" I snapped, and I slammed shut the door of the waiting room. Since the day the American military compound occupied the Agricultural High School, Madame Jun has been my regular customer. She's a former prostitute and now runs a whorehouse. She's received my services many times over the past years. She's a loyal customer who regularly sends her girls to my office regardless of the distance. In spite of her status as a long-term, faithful customer, she still addresses me respectfully as "ma'am" rather than the common "you." Nonetheless, I can discern by her undertone her clear awareness that we make a living from different roles but the same business.

The first thing Wha-young asked me, after her examination and treatment, was when she could resume her business.

"Tomorrow may be all right, but would you like me to excuse you so you may rest for few more days?"

"Oh, no! I have a sense of duty. I'm really indebted to *Mama* for already skipping so many days."

"Is that so? All right then. Starting tomorrow you fulfill your responsibility," I said as if I were chewing the words.

"Ma'am, in any event it's rare to have a *Mama* like *our Mama*," Wha-young took up for her patron as she pulled her panties up over her shapely legs and hips.

Although her face was usually thickly painted, Wha-young's face without makeup was quite ordinary. Her movement in taking her panties off and spreading her legs on the examination table was extremely refined and without a sign of superfluity, making me acknowledge a sort of beauty arising from her job. I found myself admitting that she was a beautiful girl.

The three of us—Madame Jun, Wha-young, and myself—gathered in the waiting room where a mood of family permeated the air.

"I understand the road in front of your office is going to be widened. This neighborhood will have a windfall, I must say," Madame Jun said.

"Yes, indeed. Madame Jun, if you still had your house, you might have become a wealthy woman, I bet you!" I said.

"Holy, moley, what's the use of talking about the trifling past? Was it only once or twice that I missed a perfect chance to get rich?" Madame Jun said.

"Our Mama suffered a great loss this time again, ma'am," Wha-young interjected.

"Well, I bet you she must have been unreasonably greedy again," I said.

"Ma'am, have you ever seen me being inattentive before? For better or for worse, I have conscientiously run my business. Anyway, accidents seem to happen constantly I gather it's about time for me to rid my hands of this business, and yet I have nothing to fall back on," Madame Jun said.

"Why are you so wretchedly depressed? What happened?" I asked.

"It's no big deal. It happens all the time. A girl who cost me a lot of money ran away after leaving me her huge debt."

"By Jove, you'll find her or she'll crawl back," I said.

"I'd look for her if I desired to do so. If someone had snatched her, I wouldn't be sitting still. I wouldn't stand for it. But I found out she ran away with a man whom she couldn't live without. Knowing that, my heart melts, and I have no choice but to pray for her happiness."

"You'll go to heaven, Madame Jun," I said.

"I love to see people falling in love. You know that, don't you, ma'am?" Madame Jun smiled sadly.

"Wha-young, I suggest you also fall in love with someone soon. Out of pity, you know,." I said.

"I don't think feeling sorry for myself could make me fall in love," Wha-young said.

Although I deliberately remain aloof from people at all times, I found myself freely letting myself go since we have known each other over so many years, building inevitable family-like ties.

"By the way, only those people whose houses are demolished are the losers. If the

Kyungsung Store was left intact, your office could as well run another ten more years, ma'am."

"No, I'm closing my office at the right time. Now that I've set the final date, I don't think I could go on another day longer even if someone threatened to kill me," I said.

"Do you know where Old Man Whang plans to move? Well, since he's such a miser, I'm sure he stashed a huge sum of cash somewhere..."

"Since he lives on the largest lot in this vicinity, I bet he got a good sized compensation for it. I was told that he has already bought a decent two-story house that has space for his store. He said he'd move all the merchandise to his new store," I said.

"Learning that you are retiring makes me feel like I'm losing one of my arms. Draw me a map to your house. Is it all right to come see your new house, ma'am? I'll bring a box of matches to wish you prosperity," Madame Jun said.

"No. My house is located in a refined neighborhood, and I am going to act like one of them. So why are you, Madame Jun, going to visit me?" I said as I drew a map to my new house.

"I'd love to hang out in a place where I'm not welcomed. It's in my nature..." Unyielding, Madame Jun responded.

She put the paper bearing direction carefully away and left, saying "Well, then, see you later."

There are only two days left.

The majority of my patients suffered from sexually-transmitted diseases or pregnancies which they terminated through dilation and curettage. It was not unusual by any means. I was the one who paved the road for my profession. It is too late now to correct my track record.

Only two days are left. Yet, I can't shake off my desire to deliver a live baby with my own hands just once before I retire.

As if to mock my longing, each of three women whose fetuses were aborted by my hands that day carried a less-than-three-months-old fetus, each with the impeccable shape of a tiny baby. Most three-month-old fetuses are damaged when extracted; however, that day was a strangely peculiar day. Perhaps not even a pregnant woman knows that the tiny fetus she carries, though as small as a fingertip, has distinctly human features. The ratio of body parts is different from that of a complete human as its head takes up most of the size. Speaking of the size of its head, it's as small as a green pea. Surprisingly, however, it has distinct eyes. The eyes, which have not developed eyelids yet, are open widely, reminiscent of two seeds of a portulaca being planted there.

The eyes that I executed, the eyes that would never see the outside world—gazing at these portulaca seed-sized eyes, a sudden shivering seized me as if the eyes penetrated my entire life from a certain point in the past to the present. My life, reflected thoroughly in these tiny eyes, is poorer than that of a panhandler, and my hands are stained with blood. I'm forced to face the reason why Old Man Whang disallowed my service in bringing his grandson into this world.

Is the range of its view somewhat indefinite because its eyes are not yet conscious? The eyes seem to inspect freely the yesterday, today, and tomorrow of my life. They also try to polarize the fixed idea that had been my emotional pillar. The eyes seem to dare to ridicule me, a successful woman, as a pathetic fool—a woman who refused to love a man, not even once excusing a disgraceful rape in the grass on a summer night orchestrated by a cannon firing afar and a loud chorus of frogs croaking nearby—a woman who had led a good life in spite of or because of it. Driving me into this fantasy, the eyes meddled and then transformed a proven profit into an instant loss. As if this were not enough, the eyes laughed at my professional status—I had failed not only as a medical doctor, but also as a healer since the aim of my healing intention had been far from easing the patients' suffering but only to treat them as objects for my disgusting personal pleasure.

The thought of vengence came alive whenever I aborted a fetus, these tiny eyes penetrating into a pleasure arising from my secretive revenge, an eye for an eye, a tooth for a tooth for the brutality I'd been subjected to at the peak of my youth.

The velvet chair is still by the south window in a pleasantly decorated, spacious area that is used as both a waiting and consulting room. Each day the chair has been a thorn in my side; even today it is an offensive sight. When you brush the fabric in a certain direction with your palm, the faded gray comes alive with a bright pea green hue. This pea green is a residue of hunter green from thirty years ago. The chair didn't go with the other furniture in my office when it was hunter green or when it was pea green, and now it has turned to gray. Except for the one time when Father sat in it....

What did Father say sitting in that chair? "Since old times, the art of medicine has been called the art of healing. With that in mind, practice it with good intentions." When I think of his remark, I can't keep myself from bursting into laughter as I did when Father said it. Back then I was making all the preparations in every facet of my profession to make money using my skills. From time to time I've involuntarily imagined good-looking Father sitting in that velvet chair and have dwelt on the image; but, I've never been moved from doing my job by the statement he made. I've lived only according to my own will and whim. Nonetheless, every once in a while, I feel as if the velvet chair is taking a tight grip on my soul. Not the soul filled with hatred but another soul.

That's why I've kept that velvet chair by the south window, the chair that proved to be good for nothing, the chair that never went with any other furnishing—unable to discard it or treat it as a hangdog. Although I'd made up my mind long ago not to take a single item from my office with me, as I gaze at the chair absent-mindedly, I find myself etching in my head a picture of the velvet chair parked by a south window in my new house.

Two days left.

However, it was too late in the day for me to experience delivering a baby. The autumn sun couldn't care less about my heart-wrenching longing as dusk gathered around me. I bit my lips; as I wandered aimlessly from one room to the other, I saw an object on the examination table which deeply stunned me. I saw three pea-sized embryos, which I had curetted that day, still preserved in formalin inside an empty penicillin bottle. Seized by a momentary fury, I called out for my nurse Miss Choi, frantically as if just burned by flame.

"What's the meaning of this, Miss Choi? What's got into you? What did you do that for?" I said in a trembling voice, gripped with a hint of fright like an easily scared child.

"It's not my doing, ma'am. You did it yourself a short time ago...." Miss Choi protested, widening her eyes as if she were somewhat doubtful of my mental capacity.

Miss Choi was far from telling groundless lies or playing games. I might have done it, as she said. *What made me do such a thing?* It was beyond me. *I admit it's a mystery to witness a fetus that is being extracted unimpaired; nonetheless, it's not the first or second time I've seen them. What drove me do that?* Come to think of it, once I saw fetuses in glass bottles displayed side by side as specimens according to the month of fetal development in my colleague's office. When I saw them, I was as nauseated as if I were witnessing a pickled human being in a bottle. Such was I then, and now I performed the very same thing—pickling a human—without realizing it.

"May I throw it out then, ma'am?" Miss Choi asked as she picked up the penicillin bottle.

"No, don't. Don't throw it away," I barked as I snatched it from her. My intention in keeping it was neither for a keepsake nor for a future use of the bottle. I just didn't want to throw it away while I was conscious of doing it. Until then, I had discarded these embryo fetuses without being aware of what I was doing. I regarded them as common, as something sordid, and acted accordingly without giving them much thought. *Nevertheless, what made my unconscious behavior concerning an extracted fetus include this preposterous act today?* I placed the bottle back on the table and wished Miss Choi would get rid of it secretly when I turned my head.

As I toyed with this thought, I was captivated with a certain sense of self-doubt. *Why must I get so aggravated when I get an impression of something senseless happening or witness someone's inexcusable behavior? Especially when I'm the cause!* In any event, ever since I watched that ridiculous, shabby wedding ceremony, I've nurtured this urgent desire to receive a live, full-term baby with my hands. Since that moment, I've been feeling detached from my own self as if becoming someone beyond my own comprehension. I now try to tell myself not to be so critical of me if possible and let me be. I'm scared that I might be shattered into tiny pieces like mercury—the more it's touched, the more it separates.

"Ma'am, is it okay if I give a call and give these to auntie at the dress shop and auntie at the hardware store?" Miss Choi asked, studying my face. She held up something that looked like salted roe of pollack, not yet artificially colored, lying on a plastic plate.

"What is that?"

"You're really acting strange today, ma'am. Why, it is the fetus's cord that you curetted not long ago!"

I glimpsed a shadow of doubt again crossing over Miss Choi's face. I can deal with myself being a doubting Thomas, but I can't stand someone else doubting me.

"That's right. Those women asked for them, didn't they? All right, why don't you call them? Right now!" I said cheerfully, offering Miss Choi a favor in a suddenly generous mood. Among the neighborhood women, a rumor had been convincingly spread that a placenta was a miracle drug, acting to help a woman keep her youth and beauty. As a medical doctor, I could absolutely deny this groundless rumor. Of course, I don't believe that a placenta sheds a wondrous effect on women as rumor has it. Nevertheless, I give it the benefit of a doubt, for it may well be effective if a woman has a positive mental attitude that it will enhance her youth and beauty.

Even the customers who regularly spread their legs for me could not bring themselves to tell me personally that they wished to take the placenta; I had a feeling that most of them asked Miss Choi for this favor instead. When a request was made, I gave these women permission to take the placenta to Miss Choi's room. I was concerned that it might be spoiled if I should sell it illegally; besides, I wanted to prevent beforehand the possibility of a backdoor deal.

The customers who could ask Miss Choi this kind of favor have maintained quite a friendly relationship with me personally, too. As a result of this relationship, they came to eat the placenta without restraint. Women, who could not eat it without being nauseated would secretly bring along a bottle of *soju* [Korean gin] and eat the placenta as a relish as if she were eating a slice of raw fish. When a woman has no scruples about doing anything when it comes to an erogenous drug, she has already become the most bald-faced and shady; thus, under the influence of *soju*, it is natural for her to tell a dirty story.

A cruel sense of pleasure embraces me when I look on these women. It's as if I were witnessing the zenith of their ugliness, nothing like when I have seen them lying flat on the examination table exposing their private area as though showing their faces. So it was one of the means that I used to persecute women: letting them eat someone's immature placenta and allowing them to jabber obscene stories with their fishy breath. When hatred is your motive in abetting someone in doing something, it's a form of cruelty—a most natural way. By doing this ceaselessly, I've tried to thwart the memory of the teeth-gnashing cruelty I'd been subjected to just for being a woman. I'm willing to delegate a share of my experience to strangers indiscriminately, no matter what it may take. However, no matter what I did, nothing helped shrink my resentment. No matter how hard I tried to make others look ugly and tragic in comparison, in the end I was inevitably more tragic and ugly.

The woman who runs the hardware store raved about this and that, acting giddy under the influence of two glasses of *soju* along with this unique relish as the area around her eyes reddened like a peach flower; she came out to the waiting room, wobbly in her walk and tried to sit down in the velvet chair. In loathing, I pushed her to the sofa. The dress shop owner also came out and sat side by side with the hardware store woman. Judging from the two women's agitation, I determined they wanted to say words of farewell.

"It's the day after tomorrow, isn't it?" The dress shop woman, who is prudent and does not handle liquor well, opened her mouth first.

"Ma'am, are you really going to retire for good from your practice? We're so sorry. What are we to do?"

"I know you look forward to retirement now, but you wait and see! You can't entirely let go of your learned skill. You take a short vacation and then return to us after we finish our new building. We'll offer you a place when you become bored with leisure, and you must come back with no ifs or buts. Why, ma'am, if you don't, we'll form a party and drag you back."

Due to a recent zoning project, the hardware store and the dress shop were automatically given locations in the new business district being developed by the roadside. In fact, their new locations adjoin the road. The owners are extremely excited by the fact that a new building will go up on their respective locations. Other houses were not fortunate enough to see this kind of drastic change; however, since they were an integral part of a complete zone scheduled for improvement, this entire neighborhood had a chance to see itself actually transformed after all this time.

"I'd be happy if you can just continue seeing just your regular customers even at your house. I don't mind going to other doctors, but I'd like to see my regular gynecologist..."

"Yes, I agree with you. It doesn't offend me that much when I think of spreading my legs for any other men, but when it comes to a male doctor for getting my Pap smear, I get really upset. Ma'am, what shall I do to avoid getting pregnant?"

"Don't fuck," I said, grinning and stood up. They must have understood that my remark was a continuation of their dirty stories; the two women cackled, twisting their bodies. When I was young, I used to give serious advice to the neighbor women who consulted me about avoiding pregnancy. I also gave them a chart showing the time when intercourse was least apt to result in pregnancy, and an applicator. However, these women repeated their mistakes as if they were retarded children, incapable of learning even the Korean alphabet despite daily lessons. They detested doing anything which took much concentration; they hated even more to do anything that reduced the intensity of their sensuality. I have, therefore, only one bit of advice left for them; and I've said it. Although they knew that I'd give them the same answer every time they asked, judging from the pattern of their questions, I could discern that they intended to continue to enjoy the profanity itself. After I tell them off with this kind of remark, I feel cleansed inside, as if I had spat upon them.

"We enjoyed eating, ma'am," the hardware store owner said.

"Thank you, Miss Choi," the other woman chimed in.

I heard the two women leaving the office after expressing their gratitude as if they were guests who had eaten to their heart's desire at a house celebrating some festival.

I sit by the window in my room and look down at the neighborhood where the lights are being turned on one by one.

The front courtyard of Old Man Whang's place comes into my view clearly, like an open palm. The courtyard is lighted, and I see they are packing household items. I see Old Man Whang's daughter, whom I hadn't seen the previous day. She might have come to help him move. She, too, has aged a lot. She stands there, holding Maandeuk's baby in her arms. She only supervises the overall operation, not becoming physically involved. Every once in a while, she rubs her cheek against the baby's cheek and says something to him. The baby must be smiling, because she calls out loudly so she can show the baby off to busy people passing by. As if love were surging bountifully from her heart, her face is full of immense mercy and happiness. Even if she pretends to be the baby's paternal aunt, it's natural for her to act in this way because she is in reality his grandmother. As if bewitched, from my window I follow her movements in the midst of all the disarray. I feel empty, as if only the outer shell of my body remains.

Due to my personal involvement with Old Man Whang's daughter's secret nightmare, I used to think I had her under my thumb, but that proved to be wrong. She had been freed long ago and now has become a native of a place that is beyond my comprehension and reach. It is not she but I who is still confined in a nightmare.

Only two days are left, and it makes me feel as if I were sinking swiftly, as if time were flying by with added speed. In this mood, I abandon myself in thought: a married woman is more beautiful than a single. A married woman, who has at least three or four children—daughters and sons—is much more beautiful although she may have undergone curettage more than a dozen times intending to have only two children. The woman who is even more beautiful than the woman with several children is a prostitute who has countless men, yet wishes to fall in love with someone just once in her lifetime. Even much more beautiful than this prostitute is the aged owner of a whorehouse, a woman who has been through all types of life's weather, a woman who has decided not to pursue that prostitute who followed the man she loved with every fiber of her being. I think of all these women like this, toppling my structure of ideas and rebuilding it in reverse.

Night has now deepened. In the panoramic view of the night scene beneath my window, I count the steeples of the churches—one, two, three...seven.

God in heaven, what if I wish to fall in love now! How absurd that would be? It would be nothing but a mockery, wouldn't it? God in heaven, please don't make me that ugly. Instead, God, please grant me one last chance to deliver a live baby. Please do not ask me why I desire that so much. I don't have the answer either. "Why" is not important to me now; I just want desperately to do so. Please don't ignore my plea.

I smile sadly in spite of myself as I realize that I'm praying for the first time in my life.

3. The Last Day

I was now in the courtyard in my new house. Since my house was located on a sunny side and had a wonderful view, I had a bird's eye's view of handsome houses with green grass and various kinds of colorful flowers in full bloom dotting the courtyard. My garden was not only empty, but was covered by heavy concrete. Since I had a pocketful of flower seeds, I tried to stomp my feet into the surface of the concrete and gouge it with my fingernails, but it didn't budge an inch. My hands and feet were the only tools I had. I felt stifled, not having a tool to work with, yet I congratulated myself on not bringing any tool with me to the new house. Those tools that I left behind me were forceps, Hegars, and curettes, not a hoe or pick.

I had no choice but to scatter the flower seeds in my pocket out onto the concrete. Upon dispersing the seed, I realized they were portulaca seed. The tiny seed managed to penetrate well into the concrete surface and then entered into the soil with their sole strength. Instantly, the concrete ground broke apart gently like fragile toppings on a cake. The tiny seed began instantly to spring forth as leaves and then they bore colorful flowers. Red, yellow, pink, purple...my courtyard was transfigured into a field of luscious portulaca. Then the flowers started bickering among themselves. Listening to their bitter cries and screams, I discovered they sounded just like children. It wasn't just their voices, but even their faces. Each one began to form a mouth, eyes, and nose, resembling the face of a baby. My courtyard was not just a flower bed but a living hell. Countless babies stuck their faces above the ground and cried ceaselessly with a heart-wrenching sound. *Stop it, stop crying. Stop this minute! If you don't, I'll have a bulldozer run you over and put the concrete back. Stop now, stop it now...*

Again, it was a nightmare. Although I awoke the cries continued, but they were from far away. I opened the window by force of habit. The cries that had become faint in the distance now suddenly once again became loud as if a microphone had been placed nearby and entered the room in full force. It was again the crying of the Christians who came for morning worship. It was still early dawn. Again the steeples of the churches resembled the masts of a sinking ship and the crying sounded poignantly sorrowful, reminiscent of a passenger's last SOS from an already sunken ship. The conflict between an urgent desire to wail from the innermost chamber of my heart and my determination to not squeeze out a single tear confronted me with a greater intensity than ever.

The last day!

A sense of tension facing the countdown to zero and an earnest wish that cannot be abandoned become two strands of straw rope and make me feel hopelessly bound.

I know that *that* wish will not be granted to me. And yet, I cannot stop expecting it to happen. Even on this day I continue to work as usual, but Miss Choi, in work clothes, has been packing her belongings since morning. The demolition task is already underway at the end of the road. The air outside the window is as hazy and misty as a dust storm on a spring day; from time to time, I can hear the sound of shanties toppling down in great mass. *What makes me so attached that I stay to witness the very last ugly day in this neighborhood?*

Old Man Whang, his son Maan-deuk, ordinary housewives who covet a stranger's placenta believing it to be a mysterious wonder drug although they know they are in reality the provider of the placenta, prostitutes innocent as maidens, whorehouse owners prostitutes call "Mama"—people I've helped by easing their pain or with whom I've maintained a confidential relationship—I believed I could ignore all of them and leave them behind without any strings attached. I'd never doubted that I'd been in a position of giving and they in quite the opposite. However now, in retrospect, it is I who's indebted, not they. We've known one another inside and out and involuntarily built our relationship on a facsimile family concept; therefore it's I who will miss them for the days to come, not the other way around. I'd have no one to think about but them, but once I'm out of sight, they'd soon forget me.

"Do you think there may be patients even today?" Miss Choi appears anxious to leave. I have given her severance pay, which should please her and enable her to have a few days rest before having to secure a new position. She and I have made a promise to leave my office at the same time tomorrow, but it would be heartless to stand in her way if she desires to leave a day earlier. Still, I cannot bring myself to comply.

"Miss Choi, have you ever seen even one day that our office was idle because no patient showed up?" I attempted to intimidate her by speaking sharply in the manner of a street vendor.

At this opportune moment, a girl's face, apparently that of a teen-ager, emerged from downstairs. The girl did not climb to the top of the stairs; instead, she showed only the upper part of her body, seeming to appraise the atmosphere inside my office. When her uneasy eyes made contact with mine, the girl looked about to cry, standing immobile on the stairway as if she had committed a crime. Her hesitancy as to whether she should climb up the stairs or step back made her appear pitiful. I wished she would step backwards. It was apparent to me without examining her why a young girl like herself, with a tearful face, had come to see a gynecologist. On my last day, I did not want to perform such an operation.

However, Miss Choi put on her gown in a flurry and personally helped the girl, who stood still midway up the stair, to climb up to the top. Confirming my unshakable business nature, I figured that Miss Choi was doing me a huge favor by taking this action.

Upon facing the girl at the top of the stairs, my heart began to pound. Unexpectedly, her stomach was quite large. In order to flatten her stomach, the girl was sticking out her buttock; however, she failed to deceive my trained eyes. It looked as if she were carrying a full-term baby. The girl might have come to have a baby. If that was the case, one or two of her guardians should have accompanied her, but I saw no one. The girl, who stood alone in front of me, was trembling violently, her eyes brimming with tears. I had no way to distinguish whether she was enveloped with a sense of shame or fear. Most of all, it was most urgent for me to make her relax.

"I see you're carrying a baby. Well, don't be so afraid. You look a little too young but if you are old enough to have a baby, you can deliver and raise the baby very easily. Now, now, try to tell me your story from the beginning," I said soothingly as I picked up a chart. I was known as a blunt and recklessly-speaking woman; I had no clue where this sly voice came from, and it made me wonder about myself.

"No, ma'am. I am not pregnant. Who said I was pregnant?" the girl snarled at me in a clear voice, shaking her head hard.

"Oh, really? I'm sorry to surmise...well, then, what brought you here?"

"Umm...to be examined."

"This is a gynecologist's office. Did you come here knowing what kind of problems we deal with here?" I dealt with her as if she were a child, since it occurred to me that she might be either mentally deranged or retarded.

"Yes, I know," she replied confidently, looking me straight in the eyes.

On the chart, I filled in the formal information—her name, address, birth date, etc.—and then inquired about her symptoms and reasons for coming to the office.

According to the girl, she could not recall the exact date but sometime in early spring, her period had stopped and her stomach started to become large little by little. She also said that now for about two months it felt as if something were moving inside her. She said those were her symptoms. She was a precocious girl. I was ignorant of her purpose, but I could discern an intention to ridicule me. Her eyes were dry now, not leaving a trace of tears and she was exhibiting much more gall.

"I need to examine you to find out details, but I must tell you that most likely you are pregnant, according to what you've told me," I said respectfully, not losing my dignity.

"I haven't lain with a man," the girl protested in a considerably sharp tone of voice.

"I mistook your age," I said. "I thought you younger, Miss, but you are twenty years old according to your birth date. At your age, I suggest you'd better not tell a lie that won't be credible very long. Miss Choi, get ready for the examination...."

The girl only pursed her lips and glared at me intensely. Miss Choi nearly dragged her to the examination room. When I entered the room after putting on my gown, I found Miss Choi and the girl in a heated argument. The girl was doggedly refusing to comply with Miss Choi's instruction to prepare for the examination. I told Miss Choi to have the girl lie flat on the bed as I was examining her swollen stomach. The girl did not object to my touching her stomach. Even with my naked eyes, I could tell the fetus was playing well, its heartbeat was certain, and its position was excellent.

"You're pregnant. Either seven or eight months..."

"No, it can't be. I told you I haven't slept with a man," the girl shrieked as she got up with a jerk from a table and sat bolt upright. Soon after she threw off her underwear voluntarily and laid back down on a table.

"I don't think so. There's no way it's possible. Please give me a thorough examination," the girl said.

There was something frantically urgent in her attitude. It would be merciless for me to tell her the news once again that she was pregnant. I was hesitant to do so.

"It's not true, is it? Do I have some kind of terminal illness, ma'am?" the girl said, standing up from the table without her underwear. I was as embarrassed as if I were the one being interrogated rather than the girl.

"Terminal illness? Nonsense. Both Momma and the baby are healthy. You will be Momma soon, Miss," I faltered.

The girl collapsed abruptly into my chest.

"No way. No, it just can't be! I'll die. I'll surely die. I can't live. I have no choice but to die..."

The girl convulsed. Her face was drenched with tears and her shoulders and chest shook as if in a seizure. Her tears soaked the collar of my blouse and her arms locked tightly around my neck.

"What am I going to do, ma'am? What am I going to do? I have no choice but to die. Ma'am, ma'am..."

I encircled the girl with my arms. Her body shook even more violently.

"Big sister, what am I going to do? What should I do? I have no other way but to die. Big sister, I'll die this instant." When I'd learned I was carrying an unwanted baby, I went to see my senior from medical school who was practicing in Eri, and I'd cried out in similar fashion. My agony then, a truly hellish agony, was revived now clearly in my mind. I had never experienced a compelling, earnest desire to die either before that particular time or afterward. I felt a near-murderous fury toward the man who made this girl the way she was. My tears surged, as had the girl's, and I was so outraged and dejected that every fiber of my flesh trembled, just as she had. It wasn't because of either animosity or empathy I had for the girl; instead, it was my rancor that had been piling up since that distant past.

"Miss Choi, please hand me a sedative."

Miss Choi brought a pill, and I made the girl take it. The girl wailed as she swallowed the pill.

"Miss Choi, one more dosage..."

I also took a pill and went to my office, supporting the girl. I wasn't sure whether the sedative had taken effect or raging anger itself could not last forever. The girl stopped weeping and began to tell the whole story step by step.

When she attended middle school while living with her widowed mother, the girl said, she and her family were happy even though they barely made ends meet. After her mother died from some mysterious illness even before she reached the hospital, the three siblings were scattered among her uncle, maternal aunt, and paternal aunt respectively. The girl, since she was the oldest child, volunteered to live with her paternal aunt who led the most meager lifestyle among her relatives. Since her paternal aunt and her family barely made a living by running a shabby boarding house, it was natural for the girl to help by assuming the role of a housemaid; and she grew up strong. As she got older, however, the girl decided that she would rather find a position as maid for a decent monthly pay in a suitable place than continue to be a maid for her aunt. While she looked for an appropriate job opportunity, *it* happened. It was legitimate for her to be fiercely adamant about having not slept with a man. The girl shared a room with her aunt's daughter, her younger cousin. On a night when she slept alone while her cousin was away on a school trip, she was awakened by a strong weight all over her body. Although it was dark and she was half asleep, she said that she fought back with all her might and the struggle did not seem to have lasted too long. She didn't understand how she could possibly have become pregnant so easily. The girl was taken in her sleep in the darkness of her aunt's boarding house; she hadn't the slightest idea who the person was. What good purpose would it serve, she asked, even if she guessed who the man was.

If she had any speculation at all as to the trespasser, it would be a different story because she might be willing to stab him to death and then kill herself. She stated that it would be totally out of the question for her to have any kind of relationship with the man even if she knew who he was. When I mentioned such an option to solve her dilemma, she again became extremely agitated but quieted down again without too much ado.

"What shall I do, ma'am? Now that I know for sure, how am I going to live? Shame is a secondary matter. I just want to die. No, I want to kill that thing inside my stomach. I'll kill it. I'll kill it first, and only after that I'll die."

The girl shook her head once and straightened her neck. Her eyes flashed without tears. An unquestionable murderous intent showed in her eyes. Based on my personal experience, I can testify that if the climax of hatred is murderous intent, the most cold-hearted and passionate murderous intent among any other intent is against something inside one's own body. At that particular time of my life, if my senior from my medical school had not freed me from the fetus in my uterus in her clinic, I might likewise have chosen death. By no means was I ashamed. The only alternative to killing something inside me was for me to kill myself; that's why I wanted to die. Any person who has a murderous intent tries to leave a space to save his own neck; however, I knew from my own past that the magnitude of a murderous intent against something inside her body is grave enough to cause her to sacrifice her life readily, realizing that it is the one and only way to achieve this purpose.

I came to the realization that I could not let the girl die. It would be quite adequate for me to show the same mercy which my senior from my medical school had done for me. Moreover, am I not an absolute veteran in that field many times more than my senior? However, I can swear that I'd never, not even one single time, aborted a baby who was big enough to cry aloud once it came out to the world; in other words, I'd never killed a term baby. I wasn't unaware of the fact that this kind of practice is prevalent everywhere. Nonetheless, I couldn't bring myself to join this practice. No one dissuaded me and I wasn't afraid of other's opinions; it was an exceedingly strict boundary, self-imposed and maintained.

Of all things, I hadn't anticipated that I'd be at a loss because of this self-imposed rule on the last day before my retirement. This was that last day, and I wanted to keep this day according to my self-made promise. On the other hand, since it was my last day, I conceded it wouldn't hurt to cross over the boundary stealthily only once. However, even if I aborted a baby only once, a baby developed enough to breathe and cry, I felt the nickname of human butcher would follow me for the rest of my life. Even after I suffered a dreadful humiliation from Old Man Whang, who was adamant about not having a human butcher deliver his grandson, I managed to maintain a friendly relationship with him. The reason was that I let myself rise above it since his inconsiderate remark was nothing but a reflection of his rudeness. Another reason I could treat him lightly was that I had a sense of self-confidence because, among other reasons, I'd never been a human butcher. As I was about to trespass that boundary on my last day, the first thing that came to my mind was Old Man Whang's remark, "human butcher." It made me feel numbingly rueful.

However, the living hell-like pain of carrying an unwanted baby did not belong to the girl any longer; it was revived from the deep and dark place in my heart and her pain became mine. Without a strand of exaggeration, I found myself taking the girl's pain as my own. To be more precise, I was sharpening the edge of the knife of murderous intent alone, putting the girl and her feelings aside.

I didn't have to pay attention to Old Man Whang's sentiment. I'd long depended on my own will and whims. I'd never listened to others. Now that I gave careful thought after thought to whether I could attempt to save this baby, I was no longer free to yield to a lingering hesitation.

Finally, I made up my mind and gave my permission to get rid of the baby for the girl. She shed tears of relief and gratitude. Thinking that it was her wish from the beginning, the stormy vicissitudes of my own life that I had gone through in my mind faded away stealthily. The object of my hatred was not the girl any more, but the unwanted baby who was not conceived to be born but to be a source of calamity.

I undertook my task with determination that the progress would be slow since it was the first delivery for the girl. First, I wanted to observe the result after inserting three Lamiraria around the cervix and letting the girl relax comfortably. As evening approached, her cervical canal dilated unexpectedly to ten centimeters. That is considered a rapid development for a primipara. Her cervix was smooth and the location was excellent. By giving a liquid stimulant inside her cervix, I tried to induce labor and started an injection to accelerate the process. Childbirth was smoothly led along its track. The girl started moaning as her pain became more intense. I tried to console and encourage the girl while waiting for her yelling and screaming to begin. At the full onset of pain, she finally began to roar like an animal.

Unfathomable darkness canopied the window through uncounted hours. With the thick darkness as a backdrop, my sunken eyes were flashing brutally in a sweat-drenched, gleaming face reflected by the window which was transformed into a dark mirror. My face was the spitting image of the face of a torturer. The most vicious torturer, who had consistently repaid a tooth for a tooth, and an eye for an eye for three decades, was about to go mad.

As the girl, in her last ditch fight, made a ghastly sound, reminiscent of a sound from Hell, the intense heat of venom surging from the depth of my soul also flamed. At that very moment, the baby was born successfully, and the afterbirth was satisfactorily delivered. Excluding a lingering smell of blood, the room turned to a maternity ward and became a peaceful place as if everything which had happened before was only a dream. Miss Choi, who had shared the difficult task with this innocent girl, staggered as she yawned on the verge of being submerged in slumber. My body felt as exhausted as if it would melt away bit by bit; on the contrary, an indescribable sense of emptiness made my mind clear and wide-awake.

I couldn't tell what day it was, either before or after I'd looked at my watch several times. I came out of the maternity room to enjoy fresh air not contaminated by the smell of blood. However, I could smell it faintly, permeating the air everywhere I turned. Failure to eliminate the smell of blood was irritating as I experienced a sense of freedom for the first time. I walked up and down recklessly.

From somewhere I heard some faint but certain sound. At first, I thought it was coming from outside the window, but it wasn't. The sound reminded me of the heavy front gate of a traditional Korean house being opened and shut with a squeaky noise, and I was sure it was actually emerging from a point only an inch ahead although it sounded as if it came from a far away place.

With a strange sense of anticipation, I turned on the switch in the waiting room, my heart throbbing. First of all, the velvet chair came into my view. The sound was coming from the chair. On it the prematurely born baby was wrapped in clothes and enunciated its dangling thread of life with this odd noise.

"Miss Choi, Miss Choi, what made you do something like this? Who told you to do this? Why?" I called out to her in a loud voice. Miss Choi came out of her room, buttoning her gown and looked at me closely in disgust as if to scrutinize me under a microscope.

"Ma'am, you're not yourself these days. Why, ma'am, you said it yourself. You let me take care of the mother's afterbirth and you took care of the baby!"

I did? Did I really do that? With an intent not to have it live, it is unnecessary in the case of a prematurely born baby to set matters right by taking normal and proper care of the umbilical cord. Rumor had reached me that some doctors lay the baby down on its stomach and some even submerge it in water every once in a while; I couldn't be a part of those kinds of extremes. It's the prematurely born baby's mist-like fate that its life can be ended immediately just by leaving it alone. However, the girl's baby was still alive. Without realizing it, I'd treated the prematurely born baby as a perfectly normal, warm, and healthy infant. Its umbilical cord was well treated, and it was even wearing a diaper.

Ah, from now on, I'd need to hide nothing. I wanted to have a baby, a baby I could raise and love. My yearning to deliver a live baby at least once for the last time with my own hands was nothing but indeed a mask of my deep desire for a baby. I felt my candid pining kicking off my every repression and mask, gushing forth strongly as a life force.

I held the baby, who was making a strange weak sound, deep in my arms and like a mad woman, I ran down the stairs and kicked the door open. Behind my back, Miss Choi was yelling something in a trembling voice. The city had locked its latch in the dark and was sunk in a deep sleep. A large hospital! A large hospital that has an incubator! I rushed like an arrow, holding the baby in my arms. The large hospital that was equipped with incubators was very far away.

Somewhere, a night patrolman grabbed my collar. The sound of whistles surrounded me from every direction. I showed him the thing in my arms—baby, baby, I must save my baby—and I wept bitterly. *A crazy bitch. Let her be!* The sound of a whistle scattered into pieces and became distant as the road was again wide open for me. However, the large hospital with incubators was still a long distance away. Farther away than the hospital was any ray of hope for the baby's life. In my consciousness that hope flickered, too—faintly, like a fading firefly.

The hospital was still so far away. However, in my thoughts I was already throwing myself at the feet of the doctor in charge and begging him to save the baby's life. *Sir, please save it. It's my baby. It's the only baby I have. I bore it just now. It was premature. I was punished. You see, I didn't want the baby be born. But, I'm different now. Save it. Please... The doctor wouldn't believe me. I'm too old now. I'm nothing but an old woman who cannot bear a child in anyone's eyes. All right then, I'll tell him it's my grandson. It would be even better to tell the doctor the baby is the only son in five generations. Sir, please save our only son who is the only son in five consecutive generations. I won't forget your kindness until I die. Please, save him, please!* Tears streaked down ceaselessly onto my cheeks and I was choking acutely.

However, when I finally reached the hospital and gave the baby in my arms to the doctor in charge, not a word came out of my mouth.

The baby was already dead. I detected a glimpse of sympathy which crossed the doctor's face, a reflection of the look on the face of the night watchman who had said *A crazy bitch. Let her be!* I held the baby in my arms again with utter care and left the hospital. A taxi, its beams low, passed slowly by me. The city, night having passed, was turning its body and rubbing its eyes. The baby was born yesterday and died today. Yesterday was the very last day for me to hold on to my wish for to deliver a live baby. My wish finally came to a realization on the last day before my retirement, and today is a brand new day. I had come to grips with the fact that my yearning had been finally realized only after knowing that it had turned out to be in vain.

Still holding the baby deep inside my arms, I slowly walked without stopping toward the neighborhood where my new house was located. Today is the day for me to move into my new house. I was going to move in with my baby. I was going to lay the baby to sleep in the sunny side of the courtyard in my new house. Why, my baby has died! I thought that a woman who has only a baby's tomb is much more beautiful than a woman who never had a baby in her lifetime. Next spring I will scatter portulaca seed over the earth where the baby sleeps—the seeds like the eyes of the countless babies I had killed—the eyes that had never become conscious even for a moment.

I had no idea how far I'd come; I heard the cries of Christians emanating from a church. Even in that neighborhood, there was a church, offering an early morning service with crying Christians worshipping. Church-goers were swarming around the church. Holding small Bibles in their hands, worshipers, who carried loads of sorrow in their hearts, were assembling endlessly from somewhere.

On the spur of the moment, I found myself heading for the church, mingling with the church-goers, nursing a colossal sorrow that could swallow up the wail of every Christian and the baby.

Sorrow was no longer a hard mass deep inside me. A tear drop could now indeed be squeezed out. It had been suppressed until it could flood into a spacious, open place.

POVERTY THAT IS STOLEN

Again, I found Sang-hoon's attitude a little disgusting. When I lifted the lid of the stew pot, despite the other ingredients I saw only a large anchovy on a slice of tofu. Sang-hoon saw it also.

"Why didn't you get rid of that damn anchovy's head?" he asked. "It's creepy to see an anchovy's eye." He spoke gently, knitting his brows.

Defying his criticism and also wishing to show off to him a little, I broke its head off right then and there and popped it into my mouth, chewing it with exaggerated savor. "Don't you know the head has more nutrition?" I retorted.

Even if an anchovy's huge, it's still just an anchovy. I couldn't understand why he made such a fuss about that insignificant eye. Why, it was no larger than a mustard seed! Sang-hoon had made me not only sick to my stomach but also uneasy and nervous.

In a gesture intended to reveal my displeasure, I glared at him. Sang-hoon, however, did not complain. Instead, he began to fish out anchovies and eat them, pushing slices of tofu and turnip leaves aside.

"Oh, man! Not even one anchovy has its eyes closed!"

"Why? Because they died before their time. That's why!" I said.

"If that's true, better types of fish like sea-bream or cod would die with their eyes open too."

"They do. Why even talk about it?" I asked. We giggled and finished our breakfast.

"Well? Do you like living with a woman?" I asked.

"Yes, I do. But aren't you uncomfortable having such a tiny room?"

I explained to him that in this neighborhood a family of five or six could easily live in a room this size, itemizing for him once more the amount of money we were saving by living together. Whenever I pointed of how much we were saving, I felt good, as if I were riding the wind. First, we saved 4000 *won* rent—the largest item—then our savings from paying a single bill for briquettes, groceries, herbs and spices. The list of items that now entailed less expense would go on endlessly if I wanted to name them one by one. Although I mentioned the savings from light, water, and even sewer bills by being one household instead of two, I deliberately omitted the most important thing of all: we liked each other.

This was the most important reason we were living together, yet I discounted it every time without fail. I was too shy to mention it. Besides, I wanted Sang-hoon to say that special phrase, *we like each other*, to me. Although I'd made the suggestion that we live together, I hadn't uttered those words. I was brazen enough to say, without a second thought, that we'd use only two briquettes instead of four by heating only one room instead of two, and we'd also save a half or one more briquette a day by sleeping locked in each other's arms under the same blanket, but I hadn't spoken that phrase to him. It wasn't that I didn't want to say it, but that I wanted him to say it to me first. I was waiting for the right moment.

I fixed a lunchbox for Sang-hoon and sent him off to work, then washed the dishes in a flurry. Sang-hoon worked at a factory which plated different metals. I was told that in that factory, a silver ring was transformed dexterously into gold; a pair of nickel spoons or chopsticks were changed into silver. I remarked to him that there had to be some difference between a real gold ring and a plated one. He said their skill is so phenomenal that no one could tell the difference just by looking at the products with the naked eye.

By the time I began the dishes it was time for the women from all six rooms, which were joined in a row, to do the same chore. We all washed dishes on a shelf along the narrow wooden verandah which was attached to each room. The briquette furnace and utensils, such as buckets and soy sauce bottles, were placed on the floor beneath this shelf. Therefore, this tiny verandah played a dual role as both sink and cooking area. The landlord built this nominal kitchen for his tenants by enclosing the space between the angled rafters and the block wall. The tiny bit of sky that used to be visible was hidden now, blocked by a slate wall and the overhang of the roof. As a result, the make-shift kitchen was dank, and air circulation was poor. The lingering odors from burningbriquettes and from food was stifling. The stench arising from things salty, moldy, peppery, and rancid was so bad that it made your eyes water just walking into this place. The odors permeated the room, your clothes, and even the bedding. I was sure my body had this odor, too.

Nonetheless, I refused to hate or be ashamed of this odor. My parents and two older brothers had hated this smell. They thought they'd rather be dead than endure this odor, and they, indeed, died one day, leaving me all alone. As a means of revenge toward my sorry parents and the siblings who had deserted me, I tried to train myself to get used to the odor.

I knew these women were all dying to speak to me when they washed dishes. They seemed curious about the young man I'd brought in, but appeared to have no ill intention. Judging by the way the old woman who lived in the last room of the row clacked her tongue and studied me, I knew she wanted to tell me again to have a wedding ceremony, however simple it might be, but I didn't pay any attention at all to her remarks. I could easily comply with this concern for ceremony and treat these six aunties to a bowl of noodle soup, but until Sang-hoon told me he liked me, it was out of the question. While I washed dishes, I sang loudly, discouraging them from speaking to me. Washing dishes for two people didn't take long enough to finish one stanza—*building a picture-perfect house over that green field...* The other women tenants, like me, finished washing dishes in a flurry. They had to hurry off to factories or to jobs provided by the government for the unemployed or destitute.

It was a wintry morning outside with a biting wind as sharp as a knife. The wind licked the street as if it were sweeping it, pushing briquette dust and filthy litter into a pile at the roadside. The pile then was transformed into a spiral and ascended high in the air as it scattered that dirt into every corner in all directions. The wind burned my cheeks, and everything looked dim and obscure in the midst of the sand and dust. The slate and tin roofs of the shanties stacked one after another along the hillside made strange noises as they twisted in the wind.

Although the scarves around made them look like turtles in their shells, and their faces were covered except for their eyes, as if they were masked thieves, people, to my amazement, recognized one another. It was because they encountered one another nearly at the same time each day on the street. A certain woman, on her way to work with a shovel in her hand, winked at me as she called, "I understand you're having fun these days!" Strangely, intense sensuality emanated from her even through the layers of ragged clothes. Like the time when, as a teenager, I saw an animal in heat, I experienced mixed feelings about this woman—timidity, repulsion, and mysterious curiosity. Then I became uneasy as I thought of my undefined relationship with Sang-hoon. I slept with him, justifying it by the reason that we thus saved a half briquette.

On this winter morning everything was frozen, but in every alley in the hillside village you could feel movement brisk as a live force, and everyone on the street was highly animated—like strong, spring plants pushing upward into life. How Mother had detested the unique liveliness of people who felt the claws of poverty and lived with it, refusing to yield. Mother used to remark that she was fed up to the teeth with their scorn of society and their intensity, but she never had the audacity to question their role. Thus Mother imbued her husband and sons with her scorn of such lives, and they ended up committing suicide with her. They thrust upon me the sight and smell of their poverty and ugly deaths—their eyes wide open just like the anchovy in the stew. But I felt close and friendly living with the poverty Mother, Father, and my brothers refused to accept, preferring to give up their lives. I was shrouded with a keen sense of warm pleasure even as my heart was choked. They pretended to despise poverty, but I knew they were in reality scared of it. Like a child who loves to show off, I thrust out my chest and ran headlong down the steep hill.

The factory in which I worked was actually a factory in name only, for it was only a small room with a heated floor and no larger than three or four *kan* [36 square feet]. Piles of fabric scraps cut in different sizes were on the floor and three sewing machines were placed by the window. The owner stacked fabrics one on top of another, put a pattern on them, and cut them. She then stopped her cutting and smiled weakly as she looked up at me. When I saw her cut the fabric in such tiny pieces, my heart ached. But even a doll needs a complete set of clothes. We had to make panties, skirts, and bras for them. Pockets, buttons, and even a touch of embroidery were required on the dolls' dresses. A strip of lace was required at the hem of a slip. Since this work was divided among us, it required several people to finish a single tiny wardrobe for a doll. The only thing I had to do was to sew these patterns that auntie cut out for me on a sewing machine. As I endlessly sewed doll clothes, I felt like a dress-making slave exiled to a nation of tiny people.

The owner would be exhausted by evening and ask me to pound her shoulders to relax the muscles; she would then curse these good-for-nothing dolls, who weren't worthy of so many clothes. But we knew that if the day came when these dolls stopped wearing clothes and left the factory naked, the owner's livelihood, as well as our own, would be taken away

While sewing, I enjoyed dreaming of someday learning the art of dressmaking. I dremed that one day I'd become a first-rate dressmaker who would design and make real dresses and find a position in a first class fashion salon. The daydreams made my routine job seem a lot less tedious.

But if I actually became a first-class dressmaker, and Sang-hoon was still a laborer at the factory which specialized in plating metals, I didn't know what might happen, which made me a little nervous. Although it was undoubtedly a wondrous skill to cunningly transform silver to gold, I couldn't help but think that they were too clever, that they were doing something crooks and swindlers might do. According to Sang-hoon, the vendors who bought these rings wholesale never deceived their customers by pretending they were genuine gold. Their customers coveted real gold rings but were too poor to afford them. These vendors sold them rings at a cheap price, and I gathered from what he said that they were indeed doing something good. If that were true, I wanted one of those rings.

Someday Sang-hoon will tell me he likes me, I just know it! If he says it while carefully placing a gold-plated ring on my finger, how delicious that will be! I won't tell anyone it's plated. This happy fantasy always made me smile broadly.

Unable to discern what was making me so happy, the owner doused my fantasy. "Tut, tut, that mother of yours deserved to die. Yes, the bitch deserved death!" she muttered. I couldn't imagine why she said that, why she poured out something so vile.

Mother had died only several months before, as this woman well knew, and yet she spilled her venom like that. This auntie was the first to rush to the scene when Mother was found dead. Even then she, shivering violently, said, "Look at this wretched woman. She deserved to die!"

This auntie had been the one and only friend Mother had left. Even after we were hanging by the thread of poverty, she visited us. She also was the friend who, to some degree, understood Mother's vanity. When the company where Father worked went bankrupt, causing him to lose his job in his old age without any retirement pension, it was this auntie, Mother's one and only friend, to whom Mother had gone and consulted about our future livelihood. This auntie had been widowed when she was very young and had supported herself through all the seasons of life.

When she found out we'd been living with virtually zero savings for all these years, auntie was flabbergasted. Then she challenged Mother. "What did you do with all those lump sums of cash I let you take from *ke* [a mutual savings club among women friends] several times?"

Mother tried to find an excuse, saying, "You have no idea of the lifestyle of a salaried man's family. It's bound to cause a considerable deficit every month, and I was busy making up for that deficit with that *ke* money."

Auntie said, "You deserve to live a hard life from now on. I suggest you rent out one of the rooms of your house and open a grocery store with that money. Fortunately, the location of your house is very good, and I bet you can live all right from the store if you and your husband work diligently."

Mother, however, did not take her friend's advice. "How can I open a small shop when my friends have husbands who made it in the world and now lead affluent lives? I'm too ashamed to do it!" Mother said.

To live life to the fullest, a man must have a big idea and a brave spirit. He must also know how to grasp the right opportunity and this was Father's chance. Mother pushed Father with this idea. Even when Father was working faithfully at the company and earning a decent living, Mother was fretful when she returned home from her outings. She complained that others had more know-how about living well and their assets consistently swelled, while our damned household still lived in this stagnant condition, this stalemate. She rebuked Father as a master rebukes his servant, making his life pure hell. Such was Mother. She hoped that Father, having lost his job and thus escaping the life of an insignificant salaried man, would see an excellent opportunity to become a great, risk-taking entrepreneur.

Mother wore her shoes out visiting a friend who claimed to be a millionaire and finally managed to borrow a lump sum of cash by using our house as collateral. Encouraged by Mother's aggressivness, Father rented an office space, had phones installed, acquired a swiveling chair, hired an errand girl, and assumed the role of president of the company. Mother loved to call Father at his office on the phone several times each day. *Oh, Miss Choi? It's the president's wife. Please let me speak to the president.* Mother couldn't live without uttering those words every chance she had.

Alas! Even before Mother had the tone of a president's wife down pat, Father's company went under and everything, including our house, was taken away. We were unable to pay back even one cent, not only of the interest but also the principal that Mother had borrowed with our house as collateral. Consequently, ownership of our house was transferred, and we were kicked out.

To make matters worse, due to some small amount of spending money which Mother had borrowed from time to time, household items that were of cash value had also been snatched away. Mother lamented ruefully to her wealthy friend, *I never thought you could be so cruel!* Later Mother had a maddening tête-à-tête with her friend. In the end, everything went her friend's way. I still recall vividly the day when that elegant and dignified lady, without so much as a twitch of an eye, seized all our possessions.

Despite all this, Mother's friend did not throw us out onto the street; instead, she let us lease a room.

"You deserve to go through the worst hardships," Mother's friend said, "but I feel sorry for your children and that's why I show this compassion."

Mother's friends—both the auntie who makes doll's clothing and her wealthy friend who has millions come and go through her fingertips, told Mother that she deserved to have hard times. However, neither of them said she deserved to die.

Even after Mother had no choice but to live in a rented room, she flatly refused to acknowledge that she could no longer send her children to school. She raved like a child, saying how under the sun could she not think about sending her children to college. She was human, not an animal like a dog or a pig. Father and Mother had no plan whatsoever as to how to earn a living, or even a cent, but only chanted blindly, "Study! study!" They took the deposit intended to go toward the lease and spent it for tuition on my two brothers' third-class university and my high school. And then we ended up moving to a room rented on a monthly basis, putting up a skimpy deposit.

The day came when we had to give up school—and other things as well. Finally, we found ourselves taking a room in the neighborhood on the hill, paying 4000 *won* monthly rent without putting up a deposit. Even then Mother brushed off the fact that we had become real paupers. The moldy and rancid odor of poverty made her shudder as if she were having a fit. As if the poor were creepy, filthy animals, she never really made contact with them. She was disgusted by poor people's unbending zest for life. She put them down, wondering how in the world they could possibly live in their cave-like rooms in such unsanitary conditions, even if they were of an unassociable low class, poverty-stricken, reeking with their unbearably foul odor, and human in face only.

In spite of her feelings, however, Mother was the worst when it came to house-keeping. On the wooden verandah attached to our room, dirty dishes were stacked and placed at will until the next meal time, inviting the neighborhood flies and providing them with a field day. This was Mother's way of stubbornly refusing to acknowledge poverty.

The auntie who made doll's clothes suggested to Mother several times that Mother work for her so that Mother's children need not starve, but this fell on deaf ears. As a last resort, she invited me to come work for her. I jumped with joy at this opportunity and went there to learn to make miniature clothes. It was an easy job, not requiring skill as long as you knew how to operate a sewing machine. The auntie, after watching my work for several days, said she'd pay me 10,000 *won* a month. She said she'd grant this special payment in my case, as with this generous sum she would be responsible for saving my family.

I rushed home in a single bound that day, hoping to make my family happy with the good news. That mere 10,000 *won* would actually be nothing but pocket money. After paying our monthly rent, the remainder wouldn't be enough to buy rice for the five members of our family. Nonetheless, I, the youngest, proved I could earn 10,000 *won* and thus established the idea that every member could earn at least 10,000 *won* if they would take off the mask of defending their honor or keeping up a good front and be ready to throw themselves into hard work.

"We can make it if we unite as one heart. Since everyone in this neighborhood makes a living in this way, you don't need to feel ashamed. Adults, children, and old alike earn money; they work like dogs but live like aristocrats. Some households have a TV; some feast on roast pork once every several days. In any event, they live singing songs and laughing heartily. We can live like that, too. Please! Since our family has neither the old nor children, all of us can earn money. If we don't rely on just one person but all go out to work, I'm sure there's no reason we shouldn't live adequately." I tried to encourage my family in this earnest way.

"So, then. Are you afraid we might come to depend on you? No way. Never! You wait and see." Mother said. The following day when I returned home from work, I found my family dead. On an Indian summer day, they had a briquette stove going and had every tiny crack of the room sealed tightly. Four members of the family were found dead, side by side. Without me!.

Since I began living with Sang-hoon, I'd developed the habit of stopping at the market on my way home from work, no matter how late it might be. I looked at cod and sea bream displayed on a fish stand. Although I told Sang-hoon confidently in the morning that no matter how good and expensive a fish might be, it was bound to have its eyes open when it was dead, I had to be sure. Sure enough, every fish was lying flat in the display case with its clear eyes wide open. I couldn't help feeling ready to burst with laughter when I toyed with the notion that fish have no eyelids.

I bought a salted mackerel. That mackerel, being so oily, would produce not only a great deal of smoke but also a stinking odor if grilled on the surface of a briquette. The odor would penetrate into the tunnel-like kitchen six households share and fill it with a strong, fishy stench. Triumphantly, I took quick, short steps toward the neighborhood on the hill. Sang-hoon was already home, laying flat on his back without having done anything.

"Don't you remember we agreed that whoever came home first was supposed to fix rice?"

Sang-hoon turned a deaf ear; instead, he lit a cigarette in a leisurely manner.

"Are you really going to act this way? If you want me to work, don't you think you ought to be supportive of me? Agree? I don't think we live together so one of us can benefit from the other!"

We'd been assuming equal responsibility, evenly dividing all our living expenses. As a result, we agreed to share household chores as well. Nonetheless, I felt I was losing ground by doing more housework than I bargained for, and I was angry about it.

"Please leave me alone today." Sang-hoon was dispirited. He appeared to be hiding some sorrow.

"Did something unpleasant happen at your workshop today?" I became amicable instantly.

"Maan-sik vomited blood today at work," Sang-hoon said.

"Oh, my good heavens. He really has TB then! So? What happened afterward?"

I hadn't met Maan-sik yet but knew him through Sang-hoon as someone who was pale and always had a hacking cough. He said he suspected Maan-sik had TB and complained that he had the worst time during lunch break when they ate together.

"He vomited blood out of the blue, lost consciousness, and collapsed. The owner must have panicked, fearing that he might have to deal with a corpse. He screamed at us, the innocent ones, demanding that we take Maan-sik home right away. So we followed his order, also delivering the money that the owner paid him, and returned."

"How much did the owner give him?" I asked.

"How much? He paid him through yesterday."

"That damn miser! You guys just stood there silently and watched him?" I asked.

"What else could we have done?"

"You tell me that one of your friends fell into that kind of predicament and you, his fellow workers, just watched him? Are you implying that you felt good after that? It wasn't the decent thing to do. Whatever people may say, I think it's only right for needy people to help one another. We're all in the same boat. It's not right to ignore the needy!"

When I had finished my speech, Sang-hoon did not seem to quite grasp it and appeared at a loss. When baffled like this, Sang-hoon seemed extremely dense and stupid. With his striking good looks he didn't look destitute, but he appeared to be an idiot. I had a fierce revulsion to this trait in Sang-hoon, and as a result, I was angry. I again told him that we, the poor, ought not to abandon one another. I told him we should collect money and take it to the sick person and comfort his family. I admonished Sang-hoon to tell a white lie to Maan-sik. Tell him, I said, not to worry about anything but to take care of himself. I tried to persuade Sang-hoon to do this until Maan-sik's death. When I said "until death," it sounded like an eternity, but since the man had already vomited blood, how long could he continue to live? In my bad mood, I calculated even this.

We picked at our dinner, sat there awkwardly in silence, and went to bed. It was best for us to be in bed because our room had no protection from the draft. The wind was so biting that when we left our noses outside the covers, they froze. To make matters worse, the temperature of the floor was only nominally warm, not enough to rid the room of the chill. Consequently, we had no choice but to glue ourselves to each other. When we did what any man and woman who lie under the same blanket would do, I thought, *not this, ah, ah, not like this.* This thought had nothing to do with the tension derived from our being equal novices in the area of lovemaking. I hoped to feel something warm and peaceful while making love but always ended up feeling the opposite. I wanted to cry but suppressed the desire. I used to cry often, even when I was happy, and I appreciated that light-hearted sense of everything having been cleansed after a good cry. Nonetheless, I didn't want to cry now.

The following morning I handed our joint savings book to Sang-hoon and tried to convince him that the one collecting the money should contribute first, willingly, and then take up a collection from the others, and by doing so, it would go easily. I asked him over and over to take the money to the sick man as soon as possible, whatever and whenever he collected. Even all day at work, I felt pretty good about myself, convinced that I was doing something good. The mere thought that I'd survived and was now able to help someone else made me feel proud.

However, when I returned home that night, I was so shocked I nearly fainted. Not a penny was left in the savings account. Sang-hoon said he'd taken out every penny and given it to Maan-sik. He couldn't have done such a thing unless he had gone completely mad or stone crazy. By the same token, I wouldn't have stood for it unless I had also gone mad or stone crazy.

"I'm sorry," he said, "but, I don't think you understand. Who do you think I can collect money from? All of them are poor."

"What? They're all poor! What are we? Rich? Are we? Are we rich?"

Failing to overcome my anger, I grabbed his shirt collar and dragged him, slamming his head against the wall. Sang-hoon grinned carefreely. Although more than half of that 30,000 won belonged to him, Sang-hoon didn't seem to care. I knew that he didn't have any compassion for the TB patient. Neither the money nor the sick man were of any concern to Sang-hoon. So that was the problem! Some people want to help but can't bring themselves to part with their precious money. They take out money to give debate whether to give 2,000 or 3,000 won, and then put the money back, remaining troubled over the 1,000 won difference. The conflict between altruism and selfishness could last over an hour for these people as they pondered how much they should give. Without going through any heart-rending conflict, Sang-hoon had thrown away over 30,000 won as heedlessly as he might discard a worn-out shoe. When I realized this, I shuddered.

"Who do you think you are? What are you anyway? Are you rich? Are you?" I screamed at him again to shake off the sick feeling I had. Sang-hoon just kept on grinning. I had tired myself out, but although worn to a frazzle, I couldn't fall asleep. He, however, fell asleep immediately. Under a dim twenty-watt florescent light, which was nearing its life span, I looked at his sleeping face carefully. *For goodness sake, what are you? Who are you who can sleep so peacefully after throwing over 30,000 won out the window as if it were a tattered shoe? Okay, I can live with the fact that your spirit is unbroken! However, your spirit is very different from that of the poor people. They're unrelenting, tenacious, and fresh. You're entirely different..* I trembled with fear.

I'd met Sang-hoon for the first time in front of the covered wagon of a street vendor who sold a cheap cake for 5 won. At first glance I could tell he was a mechanic at one of those domestic industries which stood nearby row upon row. In any event, I could not bear to watch the way he ate the cake. He seemed overly self-conscious of his filthy hands: he didn't pick up the cake with his bare hand but wrapped it with a floral-embosseded white paper napkin and ate it. After he finished eating it, he patted his lips with the napkin with subtle dignity.

Although he ate the same 5 won cake, with that darned napkin he was savoring some kind of superiority over the famished and exhausted factory workers who ate cakes there that evening, and his display of superiority made the sight of him an awful thorn in my side. At the time, I couldn't afford to pack a lunch and was so starved that I gulped down one cake after another. Only after I finished gobbling did I realize that the offensive guy who'd wrapped the cake with a napkin and eaten it so daintily had been watching me all this time.

"Aren't you thirsty after cramming those cakes down like that?" he asked. "Would you like me to buy you a cup of tea somewhere?"

At his invitation to buy me a cup of tea, I laughed and kept on laughing, doubling over until I was choked.

"You must have heard that line some place. Even an idiot knows how to lure a woman with an invitation to go to the tea room," I replied, still laughing. It was indescribably funny. "You and me in our shabby clothes and having these cheap cakes for a meal..."

A tea room was a place beyond our means. Nevertheless, I found myself falling for this idiot, and on days I didn't see him at a street-vendor's place, I felt empty inside as if I'd lived that entire day without a purpose. When I was told that he lived alone, I assumed he was an orphan, too; therefore, I tempted him with the suggestion that he live with me. That's the whole story of how I met Sang-hoon, and I've been living with him ever since.

Even after the incident concerning the TB patient, we continued to live together, and I was frequently irritated enough to pick a fight with Sang-hoon. I pretended I was badgering him over the 30,000 won, but that wasn't really the case. Sporadic hatred toward him for being able to live in a happy-go-lucky way each day, forgetting entirely about the TB patient, crept often into my mind and was the cause of my harassment.

One day, without any warning, Sang-hoon failed to come home. The next day and the subsequent day he still didn't return. I waited and waited for him. Then I managed to overcome my humiliation, and I went to see him at his workplace. I was told that he'd stopped coming to work, too. The owner said the most awful thing to me. He said he was sure some horrible accident must have happened to him somewhere. He said that if someone were just skipping off to another place, it was customary to borrow money from wages before the following payday. One would also owe a considerable debt in neighborhood shops. Sang-hoon, however, disappeared without claiming his earned wages. Judging from this, he must have been hit by a car and killed or stabbed to death by a gangster. The mystery of his disappearence, the owner asserted confidently, would fall into one of these two categories.

The wings of my imagination spread wildly as I pictured some such gruesome event, and I couldn't sleep a wink. I hadn't the slightest idea, however, what to do for him or how to approach it. I was more frightened of my own impotency when I pictured the magnitude of the city of Seoul. How huge and complicated it seemed! Every night I slept in a fetal position, crying in my sleep, but I went to work as usual in the morning. I had to go to work to make a living. Each day the hope that he might have returned home while I was working sustained me. Thus, I could spend the day with the belief that he'd come back. I'd then run like mad up the steep slope of the hill to my home, believing that the light was turned on in my room. This burning and buoyant expectation caused me to go to work in high spirits.

I understood vaguely that miracles always happen subtly, unnoticed by anyone. Keeping this in mind, I had to leave my room unoccupied every day to have a miracle take place in my absence. Although each expectation proved fruitless, I was filled with hope every day. Waiting was the only thing I could do.

Then one day I did see the light in my room. Sang-hoon had indeed returned. He greeted me with a cold and collected expression. He was wearing nice clothes and was clean from head to toe, which made his sitting in my room seem extremely unreal since I'd never considered, even in my wildest imagination, that he would return as such a splendid person. I'd imagined only that he would return in a pitiful condition. I was bewildered .If only I could run away somewhere for the time being and reappear again, I thought, I'd be able to get things under control.

"What's happened?" I barely managed to ask, and it came out in a subdued tone, as if hard phlegm blocked my throat. My voice was foreign even to my own ears.

"Oh, I came to pay you back. How much was it? Thirty thousand won or something?" he said kindly, yet in the business-like tone of a banker. I felt that every fiber of affection wriggling in me was vanishing for good. I was plunged into a torrent of confusion.

Suddenly a glistening college pin on the lapel of his jacket caught my eye. A thick book, which seemed to be his, lay on the table. Like a bolt of lightning, a certain notion popped into my head.

"Are you crazy? You finally did steal! Stealing big time! You also pretend to be a college student. Are you really crazy?" I yelled at him in a frightened tone.

I came to the conclusion that he had done all of this because of me—because I'd nagged him day in and day out about that 30,000 *won*. I was enveloped with over-whelming fear, but at the same time, I was so touched my heart throbbed. I was about to burst into tears and was ready to be held in his arms. He rejected me gently.

"Look here. Please don't do that. Now collect yourself and listen carefully to the things that I'm about to say. I'm not crazy, and I'm not a thief. I'm the precious son of a wealthy family and a college student, as you can see. My father is a little eccen-tric. He was somewhat concerned about his son growing up not knowing any kind of hardships in life, so, during school vacation, he kicked me out without a penny so I'd experience the worst of times and learn the value of money. Do you understand?"

How in the world could I understand? Mother got a kick out of pretending to know how the rich lived in luxury. I'd heard Mother's remark that money talks—money made it possible for a person to do anything and everything under the sun, and every pleasure available in life gathered around money in silent flattery. I'd never heard, however, of the wealthy who made it a part of their game to act as if they were poor.

"My father's a remarkable person. He's an exceptionally fine man such as can rarely be found in this day and age. He wanted to have his children experience many hard-ships instead of enjoying only a luxurious lifestyle. I could have these very precious experiences during my school break, and I owe him for this. It was a valuable experi-ence that money couldn't buy."

Oh, yes, that reminded me of something! I recalled the auntie who made doll clothes telling a story she'd seen in on TV: the son of a financial mogul sold drink-ing water or something of that nature to learn about life in the real world. I thought it a nauseating story even if it was only a TV drama. What do they think of poverty that they dare jeer at it? I couldn't care less what the rich do with their own money, but I can't find it in my heart to forgive them for making a mockery of poverty! I may forgive them for making fun of a poor girl, but I can't forgive them for bantering about poverty itself. Besides, they could never experience my kind of poverty! Poverty is fate to me.

"Father is satisfied with my endurance in overcoming a life of dire hardship for all that time. In fact, I think he might recommend that his friends try the same thing with their children. To be honest, people lean toward raising their kids with too much ease and luxury today!"

Good Heavens! I'm hearing that this poverty game is going to be popular among high society from now on. Fattened elderly gentlemen will flock togrther and make remarks like, "Haven't you sent your son there yet?"

"No, sirree, but he's in the process of obtaining a passport."

"I didn't mean sending him to that insignificant America. I mean sending him to a slum!"

Sang-hoon was speaking again. "So I told Father about you, taking advantage of his good mood. As I informed him of the actual circumstances of life here, painting him an actual portrait of how pitiful the slum is, I hinted about you as though it were not an important matter. I told him there was a certain woman who lured a man to her bed to share body warmth so that she could save a half briquette. Of course I didn't tell him that I was the man who was lured. Father unexpectedly showed a deep interest and suggested that I bring the woman home and have her do little chores around the house. If she proved to be useful, he said he'd be happy to send her to night school. It's an excellent opportunity for you. You can give up this miserable life by taking advantage of this opportunity. This kind of life is not only pathetic, but also shameful. You should feel ashamed of yourself for luring a man to your bed just to save a half briquette."

Yes, I'm more than ashamed. Ashamed! Ashamed! Ashamed! I'm so ashamed I wish I could evaporate like mist at this instant! I'm ready to disappear. Yes, I'm indeed ashamed!

"Here's some money for you. I'll be back again for you, so be ready with your clothing. I want to take you with me now but you can't go in that shabby attire," he said.

I threw the money in his face and kicked him out of my room. I raved and ranted so loudly that the six renters rushed out in their bare feet and watched the commotion as he ran away. He was so frightened that he nearly lost his wits as I screamed, showering him with profanity.

"You poor thing. You've gone mad!" Although he had mumbled sympathetically to himself as he slowly put on his shoes before he ran off, he would forget about me very soon. As he had so quickly forgotten about the TB patient, so he would forget me.

After I ran him off like that, I was proud of myself for being able to refuse his offer. However, my room was not the same place as it was even minutes before. The ceiling paper was stained by rain and, due to the moisture, sagged hopelessly along one side. The filthy wallpaper exposed the wall here and there; the vinyl suitcase had a broken zipper; a cheap Formica table had a broken leg, a worn-out transistor radio was connected to a battery larger than it was; the pot and utensils were bent and crooked. Although all these items were still in the exact same spot, they were not the things of yesterday. They were nothing but meaningless and ugly. Yesterday they had carefully defined my poverty; today they were nothing but a bunch of ugly useless objects.

After a house is demolished, the boards of which the house was built, the slate, the mud piles, the concrete blocks, and the door become a pile of meaningless rubbish. Now the belongings out of which my poverty was composed were just thrown out there carelessly as sordid and meaningless junk. I didn't believe that I could restore them again to a meaningful whole. Not even my poverty was there in my room—my poverty, which had made of all these things a coherent whole. Sang-hoon had stolen my poverty. My poverty, the meaning of my poverty, how possibly could I get it back?

Through my family's misfortunes, I had known all along how greedy wealthy people are. I had known the nature of the rich, who had ninety-nine coins and yet coveted one more. But I never dared to think, even in my dreams, that the rich would covet poverty. They couldn't be content with only their shining academic careers and their comfortable lives. They even stole poverty to find somelthing that would enhance their multi-colored life, making it even more colorful. I had no idea of the magnitude of this yearning within them.

When my poverty was stolen I felt, for the first time, a dark sense of despair, something I hadn't felt even when my family lost everything.

As if adding one more piece of trash to the pile, I threw myself into my room—into the middle of a meaningless desolation—giving up my entire being to its bone-aching cold.

A SKETCH OF THE FADING SUN

Mr. Chu and his wife were living in the Green Belt, away from the blizzard of soot and smoke of Seoul. Because of the impossibility of obtaining a permit for either the construction or extension of a building in the area and the lack of transportation facilities, real estate values in the Green Belt were low.

The air was fresh and clean. It was an ideal neighborhood for a couple: a retired man who did not have to go to work and return home at a specified time and an old woman who took great pleasure in gardening. Quite frequently either Mr. Chu or his wife had business downtown to tend separately and would return home worn to a frazzle. Though they had to change buses several times in order to get downtown, they always blamed the foul air in the city for their sheer exhaustion. Returning home, they were always grateful, once again, that they lived far away in the Green Belt. They deliberately took deep breaths as they gazed at the spacious sky and the wide open view of the mountain facing their house. A single day at home was sufficient for them to feel hale and hearty again, as if the city soot had been thoroughly purged from their lungs.

Mr. Chu would celebrate his sixtieth birthday in the coming year, and his wife her fifty-eighth. Although they were nearing the age at which one often suffers from some kind of old-age malady, the couple were blessed with perfect health. Their black hair was still thick and lustrous. Every once in a while gray hairs popped out here and there. Instead of coloring them, the couple was content to pluck them out for each other. They were the object of envy of the village natives, who were either farmers tied to the backbreaking toil of tilling the soil and tending crops, or hands hired to do the heaviest, most menial labor. The villagers, who all grew old before their time, never failed to show their amazement upon discovering the Chu's real age. Neither were they timid about openly displaying their longing and jealousy for the city and everything in it. The couple, on the contrary, harbored the exact opposite sentiment. They were firmly convinced that retirement to the country had rejuvenated them.

Neither health nor financial problems stood in their way. Mr. Chu had retired from public office after a career of several decades. Not only was he eligible for a pension, but his wife was to receive it after his death for as long as she lived. It was a generous pension for a couple who had become accustomed to a frugal lifestyle. In fact, it was a sum quite sufficient to give them a feeling of security in their old age. The couple had four children—two boys and two girls—who were their source of pride and joy.

They had never experienced such blissful contentment before. Before his retirement, Mr. Chu had held a modest position which entitled him to his pension. He suffered several turns of ill luck during his government service, a lot worse than anything suffered by a high-ranking personnel. He was required to humble himself in order to keep his job, and this disgraceful period was not brief. To make matters worse, during this trying time of his career, he also had to finance his two children who attended college the same year. Other years he had a child either marry or enter college. He had no choice but to sell his house within two years and move into a smaller one in order to provide for his children's needs. Finally, he had to sell his small, modest house to provide for the marriage of his youngest daughter; it was then the couple was compelled to purchase a home outside the city of Seoul. To their tremendous relief, they discovered that with this move they had now stopped hemorrhaging financially to support their children. Their house in the countryside, which was cheap, was actually a comfortable and proud nest for them.

When they purchased the house in the Green Belt, the day of his retirement was near at hand, so the inconvenience of commuting was the least of Mr. Chu's concerns. Instead, his spirit was uplifted to know that his wretched office days were numbered. The house was indeed a blessing to the couple. After Mr. Chu's awaited retirement, he was, thanks to the house, neither flustered nor afraid as he suddenly faced free time on his hands.

The house was ancient and built in the extremely inconvenient style of rural areas. After his retirement, the old man dedicated most of his free time to repairing the house. At first, when Mr. Chu turned his attention to it, he could not even replace a fuse. As time went by, however, he became a competent, though somewhat slow, amateur carpenter and plasterer.

In recent years, Mr. Chu paid special attention to pleasing his wife by displaying a spirit of cheerfulness in whatever work he did as he poured out his talent and care. When he'd first begun, he'd started repairs on the house with a sense of destiny, hoping he could do something to improve the shabby safety features and extremely poor exterior of the house. He repaired the leaking roof, eliminated the pipes in an *ondol* (traditional Korean floor), installed hot water pipes, and insulated every wall. Although installing the insulation required professional help, mostly he managed to be self-sufficient. The greatest challenge for him was the structural design of the traditional Korean house. In the beginning, he never dreamed that he could remodel the infrastructure; however, when he discovered that he was fairly comfortable doing carpentry and plastering work, his project became more ambitious. He knew how painfully inconvenient living in a conventional Korean house was for a woman. In fact, he'd learned this when they first moved into a modernized house in the city He remembered how openly his wife had showed her gratitude and pleasure at being free from a traditional Korean house. Even a quite respectable house in the neighborhood, whether an ordinary family house in town or a tiny thatched shack in the remote countryside, all had been designed exactly the same way for generations. After he became involved personally and finished massive repairs on the house, he realized that the basic Korean house was not only knavish but also cunningly designed to be as punishing to Korean women as a torture rack.

Mr. Chu's approach in expressing his love for his wife was subtle and without fanfare. He tried to put himself in his wife's shoes as he continued to make improvements in their awkwardly designed structure. He immersed himself in this project and eventually found himself hopelessly attached to the house; in fact, he reached the point where it was difficult to tell the difference between his love for his wife and his love for his house. He knew that he could easily face the jaws of death when he thought of his wife sitting by his death-bed. By the same token, he felt cool and collected whenever he thought of his present house being his last one in the world. He experienced a sense of sorrow, relieved by an equal sense of security.

Mr. Chu had never felt any particular need for religion. Nevertheless, he toyed with the idea that if a spirit truly lingers after one's death, he would prefer that his soul go to purgatory. He wasn't sure he was worthy of entering the Gates of Heaven. He was scared of Hell; he felt he would be dealt with unfairly if sent there. In the course of his hectic career, he had known numerous people who were more remarkable and beneficial to others than he. He had also brushed shoulders with lesser people who were harmful to others. Being of the middle category, he judged himself comfortably qualified for purgatory.

Mrs. Chu was a Catholic. He had heard her reciting prayers for the souls in purgatory, which heightened his desire to go there. He wanted to be the center of his wife's attention, care, and concern even after his death. He wanted to be in a place where he could hope for his salvation through his wife's tireless prayers.

In the same way that Mr. Chu found the middle path appropriate for his soul, he believed that the house was neither beyond nor below his financial means. At a glance, the house did not seem changed from its original appearance; however, the more functional it became, the more it manifested the old man's thoughtful affection and the deft talent that touched its every nook and cranny.

The completion of his home improvement program, which kept him busy for some time, didn't mean that Mr. Chu's life became boring and meaningless. Every morning he went to a mineral spring to bring home drinking water; the climb to the site was excellent exercise, and it became one of the highlights of his day. The village was nestled in a cozy valley at the foot of the ridges of Acha Mountain. Although it was not so well known as Dobong Mountain, Kwanak Mountain, or Bookhan Mountain, Acha Mountain still held the remnants of ruins. The path that led to the nearest ridge was picturesque, and on top of it were work-out facilities for local hikers. The ridge was not the highest, and it was less than one kilometer from the village. Even those who were older than he could easily manage the climb. On weekends the place was frequented by hikers from Seoul. They would usually bring the entire family on this outing, and on clear spring or autumn days they would picnic on the ridge. On these occasions, the valley was saturated with the aroma of barbecuing meat and the pleasing sound of musical instruments.

Without fail every day after city folks had picnicked there, Mr. Chu would scour the trails behind the rocks and hills with a vinyl basket on his shoulder and a long pick in his hand, cleaning up the waste. When the hiking season was at its peak, the chore required more than one trip. But he was neither flustered nor in haste to finish the job and took as much time as he needed to do it right. Every once in a while, the other old men in the neighborhood, all having time on their hands, helped with this project even though Mr. Chu had never asked them to lend a hand.

He would have preferred doing it alone. It wasn't that he wanted to monopolize doing something good; far from it. He just wanted to do it at his own pace and enjoy working without being annoyed. It was burdensome working with others because he felt he must cater to their whims, although he couldn't match the vehemence of their statements and thus found them annoying. They were easily provoked over disgusting waste on a hiking trail. Whenever they picked up a plastic bag or an empty can discarded carelessly, they would curse sharply. They called these littering city folks "bastards," "sons of bitches," or "thugs." "Those scum! Do they think this place is their damned garbage bin? Do they only know to bring their damned mouths? Where did they leave their damned hands?" Such were their foul judgments and profane language.

Being agreeable to these men placed a strain on Mr. Chu. Once in a while he responded with a bland remark, "I know what you mean" or something of that nature, a response he'd learned during his career. He'd used some similar indifferent sentence, such as " I hear you," to appease his colleagues or superiors. He learned it was the easiest and most convenient way to avoid direct confrontation. However, he didn't want to continue using a technique in retirement that had sustained him during his office days—another reason he didn't particularly care to have anyone accompany him.

After his retirement, Mr. Chu was content having only his wife as company. His wife seldom disturbed his peace. He loved to help her in the kitchen; his favorite chore was either cutting off the stems of bean sprouts or peeling the skin of green onions. He also enjoyed taking his turn washing dishes. Most of all, he loved watching his wife tending her flower bed and vegetable patch. Sitting in his study, he could observe her for hours through a small window in the sliding door.

Just as bringing mineral water from the spring and cleaning up the mess on the hiking trail were his self-appointed duties, his wife dedicated herself to taking care of the garden and flower bed. They neither interfered nor meddled with each other's work. Instead, they drew pleasure from appreciating each other's accomplishments.

Their house was bracket-shaped. In the sunny spot in the front courtyard, Mr. Chu built a handsome terrace to store soy bean jars. The rest of the house was in the shade. Unlike his houses in the city, this one had more yard space outside the front gate. According to the deed to his property, the registered size of the lot was, in total, 78 pyong (approximately 312 square yards). Excluding the house site and the front courtyard, the rest of the land, the backyard vegetable plot, was less than 40 pyong (approximately 160 square yards). Since their house was situated at the edge of the village, no other house stood in front of it to block the open space. Consequently, their house looked larger than its actual size.

Mr. Chu had built a cross-hatched wooden trellis for rambling roses so that they could climb up in every direction. The mountain trail led along the outside of the fence. Farther along this trail, a gurgling creek complemented the landscape. Across the creek lay an open field, a flood plain. A long stretch of deep woods beckoned beyond. When he stood in the yard outside of his house, which faced south, he had an unobstructed view of the reed-filled open field and the lush woods and felt they were a continuation of his yard.

The seasonal changes in the field and the woods were superb. Intrigued by this exquisite landscape, Mr. Chu and his wife bought the house, paying the full asking price without hesitation. He was told that the house was grotesquely overpriced, considering its location and the timing. Nevertheless, according to his own inner calculation he had won a bonanza, getting free of charge a view of the verdant forest and open field. He thought the true owner of the fields and woods was the person who could daily gaze upon them, free to frequently hike their trails and breath the fresh air. The deed to the land was meaningless.

When he had company, he would habitually point out the splendid view before taking them inside the house. The woods stretched out smoothly on the flat plain encircling the mountain like a trailing skirt. Its edge formed a sharp slope, yet, his house was located far from that gorge. The ridge, where the mineral spring was located, rose to the west of the Chu's house, and its only flaw was that it made the sun appear to set a little earlier in the western sky. Besides that disadvantage, the ridge did not diminish the stature of his house.

In spring, the woods abounded in native mountain vegetation which villagers used as food. The villagers knew many varieties of plants inside and out—more than the Chus knew. The couple learned from them; they dug some plants every once in a while and cooked them. However, it seemed that only Mr. Chu knew about the aromatic flowers that filled the entire valley with their sweet and fanciful fragrance at the end of spring.

The basin of the valley was a bed for these beautiful flowers. The flowers were hidden behind wide and healthy leaves. The tiny white petals bent their heads downward, yet they were bathed in a rich fragrance which reached remote regions, enabling one to find the valley with his eyes closed. The first time he found himself in the center of the valley, he feared he would never get out of the place. This strange sense of enchantment caused him to sink into a euphoria tinged with fear and despair.

Mr. Chu knew it was useless to ask the villagers about these peculiar flowers. He suspected no one knew they were there, gathered in one spot, and even if anyone was aware of it, the discovery would be exhilarating to no one but himself. If a plant had no medicinal value or could not be eaten, it was nothing but a nameless weed to them. Only by consulting the field guide did Mr. Chu find out the name of these beautiful plants: silver bell flowers.

At the onset of summer, the usual color of the woods exploded in verdant green. Its countless leaves were bathed in blinding sunrays at high noon. The sunlight sparkled sharply as it caressed the surfaces of the sensitive leaves. Amid these surroundings, his deep sense of emptiness reached its zenith as he listened to the rolling chorus of cicadas. Then his sense of the meaning of things and the value of life, upon which he had previously relied, would suddenly escape him, seeming to evaporate and leaving the lingering sound of hushed and mocking laughter.

At the sound of raindrops on the broad leaves, autumn would inevitably permeate the air with its touch of melancholy. The vanity of the leaves would intensify each day as they desperately camouflaged their decline. The woods reached its peak in a display of spell-binding brilliance. During this most fickle season, they could not remain truly unchanged, not even for a moment.

The leaves would fall from the branches, ousted by a mere sigh of wind in the middle of the night. The sound of the falling leaves seemed to voice the lamentation of the woods. Awakened by the sound, Mr. Chu would toss and turn. Like a boy who wets his bed at night, he was engulfed with a sense of aloneness and nakedness. He then sneaked into his wife's room and buried his head in her withered but warm bosom. He remained in that posture for a long time, being comforted by her warm body. He even sucked her old nipples, which refused to be aroused from a sorrow that was stronger than the intensity of her sensuality.

Winter had come now to the threshold. The first hasty snowfall touched the ground. It hastened to separate the last leaf from its branch. Its harsh breath shook every windowpane in the neighborhood, warning people to prepare for the coming winter months. And with the passing of that breath, the first snow was gone. Each naked branch had its own shape and form—loose, dense, stretched toward the sky or freely bent. Like a gigantic net, the naked branches revealed the flat ridge of the woods and the ground of the gorge.

The vanity of the splendid fall colors of the leaves had now changed to faded, subtle brown and subsided silently toward the earth. How in the world could the trees disrobe in this magnificent way? Even Mr. Chu was impressed by the beauty of these winter trees. He thought of the roots of the silver bell flowers sleeping beneath the fallen leaves piled thickly over them. He had plenty of time on his hands. He spent his days reading, either sitting up or lying down comfortably in his room. Whether or not this abundance of free time was responsible, he had a special affection for the winter woods; he could appreciate the woods at his leisure. In fact, every season of this year offered him leisure time. Since their move, he had never, prior to this year, been completely free of his toolbox.

Suddenly, the mountain invaded the valley, its shadow falling at a slant across the woods and the sunny side of the riverbed. Before his wife hurried off to a wedding, she asked him to listen for the ring of the telephone, and he had been mindful since then of every sound. A moment ago, the clock struck only three times; nonetheless, the sun was about to retreat. Were it not so, it would be the season for an insatiable appetite for sunlight. He felt quite impatient with the ridge for shortening by over an hour the sunlight in his field of vision.

The shadow of the mountain spread rapidly, like an evil omen. Since Mr. Chu felt he might have missed hearing the clock striking four, he now tuned his ears to the living room and waited for the clock to strike. He had surrendered to his singular compulsion that his study must be innocent of worldliness, and his room had neither telephone, radio, nor clock. If he told his wife that there had not been not one telephone call all day, she may have not believed it. Somehow, he didn't feel right. He had missed the striking of the clock. Had he missed the phone ringing as well? Just as a kid who has failed to do his homework tries to exonerate himself by some logic which he himself can accept, so Mr. Chu tried to persuade himself that he had been all ears throughout his wife's absence, reassuring himself that he would have heard the phone if it had rung.

Abruptly, a flock of birds took direct flight from the woods to the sky. *Were they sparrows? They were the color of dried leaves. Where in this void, cold and semi-transparent as thin ice, had the power of gravity hidden itself?* From his viewpoint, the birds, without even flapping their wings, had taken flight like a pendulum broken from its axis at the end of its swing. Then, sucked into the void with uncontrollable speed, they scattered as if gliding on unseen shafts of air.

Although he took pride in his knowledge of the woods, Mr. Chu did not recall seeing any nests there. Neither did he remember seeing any birds. Are these birds visiting the woods from other places, hoping to find food, he wondered. Or, did they change their color to green in the summertime, to the color of dried leaves in the fall, and in the winter to snow white, thus living successfully in hiding? Now where had they gone? No trace of the birds could be seen in the transparent sky.

Watching this flock of birds flying up from the ground, Mr. Chu was gripped with sudden fear that would linger with him for quite a while. Even in the midst of his hard-earned peace, ominous sign, like the uncanny behavior of the birds, were concealed in secret places. Then, one day, without warning, they might well emerge from the ground and fly in his direction. Helplessly yielding to the leap of his wayward thoughts, Mr. Chu was agape with wonder.

Mr. Chu heard the clock striking from the living room. It was four. It was time for his wife to return from the twelve o'clock wedding she had gone to attend.

"After the wedding, I'll go to the market. I'll be back in plenty of time to fix supper so please don't try to fix anything. If people see you in the kitchen, they might frown," his wife said just before she went out.

"What people are you talking about?" he asked.

His wife didn't mind him doing chores for her in the kitchen when she was with him. However, she detested the idea of his being alone in the kitchen. She said he might look shabby and pitiful in the eyes of strangers. He had no idea who was going to see him in a house where only the two of them lived. What people are you talking about? Sometimes he, too, presumed that others might observe and judge their actions.

When she finally returned home from her outings, his wife had no time to rest. She fixed dinner in a flurry and fed her husband. She always had her husband wash the dishes and clean up the kitchen. She, bespectacled, would sit comfortably in her room and read the evening newspapers. She would then say, good spiritedly, "*Dear, please fix me a cup of coffee.*"

Mr. Chu did not drink coffee in the late afternoon. However, after dinner was the time his wife most enjoyed drinking coffee. Even if he was busy washing dishes, he would drop everything to serve her. Sometimes he would tease her by reminding her that he had spent extra time fixing special coffee for her. He would jokingly rebuff her: *If people see you, they might suspect that you are the breadwinner for us.* She would reply with his familiar sentence, "*What people are you talking about?*"

After the clock struck four, Mr. Chu suddenly felt a sense of urgency as he waited for his wife's return. Even at her age, his wife loved to wear high-heeled pumps. Her footsteps made a quick, staccato click as she walked, like the footsteps of a young woman. His room faced directly on the yard. The yard was divided in two, half flower bed, half vegetable patch. Nothing survived now except a planting in the corner of a bed of native yellow chrysanthemum, which had a reputation for outliving the early frost.

Although the entire yard was completely bare, it was distinguished by a line of stepping stones. The stones separated the flower bed from the vegetable bed and also made a walkway. The beds appeared tasteful compared to the barren fields. When he installed a boiler system, flat stones from the former system had become useless, and he congratulated himself on his common sense in utilizing some of them for this purpose. The stones were not only pleasing to his eyes, but also to his ears. He enjoyed listening to his wife's clicking across the steppingstones. Her gait was the same as when she was in her twenties. She had continued teaching at an elementary school during their honeymoon days. However, although she was a confident, professional woman, when they went out together his wife walked a few steps behind him as if she were an old-fashioned wife. The sound of her footsteps following behind him at a certain distance was proud, independent, and strong, not the sound of blind obedience. Even now, the sound of his wife's step was sharp and decisive. Even a few steps behind him, her footsteps made him feel she was an equal to him and he liked that.

The old scholar who planted a pawliona tree in front of his little cottage to appreciate the sound of raindrops falling on the leaves might have mocked Mr. Chu as a fool if he heard that Mr. Chu placed the steppingstones so he could enjoy his wife's footsteps, forever young in her high-heeled pumps. It was one of Mr. Chu's small pleasures to watch his wife walking on the stone path as she returned home. He could see her upper body through the small window in the sliding door.

Mrs. Chu walked proudly with her head held high as if an invisible string were pulling her ears from somewhere above. She moved her head in such a natural way that she looked like a self-confident model. It was indeed a pleasure for Mr. Chu to see the pride and dignity with which his wife was born unrestricted by clothes or accessories.

Listening to his wife's staccato footsteps, a sense of pride swelled in his chest; while realizing that he had not provided her with a "golden cushion," she did not want for much in life. She had never been forced to be servile or to ask favors because he protected her from the sharp teeth of a harsh world. However, his sense of pride was tempered by a certain sense of responsibility in his role of assuming responsibility. Only recently he discovered that he could not provide everything required for his wife's happiness. Finding out that there were some things in his wife's life for which he could not be responsible was not only a grave issue, but indeed a great mental blow to him.

The birds had not returned yet. Had their flight been of their own free will? Some strong, ugly, and ferocious animal might have frightened the birds, forcing them to fly. And yet, he rejected the idea. He wanted to believe that he knew the woods as well as he knew every line in the palms of his own hands. To date, he had not seen even a hare in the woods. As he was incapable of predicting what would happen to him in very next minute, how dare he suggest that he understood the hazards in a bird's life?

The Chu's house now had four bedrooms. Originally, it had only three: master bedroom, second bedroom, and a spare room. Mr. Chu broke down the wall of the storage room, which was adjacent to the spare room, and turned it into a spacious room with a new wooden floor; it became an adequate study for him. At this transformation of her husband's quarters, Mrs. Chu turned green with envy. She expressed her desire to have a separate room for herself, also.

If a study was the husband's room, the main room would be the wife's, reasoned Mr. Chu. Mrs. Chu had a different idea. She said the main room was for the entire family in any household. Mr. Chu conceded that his wife made sense when she said that their case must not be an exception, even if only the two of them lived in the house.

In the warmest spot in his room Mr. Chu loved to lay on a decorated ottoman which had been presented to him as a gift from his first daughter-in-law before her wedding day. He indulged himself by idling there most of the day. Rarely, however, did he sleep in his room. Spending a night in the main room made him cheerful and at ease the next morning. He also ate and changed his clothes in the main room.

When he remodeled the kitchen, he installed a built-in breakfast table there. Somehow he and his wife were not crazy about eating while seated on high stools. It just didn't feel right. They'd rather bring a small eating table into the main room and eat comfortably on the *ondol* as they sat at the table, facing each other.

Only when she had a definite reason did Mrs. Chu go to her husband's quarters. Even when she brought him some well-ripened persimmons or served him ginseng or citron tea she made it a habit to indicate her presence before she opened his sliding door. Mr. Chu, on the contrary, came in and out of the main room freely whenever he felt like it. He didn't feel the main room was her territory only. There was no foreseeable hope of his changing his way of thinking, either. Thus, his wife revealed her inner desire to have her own room, no matter how small it might be, into which no one, not even her own husband, was admitted without permission.

No one occupied the second room, as it was designated a guest room. They rarely had guests who spent the night. However, since the four children had their own families now, the couple had to be prepared in case they might visit. In fact, their children were considered honored guests.

Mrs. Chu kept the guest room neat and tidy at all times. She stored clean, soft satin bedding in the closet for her children. She saved every book, each bit of memorabilia, or anything recalling any trace of certain interests that her children had cherished before they married and then discarded like worn shoes when they left home. She stacked these neatly and placed them in proper places throughout the room. Polishing and cleaning the room every day was a testimony to her treasure in her children.

To please his wife, Mr. Chu had no choice but to add a room solely for her. Fortunately, the kitchen was larger than they needed. The house had been built when people had to get firewood from the nearby mountain. Consequently, a part of the kitchen was used for firewood storage. He converted this storage space into a small room. As his wife wished, Mr. Chu installed a door so that one must knock on it before being admitted. A large window, facing the backyard, was installed in the room to defeat the darkness. It was indeed a tiny room scarcely 1 *pyong* in size.

After he built the room for his wife, no occasion arose for him to knock on her door. When he needed her, she was never in her private room. Mr. Chu suspected that she had been so irritated at not having her own private room that she had demanded it out of spite. Therefore, he concluded that in reality she had no actual need for it. Once Mr. Chu pushed the door absently while she was out. He hadn't the slightest intention of peeping into her room; he was merely checking to see if it might be locked. When his wife had insisted having a door so that any would-be visitors were required to knock, Mr. Chu catered to her wish by making sure to provide a knob with a key lock so that she could easily lock and unlock it from inside as well as out.

The door opened effortlessly. The room was overly simple and seemingly forlorn. The window, facing the door directly, was curtainless. As a dank painting framed by a naked window, only darkness gathered in the narrow backyard and the crevice of the wall between his yard and that of his neighbor.

The only furniture, in the far end of her room, was a shapeless clothes chest that might have been removed from the garret. A cross hung on the wall above the chest. On the chest were a Bible and a miniature statue of the Virgin Mary. In his opinion, those icons did not have much significance as far as her reverence for God was concerned. One of her friends had convinced his wife to be baptized some years back. However, she attended church infrequently. Mr. Chu, who hadn't been really enthusiastic about the baptism, even teased her by asking about the purpose of being baptized if she didn't attend mass regularly.

To commemorate his wife's baptism, her godmother had given her the icons in her room. Since that day, Mr. Chu had never witnessed his wife worshipping these holy objects. He suspected that his wife wanted to decorate her room with her own things, and these icons were the only objects she could claim as truly hers alone. When he reached this conclusion, Mr. Chu felt sorry for he. He had neither interest nor desire to step into her room. He was about to close the door when he spotted something that made him literally jump. Two candles, without holders, stood nakedly on the chest.

It must have been at Easter this year. After a long absence, his wife had attended church. She came home after the service and took out a hymnal and a mass shawl from her handbag. She also took out a large bundle wrapped in white paper. Since he was hungry, Mr. Chu thought the package must have been some kind of food given by the church. He unwrapped it and found two candlesticks, each fat as a child's arm.

"Why didn't they give you something to eat instead of these?" he said.

"What do you mean 'give'? I bought them. Here's something for you to eat," his wife said.

Mrs. Chu took from her handbag eggs wrapped with gold or silver aluminum foil.

"What made you buy candles? We don't have power failures now as we used to, you know. How much did you pay for them, anyway?"

"One thousand *won* per candle," his wife said.

"Very expensive, don't you think?"

"The church was selling them. Whatever profit they get, I am sure they will use for a good cause."

"I bet you bought these eggs, too."

"Yes, I did. Anyway, you are strange. Why are you craving something free today?" his wife said, as she slowly gathered up the candles.

Such was the history of the candles on the chest.

Even though his wife did not explain, Mr. Chu knew they were not ordinary candles; he knew they were blessed and holy. Naturally, he was not surprised at all to see them in front of the statue of the Virgin Mary on the chest underneath the cross. He had no idea when she had used the candles, but they were now about thumb sized. He was as embarrassed to see them, as if he had trespassed on his wife's privacy. His heart pounded as he felt a sense of shame springing from the depth of his innermost being. His curiosity concerning what she must be doing with the candles in secret behind a closed door was quite intense.

As if he were a sentry, for a few days Mr. Chu watched his wife's every movement. One night he managed to peep into her private room from the narrow backyard. He saw her kneeling down on the bare floor and fervently praying. The two candles on the chest were lighted. Since it was pitch dark, he had no need to hide himself as he observed his wife. She reminded him of the tiny poster "Safety Today," which featured a portrait of a young girl and which he had seen many times in most city cabs. Then he deliberately tried to capture a view of this scene from the same angle used in taking this portrait. Not only was it the ideal angle, but the wings of his imagination concerning his wife's prayers made this glimpse through the window seem as beautiful to his eyes as the portrait of the praying girl. Mr. Chu fancied that when someone is praying, regardless of his or her appearance, fair or plain, that person becomes absolutely beautiful. Such was his impression of prayer.

Mrs. Chu appeared to be neither smiling nor crying. Her face was miserably distorted, reminding one of a mercilessly torn picture. He was afraid that he would fail to put all the torn pieces together and thus be unable to restore his wife's proud and stoic face again. It wasn't prayer but extremely humble adulation that his wife was exhibiting, he thought.

Anyway, what kind of terrible mistake, he wondered, could she have made that caused her to beg in such servility? Although from where he stood he could see clearly neither the cross nor the statue of the Virgin Mary, he was inclined to think that even God would turn His head away from his wife's excessive adulation.

The unexpected twisted look on her face awoke in him sudden, sordid images as well. He suspected that his wife might be in some colossal financial bind and was suffering without his knowledge. Or she had become involved in an unfortunate affair with a younger man and was now being blackmailed.

That night, Mr. Chu could not sleep a wink. Even the next morning the memory of her face, like a disturbing dream, troubled him, leaving him fidgety and distracted. It was disagreeable to him to see that his wife's normal appearance returned without also repairing his vision of the torn pieces.

He could not bear her double personality any longer. One day he grasped an opportune time to bring the subject up in his deliberately natural manner. After he helped his wife wash the breakfast dishes, Mr. Chu lit a cigarette. His wife detested his smoking habit. He used to consume a pack a day, and now under pressure from her, he smoked only five cigarettes. He was afraid she was determined to have him stop smoking entirely. She would fret and fuss and make little coughing noises.

"Once you demanded to have your own private room. Now look at it. You don't use it for any particular purpose. I might use it for a smoking room," Mr. Chu said cunningly as he opened her private room door.

"Don't you even dream about using it as your smoking room. What makes you think I don't use the room? It's my prayer room. Don't you dare smoke in that room," she said.

"Prayer room? You mean you pray? You, who go to church once a month or less?"

"Yes. Anyway, do you find my praying surprising?"

He wasn't prepared to see his wife so open about her praying, far from attempting to hide it as he had anticipated. At any rate, Mr. Chu was determined to find some insight into the subject of his wife's prayer. Following his previously-composed scenario, he pretended to be astonished to see those thumb-sized candles.

"Didn't you buy these on Easter Sunday? Does that mean that you've been praying until they are this small? Honest?"

"Yes, it's true."

Mrs. Chu seemed to be a little embarrassed; however, she did not appear to be suffering from some ineffable anguish.

"What do you have to pray for every day? Is something bothering you? Couldn't you talk to me, your husband? Am I not right?"

"Matters of life and death are not in man's hands," his wife said.

"What an extraordinary thing to say! Are you trying to tell me that one of us has an incurable disease? What are you talking about?"

"No, I don't mean that. My everyday prayer is for the only wish I have. You see, I pray to God to grant that my family die in order of our ages."

"In order?" Mr. Chu said.

"Yes, that's right. I pray feverishly to God for our immediate family—our children and their children—to meet death one by one according to age. When I appeal to God to listen to my prayer, I feel an acute earnestness in my heart. I've never asked Him foranything else. I don't want God to think I'm too greedy. You have no idea how ardently I talk to God. In fact, I flatter Him with my prayer."

Then what he found in her room by stealth had never been a secret. She had nothing to hide or any desire to deceive him. It wasn't any secret in his wife's life but the comfortable lifestyle he was presently enjoying that might have short-sightedly obscured the reason for her prayer.

When they were married, his wife's family was composed of old people who had twice endured the loss of their children, and of young widows. He was told that his father-in-law, an army civilian employee, was killed in the bombing of a small town during the waning years of Japan's colonization of Korea. His brother-in-law, an army officer, was killed in action during the Korean War. Among his in-laws who survived to old age as man and wife were his wife's grandparents. They had sent their son and grandson to the other world long ago. His mother-in-law and the wife of his wife's brother were widows.

The wife of his wife's brother became a widow even before she celebrated her first wedding anniversary. She bore a son after her husband's death. She and Mrs. Chu were the same age. Whenever Mr. Chu saw his sister-in-law, who was bursting with youth, he used to feel deep compassion for her. During the war, the majority of old people had lost their sons or grandsons at the front-line. It was rather an expected and accepted phenomenon. However, Mrs. Chu took it very hard. Even after the war was over, sudden death did not leave his wife's family household. His mother-in-law passed away before she was fifty years old. The following year Mrs. Chu's grandfather left this world near his eightieth birthday.

Mrs. Chu seemed so calm and poised at her mother's sudden death that it was rather embarrassing. However, during the mourning period for her grandfather, she lamented heart-wrenchingly over his death. *It would have been really nice if you'd passed away a year ago,* he'd heard her cry aloud. *Why, Grandfather, must you leave us now?*

What kind of grotesque grieving is this? he wondered. Mr. Chu was troubled. Her tormented lamentation expressed a deep suffering which baffled him. Even more baffling was her obvious regret that her grandfather had survived his daughter's death by a year. Her continuing wails had become more and more distressing. But now Mr. Chu realized that his wife was overwhelmed by the fact that her family members did not leave this world in the order of age. He could sympathize with his wife, who was indeed obsessed with this tragic family history.

Since then, no out-of-order death had crossed the threshold of Mrs. Chu's family. Her nephew, who was born after his father's death, became a successful, self-made man and was now holding the family together. Mr. Chu believed that his wife was the only one still suffering from the events of the past. Every once in a while, she would take out a piece of patched cloth or a picture of standing Buddha that she had made in her grade school days. Whenever she gazed at her childhood memorabilia, she seemed to suffer from this repetitious pain. She then seemed totally absorbed; in moments like these, he knew that she needed to be left alone in her own private world. He acknowledged that he was neither responsible for his wife's inner-most pain nor could do anything to lessen her misery. He could only pity her.

He was roused from his reverie as he heard her clear foot steps on the stepping stones. Cheered like a child, Mr. Chu slid open his door. She looked healthy; nevertheless, she pretended to be bone-tired, as was her habit whenever she came back from downtown.

"What are you just looking at me for? Come and get my sack!" she said.

Mr. Chu jumped to his feet, dashed to the courtyard and took a cloth sack from his wife.

"Why did you buy so much?" he asked.

"Well, some of my friends were going to Karak market, so I went with them. I bought some fruit, fish, and fresh ginseng there. I'm telling you the market was huge! I must have walked about twenty *li* around that place."

"I don't care what kind of bargain you got there. Why did you go that far? You should have been more considerate! Tsk, tsk! I've been waiting for you for all these hours. I nearly lost my mind worrying about you." Mr. Chu chided his wife in his deliberate manner as he went inside ahead of her with his head high.

"Why are you picking on me about such a trifling matter? Have you ever returned home early just because I waited for you anxiously?"

"Ah, is it the same between the person who went out to earn the living and the one who went out to spend the money?" he said.

"Spending money is far more difficult than making it. You don't know what you're talking about."

"You realize you spend the money that I earned, not free money," he said.

"Don't you remember I used to work, too? Judging from my experience, I can assure you that it's much harder to spend the money than the other way around."

"Okay. That will do. Don't waste your breath on that subject any more," Mr. Chu said.

Mr. Chu enjoyed arguing with his wife; it was somewhat invigorating. He pretended to yield to her cajoling. He unwrapped the cloth sack. His wife went to her room to change her clothes. She came outside immediately and separated the groceries and fish; she then trimmed the vegetables, washed, and salted them swiftly.

"I was told that the statute of the Green Belt in our neighborhood will be lifted soon," his wife said.

"Nonsense. What kind of windfall are they expecting from the value of land? The village people live in hope of seeing the price of land skyrocket. I tell you they are dreaming the impossible. It's like a poor but optimistic scholar dreams of an imminent coup-d'état," Mr. Chu said.

"Mind you, the rumor didn't come from the village. I heard it from one of my friends. You see, her husband is an influential man in that area."

"Isn't it a groundless rumor going around during election time?" Mr. Chu asked.

"It isn't. Anyway, my friend thinks we own a *gold mine* besides our house. She said you possess the gift of foresight, although you give the impression of simplicity. I could tell she felt a hint of jealousy when she complimented you."

"I don't want to move again," Mr. Chu said.

"Well, this is what I think. Once the Green Belt becomes an ordinary place, people will pour into this area. I don't think they will expel residents like us."

"Do you mean that I have to watch the woods being destroyed by bulldozers and replaced by houses? It's nonsense. I can't bear the thought of not being able to see the woods from my room."

"In any event, whenever I think of the value of our house going up, I'm so elated. All our lives, we've been selling our homes and moving into smaller and smaller ones. Now, it is time for us to even that score."

"So, that's it! You're showing your true colors now. I know you're contemplating selling this house and moving into an apartment in Seoul. Well, you might as well hang up that dream. I don't think the value will go up. Even if its value really soars, I don't want to move again to an apartment, and that's that!" Mr. Chu raised his voice angrily. He pictured a flock of birds flying up from the woods, as if they were being sucked into the air. People say that animals are better spiritual beings when it comes to having premonitions. Mr. Chu now reasoned that it might be the sound of future bulldozers that had scared the birds, not a wild animal in the woods.

He could not allow himself to think about making a profit from selling his house. He was wracked by a sense of loss as he thought of something so precious and dear being taken away from him. His wife gazed at him in her warm and caring way, encompassing him with a gaze of understanding and generosity.

"Don't try to read my mind. Have I ever hinted that I would like an apartment? Let's brace ourselves to move to an even more remote district. I'm sure it won't be that hard to find woods and a mountain like these somewhere. A place in the Green Belt, a new village which is about to form, will have similar surroundings. So, please don't lose heart, dear."

"Do you mean that, dear?" Mr. Chu said.

"You said the woods, mountain, and the creek captivated you. That's why you bought the house. That's what you said. You know what attracted me to this place? I liked the lack of transportation facilities here. Yes, indeed! You see, I'd rather have the inconvenience of transportation than missing the woods, mountains, and creeks. I'm sure we won't have any problem finding another village we can both fall in love with."

"I'm sorry, but it's hard for me to believe that you were drawn to this village because of a poor transportation system. I hope you're not being sarcastic. Are you?" Mr. Chu asked.

"We feel comfortable in a place where transportation is inconvenient, far from the city. You still don't understand me? We don't have to expect a child who lives in a distant place to visit often as we might every day with a child who lives next door. What about our children? I think they feel comfortable living some distance from us. They have an excuse not to visit us often. Don't you see how humiliating and tiring it would be to wait for children who seldom come to see us? I can breathe easily now since we don't have to crane our necks waiting for their visit. I don't want to do that anymore."

Mrs. Chu sent her husband a tender gaze as she smiled sadly. He avoided her eyes quickly. He felt the same way his wife did, but he had no intention of being caught at it. Instead, he put his hand in the sack she had brought from the market and unloaded the last item. He found some dirt from the vegetables and several lollipops at the bottom of the mesh bag.

"Leave those lollipops alone. They are for Chul-woo," his wife said.

Chul-woo was the first child of a young couple who rented a room from a next door neighbor. The baby was so cute that Mrs. Chu took pleasure in sitting with him whenever his mother was too busy to take care of him. Chul-woo's father worked for the furniture factory, and his mother was known for her diligent work and also for her craftsmanship. As a result of her reputation, Chul-woo's mother was constantly busy with odd jobs all year round. Her only wish was that together they save money so they might move to the city as soon as possible, even if they had to rent a room. Recently, she had been working with Angora sweaters, decorating them with shimmering beads in the shape of flowers or pheasant's wings.

Mrs. Chu visited the young woman quite frequently. *How much do you receive for doing one flower? Oh, my word, is that all? The sweater looks twice as expensive with that beaded flower in the center. It's more than twice, I bet you. These sweaters are transformed into something extravagant that only movie stars can afford.* Mrs. Chu would compliment the woman's work in awe as she bounced the baby.

Then, she would leave the house furtively as she cradled the baby in her arms. Since he was an infant, he had not yet been spoiled. Chul-woo was a good baby; once he was in a baby walker, he was happy. Whenever Mrs. Chu imagined dust mites wriggling delicately on the surface of the mirror stand, the Formica table, the rice bin, the radio, or the TV set in the woman's room, she had an urgent desire to take the baby from the room. Also, Mr. Chu wanted his wife to bring the baby home rather than to remain for a long visit there. Although the baby was easy to take care of, he was frightened by strangers. Whenever Mr. Chu held him in his arms, the baby cried bit-terly, as if he had been pinched. So, Mr. Chu preferred watching his wife and the baby playing together. He was so pleasantly absorbed in watching them that his wife teased him by claiming that Mr. Chu was indeed drooling.

Mrs. Chu even furnished snacks for Chul-woo. She either cut fruit into slices or mashed it and fed it to the baby. Once she received free lollipops from a shopping center on its grand opening day. Chul-woo was deliriously happy. Since then, Mrs. Chu bought some of them whenever she went downtown. She gave him candy when-ever he was cranky. Sometime during the past summer, Mr. Chu noticed the baby's two bottom teeth. He told his wife the baby's teeth reminded him of two rice grains stuck on his gum. His wife teased him about this silly observation. Her impression was much more romantic: "They look like two lambs emerging on a pink hill."

"I don't care whether it's rice or two lambs. What are you going to do if your beloved baby's teeth go bad? Don't you know that too much indulgence in sweets decays the teeth? Why do you keep buying candies for him? People blame a baby-sit-ter for any mishaps that befall the baby; they don't remember the tender loving care the baby received. Remember that!" Mr. Chu scolded as he put away the lollipops that his wife had bought in the Karak market, laying them in a drawer.

"It doesn't matter. They are nothing but milk teeth."

"Aren't you being irresponsible just because he's someone else's child?" Mr. Chu accused.

"Well, I'm not so sure. Anyway, I'm not taking care of him to receive a pat on the back. He's so cute and I want to love him in my own way. What's wrong with that?" his wife said.

"I can see you're crazy about babies. What I don't understand is why you don't treat your own grandchildren the way you treat Chul-woo. I must say you've always been awkward and distant around the babies of your own family. I'm afraid our children's feelings will get hurt if they see you love Chul-woo so openly and whole-heartedly."

"How could you possibly compare my own with someone else's? My grandchildren are the most precious things. In any event, mind you, I feel timid about showing my love to my grandchildren. I'm uncomfortable around them," Mrs. Chu said.

"Uncomfortable? How strange!" Mr. Chu exclaimed.

"I bet you feel the same. Don't pretend. Don't you see, the parents of my grand-children put them under their over-protective wings. Naturally, we lose heart; we feel small in their presence. I don't feel comfortable using an expensive glass when I drink water from it. I may have a boorish mentality. When I try to hold my grandchild in my arms, suddenly I become puzzled as if I had forgotten how to hold a child prop-erly. Don't you agree you and I are useless in that sense?"

"What right do you have to include me in your own incompetence? Don't you dare try to treat me like a stick. Anyway, I admit I'm not good around either my grandchildren or Chul-woo. It's the same with both. However, you're not the same around Chul-woo."

"By the way, did you get any calls today?" Mrs. Chu said, evading his remark.

"No," he said. He turned his head to see the telephone on the desk and saw the handset dangling downward. Chul-woo was responsible for it. Before she went out that morning, his wife had brought Chul-woo home and played with him until she was ready to go to the wedding.

Mrs. Chu also noticed the phone.

"I wish you'd checked the telephone, especially when it didn't ring all day long. How sticky it is! Chul-woo must have wanted to make sure he left evidence of himself."

Mrs. Chu put the phone back on the receiver. It was obvious that Chul-woo had been playing with the phone while consuming a sticky lollipop. Mrs. Chu smiled broadly with mysterious mirth while wiping the phone. She had a vivid mental picture of Chul-woo playing with the telephone. After he finished sucking a lollipop, his ten fingers were sticky enough to glue them all together. He knew the inconvenience of having such hands. He would whine and place his hands under Mrs. Chu's nose. She would then lick each finger with her long tongue in preference to washing them with water or a washcloth. She did it so thoroughly that she looked exactly like a hungry demon greedily swallowing sweets.

Mr. Chu could easily discern by their expressions that his wife and Chul-woo loved this ritual. It was a sensual rapport. Gazing at the two—old and young—and this innocent pleasure of the senses, Mr. Chu would sink into heart-wrenching sorrow, although he couldn't voice why he grieved.

As soon as she put the cleaned phone onto the receiver, it rang. Its sound was strong and intense as if it were ringing with the force of a whole day's delayed calls. Instead of picking up the phone, Mrs. Chu stumbled backward toward her chair.

"For goodness sakes, what's the matter? Haven't you heard a phone ring before?" Mr. Chu said. As he picked up the phone, however, for no apparent reason his heart also sank.

"Hello?"

"Is that you, in-law? Why in the world have you been on the phone so long? Something terrible happened. Ah, what are we to do?" Before the sentence was complete, the sound of wailing came across the wire. Mrs. Chu turned deathly pale. Mr. Chu made a desperate effort to regain his composure.

"Who are you? Who in heaven's name are you?" Mr. Chu asked, trying to ignore the crying.

Fleetingly, Mr. Chu hoped this was a wrong number. The crying abruptly stopped.

"I am Boram's maternal grandmother. Aren't you Boram's paternal grandfather?" she said frantically in her metallic voice.

Boram was indeed his oldest grandson.

"Yes, that's who I am."

"How in the world can you be so peaceful at a time like this? Do you have any idea what happened to Boram's family today? The entire family was in a car accident. They collided with a truck. Ah, my poor daughter! What am I to do? I tell you these cars are our enemies!"

"I think you have the wrong number. None of my children own a car." Mr. Chu wanted to hang onto that hope.

"Didn't you know about the car? They bought it about two weeks ago."

Mr. Chu helplessly dropped the phone. He then embraced his pale and trembling wife. From the dangling phone, he could hear his in-law's heart-wrenching sobs as loud and clear as if he were listening them from a loudspeaker. Although her crying filled every fiber of his being, he couldn't understand a word she was saying.

"The driver is the only one dead. The rest are critically injured. My husband rushed to the hospital before we confirmed whether the driver was your son or our daughter. I haven't heard a word from him yet. My daughter drives, too, you know. She got a driver's license before your son did. She might have been driving. Who knows? I was going to go with my husband, you see, but I couldn't reach you all day. I've been glued to this phone. They are in Han Hospital in Yichun City. Are you listening?"

Mr. Chu and his wife, pale as ghosts, trembled violently as if they were afraid of the telephone. Seized with fear, they stared at it. Neither of them dared to touch it or to place it back on its receiver.

Momma's Stake

Part One

Once we crossed over Dresser Rock Pass, I was told, we would see Songdo. Dresser Rock Pass was the last of the four passes that stood between Bakjuk Valley and Songdo. As one might expect from the last pass, it was steep. In the eyes of an eight-year-old girl, who had already walked nearly 20 *li*, the pass appeared merciless as it towered over me. However, as if emerging through a lush woods, once the uphill trail ended, the wide open sky looked wide and deep, like a sky reflected in a spring well, making my heart throb in fear.

I kept trudging along. Momma and Grandmother each held one of my hands. Each carried a large bundle on her head. Whenever I looked extremely weary, they exchanged glances then lifted me up lightly by placing their hands beneath my armpits. As if I were on a swing set, I was carried dangling as they took several quick, short steps. Soon they would put me down. Although I knew that, carrying heavy bundles on their heads, they went to considerable trouble to do this, I wanted these rides to last longer. They seemed far too short, and each time I hoped the ride would be extended.

However, as we ascended Dresser Rock Pass, they stopped indulging me, ignoring my tired and blistered feet. Instead, they held my tiny hands painfully tight in their sticky hands, each of which had a different skin texture. I was being dragged inevitably to an unknown town. The thought of being forced to go gave me mixed emotions. I experienced a sense of fear, yet at the same time a feeling of heady giddiness as if I were in a free fall, even though I was ascending a steep pass.

Finally, we reached the top.

"Look! That's Songdo. The city!" Momma said this proudly, as if she owned the place. Sure enough, just as if Momma had taken it out from under her loose cloth wrapper, an entire birds-eye view of Songdo stood revealed in a panorama directly below us.

I was seeing the city for the first time in my life, and it impressed me more with its dazzling splendor than with its size. It looked like a ball of light. My eyes were accustomed only to such light as is absorbed by mud walls and thatched roofs and is then transformed into something soft and warm. Now, the sunlight of high noon reflected from the windows of two storied, rectangular houses and from tiled roofs. It made me edgey, as if the sunrays were countless arrows.

My ideas about the city had been formed by someone who'd come from there and whom I'd met only once, but they matched that of the city before me. That person was Momma's brother. Grandmother, Father's mother, had been thrown into confusion by her in-law's unexpected visit. She repeatedly said that she had nothing in such a remote countryside worthy of being offered to a guest from the city, which is how I discovered where he was from. I disliked him. He was wearing a black suit. He wasn't the first man I ever saw wearing a suit. Some time before that, a man had passed near the entrance to our village, riding on a bike. Since children shouted, "A policeman!" I dashed to the house with my heart in my mouth. Although I didn't see him clearly, I glimpsed a suit similar to the one I later saw Uncle wearing. An even more unpleasant sight to me than that suit were the spectacles he wore.

Momma had taken my older brother to the city long before she took me. Just before they left, he turned over all his valuables to me. My brother finished elementary school at our town seat, about four kilometers from our village. My brother, who was to go to middle school in the city, had many interesting things—a slingshot, a top, a shuttlecock, a kite, marbles, a sleigh, crayons, a magnet, and pieces of glass. Among these, the only thing I ever truly coveted was his magnet. It was amusing to watch him move the magnet over a charcoal brazier. It would attract every metal scrap to itself. The most breathtaking thing for me to witness was his finding Grandmother's missing needle that I had been hunting for all day. When I saw that needle at the tip of my brother's magnet, trembling as it sparkled in the light like a freshly-landed carp, I was overpowered by envy and wonder. Now this fascinating object was finally mine.

Before my brother left, however, he taught me an even more wondrous thing that could be performed with a piece of glass. He showed me how to focus that round piece of glass and use sunlight to start a fire. The light, passing through the center of the lens, shrank into the shape of the tip of a drill and penetrated the paper. The sensation this aroused in me was a mixture of cold and hot. When I watched it, my heart similarly tightened. Finally, as the paper sent up a column of bluish smoke, my heart received a sudden flash of heat as it sent a chill through my bones. Then I felt an urgent need to pee. That night, I dreamed of practicing this feat and ended up really wetting my bed. Perhaps that's why even to this day I tend to believe that common saying intended to teach children: "Playing with matches makes you wet the bed." When he turned his burning glass over to me, my brother didn't warn me to keep it hidden from adults. Nonetheless, I hid it from them since I'd already experienced a creepy sensation of guilt caused by playing with the glass. Naturally, I played with it only when no adult was around. However, one day I focused the glass on a heap of crisply dried straw, which of course caught fire and nearly burned down the house. I caused an awful disturbance, and as a result, the glass was taken away from me on the spot and I was paddled until my fanny was blistered.

When Uncle from the city appeared, he was wearing formidable-looking burning glasses, not one but two, one over each eye. Blinded by the glare from his glistening glasses, I failed to see his eyes. I feared and disliked a person wearing such glittering objects. Although Uncle, all smiles, held out his arms to me, I stubbornly refused to go to him. I wrapped myself in the hem of my Grandmother's chima [traditional Korean skirt]. He took a shiny silver coin from his pocket and showed it to me, trying to lure me. I stood there firm as a rock, having no idea of the worth of a silver coin. It was nothing to me but one of those sparkling objects that Uncle had. Grandmother must have been embarrassed; she pulled me from behind her and tried to push me in front of Uncle. I was so scared and disliked him so strongly that I burst into tears and stamped my foot.

"Please let her be, ma'am. I see she is very bashful," Uncle said.

"It's so peculiar. She's not usually this way..."

Grandmother wrapped me again in her chima, clucking her tongue.

I remembered nothing about Uncle except his spectacles.

The city wore the same face as Uncle.

Unlike the road uphill, the road going down was winding and much less steep. Stealthily I freed my hand from Momma's grip, clinging to Grandmother with both hands and wrapping myself in her chima like I often did at home. Now though, her chima wasn't easy to handle nor did it bring that sense of closeness I felt when I wrapped myself in it at home. Her heavily starched calico chima, which had been softened by beating on a flat rock, felt as cold to me now as if it had a sharp edge on it. My gesture of breaking loose from Momma's grasp and holding onto Grandmother was my way showing my vexation with being taken to the city against my will.

Grandmother had taken my side. Momma wanted to take me to the city, but Grandmother was opposed. Even after Momma returned to the countryside to take me back to the city, she and Grandmother continued to quarrel about it. Neither of them bothered to ask me where I preferred to live. Even though I'd never been to the city, I just hated it. The house in Bakjuk Valley was paradise to me. The back court- yard had a small hill choked with strawberry vines. Cherry, pear, plum, and apricot trees blossomed and bore fruit in season. Our ancestral grave site was nestled behind the hill. The valley, boasting of its clean water, was attired in splendid robes of chest- nut and oak trees. When we prepared for a feast, the tent that was set up and the straw mat laid on the ground were large enough to accommodate all the village peo- ple at one time in the main courtyard. The ground in the main courtyard was flat, and all around the mat was a decorative flower bed containing Grandfather's favorite chrysanthemums. Small, clustered, lush, and aromatic, Korea's native chrysanthe- mums did not lose their elegance until the dead of winter.

Grandfather's clear, bell-like voice would become even richer and more resonant when the chrysanthemums bloomed. However, his voice had not been heard for some time now. He used to read a famous Chinese poem that was revered by Korean schol- ars; Grandfather loved to recite a part of this poem in his singsong voice. But the sound of his pipe hitting the brass ashtray or a dry cough were now the only sounds indicating that someone occupied the male quarters of the house. Even after the onset of summer, its sliding door was shut. After he lost his oldest son, Grandfather had a stroke which partially paralyzed him, and he confined himself to home. Father's death was the cause. Every bad thing I could remember in that paradise began with Father's passing.

One day Father was afflicted with an excruciating abdominal pain. He fell onto the wooden floor, then down to the stone terrace, then rolled over and over to the ground, three steps below the terrace. He writhed in torment as he dug his fingernails into the dirt. The herb doctor was summoned immediately. He opened up four places in Father's hands and feet with acupuncture needles so blood would flow smoothly. While herbal medicine was being prepared, Grandmother, who couldn't sit still, gave Father barley malt to drink. Grandfather offered Father an *youngshimwhan* [heart med- icine], and Momma dribbled a dissolved *chungshimwhan* [heartburn pill] into his mouth. Despite their efforts, Father showed no improvement. The hastily prepared herb tea also proved to be ineffective. Grandmother and Momma rushed to a sorceress and consulted her. According to the sorceress, severe retribution from infuriated earth gods had been cast upon the house site. The sorceress advised them to have a lavish exorcism performed. The sorceress guaranteed Father's instant improvement just as soon as they set the date for the exorcism. They immediately set a date, then returned home. Father had just breathed his last breath.

That was less than three years after our new house was built. All the villagers were awestruck upon learning that the earth gods were indeed fearsome, just as they'd believed. Although Momma visited the sorceress as Grandmother requested, Momma held quite a different concept. Her entire family lived in the city, and she had already been exposed to the world of civilization before she got married. She knew Father's ailment could have been taken care of as easily a splinter in a finger by an operation. The diseased tissue could have been surgically removed. But this could have happened only if a city doctor who practiced western medicine had tended Father.

After Father's death, Momma dreamed of leaving for the city. Her dream came true when my older brother finished elementary school at an opportune time. Before the third anniversary of Father's death, Momma left for the city with my brother. As the oldest daughter-in-law, Momma had an obligation to provide food for her parents-in-law, along with observing sacred memorial services to our ancestors. In lieu of Momma's fulfilling her duty, she gave up her inheritance. Not even a spoon in the house could she touch. Relying on her only talent, her sewing skill, Momma left Bakjuk Valley freely, clutching her young son by the hand. My leaving seemed to be creating ill feelings between Grandmother and her daughter-in-law which had not arisen between them when Momma left with my brother.

The old folks had known all along that they could not possibly deter their daughter-in-law from this daring and undutiful plan. Even if they voiced their disapproval, they knew it would accomplish nothing but bringing more disgrace to the family. They surrendered to her will, merely wishing to keep their family's honor and respect. They held a secret ray of hope, based on her strength and determination, that she would successfully raise her only son in the city and for his future success as well. Consequently, Momma's first departure was comparatively smooth and quiet.

However, Momma's determination that her son succeed at any price was a heavy yoke to a boy who had just finished his elementary schooling, and the expectations of our grandparents made it even heavier. I was very close to my brother and loved him deeply. I could somehow feel the weight of the heavy load he carried, and I was sorry and uneasy for him. I couldn't feel even a scrap of the abstract yearning which a young girl should have felt for Songdo or Seoul, which the villagers called "the city." The city simply engendered fear within me. This might have been because of the expectation for success that must be accepted unconditionally if you went to the city.

For one reason or another, two uncles on Father's side had not yet had sons of their own. Moreover, they were not doing anything special with their lives. However, my brother, the eldest grandson of the family, was bright and strikingly handsome. He had skipped one grade and finished elementary school a year earlier than his peers. His reputation as a child prodigy spread throughout the near-by village. My brother, still only a boy, was expected to assume responsibility for restoring the declining family fortunes.

Although I missed my brother greatly, I had no desire to go to the city to see him. I did not miss Momma that much, either. I was too young to understand the meaning of the word "responsibility." I put two and two together and sensed that the grown-ups and the city had conspired to trap my brother with an ugly noose. While Momma was away, I was the apple of my Grandparents' eyes. I also received the unconditional affection of my aunts and uncles. Nothing was too much for me to ask. I was as free as the grazing cattle. The last thing I worried about was being trapped as my brother was.

One day, however, Momma showed up to take me to the city. I wrapped my arms tightly around Grandmother's neck and glared intensely at Momma, whom I had not seen for a long time. I was stubbornly determined not to go with her.

Thus began the quarrel between Grandmother and Momma. At first, Grandmother tried to convince Momma that she hesitated to send me away because she wished to ease Momma's burden. She felt Momma would be better off without another mouth to feed in a strange place where she was trying so hard to make ends meet. She pointed out that it wasn't an easy task to raise a little girl without her parents.

"That's the reason I want to take her with me. I believe a child should be with her Momma for better or for worse. I can't allow my fatherless child to grow up missing her Momma, too."

With Momma's argument so strong, Grandmother changed her tactics from reasoning to pleading as her eyes welled up with tears.

"You heartless one. Don't you see that she's the only joy and pleasure we have? Watching her move about and listening to her chatter adds happiness to our lives. If I knew for sure your second sister-in-law would have a child soon, trust me, I wouldn't feel this way. Your third sister-in-law will be with child soon, I feel sure. Then you can take her. I won't stand in your way."

"No, Mother, it just can't be. This is the right time for her schooling."

"School? Send a girl to school?"

"Yes, even a girl needs to learn."

"You—what did you do in the city? Did you strike a gold mine? Or, have you lost your mind? Otherwise, for Heaven's sake, how can you possibly send a girl to school? I mean, a girl, to school!"

The quarrel between the two women flared as if oil were poured onto a flame. When this happened, I always took Grandmother's side in any way I could. To me taking her side merely meant wrapping myself in Grandmother's *chima* and glaring at Momma.

One day a small incident occurred that made it inevitable that I'd go with Momma. Since her return to the countryside, it was her daily duty to comb my hair. I didn't have enough nerve to refuse her. My hair was not quite long or thick enough to make a single braid that could have been attractively tied with al ribbon. My hair required several tiny braids. These were gathered all together at the end and tied with a ribbon. Such was my hairstyle. Combing through my hair was murder! The artistry of my hairstyle was also dictated by the shape of my face—in some places straight, in some places crooked. The one and only time I ever thought of Momma during her stay in the city was in the morning when my hair was being braided. Grandmother and my two aunts were still far, far from being as perfect as Momma with her masterful skill.

From the crown, Momma would separate my hair exactly into six even strands and braid them so carefully and firmly that not even a single hair was out of place no matter how roughly I played at skipping and jumping. Since Momma had left for the city, I imagined that my hairstyle made my face look a little askew and somewhat homely. When I looked at myself in Aunt's mirror, I vaguely sensed the absence of Momma's touch in my face. Then I would be gripped with a momentary whirlwind of agitation, but never really driven into anxiety. Mimicking a boy was a lot easier for me than acting like a typical girl; consequently, I didn't need to break a mirror by looking in it.

Although I deliberately kept my distance from Momma, nursing hostility, I let her hands dress my hair. My intentions actually had nothing to do with a girlish desire for a more handsome hairstyle. I deeply loved the tingling feeling of affection that I received from Momma's firm yet soft fingertips. At such moments, I wasn't troubled that much about Momma's winning over Grandmother and taking me with her; in fact, I anticipated it.

One day, however, my enthusiasm was shattered into pieces by Momma's scheming. She pretended to comb through my hair and then without any warning she chopped it off. To make matters worse, she cut it from the angle of my back hair, rather than from the nape. It certainly was a sight to see. I looked at the back of my head in a large, tarnished mirror from which the mercury was missing. I couldn't even cry. The back of my head was hollowed like the mouth of a furnace and its whitish, bare skin was exposed. It was like Momma had thrown mud in my face. Starting first with disfiguring my hair, Momma succeeded in making me feel totally dispirited. She then began to touch up the damage in her careful manner. It was too late; the milk had already been spilled. The side hair was trimmed off, using the short length of the back hair as a guide; my ears were exposed, and the front hair cut in straight bangs, erasing the part in my hair.

"Don't you like it? It's so easy to comb and wash. It looks so much nicer, too. If you go to Seoul with your pigtail, the children will tease you, calling you a country bumpkin. You might not be able to go to school. Every girl in Seoul has this short hairstyle and they go to school with backpacks. In Seoul you must attend school. You must finish your education and become a modern woman. Do you understand?" Momma kept whispering this into my ear.

I hadn't the foggiest idea what a modern woman was. It was crystal clear, however, that Momma was conspiring with the city to cast a noose around me, just as she had done to my brother. We were expected to succeed in the city. For some strange reason, however, I had no words to contradict her. I merely squirmed. My short hair was indeed something to see, stamping me with the brand of the city. I knew I couldn't stay on in the countryside with that hideous hairstyle.

As the wings of my spirit were being clipped, so were Grandmother's. She began to gather many things for Momma to take. Unlike the time she left with my brother, Momma received much more generous treatment now. When we went to bid our farewell to Grandfather in his quarters, he cast a sidelong glance at my short hair and turned his head in disgust, his face looking as if he had chewed an insect. Nonetheless, he gave silver coins to Momma for me. He gave five pieces of much-creased paper money, smoothing them carefully before he handed them to her. He then gave Grandmother an order to carry me on her back to the train station. Grandmother told him she had already planned to do so even before she was told.

"That man is nearly dead," she mumbled under her breath.

Grandmother ignored Grandfather's order; she had me walk as she carried a large bundle on her head. Grandmother had Momma carry an even larger bundle; she was anxious to give Momma even more gifts. Despite many more quarrels than the time she saw my brother go, Grandmother seemed to maintain good rapport with Momma. She had already succumbed to the idea that her grandchild was being taken to the city. I sensed that hope for my brighter future in the city had sprung afresh in her breast.

However, when I freed myself from Momma's clutch and was wrapped behind Grandmother's chima, the strain began to build up between them again. As I witnessed their intimidatingly cold glares, I was convinced that I had managed to express my feelings to both of them quite well. I was determined that I would never let myself go from Grandmother's chima hem if only she would take my side a little more aggressively.

The first impression of Songdo was simply magnificent. I imagined Seoul must be even more grandiose. However, the city had its own noose. I was scared of the trap that would transform me into something different. I had no desire to become the modern woman whom Momma hoped I would become.

"Let's get some rest," Grandmother said. Her tone of voice was reminiscent of an icy wind.

"Yes, Mother." Momma's voice was as sharp as Grandmother's. I had a feeling that they would start another fierce quarrel concerning me.

Several large rocks, which reminded me of dresser tops, were scattered along the hillside that descended from Dresser Rock Pass. Some were standing straight up, others lying flat. Dresser Rock Pass took its name from the shape of these rocks. Between them was an ideal place with an ice-cold, mouth-numbing spring, an oasis where traveling merchants or wayfarers who had come a long distance to reach Songdo could take a break and quench their thirst as they enjoyed a bird's-eye view of the entire city.

Grandmother put her bundle on a rock shaped like a pounding board for making rice cakes. Momma followed suit. The air between them was tense and bitter cold. Anticipating a grave quarrel between them, I clutched Grandmother's *chima* hem even more tightly. Suddenly, she pulled me away from her *chima* with the force of a high wind. Then, immediately afterward, something incredible happened. She lifted me up lightly and then placed me on my stomach upon a flat rock. She lifted my *chima* and pulled my underwear down. At that time, I was wearing bloomers that were easy to be pulled off for doing business. Grandmother began to spank my buttocks with slaps as if she were pounding steamed rice into cakes. I had never felt such severe smacks before. She continued with her relentless flogging. "Momma, Momma," weeping bitterly, I cried out for Momma to rescue me. However, she pretended to be deaf to my outcry and merely stood there, vacantly looking over Songdo.

"You, my enemy, my mortal enemy. Please stop hurting your Grandmother. You, my enemy." Grandmother kept on shouting as she showered me with more blows. Her yelling turned eventually into wailing.

"That's enough, Mother." Momma's tone of voice was calm, yet had a suppressed fury. Grandmother stopped. I got up slowly and I was nearly crawling as I pulled up my bloomers. Grandmother's eyes were as red as the core of a pomegranate.

"Grandmother, are you having eye trouble again?" Gazing at her bloodshot eyes, I cried out, still pinning my hopes on her as my last source of rescue.

"Maybe," Grandmother said bluntly as she pressed her eyes with a cotton handkerchief.

"Who is going to catch leeches and bring them home if not me?" I said.

Grandmother suffered frequent bouts with some eye disease. People said this sort of eye trouble, which caused her eyes to only be severely bloodshot and not filled with pus, was due to bad blood. The quickest and most effective method to cure this, according to folk remedies common among the villagers in those days, was to have a leech suck up the foul blood. It was my responsibility to catch leeches either in the rice paddies or in a Japanese parsley field, saving them in a washbasin. Grandmother would roll back her eyelids and stick a leech on each one. After the leeches sucked up blood to their heart's content, their bodies become inflated, they wriggled like grubs, and then fell from Grandmother's eyes. She would declare that her eyes felt so refreshed, so much lighter, and would give me full credit for my leech gathering service.

Regardless of the quick wit I had summoned to remind her of my services, my attempt to restore her as my ally was in vain.

"Oh, my wonderful child, you're terribly kind to think of your Grandmother. Let your Grandmother enjoy the sweet taste of having a dutiful granddaughter. But once you go to Seoul, you'll bring back modern medicine for me. Why in the world will I need leeches to bite me then?" Grandmother said, with a faint smile. Her smile seemed somewhat forced to me.

"Yes, Mother, you're right. I was told there's a miracle medicine available for an eye disease like yours. When I bring the children back during school break, I promise to bring it to you." Momma hurriedly chimed in response to Grandmother's remark.

The three of us resumed walking. Grandmother didn't hold my hand; instead, she walked a step ahead of me, her calico *chima* fluttering in the wind. We were slowly approaching the heart of the city, entering from the outskirts. As we came nearer, the light in the city faded. The orderly layout of the city was apparent—the main street, alleys, shops, and houses stood each in a line so straight it looked like it had been drawn with a ruler.

"Please don't pause to stare. We'll be late for the train. For crying out loud, girl, don't tell me you are already dazed at the mere sight of Songdo? This is nothing. Just wait. You'll see, you're going to see Seoul very soon."

Momma kept pulling me.

"Let her be. Is the sight of Seoul so superior? You have to remember, this is the first time she's seen Songdo." Grandmother once again supported me.

"She acts like an absent-minded bumpkin."

"You're in too much of a hurry. Don't go off half-cocked. Do you really believe she's already become a city girl?"

Grandmother put Momma to shame. Momma remained silent. However, for the first time in my life, I found myself nurturing a sense of distance from both of them. Perhaps it could be called the solitude of impasse. I wasn't by any means enthralled by what I was witnessing in the city, as Momma and Grandmother thought. Everyone was stylish, and I sporadically noticed men in suits, shining tiled roofs, rectangular two-story houses decorated with windows, and paved streets which were so strange to me as to be awesome. Colorful, mysterious things were displayed row after row in every shop; and life-brimming, cheerful noises sounded all around us. The hustle and bustle of the city, as if it existed in unconditional obedience to some mandate, cast me into a sea of bewilderment. Such order was indeed a strange sight to me. Even before being taught, I could sense instinctively that one must adapt to this kind of particular order if one were to survive as a city person. I was wild by nature, having been raised in the country, and I was seized with a sense of insecurity.

Momma mentioned that Songdo was nothing but a small town indeed compared to the splendor of Seoul. When I whined about my achy legs, Momma praised Seoul once again: "If we were in Seoul, we could be sitting comfortably in a streetcar and going where we pleased."

The Gaesung train station was bigger than any of the huge houses I had seen near an intersection in Songdo. Its round roof, the red bricks, the high ceiling, the railroad tracks stretching to some mysterious, far-away town, an overpass floating in air, the many steps to climb, people always running rather than walking—as I was watched all of this, I felt a wave of cold electricity flash through my body. Instead of easing my shock with some word of comfort, Momma pretended to ignore me completely.

The architecture of Gaesung train station was like that of the station in Kyungsung. Nonetheless, I knew that Gaesung would look like a child's toy compared to Kyungsung. Grandmother and I sat on a long bench while Momma went to buy the tickets. Since I had been spanked at the Dresser Rock Pass, my relationship with Grandmother had become somewhat strained. She put her hand into the corner of her bundle to take out something and offered me a glutinous millet cake. I truly craved one of the sweets wrapped in attractive paper that I saw in the display case in the shop. My mouth watered as I gazed at them. In spite of my hunger, I refused to take a millet cake. I shook my head violently. I was ashamed of Grandmother's rake-like, harsh-looking hand and hated the millet cake, which was shaped like an old, large sweet potato.

"Child, you aren't still upset, are you? Don't you realize Grandmother spanked you for a reason..."

Grandmother pulled me up with a sudden jerk and put me on her lap. She began to remove my bloomers. I writhed, kicking my feet. Grandmother rubbed my buttocks.

"My poor child! Look at her blistered fanny," Grandmother mumbled. "Some woman must have thorny hands. Grandmother has curing hands. Let me rub your buttocks. Grandmother has curing hands. Let me rub your buttocks. Goodness, gracious, some woman has thorny hands."

Momma came back with two tickets and gave one to Grandmother. I found out that Grandmother's ticket was only good for her to go inside the train to say good-bye.

"You mean to tell me that they charge for a ticket to go inside the train? Especially when I can walk by myself? What in the world! City people are terrible..." Grandmother shouted so loud that people nearby were startled.

"No one twisted my arm to make me buy it. It's not that much. It's very cheap."

Grandmother and Momma put the bundles on their heads again and stood in line. We entered the ticketing gate, crossed the overpass, boarded the train, and found our seats as others did in such a flurry that it seemed to happen in the twinkling of an eye. Momma placed her bundles on the shelf and had me sit by the window. I saw Grandmother outside. If not for the window between us, I could easily have touched her with my outstretched hand. Yet, she seemed to be standing in a remote place far away from me. I was emotionally very close to Grandmother. It was the very first time she'd ever looked at me from a distance. It wasn't because of the actual distance between us, but perhaps because of my realization that I was becoming detached from her. The train didn't move for a long time. Since Grandmother was still standing outside the window, the waiting period was dreadfully unnerving.

The train started to move. Unlike other well-wishers who moved along with the train, Grandmother stood still. She was soon out of sight. I breathed a sigh of relief. I bounced in an attempt to test the wonderful elasticity of the chair with my backside. With one hand, I touched and caressed the back of the cushion. It felt as soft as the first fuzz on a chick or a green barley field in early spring.

Whenever the train stopped, Momma pulled my hand and made me count the stations we still had to pass on the way to Seoul. Since Kyungsung was the tenth stop from Gaesung, it was easy to count them on my fingers. As the train approached Seoul, I found myself regarding Momma as if she were queen of this majestic palace — Seoul!

Momma talked calmly about the modern woman I must become once I was in Seoul.

"What is a modern woman?" I asked.

"Just because you live in Seoul, you don't automatically become a modern woman. Only after you learn a lot do you become one. Once you become a modern woman, you have a modern hairstyle, a bob, not chignon like mine. You wear a straight black skirt which shows your calves, and high-heeled shoes, and you carry a purse."

I had no idea what she was talking about, and Momma knew it. She looked around the compartment with hawk eyes and pointed out to me someone who had a wavy bob and held a purse in her lap. Momma wanted me to see the real thing with my own eyes. She tried hard to make me absorb the meaning of being a modern woman. Strangely, not even one woman in the compartment matched her entire description of a modern woman. It wasn't that difficult for me, however, to imagine a *completely-* modern woman. I was disappointed in Momma's expectations for me. My desire was far from being this modern woman. I yearned to have a long braid of hair with a gold-trimmed, crimson ribbon at the end of the braid. I wanted to wear a long matching *kori* [back-slit] *chima*. Under the *kori chima*, the tips of my *bosun* [typical Korean socks worn by women] would barely show as I walked in my *kotshin* [floral-decorated shoes]. I wanted to wear a yellow *chogori* [typical blouse worn by Korean women] fastened with a plum-colored tie. I was completely captivated and intrigued by beautiful colors then, so I wasn't at all impressed with a black skirt, black shoes, and a black purse—Momma's description of the modern woman.

"What does a modern woman do?" I asked since I was yearning to be dressed in beautiful colors and fly high on a swing or play on a teeter-totter.

Momma didn't answer right away. She seemed to be at a loss. Grown-ups wore this expression quite often. I saw them wear this expression when they pretended not to be sick or saddened although they were ill or full of sorrow. I guessed that Momma was merely pretending to know something of which she was totally ignorant. I gazed at her with a playful smile.

"A modern woman has a good education and knows everything about the world's affairs. She can do anything she makes up her mind to do." Momma stuttered a little as she said this.

Since my expectations had been great, my disappointment at her response was much worse than when I merely flirted with the image of a modern woman in my mind. It was my first revelation that a modern woman was truly of little importance. However, I lacked the courage to tell her that I could simply dismiss the idea of becoming such a woman. The train was rushing toward Seoul at an alarming speed.

Dusk was gathering when we got off at Kyungsung train station. As I had anticipated, the station was colossal; in fact, its size overpowered me so much that I dared not embrace the entire view at a glance. Pushed and pulled by the tidal wave of the crowd, encountering such throngs of people for the first time, I was gripped by fear of losing Momma. She was carrying three bundles, one on her head and one in each hand. She was too encumbered crossing the overpass to hold my hand, and she didn't like me to cling to the hem of her *chima*.

In a frantic flurry, we snaked through the crowd and came outside. Coolies with A-frames swarmed around us. One coolie tried to snatch a bundle from Momma. She told him, pointing with her chin, that her house was right across the street. She broke loose from him and hastily escaped from the encircling coolies. As if I might also be pushed aside by Momma, I desperately clung to her. The A-frame coolies did not give up on her that easily either. They all followed after us.

Momma slowed her pace. She hesitated at first and then began to bargain, pretending she was giving in.

"How much to Hyunjo-dong?"

"Why, ma'am, didn't you say your house is just across the street? No way is Hyunjo-dong that close." I could see contempt written all over his menacing face.

In the midst of the city's throng, Momma looked tiny and shabby. Her elegant chignon combed with camellia oil was now disheveled, as she'd carried the heavy bundles on her head off and on during the journey. Some of her hair even stood up straight. A vague, surging sorrow nearly choked me, yet I didn't allow tears to come.

For some time, Momma and the man haggled over his fee. The coolie insisted that her house was on the top of the high hill, and Momma tried to contradict him, although she conceded it was located on an elevated area. I had no idea in what kind of place she lived. Those coolies who had followed Momma left furtively one by one. The oldest coolie was the only one who still lingered. Momma succeeded in bargaining with him on his fee, and he loaded her bundles onto his A-frame.

"I'll let you carry them for me because I want to be kind to an old man," Momma said, as if she were doing him a great favor.

"If I'd had a single customer before you, ma'am, I wouldn't go to that high hill even if you offered me a thousand coins," the old man said.

That wretched old man mentions a high hill every time he opens his big mouth. What a sorry fellow! Momma muttered under her breath as she looked at his legs. Since the man's head was hidden behind the three large piled-up bundles, we could only see his legs. I was glad they had agreed on a fee. Quite relieved, I could hold Momma's hand. Although we walked fast to keep up with him, the man always kept a few strides ahead of us.

"Momma, where are the streetcars?"

She silently pointed at a vehicle which was running on a rail with something like a large wen on its forehead. Compared to the black train, which had seemed to have neither beginning nor end, this vehicle looked like a box that could be easily handled. If the train were a python, the streetcar was a cabbage worm. Children were laughing as they looked outside from within the streetcar. Momma deliberately talked about different things to shift my attention from the streetcar. She told me about an automobile that ran without a rail, a rickshaw pulled by a man, and a red fire truck. Momma couldn't stop talking.

"Momma, my legs hurt. Let's ride a streetcar," I said flatly, and I abruptly stopped walking.

"No. We're practically in our backyard now. From now on, you mustn't behave as you used to around Grandmother. You cannot have your way all the time. If you make a scene, I'll spank you."

Momma bore an intimidating look. She gave a coin to a street vendor to buy *Poolbang* [cheap round cakes] which were being prepared in a portable oven. The vendor poured batter and put some red bean paste in cups which were much bigger than those in Grandmother's muffin pans. Then he baked them. We received two warm cakes from him. The sweet taste of red bean paste melted in my mouth. Although its taste was not as strong as that of taffy or honey, it held me spellbound. Mesmerized by its taste, I forgot my desire to ride a streetcar. I savored every bite and tried to eat slowly, but the cake disappeared in a flash. This exotic taste stayed in my mouth for a long time. It was quite alien—totally different from anything I'd tasted ever before.

Momma and I walked along the main street. Then, at the streetcar's final stop, Momma entered an alley. From that point, the A-frame coolie became so sluggish we walked ahead of him. The alley was winding, dirty, and complicated as intestine. It was endlessly long and rough. Then I understood why Momma had hired a coolie, pretending to give in to him although she could easily ride a streetcar with her bundles.

"I hope you give me a tip to buy a bowl of *makkoli* [cheap rice wine]," said the coolie, who was far behind us now, huffing and puffing as if trying to win a bonus.

Momma was deaf to his plea. Narrow steps, like an upright ladder, greeted us as we topped a winding rise in the road.

"Madam, madam, how could you say this is not uphill?" the coolie complained, panting heavily.

It was a strange neighborhood. Dwellings, the size of outhouses back in the countryside, clustered together like randomly dumped boxes. The very first thing that had struck me back in Songdo was the dense concentration of people and houses. The concentration itself did not depress and overwhelm me; it was rather the order controlling it. Order was something that conferred beauty upon density. There was order there. At first glance, it was a depressing sight to a girl who had been as free as the grazing cattle in the pasture. At the same time, it fascinated me.

But I didn't see anything in this neighborhood, through which Momma was climbing laboriously in silence, to remind me in the least of the beauty of that order. It was dirty and indiscriminately jumbled. The road, for example, would not have been so pathetic had it been built before the houses. The houses themselves were just nominal, nothing but a pile of shabby boxes thrown on top of one another. They had abandoned the idea of betterment and had managed to make a passage—the so-called road—to use for trifling survival. The box-sized houses shamelessly revealed their filthy insides, from which came loud bickering. The foul and congested alley stretched on endlessly.

"Is this Seoul?" I asked cynically.

"Nope." Out of the blue, Momma shook her head decidedly. Her answer stunned me more than if she had said "Seoul itself."

"We're not really in Seoul. This is outside the gate. Until your brother becomes successful, we'll go through hard times together here. However, someday we can live in Seoul, showing off your brother's success. Do you understand?"

Momma sounded so authoritative that I nodded immediately. In reality, however, I understood nothing of what she said. When she came to the countryside to take me with her, I was impressed by the dignity with which she carried herself. Anyone could tell it was something she hadn't had before she moved to Seoul. This arrogance had been learned in Seoul. When Momma, whom my grandparents understood to be living well in Seoul, left with my brother, she didn't face too much objection from her parents-in-law. Momma's lofty air helped her succeed smoothly in taking me, too. Now I discovered that Momma was living outside of Seoul. Although the neighborhood was within the prefecture, the official term to define the location was "outside the gate," which meant it was not within the boundary of the four city gates: east, west, south, and north. Since I was kept in total darkness as to the usage of the terminology, I interpreted the phrase by its literal meaning—outside the gate. As if I were suddenly degraded to the status of a beggar, I was shrouded with sadness and dejection. I felt as though I were being kidnapped after falling for a sleek lure. All my affection for Momma abruptly froze. At the same time, I drowned in a yearning for everything I'd left behind in the countryside.

The thing that dismayed me more was that she didn't even own one of those piled box-like shanties. Momma was renting a room near the entrance in a thatched-roofed house on the very top of the hill in Hyunjo-dong. I had never seen or heard of renting a room to live in. What stunned me more was that Momma, who did not hesitate a bit to speak right up to her godlike in-laws, bent over backward to please the owner of the house. She bowed her head even to their toddlers.

The A-frame coolie continued to demand a tip for a bowl of *makkoli*, on top of the previously arranged fee. From the beginning, I'd felt certain the coolie's plight was hopeless. Momma unloaded the packages and paid him the agreed fee. She didn't lift her eyes to look at him, and she ignored his rude remarks. Suddenly, the coolie waved his A-frame stick at Momma, bawling out his demand for a tip. Momma didn't know what do to and pleaded with him to be quiet. She was worried about disturbing the owner of the house. The coolie shouted even louder, knowing that he had found

Momma's weakness. Momma hurriedly gave him a tip.

That episode was a good example for me.

Because the house had not been newly thatched with straw for a long time, millipedes infested our room. I was not allowed to go far from the room. I could neither laugh nor talk loudly. Thus began the saga of my life in the city.

After that morning, Momma lectured me with a menacing look. Except for a warning not to go too far away lest I get lost, she talked mostly about the renter's first rule. The renter must live in harmony with the landlord's family. I marveled at the capability of the people in the neighborhood to return home every evening without fail. I listened carefully to her warnings about getting lost. At that time, the nightmare from which I would frequently awake, soaked with cold sweat, was usually an episode of being lost. Momma filled my ears with warnings like these: try not to play with a landlord's child if you can help it. If she invites you first to play then it's all right, but never ask first. Don't ever fight with her. If she hits you, just take it, even if you did nothing wrong. Don't show you are envious of her toy when she plays with it. Don't even look at the toy. Don't look at her when she eats her snack. However, I couldn't unconditionally follow Momma's many rules.

As time wore on, I managed to find ways to get a coin from Momma. Frequently I did something to the landlord's child in her presence, causing Momma to nearly faint. I never forgot the mouth-watering taste of the sweet red bean cake Momma had bought for me from the street vendor in lieu of riding a streetcar on the first day I arrived in Seoul. It wasn't as sticky and the taste wasn't as strong as that of taffy or honey. It was a soft, clean, tongue-melting taste. Its flavor was a symbol. At the first bite, in a way that mystified me, this sugar-coated object represented the city. A coin could be exchanged immediately for some sweet thing. Even if it were not a cake filled with red bean paste, I could buy a mint, a caramel, or a plain candy at the small shop. Having these sweet tidbits right at my fingertips representing the city's sweetness enslaved me beyond words.

This bondage to buying and eating candies between meals made Momma and me miserable, and it lasted for quite some time. The face I saw in the mirror had eyes with no luster. I was becoming haggard and cunning.

One day I did something awful: I broke a display case at the store where I shopped regularly for my sweets. On the left side of the store, several wooden boxes with glass lids were displayed, full of either candies or cookies. The owner took the customer's coin and then let the customer help himself. I wanted to get a new candy from the second row. I pressed my hand against the counter as I leaned over the glass on the first row to open the lid of the candy jar in the second row. My body weight caused the large glass to shatter into pieces with a loud splintering. Frightened, I burst into tears. The alarmed storekeeper rushed to me and examined my hands to see whether I was hurt. He then scolded me for pretending to be hurt. He took out the candy I wanted and handed it to me. He then asked me to leave his shop right away. I was immensely grateful to him because he didn't holler at me for breaking the glass. I came home to eat the candy and even before its sweet taste was completely gone from my mouth, I heard quite a commotion outside. Fighting occurred frequently in our neighborhood. Next to having a snack between meals, watching fights was my favorite pastime. Exulted, I dashed outside.

Momma was fixing supper. I saw that her hand, placed at her waist, held a stick. She was haughtily facing the merchant, who was rudely shaking his finger at her. He was demanding compensation for the broken glass, and Momma was furious because she was being pushed around for something she didn't know anything about. She insisted she wasn't responsible for breaking the glass and confronted the man's rudeness, claiming she had no idea what he was talking about. She cried out that he was treating her without respect. The merchant and Momma looked equally over-confident, defying each other. The shop owner knew for sure that Momma was my mother. Momma believed that I wouldn't keep her in the dark if I'd created such a disaster.

I realized that I had no power to help Momma and was stricken with an acute sense of guilt for causing Momma to be driven into such a self-defeating, embarrassing situation. Rather than being a witness against Momma, I wished to disappear totally from the scene. The shop owner, however, had no intention of losing me, an excellent witness for him. He grabbed me brutally by the back of my collar and presented me in front of Momma.

"Who is this girl? You wouldn't dare deny she's yours, would you? You're not going to refuse to pay a nominal fee for the broken glass and try to contradict me, are you?"

The merchant put my face nearly against Momma's during his insinuating remarks. That was the first time I'd seen her face that close. I couldn't see anything except that I was the spitting image of Momma when I put my face close to a mirror. My heart filled with a strong and very strange feeling.

"Put her down this instant!" Momma's imposing tone of voice was full of so much dignity and pride that it made me nearly shudder. "I'll call the glass repairman and have him replace it. Get out of here now!"

"You should've said that earlier."

I got away clean although I had been preparing to face the music.

Must we live with this despicable low class breed, she lamented, mumbling. Momma frequently used the term, "low class breed." The landlord lived with his aged parents and a handful of small children. He had a concubine who shared the same room with his lawful wife. Momma shivered at this arrangement, muttering, *How can anybody stoop so low? I can't deal with these people...* Momma looked one hundred percent dif-ferent—lofty and dignified—when she criticized them, compared to her blindly servile manner in the presence of the landlord and his family. But Momma could look unmis-takably regal. When she came to the countryside to take me to Seoul, she had an air of dignity about her. Momma might have been somewhat arrogant then, considering the city as her glorified domain. But why was she so haughty now? What was she trust-ing in this time? I wondered. Could she be relying only on the status of her scholarly, though nearly helpless, paraplegic father-in-law? He owned countless orchard trees in the backyard and the chrysanthemum-decked front courtyard. He had a spacious and clean house with a thatched roof. He also owned a hill, where our ancestors were buried, vegetable fields, and rice paddies. Momma lived with confidence derived from trust and pride in her father-in-law, whom she had betrayed by bringing my brother and me to the city. If her father-in-law was the source of her pride, then Momma's arrogance was nothing but vanity.

I thought that the incident of my breaking the glass was over, but that assumption proved to be wrong. A few days passed. My brother told Momma that he'd take me to the nearby hill behind our house. It was an unprecedented action. When he lived in the countryside, my brother was a typical urchin. We were very close. During those two years away in Seoul, my brother had been transformed into a melancholy and tac-iturn boy. He was taller than Momma. He had broad shoulders. He wasn't the poor boy I remembered when he'd had to leave the countryside against his will. Then he was carrying a heavy burden, imposed on him by other members of the family: to restore the fate of the family. He was made to feel a deep sense of duty to succeed in the city.

Although he was only eight years older than I, he now showed distinct signs of maturity as well as a commanding bearing. He even displayed a voluntary willingness to assume responsibility for the family. Since I'd come to live with him, I hadn't been able to show how close I felt to him. Instead, I studied his moods and kept my dis-tance.

"What's the name of this mountain?" he asked in his subdued tone of voice as we climbed the bare, rocky hill hand in hand. His manner was friendly.

I shook my head.

"It's called In Wang Mountain," my brother said in his melancholy voice.

"If so, tigers must live here," I said. Once I'd heard a song on the radio from my landlord's living room. The song had a lyric something like, "the tiger on In Wang Mountain roared..."

"In the old days, perhaps," my brother said briefly. I was proud of my brother. He was tall, had a broad forehead and thick eyebrows. Pleased that this handsome young man was my brother, I walked beside him, shrugging my shoulders in glee. We climbed up to the ruins. We had a panoramic view of the city.

"Is it inside the gate from there?" I asked, pointing to the Independence Arch which stood straight in the center of the street. Even then, a concrete gate was necessary to distinguish between within and without the city limit.

"When do you think we'll live inside the gate?" I said. I wanted my brother to comfort me, to erase the inferiority complex which I had learned from Momma because we lived outside the gate. I blindly believed in him, hoping that he would tell me, without reservation, "Oh, as soon as I become successful..." My confidence in him was so real that even before he answered my question, I jumped and skipped in a good mood. A secretive yet warm affection between us seemed to be rekindled, connecting us once again. But my brother ruined these feelings by saying something I found incredible.

"Are you ready to be whipped? Pull your pants up to your knees." My brother had already then turned his back and made a switch from a branch. I had no idea whether he was in jest or in earnest. He turned around swiftly, holding a smooth switch in his hand. He was expressionless and ashen-faced as if all feelings of joy or sorrow had faded, along with the color, from his face.

"Are you going to beg for a coin and buy a snack again? Are you? Do you have any idea how hard it is for Momma to earn that money? How can you nag Momma like that? You spoiled brat! Don't you see Momma sews for kisaengs [similar to geishas] and receives money from them? Our Momma works for the lowly kisaengs. Each day you waste enough money to buy a bundle of firewood. Even if you're too young to understand, you just can't do that to Momma. Promise me you won't nag Momma again. Promise." My brother switched my skinny calves pitilessly, scolding me in his tearful voice. I was stoic about his switching. I could endure physical pain more easily than bearing the burden of giving in.

"Aren't you gonna give in?" My brother wasn't spiteful enough to force me to say that I gave in. His rebuking tone swayed a bit and faded. He threw away the switch and gathered me in his arms.

"You're not going to nag Momma, are you? Not again, not any more?" He sounded sad as if he were begging. My head against his chest, I kept on nodding emphatically.

That was the end of my exploration of the sweetness available in the city. Instead of giving me a coin, Momma bought candies and hid them; she would reward me with candy whenever I pleased her with good behavior. My brother would write my name, address, and the names of our family in Chinese on a tablet as a sample and had me write them ten times over before evening. Sometimes, he would have me write them twenty times. That's how I learned to write numbers and Japanese characters and slowly became familiar with them. I was being prepared for school, and I was a fast learner, faster than my brother expected. He wanted me to spend a great deal of time practicing Chinese characters, but I had already mastered the Thousand Character Text when I lived in the countryside.

Don't go to the landlord's area. Don't go to the entrance of the alley. Don't play with the landlord's child. Don't play with the neighborhood children. I haven't found anyone worth playing with you.

Every waking moment of the day and night, Momma repeated these admonitions, holding me to a very narrow and lonely area with her persistent warnings about my social activities. That was all she did—limit the boundaries of my daily movement and friendship. She hadn't the slightest idea what a cruel punishment it was to impose on an eight-year-old girl. If I'd obeyed her orders blindly, I would have glued myself to that tiny room at all times. On top of that, I wouldn't have had any friends besides Momma and my brother.

From early morning on, Momma sat beside a charcoal brazier sewing for someone else. If my brother was correct about Momma, she was sewing for *kisaengs*. I didn't really know what *kisaengs* were. Judging from my brother's talk and Momma's attitude toward them, I was positive about one thing—they were a despicable breed with whom we should not associate. All of the clothes that Momma was sewing were soft, smooth, and beautiful. It pleased me greatly to merely touch or look at them. They were the very dazzling wardrobe I'd dreamed of wearing some day, a lot more captivating than the white blouse and pleatless black skirt that I would be expected to wear before long. What kind of person would be wearing such fine clothes? I wondered. On the way to Hyunjo-dong from Kyungsung train station, or while living in Hyunjo-dong, I hadn't seen any woman this well dressed. I concluded that there must be other neighborhoods existing outside the gate, other than our neighborhood, whose inhabitants were also beneath us.

Momma's rigid taboo about associating with the lower class aroused my curiosity. This sensation, this taste of guilt, this secret tingling in my heart was more stimulating than the taste of candy.

I'd quickly finish the homework my brother assigned for me each day. The rest of the day, I talked to Momma incessantly, mainly about her needlework projects and the colorful scraps falling from them. I became an expert at telling the difference in the fabrics—silk, satin, satin damask, taffeta, and so on—as soon as I laid my eyes on them. I even became a critic of Momma's workmanship by finding fault with her skill, making a critical comment that the back part of the collar was set too tight, or the front of a *chogori* was too round, and so on. In doing so, I also learned to tack, backstitch, hem, and blind stitch. I folded rectangular scraps in half and made an ornamental purse. With triangular scraps, I managed to make a rectangle and as I was playing with different shapes, I made a fairly large patchwork wrapping-cloth. I felt quite comfortable with my mastery and was confident that Momma would praise me. On the contrary, she snatched thread, needle, and scraps away from me. From that day, my playing at needlework became one more forbidden item on Momma's list.

"You have to be smart at books. Don't you ever dream of being good at needlework. If you're good with your hands, making a living will depend on your hands. If singing is your talent, a singing career will be your future. If your face is your trademark, it will provide you a livelihood as well. If one has no talent, one can still live the way one is constituted. Your momma is not crazy about a talentless person. On the other hand, your momma doesn't want you to live off your hands, looks, or singing. You must study a lot and become a modern woman. Do you understand?"

Momma didn't tell me what a modern woman did for a living. Her view of a modern woman was like this: she must get the highest education available and know about world affairs. She could do anything indeed if her mind was made up. Most of all, she was a free-spirited woman. Consequently, she didn't have to be concerned about her livelihood. Anyway, another way of killing time was again taken away from me. A notebook, a pencil, and less than one *pyung* [3.954 sq. yds] of space was all that was given to me to occupy my day. Momma asked my brother to assign me more penmanship each day.

Despite the increased amount of my assignments, I finished them in a heartbeat. My present handwriting looks like chicken scratch, the result of my writing fast during those practice sessions, especially when writing Japanese characters, which were simple and meaningless. I wasn't sure if my brother was too busy with his own studies to teach me more than the sound of each Japanese letter. I was bored stiff at not being able to enjoy the meaning of a new word by connecting different letters.

No rule or regulation is strong enough to completely suppress an eight-year-old girl. I started to draw on the blank space in my tablet, and kept on drawing a wavy bob-haired modern woman dressed in a white *chogori* and a straight black skirt, wearing high-heeled shoes and carrying a purse. I wasn't particularly intrigued by then with this unusual look of a modern woman. Even in Hyunjo-dong, which Momma looked down upon as a place "outside the gate," I'd seen many sophisticated women who were more avant garde than Momma's description of a typical modern woman. I even saw women dressed in Western attire; some had short, blunt haircuts. Momma's view of a modern woman was actually a thing of the past.

Nonetheless, it remained a secret from me what this modern woman—according to the concept with which Momma had blindly imbued me—could do. Momma's vocabulary was not that difficult, yet I could not comprehend it. This secret concerning a modern woman's accomplishments might have been a rope to save me from drowning in the boredom of drawing the same object every day again and again. Gradually I used the entire sheet of paper to draw, instead of drawing tiny pictures only on the margins of a notebook page. Accordingly, I used up my notebook faster, causing a problem in our poverty-stricken household. But, neither Momma nor my brother had the heart to take away the little measure of joy I derived from it.

One day my brother bought chalks for me. He told me to use a writing tablet only for practicing penmanship and use chalks for drawing on the walkway. He drew something with it outside the front gate and then wiped it off with his shoes. He wanted to give me an example. He was a dutiful son to Momma. He must have felt uneasy about my wasting the tablet which had been purchased with Momma's hard-earned money, so he came up with this alternative.

I was more elated and uplifted at being free from quasi-confinement within the tiny room than at being introduced to the use of chalk. I could breathe easily again. The thatched house which included our room was located on a high embankment. Outside the front gate was an uneven alley, a branch from the main alley that eventually wound its way up to In Wang Mountain. This dead-end alley was narrow and steep and passed right by the cliff. However, the view from the alley was terrific. From the top of the hill, I could see the main street with a blue box-like streetcar coming and going. I could also see across the main street an astronomically huge house with high, red brick walls. A king might be living in that over-sized house, I thought, because sentries were on guard at all times, twenty-four hours a day. The streetcar was a most beautiful thing to watch—the bluish sparks rising once in a while from the friction between a rail and the connection lug, which looked like a large wen on the forehead of the streetcar. At dusk, this sight was especially breathtaking. Whenever I watched this phenomenon, I felt something like a delicate power or heat colliding with the unknown inside me, emitting sparks, and I trembled. The force within me that I couldn't name was boredom, which had burrowed deep into my bones. I suffered from a chronic disease called tedium. Neither Momma nor my brother could fathom the depths of the ennui that had pierced me to the marrow, sapping my vitality.

One day, I was playing by drawing and erasing images of a modern woman on an area of smooth, even stone by the front gate.

"Will you play with me?" a tall girl asked, standing in front of me. Although we 'd never played, I knew of her. Her house was located on a lower embankment below the cliff, and from the top of the cliff, I could see the inner courtyard of her house. The courtyard was narrow, muddy, and crowded. Every room in that house was rented, and the women who rented the rooms scurried about preparing the meals, nearly bumping each other's huge buttocks. At times, they had fist fights, rolling up their sleeves.

The tall girl was the daughter of a tinker who rented one of the rooms in that house. Every morning her father climbed down the hill, wearing a soft hat with a grotesquely crumpled rim and carrying a wire-handled can on one arm and a mesh bag on one shoulder. As he descended, he chanted at full voice, dolefully and with a touch of rhythm, "Mend nickle, silver, pots and pans, buckets and kettles!" There was a live charcoal in the can, which had a ventilating hole like in a portable cooking stove, and a long soldering iron. In his mesh bag, he kept solder, tin scraps, tiny bits of nickel, silver, a pair of large scissors, a hammer, and so on. I had no idea when he returned home in the evening. I'd never seen him after he left in the morning. Compared to her father, her mother was lazy; on top of that, she seemed to dislike sewing or repairing anything. She and her children often wore clothes with holes or rips.

On this day, the girl was wearing a *chogori* with a tear in the elbow, exposing layered dark cotton inside. The upper waist line of her *chima* had a length of open seam. She was much taller than I.

Before I could respond to her request to play with me, she took my chalk and began to draw a person. It wasn't a modern woman she was sketching. She drew several men wearing long pants, and she started to tie them with a rope.

"Why are you tying the people?" I asked.

"Because they're inmates."

"What's that?"

"They live in that huge house. They're bad," she said, pointing to the royal-palace-like, high-walled, brick house across the streetcar tracks. She could draw not only a prisoner, but also an airplane, a streetcar, a rickshaw, and also a bird and a fruit. She stole the show when she displayed her ability to draw convincingly a goblin and a fairy, which I had never laid eyes on before.

"What grade are you in?" I asked to show my admiration.

"I don't go to school. I know all the Korean characters. Why should I go to school then? My father said that it's enough for a girl to know the characters."

I, too, had mastered the Korean characters from Grandmother; however, I had never thought of it as a complete learning of letters. The power of Chinese characters taught by Grandfather was overwhelming when I was in the countryside. Since my arrival in Seoul, Japanese characters also dominated the Korean characters, which were used only furtively. I envied the tall girl's simplicity in showing off her mastery only of the Korean characters. At the same time, I felt sorry for her.

"Then, when you grow up you're not going to be a modern woman?"

"I'm going to marry a cop," the tall girl said as she drew a policeman, carrying a dagger around his waist. She broke the chalk in half in a twinkle of an eye without my permission and handed me the other half as if she were doing me a great favor. She then suggested that we each draw the other's face. When I drew a portrait, the first thing that came to my mind was a woman with a wavy bobbed hairdo. This notion made me draw only a profile. Even if I had a model in front of my eyes, it was extremely difficult to draw someone's face from the front view. The tall girl drew a circle effortlessly. She filled it with my eyes, nose, mouth, and my short hair. There was nothing she couldn't draw.

"I'm so bored." She became bored quite easily since no object was a challenge for her to draw. I felt I was to blame for her boredom. I felt so uneasy that I wanted to rescue her from boredom as much as to please her. She didn't miss taking advantage of my uneasiness. A ripple of a smile, reminiscent of boiling water as the heat beneath it diminishes, gathered around her mouth.

"Will you take off your underpants? I'll do the same." Even before I responded, the tall girl was pulling her worn-out underpants below her knees. She sat up straight, her knees spread apart near her chin. She suggested we sketch each other's genitals as we had done with our faces. I couldn't kill her brilliant idea, even though I knew that if Momma caught me, she would whip the daylights out of me. The realization that we were doing something bad dispelled the sense of boredom that had been slouching within me and now the strain from playing this game made me feel as if I were walking a tightrope.

The tall girl and I drew our genitals on the ground. As soon as I sketched, I erased it with my shoes. Quickly, I pulled up my underpants. She did the same. Her game, however, did not end there. She began to draw the same thing in several places on the wall and the front gate of our landlord's house. She drew well even without an actual model. I was touched by a deep sense of humiliation, in spite of how young I was. I pushed her aside and tried to erase them. No matter how hard I tried, the chalk drawings on the aged plaster wall and the tarnished wooden door didn't yield to my effort, as it did on the ground. Failing to destroy the evidence of our wrongdoing, I was about to cry. The evidence had to be destroyed! My face was flushed and hot as I pleaded with her to erase them. She must have thought that I was just embarrassed or ashamed. She acted as though she couldn't care less.

"You stupid, these are not yours. These belong to your landlord's family."

"How would others know?"

"They'll know. I'll put a name on each drawing."

The tall girl added hair, and beside each drawing, she really put the names: "Oak-boon's Grandmother's pussy," "Oak-boon's Momma's pussy," and so on.

I realized this matter was out of my control. At the same time, I felt brave enough to let things run their own course, and I even felt a kind of tingling pleasure of revenge. Oak-boon was the landlord's daughter.

Thes drawings brought immediate serious consequences for my family. After the tall girl returned to her house, I was caught on the spot by my landlord, who was coming home from work. He called for his wife and concubine in his loudest voice. The two women exclaimed, "How disgusting, how disgusting!" as they stamped their feet. Momma dashed out soon after and started to beg, her face colorless. My brother rushed out also. My brother was the only one with any composure. He displayed poise and calm as he tried to make sense of the situation. My brother was a tower of strength, maturity and courage.

"My sister didn't do it. She doesn't know the Korean alphabet yet. Before you know the whole story, don't treat my sister like a criminal."

My brother challenged the landlord boldly, trying to get me out of his grasp. At that time the landlord had me by the shirt collar, and I was shaking like a leaf in the north wind.

My brother had a clear head, and as his argument prevailed, the landlord's spirit began to bend. His rage was beginning to wane. I could feel it in the landlord's hand, which was still holding my shirt collar. I smiled secretly in satisfaction. It proved, however, to be a hasty conclusion. The landlord thrashed me and then grabbed my brother by his throat and started to slap him.

"You son-of-a-bitch! How dare you butt into adult matters. How dare you! You can't get on your high horse and tell me off! You scum of the earth!" the landlord spat out. Before he stormed inside, he ordered Momma to clean off those revolting, hideous drawings. My brother had spoken sensibly, but they were unwilling to accept his explanation.

It wasn't just the slapping that enraged Momma; her self-esteem was bruised by the landlord's outburst. My brother was Momma's religion. She didn't even walk in the area where my brother laid his head to sleep. My brother's filled notebooks and old books were kept stacked on the shelf as if they were a jar containing an ancestor's tablets. Such was her son to Momma, and such a son was now accused of being a son-of-a-bitch, which was the most contemptuous name anyone could be called. Although Momma superficially acted in a humble manner in front of the landlord, deep inside she despised him as someone with whom she wouldn't want to associate because of his contemptuous family lineage. Momma filled the wash basin with water and washed off the disgusting drawings with a scrub brush. Her hands trembled, and she could barely suppress her furious sobbing.

That night, Momma wept under her bedcovers, and she wrote a letter to her in-laws in the countryside. In it, she described the hardships, sorrow, and pain of being a renter. She also pleaded for help in buying a small house in this neighborhood, which was known as one of the least expensive locations in Seoul. She mentioned that she would attempt to get a loan from a financial institution. Momma had never planned to buy a house there; it implied her willingness to make a great concession. She was supposed to put my brother through school with her meager income and then watch him take the world by the tail. And then she would to buy a house "inside the gate."

When Momma came to take me to Seoul, she appeared to be a perfect Seoul person, but this was a sham. She was living "outside the gate" and was stricken with an inferiority complex and nervousness because she wasn't yet a complete citizen of Seoul. Momma's only consolation for living "outside the gate" and at the mercy of this "unassociable breed" of neighbors was rooted in her deep dislike of the countryside and her sense of despair whenever she thought of us being reared there. It was truly a strange correlation. Instead of escaping from the tight grip of this contradictory relationship, Momma was sinking ever deeper and deeper into the mocking mire of contradiction.

Naturally, this incident gave Momma another excellent excuse to order me not to play with the tinker's daughter. I couldn't help but think Momma and my brother took away everything to which I was attached. This time, however, the thing I was interested in was not something to eat or play with. It was my friend. The tall girl, my friend, called my name outside the gate in her child-like, rueful voice, inviting me to play with her. When I heard her call, my eyes became shifty as those of a mouse and I tried to find a way to divert Momma's attention. My entire body brimmed with tension.

As Momma sighed loudly for me to hear, she gave me reluctant permission to play with her for a little while. Momma knew I was trying desperately to find the right opportunity to deceive her. Her judgment was right in granting me permission to go outside. I was immensely captivated by the tall girl, and I found myself moving little by little away from the vicinity of home as I got closer to her. The inner parts of the bleak alley, the stone steps, and the slope to which I'd never dreamed of growing accustomed were becoming clear to me one by one, as if I'd just mastered a new vocabulary. To be familiar with the inner layout of the area was a blissful experience for me.

Each day I'd play farther and farther from the house. One day, at last, I went to the main street where the streetcars could be seen coming and going. The tall girl suggested boldly that I steal money from Momma and ride a streetcar. Merely thinking of riding a streetcar made my heart leap and throb. However, after lengthy, serious consideration, I said no. It was the first time I'd disagreed with her. It was also the first time I felt a sense of self-satisfaction because of my decision.

The tall girl said it was no problem since she had ridden a streetcar countless times. To my relief, she didn't seem to be offended at all by my refusal.

She said she'd show me a more exciting thing than riding a streetcar. We crossed over the track. There was a spacious walkway across the track. As we climbed the steps from the ground, an iron gate and the main street came into view. Sky high brick walls, on the left and right of the iron gate, stretched out endlessly. It was the wall of the palace-like house that I'd viewed as I looked straight across from the hill outside my house. When I looked down from the hill, I could see several huge houses inside the wall. From the main street, however, I could see only the wall.

The thing my friend thought more exciting than riding a streetcar was to ride a slide. From the spacious walkway by the roadside to the steps connected to the red brick walls of that huge house, there were fairly good sized banisters, where water flowed down, on both sides of the tracks. The banisters were wide enough for a child's buttocks and the surface was slippery. There were other children in the neighborhood riding these slides, squealing in delight. Sliding was an exciting game; it was a great thrill, and it made my fanny tingle. I was so absorbed in this soul-snatching play that I entirely lost all sense of time. For several days, I was infatuated with this game. I had no idea that my underpants were nearly shredded. The surface of this slide was not smooth and even as on a regular slide.

I was worried about Momma's reaction to my shredded underpants; however, she was much less upset than I had anticipated.

"Where did you go to ruin your pants this way?"

"Near the huge house with a slide down yonder," I said.

"Really? A kindergarten in this neighborhood? Anyway, from now on, don't play with just one thing. Why don't you try the swing set or monkey bars?"

Although Momma's intention was to transform me into a modern woman, she had taken away from me a spacious backyard in the countryside. She had also denied me the boundless affection that every member in my grandparents' house had focused. Then she tried to confine me in a dirty, tiny, rented room every day. Now she was remorseful about her treatment of me, and her voice was full of heart-rending pain. She seemed to be glad and proud of my finding a playground where I could spend time freely.

Momma patched my pants with a piece of thick, sturdy cotton in and outside of the damaged spots. After that, I was mindful not to wear them out so much. I watched how the other children managed to slide without harming the fabric. I learned to do the same by lifting up my buttocks slightly as I put more weight on my soles.

One day, one of the children playing with us yelled out, "Inmates!" Everyone scattered, ran, and hid behind the gray building by the walkway. I was without a clue as to what was happening. I was the last one following after the crowd, and I was filled with such creeping fear that I was ready to cry or scream. Although I didn't know the meaning of "prisoner," I'd heard it several times from my playmates. However, it was the first time I'd seen them. Even though I only had a glimpse of them, the impression was more ominous than fearsome. They looked the same when I saw them more closely from the behind the gray building where I was hiding.

They were clad in outfits the color of dried blood. They had iron shackles around their ankles, and their heads were buried in their chests. They looked weary as they took seemingly deliberate steps. I saw some men carrying daggers around their waists, watching the prisoners with hawk eyes. The slow-paced, weak parade seemed to be endless along the red brick fence beyond the stone steps. I couldn't discern in them any sign of will or strength enough to hurt anyone, especially in their present pathetic condition. Nevertheless, our hearts sank and shrunk with fright. We were scared to death of them. It was fear engendered by superstition. Naturally, the gestures to compensate for this fear were based mostly on superstition. Some children spat and some stomped their feet, and some made an obscene gesture, "shooting the bird." In confusion, I tried to mimic them. It left a bitter taste in my mouth.

The children resumed playing on the slides. I didn't believe I could have that delicious sensation again, so I returned home alone.

"Momma, what is a prisoner?

"Why do you ask?" Momma kept on sewing with a disinterested look on her face as if she didn't want to answer my question. So I let the cat out of the bag, informing her of the huge house, the prisoners and every little detail of what had happened that day.

"Wait a minute, are you saying that the playground you told me about was the prison yard?" Momma was so dumbfounded that she turned pale. After a while, she managed to regain her composure.

She seemed to abandon herself in a sea of deep thought. Her unique air of superiority diminished. Instead, she appeared to be lonely and shabby, as if she had lost even the last grain of energy to sustain her lofty dignity. I could tell that her pride had lost its brilliance and I felt great pity for Momma. I wanted to comfort her. However, Momma always had this look of anger or aloofness about her even when she wasn't angry or aloof. She disliked the fact that she had to live with her "unassociable" low-class neighbors and shivered at the thought of having the prison practically in her backyard. She was so distressed that she was emotionally paralyzed. If one's thoughts are so bent as to habitually brand others as contemptible, one must have at least an ounce of an optimistic outlook concerning one's own life. Keeping that in mind, I suppose it was the last blow for Momma to realize painfully that her young daughter had no place to play except in a prison yard.

Momma gazed from the neighborhood "outside the gate" to the neighborhood "inside the gate" with an even more poignant longing and expectancy. Her pining to live inside the gate some day played a heavy role in her drastic decision to choose a school for me. Momma suddenly began to criticize the school over Mooakjae hill. Every child in our neighborhood was expected to go to that school. She insisted on sending me to the school in the district "inside the gate" at any cost. Back then, even elementary schools gave every child a test and accepted only those who passed it. However, the authorities enforced a law stating that the rules and regulations of each school district must be observed. It was forbidden for any child to attend a school in a different district.

Quite a few of Momma's relatives lived in different districts throughout Seoul. Many times Momma had gravely affirmed her unchallenged resolution that she would refuse to look them up until her children graduated and were successful. She had us believing that she'd endure any hardship until that glorious day. Then Momma abruptly resolved to search for relatives. She went to see relatives who lived "inside the gate," the South Gate, which was not that far from our neighborhood. My brother turned his face away, smiling awkwardly at Momma's unbecoming behavior.

Momma finally succeeded in finding a relative willing to let her give my temporary residence as their house. They lived in Sajik-dong. The school I was supposed to attend was Maedong Elementary School. Momma was elated at this choice bit of luck. They lived not very far from us, located within walking distance from our house. She congratulated herself on finding this relative inside the gate and repeatedly let me know that I was lucky indeed. However, I was disappointed to learn that I was to go to a school that didn't require a streetcar ride. If I had to walk, instead of riding a streetcar, at least I wanted to taste a sense of pride as I entered the gate, holding my head high as I passed by Independence Arch.

For some strange reason, Maedong Elementary School was situated at the foot of a hill, a remnant of the slope descending from In Wang Mountain. Just like Momma, I felt a sense of alienation living outside the gate, not being included among residents of Seoul. The idea of going to school inside the gate reinforced my high anticipation of finally seeing the city. The path through the gate led toward the top of the mountain, the other side of the bustling, thriving main street. My anticipated view of the great city was not only disappointing, but also unreliable.

For me to go to the school inside the gate, a prospect I wasn't that crazy about, I had to pay the high price of undergoing a surprising number of hardships. For the school entrance test day, Momma spent far too much on my clothes. She also tried desperately to flatter the relative whose address I was to use. It was difficult for her to be an apple polisher since it made her ill to do so. It was nothing compared to my share of hardship. I had to memorize the address of that relative from the first day my temporary residence was reported. That didn't mean that it was all right for me to forget my own address. If I got lost, I was supposed to give the authority my home address. When I was being tested at the school and when talking to my teacher once I was accepted at the school, I was supposed to use my relative's address. It became a heavy emotional burden for me.

It wasn't that complicated to memorize two different addresses. In reality, it was no big deal. Besides, I knew the chances were very slim that I would have to recite either address. Nonetheless, Momma was a woman of strict morals. She was afraid that I might confuse the two addresses, and she had qualms of conscience about using somebody else's address for me. Occasionally, she'd check my alertness. *Where do you live? You are lost now. Where do you live? You are standing in front of your teacher now.* Momma took this tack in questioning me, fearing that I might make a mistake and confuse the two addresses. In fact, she overdid it and indeed caused me to make mistakes. Another problem was the hill that connected Hyunjo-dong and Sajik Park. The hill was canopied with more trees than In Wang Mountain. The trail had been nearly deserted. Rumor had it that lepers lived in caves throughout that area. Momma grossly exaggerated the rumors about these lepers, intent on warning me about them. Her scheme was more than effective. I was scared to death of that hill. In fact, it frightened me more than the ancient story I'd heard about a tiger who had made a bargain: "Old woman, old woman, I'll spare you if you give me a piece of rice cake."

I was told that the lepers dressed like a group of beggars I'd seen in the country; and they wore crooked hats, burying their faces in an effort to hide their browless eyes. They grinned from ear to ear, and their lips were bluish. They lured children into their long, dark cave, where they cut out the child's liver and ate it raw with a hearty appetite. Then they wiped their mouths as if nothing had happened. I had nightmares about this story. I planned to deliberately fail the test, or refuse to go to school unless Momma would agree to accompany me. Next I thought about saying I was sick so that I could stay home.

Whenever I deliberately gave her a wrong answer about my address, whenever I could not come up with the right answer to questions that Momma asked me to prepare for the entrance exam, her disappointment would be evident. I felt so sorry for her that I was forced to abandon my schemes.

"Child, please remember that it's a different matter to send a girl to school than to send a boy. I don't expect you to help your family. Far from it. I send you to school with only one thing in mind—for you to have a good life. That's all, my child. When your brother becomes successful, all of us in our family will rise up and see the light once again. However, when you become a modern woman after getting a high education, you'll enjoy an easy life. Do you understand, my child?" Momma tried by tearful persuasion to infuse me with her viewpoint.

At moments like these, Momma's eyes were so urgently feverish that I didn't dare avoid or ignore her intense gaze. I still had no idea what a modern woman, whom Momma sincerely expected me to become, was supposed to do. I didn't think I would ever find out, either. Momma had tried to save her husband, who was afflicted with either a severe stomach ailment or appendicitis. However, being forced by Grandmother to make the trip to consult with a sorceress, she'd lost him. She abandoned her duty to care for both parents and grandparents of her husband and to offer sacrifices to our ancestors so that she could escape from the ignorance of the country life, where people didn't know the difference between good medicine and using a leech to heal an eye disease. Momma's enmity to the ways of the countryside, and her intense aspirations toward knowledge and liberty touched me to the core. My heart went out to her, and I felt a big lump in my throat.

I passed the entrance exam. In an exaggerated letter, Momma notified her in-laws about me as if I'd passed the government service examination. My grandparents finally came to realize that since their only two grandchildren had been planted like seeds and now filled a distinct niche in the vast field of Seoul, they couldn't afford to be so stingy toward Momma.

Just as is true today in the field of economics, a large sum of money by the standard of the countryside, sent with great sacrifice from a barely-manageable household, was considered small change when it reached relatives in Seoul. Momma succeeded in getting a loan from a financial institution, which, added to the gift from the grandparents, enabled her to make a half-payment on a house. Needless to say, the only house we could afford was on top of the hill in Hyunjo-dong. It was located on even higher ground than the room we had rented. The new house was at the top of the hill where the neighborhood ended, just where the hill thrust up against In Wang Mountain ridge.

It was a tiny house, but it had a decent tiled roof. Momma was still contemptuous and detested this neighborhood "outside the gate." These people were ignorant of the wide world that lay beyond their gaze; they only knew the height of the hill, as it was their unshakable habit to climb up the hill day in and day out. In spite of her unfavorable sentiment toward the neighborhood, Momma loved her own tiny house with all her heart. The former owner was a sieve salesman. The house had worn-out wallpaper which had lost its original color and design. Distinct and creepy remnants of bloodstains from bedbugs covered the wallpaper in every room.

"Good heavens! It's a wonder those people have any blood left in them after being bitten so badly. How repulsive!"

Momma ripped out a sliding pocket door; she also took out the doors of each room. As she trembled violently in disgust, she washed them squeaky clean with caustic soda. The countless remains of the tiny bedbugs which had lived through the winter poured down like dandruff.

"Don't let their appearance fool you. They're still alive, I'm sure of it. How dreadful! After they fill their stomach with my children's blood, my son and daughter will look just like these scales…" Momma's monologue continued as she shivered.

Nevertheless, she couldn't prevent herself from being very proud of having her own house, even if it was on the very top of the hill. She cleaned even the supporting column with caustic soda and sprayed strong pesticide in every corner of the house. She also replaced the wallpaper and floor. At first, my brother and I were puzzled about how we were going to live in this worrisome house rather than sharing Momma's genuine joy in having our own home. We changed our tune, however, as each day brought new visible changes. As soon as we returned from school, we'd help Momma with the improvements. In fact, we enjoyed working on the house. On the first day we moved in, Momma bought a brand new large iron pot. She made a kitchen range all by herself, and she placed the pot on the kitchen range. Nothing seemed to be difficult for her to do. Momma was an excellent wallpaper hanger, painter, and even a plasterer.

On the first night we spent in our own house, the three of us lay down side by side. "Finally, we have our own place here in Seoul, even if it is outside the gate," Momma commented with deep emotion.

Our tiny house was equipped with everything we needed. It had six separate, equally divided partitioned areas—master bedroom, sitting room, second room, kitchen, third room, and a good sized space near the front gate. It even had a front courtyard. The only flaw in the courtyard was its shape; it was a triangle rather than the traditional rectangle. Momma called it fondly our "ornamental courtyard." Our own house did not face the cliff as our rented house did. Instead, it faced the usual alley. The wall, the longest side of the triangular courtyard, was connected to the back of the wall next door. The wall was supported beneath by a precariously high embankment.

Whenever it rained at night, my brother would awaken off and on and would be in and out of the house. He said he was too worried about a possible collapse of the embankment to sleep.

"What makes you think the strong embankment would collapse now, son? It's never collapsed before." Momma would tease him for being too anxious. She didn't seem to be too concerned. Other than that, we had nothing to worry about.

I planted different kinds of flower seeds—four o'clock, balsam, and rose moss—in the front courtyard. After we moved in, I was even more isolated than before. My friendship with the tinker's daughter proved to be a thing of the past. I was the only one who went to school outside the assigned district. Naturally, I was an outsider to the children who went to the school in the neighborhood. They deliberately shunned me. As if she had been hoping for this treatment, Momma appeared to be pleased. Although she lived outside the gate, Momma clung single-mindedly to an eventual life inside the gate. She expected me to be a child who was on a different level from the neighbor children and become like those inside the gate. She made me lie, which she herself had taught me was bad. Not only that, she didn't mind borrowing a relative's address for me to go to school. She endured humiliation and complexity for my sake. Furthermore, even if she realized it was dangerous, she made me walk every day along the trail where it was rumored that lepers roamed. Momma made me go to school anyway. I could easily understand her motive for sending me to a school inside the gate. For Momma to bridge harsh reality and an ideal she couldn't yet realize, she was unknowingly using her children. It would be safe to say that she was somewhat ignorant of the conflict her children were experiencing as well.

Neither in my neighborhood nor at school did I have friends. My classmates lived near the school; this fact alone made them an insular group. From the beginning, they stuck together; they had fights with each other; they took sides and changed friends at their convenience. This pattern occurred among those within the group only. They were hostile, cruel, and cold toward any child who did not belong to their group. Frequently, I looked at myself in the mirror, trying to discern why I was being ignored completely by the other children. *Did I look different? If so, how?*

Momma tried desperately to have me believe that I was on a different level from the neighborhood children. She tried to infuse me with her sense of superiority. And yet, once I climbed over the hill and stood with my schoolmates, I was drowned in an ocean of inferiority. I wondered frantically if Momma had ever dreamed, even once, of my emotional state. To me, superiority and inferiority were trees of the same family, both bearing a sense of alienation.

My first grade teacher was the very first modern woman I encountered. She was equipped with all criteria of Momma's concept of a modern woman. Her hair was parted in the middle and the back was brushed into a bob. She wore a white silk blouse and a black, straight skirt. She also wore a pair of black high-heeled shoes. I saw her carrying a black purse on her way to and from school. She'd even convinced me that she knew all about worldly affairs—big or small. She never failed to answer the complicated questions we asked. She not only displayed her immense knowledge, but also showed her unbiased affection for her students. She had scattered freckles on her face. She didn't wear any make-up. She was all smiles and always surrounded by students.

Whenever I saw my teacher on the assembly ground, she could scarcely walk for being encircled by a group of children. She reminded me of a mother hen with her chicks. From a distance, I watched her being showered with respect and love by the other children as I bit my nails. It was my habit to bite my nails—during class hours, walking to school and returning home. I didn't need Momma to clip them.

Every single child was dying to hold my teacher's hand; once anyone had that opportunity, he or she refused to let go. Since she had only two hands, she made an effort to give everyone an equal chance, and my teacher showed her love in this way. "All right, then, please hold your hand up if you haven't held my hand yet." She would issue this invitation. Then the children would hold their hands high up—"Me, me." She'd pick out only those who had really never enjoyed this rare treat. She would either hold their hands tightly or stroke them fondly. However, I never held my hand up; I bit my nails instead.

I wasn't particularly fond of my teacher. Especially, I wasn't crazy about her dazzling bright smile, which made her appear to love everyone. I knew her smile was fake since I knew she had no reason to love me.

As it became warmer, I was attracted to In Wang Mountain. Most neighborhoods in Hyunjo-dong area suffered from a severe lack of water. No house had the luxury of tap water. If the household had no one to carry buckets of water on a yoke, it had to buy water. Momma, a jack of all trades—plasterer, wallpaper hanger—was unable to carry the water bucket. Even if she could do it, it took a half day to get two buckets of water from the public water spigot at the bottom of the stairs. Miles and miles of water buckets were in line to get water all day long. Before we went to bed, Momma unbarred the front gate for a water-seller. The water-carrying yoke made a unique creaking sound whenever the water-seller moved. As its sound came nearer, the gate would squeak open; then as it was being poured, the water made a big gurgling sound in the water jar. I would wake up to these sounds; only after I went back to a deep sleep would a new day dawn.

The purchased water was reserved only for drinking. Whenever it rained, Momma would use every utensil and jar available to save the rainwater, as if she could not bear to waste even a single raindrop. She did her laundry and had us wash with rainwater. If we found larvae in rainwater and were horrified, Momma made sure to have us strain the water. Even after we washed our faces, she didn't let us throw away water—not even a drop. She would make us wash our feet in that water; she would make me wash her soiled rags afterwards. After that, she would make me water my flower bed at the corner of our ornamental courtyard. This was our daily routine for the complete usage of water, and Momma supervised us sternly every morning.

So much for water rationing. In the meantime, the monsoon season came and went. I was in a state of euphoria when I finally saw clean water gurgling down from the gorge of In Wang Mountain. As soon as my classes were over, I'd climb the mountain and wash my face and feet in that cool, clean stream. I even climbed all the way up to the ruins. From there, I could look out over into Seoul in a leisurely mood. At times, I would go up to the stream to wash rags, carrying them in a basin. I'd wash them spic and span, and it pleased Momma immensely, so she didn't mind how long I stayed up there. Sometimes she even gave me a sliver of soap and said, "Try not to waste so much soap and scrub them real good."

I would do laundry as I waded in a cool, clean stream at a laundry site on In Wang Mountain. Whenever I heard the drum roll—tum-tum—of an exorcism at the nearby Most Reverend Priest Shrine, I'd cock my head a little, enveloped with a preposterous thought such as "What's the meaning of life?" Then I'd feel an adult-like numbing sensation to my very fingertips as I struggled with these concepts.

One day I was rinsing off soiled rags at the same laundry spot when I saw thick, bloody water flowing down. Holding my breath, I waited until the contaminated water flowed by. Even after the stream of water entirely recovered its cleanliness, this nerve-wracking thought would not leave me in peace. The power of curiosity to witness an eyebrowless leper washing off a child's liver in the clean stream finally surpassed my fear. Muffling my footsteps, I started to walk upstream through the woods, avoiding the bank.

I didn't go far before a girl came into view. She looked larger than I, and she was lying down flat on her back upon the surface of a wide rock beyond the stream. She was singing, an indication that indeed no one had taken out her liver. I didn't know what she was singing; it sounded sorrowful and tearful. The wide rock on which she was lying was covered with drying laundry. Strangely, they were neither clothes nor common rags. Instead, they were pieces of worn-out hemp cloth. The residue of dark blood stains was distinctly seen on them. To have a better look, I approached closer. The girl sent me an inviting smile.

"What's that?" I asked.

"You silly, you don't know? They're feminine napkins—my mom's."

Although I had no idea what that was, I nodded emphatically as if I knew. I didn't want to be regarded as stupid. Then I climbed down to my spot.

That night, I made a detailed report to Momma about the things I had seen and asked about the feminine napkins.

"Oh, God Almighty! How revolting to wash that filth in daylight! Moreover, to have her daughter wash them! How sick and disgusting! They must be the lowest of the low breed. From now on, you stay away from the mountain. What kind of neighborhood is this? I can't let my child go out even for a moment? How in the world...."

Instead of explaining what feminine napkins were, Momma once again spewed her contempt on those who were her "unassociable" neighbors.

I felt nauseated whenever I heard Momma use the words unassociables, untouchables, or contemptibles. The girl I had seen lying flat on the wide rock singing an elegy and watching the floating clouds had made a good impression on me. She didn't seem like one of those Momma described as contemptibles. I felt that something—a form of uneasiness—was chasing me constantly; I envied the girl's natural and carefree air.

Even after she had her own house, Momma didn't hesitate to criticize her neighbors as either despicable or the lowest of the low, just as she had done while renting a room. She tried hard to isolate me from them. I was not allowed to go to the mountain stream to wash rags anymore. I used to stroll the hillside. Even that was taken away from me when Momma found out that I had a piece of rice cake after the exorcism at the Most Reverend Priest Shrine. It just slipped out of my lips and she placed me in detention. With In Wang Mountain behind and the prison in front of our house, those hotbeds of the forbidden, my playground remained a restricted area.

Momma had three categories for her neighbors—the unassociables, the contemptibles, and the untouchables. There was no consistent basis by which she defined each category. It might have something or nothing to do with the family name, their living conditions, manner of speech, or occupation. It depended on her mood. She was extremely fickle.

Every neighbor, even the untouchables—according to Momma—called the water-seller simply "Old Kim." They didn't use their best grammar around this old man. However, Momma called him "Mr. Kim" and showed her respect by using respectable words. He, the water-seller, was supposed to be treated in turn by his customers. Momma's turn came once a month. Most of households treated him with kimchi [pickled cabbage] and a bowl of soup; they had him eat on a simple, modest table either near the kitchen or on a narrow side porch. Not many people paid any attention to him.

Momma, however, was quite the opposite. She awaited eagerly for our day to have him. She acted as if she were preparing a feast. The eating table was so crowded with delicious foods that its legs seemed literally ready to collapse. She then invited him to sit at the most respected guest spot in the second room. Sometimes Momma made sautéed beef or stew with herring or a frozen pollack. She would also prepare potherb along with salted fish. His rice bowl looked like a mound, reminiscent of the rice bowls that the day laborers were accustomed to receiving in the countryside. She even squashed rice down so that the bowl held a more generous serving. The old man filled his stomach and showed his gratitude by rubbing his hands as he kowtowed. He also remarked that Momma treated him as if it were his birthday. In turn, the old man repaid Momma's kindness by supplying one more bucketful of drinking water either on national holidays or on important days for our family. He emptied the water into an extra jar and did not call our attention to it when he showed his gratefulness in this quiet way.

I was thrown into a serious state of anguish by this situation. I could not comprehend Momma's attitude toward this old man. Even the neighborhood children addressed him disrespectfully as "Old Kim." Furthermore, they used the low form of speech when talking with him. On the contrary, Momma, who assumed an attitude of arrogant superiority toward her neighbors, treated the old man with high respect and used polite expressions in speech. She even tried to feed the old man with better food than what she gave my brother. I knew the old man was a widower and Momma a widow. The very possibility that Momma might like the old man gave me a violent shudder. It was an unspeakable disgrace. As if possessed by an evil spirit, I couldn't shake off this thought once I became obsessed with it. When I was awakened by the sound of splashing water pouring into the jar in the morning, the first thing I did was grope for Momma. I would then hold her tight, putting my arms under her armpits. My behavior had nothing indeed to do with my expression of love for her. Instead, my intention was to counteract her plan to go out to see the old man.

At last, I confided my agony to my brother.

"Momma respects Mr. Kim. Do you know why? Although Mr. Kim is a water-seller, he sends his two sons to college. Do you know what a college is? A school of high academic standing! They carry leather satchels and wear square college caps when they go to school," my brother explained, grinning.

Thus, my suspicion of Momma subsided easily. Besides the old man Mr. Kim, Momma respected the head of our *ku* [zone or district] subdivision. He was as tall as a lamppost. In my opinion, the degree of her respect toward this tall and lanky man was not so high as to the old Mr. Kim. In fact, it was incomparable. This head of a subdivision had the same family name as Momma's maternal family—Blue Pine Sim clan. Although he had proof that he was obviously related to her on her maternal side, they had a silent agreement between them to acknowledge each other only from a distance, since both of them were certainly less than proud to live in this kind of neighborhood. When Momma witnessed him after his speech as head of the neighborhood, laughing foolishly and even making a few jokes around a group of women, she instantly changed her tune: he became despised and included as one of the despicables.

School broke for the summer. Momma bought some fabric for me at the night market. She then went to the Whashin Department Store and browsed. She picked out the prettiest dress as if she were going to purchase it, scrutinizing it in and out. She measured its pattern and style with her eyes and tried to make my dress as close as possible to the dress in the department store. She also flattered me by taking me all around downtown Seoul in a streetcar; she even took me to the zoo for the first time. Although it was burdensome and tiring for me to digest everything at once, Momma strove to feed me everything I could ingest about the city in such a short time.

As she had demanded that I worship and keep the best characteristics of Bakjuk Valley as our foundation when we lived at Hyunjo-dong, Momma tried to fabricate an air of the city about me when I was ready to visit Bakjuk Valley.

I was unsure whether or not I liked the dress that Momma had made for me. She assured me that the dress would be a masterpiece, and it was nothing compared to a ramie topcoat she had made picture perfect with her exquisite skill. Consequently, I had to abandon my criticism.

Grandfather cast a furtive glance at my dress and criticized it bitterly, remarking that I looked like a girl playing a violin in a circus. That was the last time I wore that dress during my stay with my grandparents. On the day I was to return to Seoul, I put the dress back on.

During winter break, Momma tried even harder to show me off with the flashy look of Seoul. One of our relatives gave her a pair of skates and a rabbit fur neckpiece. I didn't mind wearing the neckpiece since it didn't require anything special but to put it around my neck. However, it was a different story with the pair of skates. Momma asked me to skate instead of riding the sled, and she put them on my shoulder. I had never skated in my entire life. Once or twice I had seen people skate. It was a truly enrapturing and splendid feat. I thought the secret of this bewitching performance depended solely on a pair of sharp-bladed shoes.

There was a vegetable plot in front of Grandfather's front courtyard. Beyond the vegetable plot, a road stretched out from the village entrance. Across the road, there were miles and miles of rice paddies. The frozen paddies had been transformed into instant rings of ice where village urchins were sledding in high spirits. I wanted to make a big splash, wearing a pair of magic shoes into the center of the ring with my head up high. To my dismay, however, I failed miserably to balance my body. To make matters worse, my two legs split apart. I tried desperately not to fall down in that comical position, looking absolutely ridiculous, fighting not to fall. The urchins gathered around me with their sleds to look upon my mishap. It was a servant who rescued me from my embarrassing moment. He put me on his back without a moment's notice and strode to the house. I didn't mind his doing this. However, when we reached home, the servant put me down in Grandfather's quarters.

A barrage of blows from Grandfather's long smoking pipe was delivered on the crown of my head. I felt as though a flower of flame sparked in front of my eyes.

"You, you wicked girl! I let you go to the city to learn modern education as your Momma had me believe. Now look at you! Is that all you learned? The Sorceress' Knife Dance of Dukmul Mountain? What is the meaning of this? How outrageously you behave! I must have sent you to the city to disgrace our family. Surely, I must have!"

Despite my suffering from a pounding headache, I couldn't control the laughter which was ready to burst out any second. It was an extraordinary sensation; it was amusing to realize how limited and shallow Grandfather's imagination was. He interpreted my skating attempt as a sorceress's dance. Dukmul Mountain, which was located in Songdo, was known to have a shrine to General Young Choi. The Sorceress' Knife Dance at Dukmul Mountain was a household word.

Grandfather had every reason to be upset. And yet, as if he were a frog in a well who knows nothing of the great ocean, I felt sorry for him. I'd already seen and learned many different things, but Grandfather's Bakjuk Valley had been his heaven and earth all his life. He would pass away after a lifelong confinement in his small world. This pensive thought was somewhat absurd. I blamed it on the city in which my intelligence had been nurtured.

Winter vacation was over for that year. Before I returned to Seoul, Grandmother made a special starch jelly coated with sesame seeds, a product of her love and care. She wrapped the pieces carefully and urged me to present them to my teacher. Momma put them in a handsome box and wrapped it in an attractive cloth. I did not give it to my teacher. Instead, I took my friends—for I had been making friends for some time one by one—to Sajik Park. I shared Grandmother's starch jelly with them.

I knew my teacher tried to divide her affection equally among her students. Yet, she hadn't the faintest idea that there was a child in her classroom who was still left out and hadn't held her hand. The taste of my revenge over her hypocrisy was indeed sweeter and more pleasing than that of starch jelly coated with sesame seeds. Oddly enough, though, a bitter taste which didn't come from Grandmother's jelly lingered in my mouth for a long time.

At the time that we placed our stake at the ridge of In Wang Mountain, we were convinced that we would move inside the gate as soon as my brother became successful. However, we couldn't get away from the mountain's tight grip for ten years. My brother finished school and got a job at a large firm. He was still an extraordinarily dutiful son to Momma. He wasn't, however, successful enough to buy an impressive house inside the gate. The only difference in our lifestyle was that Momma didn't have to make a living by sewing for others.

As World War II was drawing to its conclusion, Momma had to visit Songdo frequently in order for us to have something to eat besides bean cake. The incidents of passengers being frisked for rice on the train were getting worse and worse. Momma went to Songdo with empty hands and returned to Seoul the same way. There was a difference in her, though. Slender Momma came back as stout as a fattened cow. She usually took a night train and came home just shy of midnight. She would squat down under a dim black-out lampshade and take out small units of rice sacks from various parts of her body — stomach, waist, chest, and hips. When, with my eyes half closed, I'd watch her empty rice in a metal pail, I had to clench my teeth. I was overcome with a keen sense of despair and sadness that left a lump in my throat. Momma took a great risk to bring rice to us the way she did. I never more fully appreciated the old saying, "Hunger can make a decent person a common criminal" than during that trying period.

The air was filled with rumors that the Japanese police would jab a stout woman with a spear. A ghastly rumor surfaced that a policeman had stabbed a pregnant woman. It was true that the policemen in every train station in the countryside carried rods tipped with strange-looking pieces of metal. They showed up frequently and drove the passengers into a state of panic. The strange looking piece of metal resembled the spade poked into a straw rice sack by a rice vendor to scoop out a sample to show the customer its quality. Nevertheless, it was an object of fear in that awful time, and the cause of many bizarre rumors.

Even in Grandparents' village, the clerk from the town office went from house to house with that spade-like tool and stuck it randomly anywhere he thought people might have hidden rice. Momma brought us an account of a tragic episode. The clerk plunged it into a pile of straw, and when he pulled it out, it was covered with blood. According to Momma, a man had hidden in that straw pile in an effort to avoid the draft, and he perished tragically.

As the Japanese began to face the reality that the days of colonialism were numbered, people became panic-stricken. No one knew what tomorrow would bring. In these uncertain times, I became a middle school student. By then, I'd passed the stage of believing that a leper would eat a child's liver. Such an old wives' tale was fanciful compared to my nightmare about Momma's stomach being pierced by a policeman's spear.

Toward the end of the War, the fear of being drafted into the group of comfort women [women forced to serve as prostitutes to the Japanese soldiers] added to the difficulty of the times. I often heard Momma talking late into the night above my bed with my brother about my safety. As I listened to them, I was shrouded in a sense of utter despair, questioning the meaning of my existence. Momma must have placed her life-long wish for me to become a modern woman on the shelf: With my brother, all she talked about was my getting married. She lamented that I was too young to be married but eligible to be drafted as a comfort woman. My taciturn brother had to try and console her with words: *It's not so,* or *I'm telling you it's not like that.*

One day, we had to leave Hyunjo-dong, where Momma had put down her stake in preparation of getting us into Seoul, but not because we were moving inside the gate to buy a decent house, as she'd desired from the beginning. No, we were readily fleeing to the countryside under order of mandatory evacuation of Seoul that the Japanese government imposed when its defeat seemed certain.

After six months of refugee life in the countryside, I saw Korea liberated from Japanese rule. My brother, who'd gone ahead of us to Seoul, where we soon joined him, must have made a modest fortune during the commotion. He succeeded in making Momma's wish come true by buying a nice house on flat ground inside the gate. After that our living conditions improved, and we led a very comfortable life. We also moved several times— each time to a better and larger house.

However, we couldn't forget our house with the "ornamental courtyard" in Hyunjo-dong. This was especially true with Momma as she got older. She had a strong urge to compare everything to the days in Hyunjo-dong.

"Son, don't you think we're very wealthy now compared to the time when we lived in Hyunjo-dong?" Momma would comment, displaying her strong memories of that neighborhood. "You mustn't indulge yourself now to compensate for how poor we were then." Momma couldn't separate herself from that time and place. She would make comments like, "We had the best time there, and I miss it." or "Our neighbors were indeed good and down-to-earth people." How much she used to despise her neighbors! Now, years later, she was thinking of them wistfully.

Strangely, Momma, who yearned for those days when she had the hardest of times raising us, had lost the preposterous aristocratic bearing that had been her trademark then. How easily then she'd treated her neighbors with dreadful contempt, branding them as the lowest of the low! How she'd tried to sustain her preposterous pride by putting them down!

Momma had no problem remembering the old days, and yet she had turned into a forgetful, weak, old woman who had no idea where she had just placed her purse. My brother and I were sad about the changes in Momma. It occurred to me that what she had really lost may have been her foundation. Her roots might have been planted deeply in the "ornamental courtyard" in Hyunjo-dong, not in Bakjuk Valley.

Frequently, Momma reminded us how well off we were now compared to those bygone days. As long as she cherished those times in her heart, I knew we were tied to the first stake Momma had placed in the city. If she'd thought we were free from that tie, I don't think Momma would have bothered to compare her present life with the old. To discern the moderate difference between the present and the past was something like trying to measure the length of a rope while loosening the end that was fastened to a stake.

After the liberation from Japanese colonial rule, changes in Seoul could be described with appropriate superlative adjectives as "most brilliant" or "spell-binding." People say it was difficult to find one's old street—not after ten years but after a mere three years of absence abroad. Despite this phenomenon, Hyunjo-dong, where our "ornamental courtyard" was, remained the same. I didn't find it strange. In fact, far from it. The stake that Momma placed for the first time in that neighborhood became a meaningful monument to us. It was quite natural for a monument to stand without any sign of improvement, or even become covered with moss or fall into decay.

A few months ago, I passed by Youngchun in a taxi with my friends. When I passed the area, I looked at Hyunjo-dong as I'd always done, with my private emotions—affection and tender reminiscence. On that particular day, I looked out the window and felt my heart sink as I witnessed the change in the neighborhood. Near the same area where I used to live, tenement houses, row after row, were being built. In truth, I must admit that this neighborhood had remained the same for too long. Even in the eyes of a country bumpkin who came to the city some forty years ago, this place was a pathetic neighborhood with a much-too-concentrated population. This untidy and disorderly place hadn't changed at all. In spite of myself, though, when I saw the rows of new houses, my already-morose heart became even gloomier. The old neighborhood stood alone, steadfastly untouched among the easily changeable and thus became a monument. Now I felt as though I'd lost my last cherished possession.

On my way home that afternoon, I parted with my friends at Youngchun and started to climb the road to my old neighborhood. The road has considerably changed. The red brick building we used to call "Whasan School" still stood there, bearing the same, old familiar appearance. It served as a convenient landmark for me to estimate directions to the road I was trying to find. Around the house in which we used to live, rows of tenement houses, like a folding screen, stood tall, blocking the view of In Wang Mountain. I was drowning in the sea of sentiment, as if the autumn wind was blowing in my heart, and I wandered around the neighborhood aimlessly.

Momma's stake had finally been pulled out.

After such a long time, indeed forever, I was engulfed with a desire to walk once again on the route I used to take to school when I was a little girl. It was just the route to school for me, but to Momma it was a castle wall that determined the boundary: inside or outside the gate. That hillock is now part of the only green spot still existing in the heart of the city. Once I crossed over the top of Hyunjo-dong and was about to enter the road to the hillock, a wall blocked me. The newly renovated wall stretched from In Wang Mountain and faced the West Gate. In the side of the wall, there was a small gate.

For the first time, I saw the object that Momma had imagined, distinguishing between the inside and outside of the gate; I'd never dreamed of actually seeing it. A barbed wire fence had been erected in the direction that led inside the gate, and the old road was gone. Instead, the area was canopied with the lush green of trees as if prohibiting the pedestrians' entrance. I hadn't seen a "No Trespass" sign anywhere; yet I felt it was a forbidden area. Gazing at an even more underdeveloped woods than that of the so called "den of lepers," I pictured the Demilitarized Zone, which I've never had an opportunity to visit.

I gave up the idea of climbing over the spine of the hill for old time's sake. I climbed down in the direction of Sajik Tunnel, following along the newly-built wall.

I took off my sandy shoes, shook off the grit, and laughed in spite of myself. Momma had persevered and placed a stake on strange and barren soil not even the tip of a shovel could penetrate. How fervently she'd pleaded with me to become a modern woman, and I've become sophisticated and fashionable. Nonetheless, I'm absurdly inadequate in terms of the concept of a modern woman with which Momma attempted to imbue me. Momma's concept in the old days was bold and daring. Even today her ideas and thoughts are not less so. Her willfulness did not end there. She planted roots for me continuously. She encouraged me to ignore the ordinary things in the city without second thought. She then coached me in how to imitate a child from the city when I returned to my roots—my hometown.

Discord between the far too old fashioned appearance upon which Momma based her model for a modern woman and her own ridiculously high ideology, the contradiction between noble roots and worldly vanity, eternal awareness of being outside the gate—all these were still part of my consciousness. Come to think of it, my consciousness still has that stake. Even if I feel I'm far away from it, it may be that I'm still attached to a length of rope that has just been loosened from the stake.

At the point where the restored wall embraces the road, I separated myself from it. The wall was reconnected across the road. I looked back at the wall, which reminded me of a typical fenced wall surrounding the estate of some newly-made millionaire. Where now is the mossy stone by the ruins where my brother whipped me? I wondered.

I still cling to the phrase, "modern woman." Like a restored castle wall, I feel it's ridiculous and meaningless in today's world. Both the wall and the phrase are capable of being either old or new, but I'm not going to attempt to restore the phrase and its meaning. Still, I feel as well that bygone days ought not to be denied.

Momma's Stake

Part Two

I believe that every disastrous event, large or small, that's taken place in my home has occurred during my absence. Mishaps has always awaited me when I returned from any wonderful outing. When my body and psyche, hand in hand, were someplace other than my abode, when I felt the least concern about my house, then catastrophe never failed to strike.

One such incident occurred soon after my first child was weaned. This, I felt, signaled my freedom from the most difficult and time-consuming part of rearing a child. Motivated by a terrific new sense of freedom, I went to a meeting of an alumnae *ke*. I plunged myself into playing *hwatu* [flower cards]. Until then, I had no opportunity to play any game. My time had been fully occupied in taking care of my baby or being at the beck and call of my husband's parents or grandparents. Captivated by the game, I'd peek over the players' shoulders whenever I could steal a moment here or there, and such had been my previous flirtation with *hwatu*.

Now I took my seat at the table and allowed myself to become completely absorbed in the game. I was totally enchanted, feeling myself under a spell cast upon me by some inexperienced sorceress who did not understand the intensity of her magic. I was so engrossed in winning money that I lost all sense of time.

"Look at her," I heard someone remark. "I wonder what will happen when she goes home this late. Doesn't her mother-in-law live with her?" This brought me around suddenly.

However I was not naive enough to be daunted by the threat of my mother-in-law's displeasure. She might furrow her eyebrows about my having so much fun with friends that I lost all sense of my need to return home, but such a reaction didn't worry me. I was far too engulfed in my new sense of freedom to give a thread of thought to my household even for a second, and this was strange to me.

The first child requires more time, energy and care than is accorded those that follow. I had indeed given every fiber of my being to the nurturing and care of this, my first child. I couldn't stop worrying about her, even in my sleeping hours.

It wasn't freedom that made me fall for *hwatu*, but because of *hwatu* I didn't think of my family. Soon an unpleasant and eerie thought engulfed me. *Is there a hidden web of wicked deceit in this enticing card game that entrances me so? Is it the hand of evil drawing me inexorably, not just the lure of gambling?*

Immediately I told myself that such a thought was preposterous; nevertheless, the sour feeling I had was as real as the touch of a tangible object. In an attempt to shake off this sense of foreboding, I tried to calculate my winnings. I'd made enough, I reasoned, to pay a food bill. I was having a wonderful time playing, and my winnings were a bonus, a windfall. I tried to shift the unpleasant sense of impending disaster into a more positive concept based upon my nebulous earnings.

I learned later that the dismay which had overtaken me concerning my wasted time was indeed a premonition. While I played *hwatu*, my toddler tipped over a kettle of boiling water, spilling it on her leg. She suffered from second degree burns and was rushed to the emergency room. The emergency staff was treating my baby when I arrived at the hospital. It broke my heart to listen to her painful moaning. My mother-in-law was also weeping. As soon as she saw me, my mother-in-law began defending herself for having failed to take care of my child properly. I'd expected her to scold me for my day-long outing and for showing up so late.

"It happened in the twinkling of an eye. I was getting hungry and it was late evening, so I boiled two eggs, one for me and one for her. I put the kettle on the table and turned my back to get some salt..." She couldn't finish her sentence. Like a little girl, she curled her lips and wailed, "Ah, ah," sobbing dolefully.

"It's my fault," I managed to say in a trembling voice.

"People say life's least rewarded task is baby-sitting a child," she stuttered between sobs.

"I told you it's my fault," I said firmly.

She continued as if I hadn't spoken.

"The doctor said she'll be all right if no infection sets in. Since her skin takes after mine, I don't think she'll have an infection. When I was little, I did exactly the same thing. I spilled a bowl of boiling soup over my left foot. I was terribly burned. I was told that when my socks were taken off, my skin peeled off from the burn. Back then, no medicine for such a burn was available. Soy sauce was the only remedy. Truly those were ancient times! Yes, indeed! Anyway, I was told that they applied soy sauce several times to my foot and before long it healed as if nothing had happened. I tell you it's good to have skin like mine. Nowadays, wonder drugs are available any time and any place. The nurse gave her a shot." My mother-in-law spoke in broken phrases, studying my face all the while. It was a trial for me to endure her chattering.

Her words were irrelevant as I gazed at my baby. Regardless of our presence there with her, she alone had to go through the agony which I was sure the burn was causing. I was about to lose my mind at the harsh realization that there was nothing I could do for my child; it was cruelly unfair that I couldn't share even an ounce of the pain for this child, who had come into the world because of my participation in her conception. She was facing excruciating pain all alone for the first time in her life, and I, who was responsible for her existence, could do nothing.

My child was too tiny and too young to understand the profound meaning of the common saying that each of us is a stranger to all others and thus ultimately alone. The eerie feeling I'd experienced earlier was more meaningful now since the disaster had happened to my toddler during my outing as I savored my self-proclaimed freedom at the game table. I now regarded this weird feeling as a prophetic warning sent through some mysterious link, concrete yet invisible, between my child and me. If I'd realized sooner that this stubborn feeling was a warning, my daughter wouldn't have experienced this shameful accident. I was deeply sorry for my stupidity and made a firm pledge to myself not to make such a foolish mistake again.

My daughter's burn healed nicely. I wasn't sure whether this resulted from her having skin like my mother-in-law's or from the effective dose of a wonderful medicine. It didn't matter; no trace of a scar was left on her leg. After that, I gave birth to a child every other year, giving me five children to rear. During those years, my children have gone through many other illnesses and accidents besides burns. Fractured bones, injuries from falls, traffic accidents, poisoning from medicine, and countless other mishaps have made my head swim. My heart pounded with anxiety over their misfortunes. Just as with my first child, every accident occurred without fail when I was enjoying a brief outing from home.

Since such accidents happened so periodically, I stopped listening to my mysterious premonitions. Since incidents, both good and evil, hasppened in the same way, my feeling of guilt became somewhat vague. If it were truly a premonition or a warning, I told myself, this eerie feeling would overtake me before the accident. Later, recalling all these accidents, I realized that most of them came after that weird feeling had held me hostage. Even if I admitted grudgingly that every single mishap had taken place while I was out, why did those accidents which didn't directly harm my own flesh and blood—my mother-in-law's fall, a boiler explosion, being a victim of theft and so forth —also happen when I wasn't home? The reason is actually far from mysterious: I discovered that the character of an accident is to take advantage of a person's absence when that person is in charge of the safety of the house.

This awful knowledge was irrelevant to the mysterious tie that exists only between blood relatives. Instead, it was closely tied to my thoughtlessness. My temporary indifference to my home meant that I abandoned myself wholly to personal matters undertaken solely for pleasure. When I was able to swim out of this rare, selfish indulgence, I was shrouded in a sense of guilt and embarrassment which evoked the premonitions. I arrived at the conclusion that women hold a singular position, one entitling them somewhat to be worshipped because upon them rests the security of the entire household. I didn't want to place the blame for all such disastrous incidents on myself, compounding my own sense of guilt and perplexity. Rather, I decided that my sense of impending doom arose from the conjunction between some supernatural power and my own innermost being. Once I formed this rationalization, my eerie feelings diminished.

In reality, the reason for the shrinking of my eerie feeling is simple. My children are now all grown and have left the nest. My mother-in-law passed away some time ago. My husband and I have moved into an apartment complex which seems designed to stand unoccupied. Consequently it has become my daily routine to leave my apartment unattended. It seems quite natural to me that nothing, not one excuse for an accident, is hovering at home. The main stage of my family's forthcoming accidents has been moved outside my house.

Oddly enough, after my eerie feeling of foreboding lost its magical effect, I began wanting to experience it continuously. This eerie feeling wasn't just a frivolous sentiment arising whenever I left the house. I realized that it happened only when my body and heart left the house at the same time. It wasn't a problem to leave the house physically; however, it was a different story when I left it mentally as well. Alas, I was one of those women who, having assumed the role of mother and wife, could not entirely lose concern for her house and everything happening in it.

Having created my own superstition, I believed that the cause of all these accidents was my total indifference to my home once I left it. To lighten the burden of guilt and outsmart superstition, I deliberately worried about my home often and called to check on it. Although I made this deliberate effort, at times I failed to think about my house at all while I abandoned myself purely to enjoyment. I'd later come to my senses. I was infatuated with this eerie feeling.

The new pattern of my domestic life was nothing but a jumble, a somewhat meaningless and monotonous bog. I was now master of routine household affairs and the creepy feeling only became an astounding stimulus to make my family's dust of ages appear as something of striking beauty. My heart would pound as if I were a frightened actress standing on stage for the first time. Drained yet renewed, I was then able to return to my daily routine. Even if it might be only a momentary delusion, it was uplifting to have my boredom transformed into happiness, old dust shimmering like golden powder. It was indeed bliss beyond expectation.

While young, I boasted of my extrasensory perception of something ominous; I loved this unpleasant feeling, which proved to be infallible. Now, from a new viewpoint, I felt that I was mistress of my household and I enjoyed its every aspect. The sense of mastery I derived from running my household with total control might, in fact, be rooted in my extrasensory perception when I was a lot younger.

"What would you do without me? Who'd take care of the house?" I would complain upon returning home after a three-night-four-day trip. In this mood, I'd clean the house, swirling the feather duster aggressively. Perhaps my psyche was a falsified rumination of my glorious younger days. A pile of grayish dust on the top of a TV entertainment center and a pair of socks left in the corner of the room would be the only objects which now waited attention upon my return. I'd be somewhat depressed to face such a minor degree of emergency.

To camouflage this sentiment and not to lose ground, I'd deliberately orchestrate a routine bluff: "What would they do without me?" My children would then cast an incredulous glance at me. *You're hopeless, Mother.* Their eyes would shoot the silent message from one to the other. Then they would cackle in unison.

I infrequently complained that I'd love to lead a life free of the burden of trivial housekeeping. I wanted to be a lady of leisure. In fact, I may have used the phrase "a day free from housekeeping" even more often than I muttered "What would you do without me?" With due respect and in all honesty, my constant reiteration of these phrases was a habitual exaggeration. Deep inside, I knew it was my true wish to take care of my family all my life.

I set aside a day to be spent at my friend's farm villa. Snow was falling even before I arrived. Gigantic trees outside the entrance to the villa where I was to enjoy my furlough changed its appearance. During the afternoon, a common snowfall became a blizzard. The clinging snow changed the simple lines of the silhouettes of the trees into the elegant lines of an Oriental painting. They appeared warm, soft, and hazy. The branches of the young and tender orchard trees, canopied by the heavy snow, yielded to the weight, sighing painfully as they cracked or perhaps even broke.

Within the villa, fresh and fragrant pine branches were consumed greedily in the fireplace, distributing warm air evenly throughout the room, producing a cozy atmosphere. In the front courtyard right outside the window a thick cloak of snow draped the cherry trees, transforming the landscape into a tapestry that enchanted me—a magnificent spectacle.

My friend lived on the outskirts of Seoul, yet close enough for her husband to commute downtown every day in his car. I'd never dreamed a scene of such splendor existed so near downtown Seoul.

The previous spring when the cherry blossoms filled the air with sweet fragrance, I'd been invited, along with other friends, to her farm villa. The front yard and the narrow orchard trail were crowded with our sedans. The cherry trees were in full bloom. Everywhere one heard the gay laughter of children who'd accompanied their mothers. Her farm was touched by the finger of modern city life. One felt that this suburban farm was built mainly to attract and cater to tourists. Now I found myself in love with two different views of the farm house, two different farms—one in spring-time and the other in a winter wonderland. Each season showered me with its unique nuance. Since her farm was two different farms to me, the distance there was also different. Like the disciple in the history books who, fleeing from war, finally reached Keroyong Mountain after indescribable hardships, I was baptized with a sweet and peaceful fatigue.

Listening to the crackling sound of the burning pine branches, I entertained the thought that the branches knew the art of expressing shining joy through the music of this pleasing sound. Snow was still falling. The lace curtains appeared to dance outside the window. This impression created an illusion that the room itself was floating. If the room indeed moved and traveled elsewhere, it might not be a mere movement in space but in time. I happily submitted to the movement. The snow blanketed not only footprints, but also every human accomplishment. It thoroughly cleansed everything of humanity, returning the entire world to its genesis.

My friend brought out a full-moon-shaped glass carafe filled with red liquid, which she poured into a crystal wine glass.

"Taste some," she urged. "It's cherry wine."

The wine was a splendid, transparent ruby red.

"You know what? I find great pleasure in farming. It's simply the best!" my friend confided. "At first I thought of cherry trees as nothing but plants. Was I wrong! They proved to be generous fruit-bearing trees, producing an abundance of cherries—about three large baskets full. They provided plenty of fruit for all of us. The housekeeper's children loved to snack on them to their heart's content. I also sent them to relatives and my husband's friends. When friends visited us, I sent some home with them. I bragged about my fruit, I suppose. The bottles I used in Seoul are too small and now I use large jars. Now I make wine in a large jar and bury it underground. I have more than enough. Drink it to your heart's content, my friend."

"Don't treat me like a goddess of wine," I teased. Nevertheless, I kept sipping, fearlessly savoring that sweet, beautiful wine.

From spring to winter, from cherry blossoms to snow flowers, these cherry trees bore three to five large baskets of reddish fruit which was eventually transformed into fabulous wine. My thoughts leaped to the hard times these impregnated trees were then enduring, bearing their blankets of heavy fruit; I was enveloped with uncontrollable admiration for them.

"Let me tell you about farming. It's simply...." Once again my friend was preparing to brag about her farm experiences. Suddenly it occurred to me that her invitation, extended to us at the time when cherry blossoms were in full bloom, was intended to show off her lavish way of life as well. At this thought, I felt somewhat ill.

"Have you been a farmer long enough to brag about it?" I asked. "You make me feel green with envy. Why don't you tell us all about it only after you have gone through both good and bad times? I want to hear you complaining, too. Otherwise, a person like me won't be comforted at all. Don't you see that I still live in a place like a small chicken coop?"

"We've been here less than a year. But what makes you think that I shall experience something bad even if we decide to live here several more years?" my friend interjected.

She was right. My friend and her husband were the landowners and the actual farming was done by hired hands. They expected no revenue from the farm. She explained that having hired hands for her farm was quite different from having tenant farmers. The only satisfaction my friend and her family wished to derive was eating the fruit to their hearts' content. They also enjoyed the panoramic view of their land, thus being reminded that they did indeed own it. That sentiment was reward enough for them to live contentedly on the land.

My friend's husband had a business in downtown Seoul. The business provided the family very comfortably with bread and butter. For some time my friend had been suffering from an ailment which physicians couldn't diagnose. The farm was purchased partially because of this, providing a place where the air was fresh and clean. Whenever she bragged about her farming experiences, it only meant a simple harvest from a few cherry trees in the front courtyard.

My friend suffered from some kind of nervous disorder. I didn't think of her health problem as anything serious. Yet she went overboard to tend her illness; in fact, I thought that moving to the farm as a means of improving her health had been too extravagant. At this serpentine thought, I was somewhat dispirited and disparaging. The magic spell of the cherry wine, however, lifted the gray veil of my depression swiftly.

As the effect of the wine spread through every fiber of my body, I grew tipsy. At the same time, I felt as if I were in Never-Never Land. I laughed often and became more and more gregarious. Under the influence of alcohol, my innermost private thoughts, preposterous fears, and hidden resentments were transformed into a free and open book and were exposed.

Just like clean, clear spring water which keeps flowing regardless of being dipped from, a flood of words drowned me. I was not in the least concerned as to whether the listener would regard my jabbering as spring water or filthy water. I was preoccupied with new-found pleasure derived from the sense of freedom which sprang from my ability to express my innermost thoughts in spoken words with no inhibitions. I felt completely liberated by the power of words. Perhaps I wished to cherish a taste of total freedom by letting myself go.

Freedom in my routine daily life could be compared to a star hanging at the tip of a branch. The star seemed close enough for me to pick from the branch if I climbed, yet any such effort was in vain. The higher I climbed, the greater seemed the distance to the star. At the same time, the distance to the ground also increased, and I was left with only an awareness of approaching danger.

I didn't fret as I took advantage of the intoxication which enabled me to rant and rave, unveiling my true feelings. I wasn't particularly proud of my rash jabbering, but I enjoyed being absolutely free of the facade which was part of me in the routine of my daily life. So be it!

I didn't blame my friend for her ceaseless boasting about her farm. It produced the best wine, and that alone was more than enough. The spirit of the cherry wine was captivatingly aromatic, delightful, and translucent. It was a pleasing sight, and its taste was sweet and strong. The wine captured me with its magical taste, keeping me in euphoria all day long.

My friend's husband came home from work in the evening. The snowstorm had subsided by then. Nothing could be recognized—rice paddies, vegetable patches, roads and creeks were all buried under the heavy snow. The snowy road was only a slight stain on the far-reaching white satin blanket. Two blinding headlights and the deafening sound of an engine signaled his return. Somehow he looked untamed as if he were a wild animal returning to its lair by instinct after facing great risk. I was touched by his courage and paid him the compliment of generous recognition. One of my strengths is that I don't get drunk regardless of the number of wine glasses I empty. I stay only tipsy.

My friend's husband blushed at my compliment. He volunteered to take me home in his car since he was afraid for my safety on the slippery road. My friend was very moved at his suggestion. She locked her arms around his neck and jumped up and down in gratitude.

"Do you really mean it? Will you please do that for her?" she said. "To tell you the truth, I've been worrying about her. How could I have a good night's sleep after sending my honored guest, my precious friend, out to ride that uncomfortable city bus!"

"Forget about the public buses. They've already stopped running. I think they were scared to drive in this weather. If she wants to spend the night, that's a different story. But if she leaves tonight, I bet my car is the one and only means of transportation. So that's where..." Her husband paused in mid-sentence.

Even though I was still moderately intoxicated, I had the good sense to detect the rest of his unexpressed thought: they wanted to get rid of me. I jumped to my feet.

"I hate for you to drive when you're drowsy," my friend said. She then followed us to the car. She and her husband occupied the front seat. Relieved, I was able to sink into slumber in the back seat. I have no idea how long I slept. I woke up only after my friend and her husband put me in the elevator and left. I opened my purse and tried to fish out a compact. A pack of chewing gum caught my eye first. I hadn't the slightest idea how it got there.

"Chew these. It'll help refresh your breath." I faintly remembered my friend making this comment as she thrust the gum into my purse. I didn't remember exactly where or when. I appreciated her thoughtfulness and kindness of heart in taking care of me. She didn't want me to arrive home with foul breath in front of my husband and children. Until this moment I hadn't given a single thought to my house. I'd experienced absolute indifference to my family.

As I realized this, that familiar eerie feeling rushed through me. This was the most eerie feeling I'd ever felt—as if a cold-blooded, creepy insect were crawling on my skin. In the face of this reality, the day's excursion became as vaporous as a daydream. My legs buckled. It wasn't from the wine. I was now completely sober. I thought of my age; I was now well over the hill, on the downhill side where mishaps or accidents would be too much for me. Maybe it was my turn, no, my right, to be the object of concern to my family. At my age, that would be quite logical.

Lately, this eerie feeling had been less dependable than before. Despite this, I had no doubt in my mind that some kind of mishap had befallen one of my family. My premonition was especially strong and convincing. Yet when the elevator door opened, every member of my family was standing there safe and sound, looking like immovable statues.

They stood there as motionless as statues even after they saw me. Their stone-faces, as if they wore masks, were unchanged as well. They appeared to regard me as a stranger. It was my fault—completely mine alone. I didn't think I could endure the sense of total isolation with which their solidarity engulfed me, leaving me totally alone.

My daily life was decidedly mediocre. Returning to my routine pattern of life after temporary freedom, I realized that my existence could be completely ignored by my family. Sudden enlightenment enveloped me. I suddenly realized that I loved my boring life!

As usual, I did my utmost to please them, forcing myself to smile brightly. This gesture was pathetically awkward as I pulled my facial muscles determinedly upward as if learning to beam out at them for the very first time.

"I must be very late. Oh boy, what a snowstorm! The city bus stopped running due to the weather, you see. My friend begged me to spend the night at her house, but I didn't want to worry you. They brought me home in their own car. Her husband drove. They don't have a chauffeur, you know, even though they are rather important people. Anyway, they brought me here at the risk of their lives. Oh boy, what snow!" I jabbered on, looking at the long hallway over their shoulders.

"Momma, please don't be alarmed," my oldest daughter said.

"Dear, don't panic," my husband echoed.

"Something happened," my son chimed in.

"Don't be dismayed, Momma," the youngest said.

The power and effect of words are well known. This was especially true when it came to the single word "alarm," which startled me a great deal. I had to quiet my pounding heart by assuring myself that my family looked healthy and were all right there in front of my eyes. I told myself not to be frightened. I reminded myself that I wasn't afraid of anything as long as my family didn't suffer bodily harm. *I'm far from being scared, yes, indeed!* I kept reciting this in my mind. *Even if my family has conspired to deny me, I'm not going to be alarmed.*

"Your mother is hurt, Momma," my daughter said.

"She slipped on the snowy step to the courtyard," my son interjected.

"I'm afraid your mother is seriously hurt," my second daughter said.

"She lost consciousness and is still unconscious," my youngest said, suddenly tearful. "We've been waiting for you to come home. We've been watching for you now a long time."

"We couldn't wait any longer, so we were just on our way to the hospital. Do you want to come with us?" my husband asked.

They kept talking, each member of the family contributing one sentence after the other. Although they didn't sound critical of me, I was so ashamed that I wanted to hide from them.

"No, thank you. You go ahead, I'll be there soon. My heart trembles so much," I said tearfully. "My legs are about to give out, too." I covered my flushed face with my hands.

"Poor Mother! She's in shock. We didn't have to tell her everything at once," my oldest said.

"Why not?" asked the second. "Don't you see Mother must find out one way or another?"

"All right, all right. You may have a point there. Anyway, I've seen a child hide his misfortune from his parents, but you know, I've never seen a parent attempt to hide his misfortunes from his child. No matter what the magnitude of the misfortune parents face, the child is always informed."

I listened as my children argued. My husband went ahead to the hospital with four of the children, one remaining behind for my sake. Leaving my child all alone, I went to my room and locked the door behind me before collapsing on the floor. It wasn't from the shock. It was rather from a deep sense of self-shame and an increasing drowsiness.

Deep inside I was glad and relieved to find out that it was Mother, not one of my own family members, who had the mishap during my pleasure excursion. I couldn't deny this, although it made me profoundly ashamed and embarrassed. I was so overcome with uncontrollable sleepiness that guilt took a back seat. The daughter who stayed behind to comfort me seemed to be at a loss. She didn't know how to comfort me or what to do with herself even after I pulled myself up from the floor and opened the door. I succeeded in deceiving her by acting as if I were grief-stricken. Only then was I able to fall into bed. It was a slumber sweet as the sheer pleasure derived from an immoral liaison.

I woke up from my short but deep sleep. The first thing that flashed into my mind, like a revelation, was that my mother was my flesh and blood just as my children were. My mother and children were each a part of me, as it were. They were equally important to me—not one more or less than another. Despite this, I felt as relieved to learn that it was my mother who faced calamity as I would have felt if I'd handed my emotional burden over to a total stranger.

I was Mother's only living flesh and blood. I had five children who were the very essence of my life, the source of my pride and joy. My poor mother, however, had only me. A mother's love for her children is equally boundless regardless of the number she has. Her unconditional affection and care for them does not decrease according to their number; as the saying goes, "You bite any finger, it will hurt regardless of the size." I'm the only finger left to my mother. I thought of how ardent her love and attachment must be for her only flesh and blood—me! This fact simply awed me.

I thought of my brother, whom I lost during the Korean war. He was widely known among our relatives and neighbors for being a dutiful son. An unforgettable image from his boyhood, which had been etched in my heart, now lingered in front of my eyes. I recalled those days when Momma, my brother and I were poverty-stricken, how I begged money from Momma for a daily treat and one day broke a glass display case in the candy shop. This was a great financial burden for my mother, who supported us. I remembered how my brother took me to In Wang Mountain and whipped me, then held me as we both burst into tears.

As if the rhythm of that whipping awakened me, the drowsiness rushed out. I felt as though my brother were standing right beside me. I hadn't felt his close presence for a long time. I shed tears anew, thinking of the tears he shed on the mountain. The closer I felt to my brother, the greater sense of loss I felt.

With my brother gone, I'd assumed the yoke of responsibility for Mother, no matter what happened to her. I was to be the first and only one to take care of her. With that in mind, I headed for the hospital with renewed energy.

To my pleasant surprise, Mother had regained consciousness. As soon as she saw me, she even managed to smile feebly. My two nephews, my late brother's sons, were by Mother's bedside. They were now a lot older than my brother was when he died. My dignified nephews were now married and had their own families. The emergency room where Mother was being tended was dotted with my own large family and that of my two nephews. I felt better upon seeing them all there. I'd been thinking of my brother as I made the snowy journey to the hospital. The fact that the dead cannot get older renewed my loneliness even as it moved my heart deeply.

Brushing past them, I went to Mother and grabbed her hand passionately, as her own flesh and blood should. Later my family told me that my heart-felt action was something that would, as people say, move the heart of the dead. Tears welled up in Mother's eyes and then cascaded onto her cheeks. Deeply saddened by the harsh reality that I was the only immediate family left for her, Mother wept and I did the same.

"What happened?" I asked tearfully.

"I was watching through the window as Seok's father cleared the snow. I wanted to help him, so I went outside and was about to take a step into the courtyard when I slipped. My heart's young, but..."

Seok's father was the eldest son of my late brother, Mother's oldest grandson, my eldest nephew, whose family had been taking care of Mother.

"What does she mean 'help?' I bet she wanted to nag about something," Seok's mother mumbled under her breath.

"Are you trying to tell me that both of you were there and you let this happen to her?" I blamed my nephew and his wife without realizing what I was doing.

"Grandmother wants to put her nose into every little thing. I didn't give any thought to her coming out. I merely thought she wanted to give me instructions or something of that nature." My nephew hurriedly supported his wife's critical statement.

Mother was well into her eighties while my nephew and his wife were in their early thirties. We live in a world where in-laws aren't welcome to live with the younger generation. To make matters worse, taking care of an ancient grandmother-in-law, separated from her by two generations, is not an easy task. Nevertheless, it was the very first time my nephew and his wife had revealed their true sentiment toward Mother in this harsh way.

The emergency room was filled with the sounds of human suffering and the moaning, groaning and weeping of each family member.

"Where is she injured?" I asked.

My nephew's wife lifted the sheet and pointed to Mother's leg. Her left leg was grotesquely twisted from her hip bone down. It was terribly swollen, giving an impression that somebody's borrowed leg was attached to her body. It looked strange and awkward. In a single glance I could tell that her condition was quite grave.

Mother was eighty-six years old.

"I wish they'd go ahead and put a cast on my leg," Mother murmured softly as if she were trying to comfort all of us in the room.

"Aren't you in pain?" I asked.

"Of course I am, I wish I could faint again," she said.

"Oh, Mother!" I exclaimed.

The nurse came and asked for all of us. We, in a pack, rushed to the doctor in charge. The resident in the ER was very young and appeared to be exhausted. The red hand of the electric clock pointed to a time well past midnight. Mother's X-rayed hip and thigh on the light board were waiting for his judgment. They looked pitifully bony.

"First of all, she needs to be hospitalized. Depending on her progress, she might have to have surgery," the young resident said.

"What are you saying?" I asked.

"Well, when I said 'progress', ma'am, to be blunt I meant that we should check whether she'd be strong enough to undergo surgery. I didn't mean to suggest that there was any possibility that the leg would heal naturally."

"She's eighty-six years old. How can she go through surgery? She wants a cast. It doesn't matter how long it takes. Please put a cast on her leg," I said.

"I didn't make my point clear," he said coldly. "I suggested surgery because of her age. Her bone is too fragile and old to grow back if put in a cast. It's like being in a living coffin having a cast at her age. I'm sure she'd die with the cast still on her leg from this or that illness which would probably strike."

"She understood that she'd have a cast. Well, sir, would you please consider doing it for her?" I said pleadingly.

"Patients neither diagnose nor prescribe," he said flatly.

"Are you saying that we have no right of choice whatsoever?"

"Yes. The only way to help her is by getting her ready for surgery."

"Do you think she'll walk again after the surgery?" I persisted.

"It depends on her condition."

"So you're saying that you can't guarantee the result of the surgery, aren't you? It doesn't make any sense," I said, raising my voice as if I were ready to put up a fight. However, the young doctor didn't seem as excited as I was. I could detect that his distant attitude had more to do with his work-related exhaustion than with a naturally cold and intellectual disposition.

"I advise you, ma'am, " he replied, "to consult with the head doctor for the details tomorrow. First, you need to do some paper work for her admittance to the hospital."

"How could you make such a strong recommendation for surgery when you're not the head doctor?" I demanded.

"Well, ma'am, it's the only thing that can be done for her based on today's medical knowledge. It's the only way," the doctor said wearily.

"How can you say that when you can't guarantee the result of the surgery?" I snorted.

"I didn't say that it's a safe way. I just said it's the only way. What I'm trying to say, ma'am, is that it's indeed the only way. What I'm trying to explain to you is that it's indeed her last resort. The fewer the options, the more dangerous the complications which may result." The doctor finally lost his cool and collected manner.

"Aunt, what are you doing? As long as Grandmother is under the hospital's care, we must follow the doctor's orders," one of my nephews interjected. Until then the two nephews had been merely spectators, standing rather behind me, but during the doctor's last speech they had both moved to my side.

"You don't know. You know nothing, I tell you!" I barked, giving in to the uncontrollable fury and frustration surging in the depth of my heart.

"What are you talking about that we don't know, Aunt?"

"Your grandmother is eighty-six. Do you honestly believe that she'll make it through surgery?" I demanded.

"We have no other choice. The first thing we need to do is have her admitted. We'll consult with the head doctor about the details tomorrow. Aunt, we're in the emergency room now!" my nephew reminded me.

My two nephews harshly pulled me out of the ER as if I were inciting a riot. At the time, I hadn't dreamed even in my wildest imagination that talking with the young doctor would be such a detailed discussion concerning Mother.

As in any other large university hospital with the same scheduled walk-through, the following morning the head doctor made a round of visits with his usual entourage

—residents, interns, and nurses. I knew the head doctor at a glance by his air of dignity and authority. I wondered if the embodiment of the word "authority" had the power to discourage a person who wished to express herself freely. I stepped aside in humility and waited for the doctor to say something. However, he went outside after he spoke briefly to his entourage in a foreign language that sounded like babble to me. In a flurry, I went after them but they were quickly out of sight. I was fortunate to at least run into the young doctor who'd been on duty in the ER the previous night. Even before I opened my mouth, the young doctor informed me of the date for Mother's surgery. He said it might be three days later, then walked into the room of another patient.

For three consecutive days, I went to the doctor in charge and finally managed to find out about Mother's prognosis. The area where her bone was broken was a critical place to heal. This much I was told. I also learned that Mother was too old to produce in her own body the fluid essential to the bones mending as nature intended. The surgery to insert a metal pin to connect one bone section with the other was virtually inevitable for Mother. The surgery was much more complicated than one would expect. The doctor in charge didn't volunteer all this information at one time. Far from it. He was extremely reluctant as he blurted out one segment after another. I was able to put the pieces together in some sort of order, moving between common sense and wild imagination. I did the best I could with the doctor's jargon.

I had no idea whether I was intimidated by the doctor's authority or by his power of silence. In any event I failed miserably to express effectively the many lingering questions I had. Just as the doctor in charge kept us in the dark, Mother's family seemed to her to be doing the same.

"My dear," she said, "you know in the first place I should have gone to the local orthopedist. I understand they're the best when it comes to taking care of fractured bones. I'm afraid it was unnecessary for you to bring me to the hospital and end up spending a lot of money on me. I don't understand why they don't hurry up and put a cast on my broken leg. Why do they draw blood from an old woman who's nothing but skin and bones? I don't understand why they do it every single day. What kind of tests are they doing? For crying out loud, how many tests do they need?"

"It's not the pain I'm complaining about," she continued. "I can take that with no problem. I'm just worried about the cost. I don't think anything is free here. You know what I think? I think they'd feel cheated if they sent me home with only a cast. I bet they made up their minds to suck every last penny out of me. I urge you to go to them and let them know you're in a financial bind. Oh, my poor leg! Is this really my leg, or is it an enemy? If the pain persists like this even after having a cast, I beg you to let me die right this minute. Let me die! I've seen my son killed and have lived a prolonged life. I'm so ashamed. Why am I going through this unbearable suffering? What kind of sin did I commit that I have to face this?"

Mother was in grave torment, yet, she had a ray of hope if the doctors would only put a cast on her leg. She was incapable of imagining that something worse than applying a cast would come to her. None of my family volunteered to tell her the truth; instead they dragged the situation out as they studied my mood. I knew it was natural and expected that a daughter would be responsible for giving gentle persuasion and comfort.

Finally the date for the surgery was imminent. The doctor had a sign put at her bedside on the night before surgery ordering a fast. I had no choice but to tell Mother the whole truth.

"Operation? Who gave them authority? Who do they think they are? No way. I won't have it! How dare they touch me with a knife? Not under the sun! I've lived too long and I know that. I also know that I've lived the hardest and most tragic life of anyone I know. I don't wish anyone to go through a life like the one I've lived. Anyway, I've managed to live this long, barely clinging to life. It isn't that I'm afraid to end my life with my own hands, mind you. But I'm absolutely mortified that God, Who gave me life, will punish me for wanting now to take charge freely of my own life. Even if I'll surely die without an operation, so be it. I'm pushing ninety. If you let that happen, I assure you no one will speak ill of my children or grandchildren for it."

Mother's flat refusal to go through her surgery was nothing to be taken casually. Her oldest grandson had already signed the papers. The medical staff had already arranged to take Mother to the operating room the following morning, regardless of her consent. It was an automatic procedure. Nonetheless, I didn't want to add such humiliation to Mother. Minus her swollen leg, the rest of her body looked light and powerless, like less than a fistful of dried weeds. As long as she had a sense of self-respect in spite of the small size of her body, I mused, Mother had every right to know the odds that she was going to face. As Mother's one and only child, the feelings I had for her were a mixture of love and hate.

Undergirded by this sentiment, I was honest, direct and truthful with Mother when I explained explicitly, as best I knew how, about the surgery she was going to have.

"Please try to think of your leg as if it were a broken stick, Mother." I was relaxed enough to compare her broken thigh bone to a stick! "Now suppose, Mother, that you have a broken stick which is of no use to you unless you can hold the two broken ends together. Which do you think is better and stronger? Would you glue them together with a specially designed bonding, or would you use a piece of metal and tighten them together with a wrench? Also, what would you do if you didn't have plenty of the specially designed bonding, or had none at all? What then? Please try not to be afraid, Mother. Your doctor will connect the two segments of your broken bone together with a piece of metal and make it strong. Even if you live only a few days, without your limbs it is not living. Don't you agree, Mother?"

Strangely, a ripple of sunny smile spread over her face. Her lackluster eyes quickly turned into brilliant gems like the eyes of a dreamy girl. "Are you saying that *sangol* is still best for broken bones?" she asked.

"Excuse me?" I didn't understand. Mother was talking in riddles. The sudden change in her perplexed and displeased me. I found myself yelling at her, my emotions in disarray. When she spoke it was in her sweet, yearning, reminiscing voice as if she were reciting a portion of a children's story from her childhood. "No matter how much the art of medicine might have advanced, I believe that *sangol* is still the best cure for broken bones. I really do believe that. Yes, indeed! I'm telling you *sangol* is a miracle!"

"What are you talking about, Mother. Please pull yourself together," I pleaded, shaking her fragile shoulder.

"You can cure a small broken bone by eating some *sangol*. It's that simple. Since I have broken one of the largest bones in my body, I suppose I need surgery to put the *sangol* in. My children, I am not afraid of the operation, not at all! You needn't worry about me a bit. I know for a fact that any small bone connected by *sangol* becomes even stronger than it was before. Come and look at my wrist. It's living proof!" Mother lifted her right arm high, smiling warmly. From anyone's viewpoint, Mother's right wrist looked abnormal. The bone was slightly sticking out and lop-sided just beneath her tissue-like skin, making her arm look larger than normal. Suddenly I recalled the story behind her distorted wrist and sensed the meaning to my mother of *sangol*.

The first winter after Mother, Brother and I moved into our first house at the Hyunjo-dong in Seoul was brutally severe. Our house with its triangular courtyard sat on a hill. The winter was without precedent cold and harsh. Snow fell for days on end, like rain in the Monsoon season. Even Mr. Kim, our faithful and diligent water carrier from the Hamkyung Province in North Korea, yielded to the cruel grip of the weather. He gave up battling the fierce snow, skipping deliveries of drinking water to us. This caused us no great hardship as we gathered snow from the drifts in the front and back courtyards, from the terrace that held the soy bean jars, and from the rooftop. The boundless supply of snow was poured into a huge iron pot and placed over the wood fire. Accommodating our daily needs for water proved quite simple. We worried only about whether we could afford to buy firewood every day for this purpose.

Each day Mother bought one or two bundles of thinly spliced, dried firewood, tied with straw rope. She refused to buy from our neighborhood store. Instead, she purchased them in a firewood market located at the streetcar depot some distance from our house. Mother hinted that she got her money's worth from the market. In reality, the firewood obviously weighed more than that purchased at the neighborhood store, although both bundles appeared to be the same size. The market offered free delivery, carried on an A-frame, if a customer bought ten bundles or more at one time. However, Mother seemed to have no extra money to take advantage of this special offer. Mother went in person to the distant marketplace to buy just one or two skimpy bundles at a time.

The blizzard continued. The slippery, snow-covered slope became a hazardous place for pedestrians. My brother volunteered to go to the market for Mother. She absolutely refused.

"Your mother doesn't expect you, such a dutiful son, to fetch firewood from the marketplace. You're my only son, and I expect a lot more than that from you. You make the best grades you possibly can and become a successful person, making good money. Then we can afford to buy real firewood in Chungryangli Market. We can then buy sections of logs and split them into fairly good sized portions with a saw, piling them in our storage room. I bet then we can spend a harsh winter like this without being cold, my son."

"Mother, let's live right now the best way we can and face the future when that time comes," my brother said. "What will people say when they see you going to market instead of me, a big boy? Anyway, I can't let you do it. I don't feel right about it as a son."

"Let me ask you this question, son. Do you think it's proper for your mother to send you to do a trifling errand, ignoring completely the fact that you'll do something great in the future?" My mother spoke flatly, rejecting my brother's arguments. My dutiful brother had no choice but to succumb.

One bitingly cold day, Mother slipped on the snowy road as she was carrying a bundle of firewood on her head. She returned home in pitiful condition. Scattered scratches were visible. They were not a pretty sight, but were not threatening. However, her wrist swelled rapidly and looked extremely painful. We were very concerned about it.

My brother and I couldn't sleep as we listened attentively to Mother's faint moaning and groaning. I was sure she was doing her best to stifle the sound. I was uneasy as if I were suddenly witnessing a strong pillar cracking. Next morning, however,

Mother resumed her daily tasks. She was cheerful and strong, not hiding anything. However, she seemed to have a hard time doing her usual sewing. She asked the old woman who brought sewing jobs from the *kiseng* to take back the unfinished garments. Mother apologized profusely for her inability to finish the task. The old woman was beside herself when she saw Mother's swollen wrist. She then gave Mother a long list of renowned acupuncturists in the city. Mother, however, appeared deaf to the old woman's fuss.

"I'll be all right, you'll see," Mother said. "I can use my wrist a lot better than yesterday. Thank you."

The old lady left, only to return with a handful of cape jasmine for Mother.

"Why don't you try some of this on your wrist?" the old lady said. "You can make a poultice from it. I'm telling you nothing is better than cape jasmine to lessen swelling."

"What good will it do to only control the swelling?" the old woman mumbled. "The broken bone must be reconnected and *sangol* is the best for broken bones. That woman will consider nothing that costs money unless it is for her children. Why can't she understand that taking care of herself is for the sake of her children? I declare she's not very smart."

My brother also heard the woman's monologue when Mother was not around. He asked me whether I knew where the old woman lived. Without Momma's knowledge, my brother and I went to see the old woman. He asked her what *sangol* was and where he could find it.

"Did your momma send you?" the old woman asked.

My brother shook his head.

"No? I just knew it! What good children you are! I think you're doing the right thing for your momma. Children like you, I must say, make having children worthwhile. What's the use of sitting on a gold mine if one has no children? I tell you, that kind of life is vain. Yes, indeed!" The old woman's story about this *sangol* began with this fussy chattering.

Although her story seemed grossly preposterous, it was captivating, like something from mythology. In any event, my brother and I had already stepped onto the trail of the mythological. When a person is at the end of his rope, left alone in the cold without knowing where to turn, a story from mythology, with its overwhelming power, may suddenly emerge and fling open its gate, motioning with both hands for a person in such extremes to enter and become the master of this enchanting world.

According to the old woman, *sangol* could be obtained in a certain cave not very far from our neighborhood. We were told that this was the one and only place in Korea and that the cave was located at the mesa of the Mooakjae Hill. The old woman described *sangol* as bits of metal shaped like dominoes, smaller than a millet seed. She added that this tiny piece of metal had to be rectangular and without a speck of blemish; otherwise, there was no medicinal effect. She said that sellers made sure to put only the flawless pieces on the market. Nonetheless, customers should inspect them with hawk eyes before purchasing.

The old woman insisted that the success of this impeccable mineral in healing broken bones was amazing. She told us of a man whose bones were healed during his lifetime with *sangol*. After he died and was ready to be buried, they saw the clusters of tiny, sparkling metal pieces which connected the bones in the body. These metal pieces were attached so tightly that no one could remove them with only ordinary human strength.

Since we were already strong believers in mythology, my brother and I unwaveringly believed that this metal piece, taken by mouth, would travel as the old woman said, directly to the broken bone and actually play a vital role in connecting the broken bones.

"Is it expensive?" my brother asked, blushing.

"Expensive? No. It won't cost a lot of money. It's a natural resource like dirt or sand. The cave owner might charge a nominal fee, though. Not only people who have failed to get relief from either a local hospital or an acupuncturist come to the place, but also people who can't afford to go to either one come to this place."

"Let's go," my brother said.

My brother and I cautiously trudged up the Mooakjae hill, braving the snow drifts. The snowy, winding pass was extremely dangerous in the dead of winter. Fortunately, the Mooakjae hill was located comparatively near our house. It was not as if we had to cross over twelve rising hills. For us to savor the true feeling of the strange, mythological event, I conceded, the rough road was an essential part.

We asked countless times for directions and finally reached the cave in the midst of the mountain. Inside the cave, we found a shutter attached to the wall of rock. A lighted candle was necessary in spite of it still being daytime. From a first glance, I could tell that the cave was unlike a bunker or rock cavern. The entire cave was covered with glistening metals, like a mosaic. These tiny metal pieces seemed to be billowing as the candlelight flickered. I felt as if I were in a fantasy world.

The owner of the cave was a young man, attired in a white cotton *durumaki* [man's topcoat]. Had he been an aged man with a white beard, my brother and I might have thrown ourselves at his feet and pleaded pitifully for this wonder drug that would heal my mother's broken wrist. The young man, however, spread the wings of our imagination and we looked upon him as someone from myth. Unlike the common folks we brush shoulders with each day, this man was exceedingly thin. His absent-minded appearance made him appear somewhat spiritual. Compared to this man, I realized that my brother was an adult, and my heart swelled with renewed pride. I looked up at the man as I clung to my brother.

My brother bowed to the man with utmost politeness, then explained the nature of our visit. The man went to a small tray on which two candles were placed and began to pick out *sangol*. As the old woman said, although the cave was a Mecca for boundless *sangol*, every *sangol* produced in the cave was not effective. It had to be exactly rectangular in shape, straight-sided and flawless. Only then did it become a wonder-working agent for curing broken bones. However, he didn't say that they would go directly to the area where the broken bones were located and attach to the bones in order to connect them.

The way the man picked out the *sangol* was singular. He knelt reverently in front of the small tray. He then nodded as if he were dozing off. From the pile of one bowl full of *sangol*, he picked out several pieces. He wrapped them in a piece of white paper. His extreme thinness combined with the absent-minded expression on his face made him look even more spiritual. To me, he was selecting them not with his physical eyes but with the eyes of his soul. He concentrated on doing this effortlessly.

I looked up at my brother. With a serious expression, he was making a polite bow, his hands in front. I followed suit.

"To start with, I'll give you enough for ten days," the man said as he wrapped them in ten different white papers, each dosage in a separate wrapper. His voice was dry and without energy.

"Come here, children," the man said, "and show your devotion to the spirit of the mountain god. He'll bless the *sangol* and consecrate it to its great purpose of healing."

Two candles were lit even in the innermost chamber of the cave. On a natural stone platform, a scroll was placed containing the image of the mountain god. Coins of various denominations were scattered on the platform. The Buddhist offering utensil, a water bowl, sat near the front of the platform.

"Go ahead, children," the man urged, "bow to the god. If you brought money for the medicine, you're welcome to offer it to him. Remember to pray to the god to answer your earnest request. Do just like this." He bowed deeply and repeatedly.

My brother obediently bowed over and over again. I loved my brother with my whole heart and soul, yet I was somewhat detached. Because of the age gap between us, I treated him with absolute courtesy. He was ten years older. It wasn't just the age that made me feel uneasy around him, but also his strength of character. He was an extraordinary man. No unspeakably ignorant or tricky superstition dared to confuse his superior intelligence and self-confidence. These traits defined his individuality. Brushing elbows with the humble, common folk in the slum in which we lived seemed in my opinion to make his noble character even more outstanding. My heart swelled with pride, as if I were wearing a dress dotted with shimmering precious stones.

Such was my brother to me. Now I was actually witnessing him humble himself as he kept bowing deeply in front of the god's scroll. Although only a child, I could tell easily that the whole thing—god, spirit, altar—was vulgar. Oddly enough, my brother's surrender to this superstitious ritual did not make him look in the least ridiculous. Far from it. In fact, it enhanced his appearance of self-assurance. If one's devotion is at its peak, even contradictions may be reconciled. I was in emotional disarray, but I voluntarily bowed politely with my hands in front and watched my brother perform this ceremony.

I had no idea whether the money my brother placed on the stone altar was sufficient. One thing was sure: his undivided attention and dedication to the god completely satisfied the young man in attendance.

"Before, I told you to have your mother take these for ten days," the man said. "Judging from your dedication, I tell you that she'll be whole in no time. You won't need to wait more than ten days, I guarantee it. Yes, indeed, this little piece of metal is a spiritual thing and works better with a touch of spirit than using only its medicinal power. Your steadfast dutiful devotion to your mother will move any god. He's bound to hear you. Moreover, my god is especially strong in spirituality."

Needless to say, Momma was deeply touched by my brother's obtaining the *sangol* for her. She was, incredibly, happier than before she twisted her wrist. On the tenth day Momma announced that she was well on the road to recovery. The swelling and pain in her wrist were decreasing every day with hourglass precision.

In our view, her wrist was still abnormal. Momma, however, tried to convince us by explaining that the pieces were clustered around the bone to heal it. That's why it looked strange. To convince us she was well again, Momma resumed her sewing job for others. She did it as dexterously as before. Momma insisted that her bones were even stronger after she took the *sangol*. To demonstrate this, she made a point of lifting heavy objects when she knew we were watching. She didn't change her daily activity of going to the Youngchun Market to bring home a couple of bundles of firewood. My brother insisted on doing this chore for her until warmer weather prevailed. Momma was deaf to his plea, as expected.

"Don't worry about me, son. If I slip again, I'll put my weight on my right hand, and it'll save me. Don't you see that my right wrist is stronger than steel? It's not like it used to be!" In spite of its grotesque shape, she boasted of her right wrist, waving it in the air.

The next morning, Mother was told to take her dentures out before she went into surgery. Mother kept smiling. Without teeth, she looked like a new-born baby. She was in her late eighties and facing a serious, difficult operation. Despite this grave fact, Mother's emotional stability enabled her to smile like a carefree infant. Her amazing inner strength drove me to the edge of overwhelming sadness.

In the movies or a TV mini-series, the scenes of the surgeon interacting with the patient's family just prior to surgery are quite moving. Surrounded by the nervous family, the doctor momentarily sheds his armor of authority. At that particular moment the doctor shows his human attributes—warmth, compassion, and devotion. No one can ignore the fact that there may be a remote possibility of a mistake occurring during the operation. The reality that one human being's life is being thrust into another person's hands rather than upon an infallible machine gives one a great sense of relief. In this depiction of human trust, I suppose, the patient's relatives are free to nag, plead, ask favors, and even demand a guarantee. This kind of human behavior would be unthinkable, unacceptable, and disgraceful under normal circumstances. Still, the doctor shows an unprecedented generosity of spirit to the patient's family, whose members display the fragility of humanity as they go through rough times. Perhaps it is less generosity than sympathy or sentiment.

Like some character in such a movie or mini-series, I hoped to enjoy momentarily this kind of warm human relationship with Dr. Hong, who was in charge of Mother's case. Mother was nothing but skin and bones. Every sign of youth had disappeared from her a long time ago. Nonetheless, she still had a woman's body, and it was unusually cruel to imagine abandoning her to the hands of the doctor while she was under the influence of anesthesia. This was sufficient for me to talk to the doctor. I needed his emotional support.

The operating room in that mammoth hospital was not a room but a field. On that battlefield, they operated on approximately twenty to thirty patients daily. Just as goods are produced and delivered by the conveyor system, so the general hospital, a colossal mechanism, admitted and released patients, in and out of the operating arena according to a timetable. It also took care of every patient's needs in a professional manner. When time came for a certain patient, that patient was wheeled into the operating room and then sent back out automatically after a certain period of time elapsed. Before Mother disappeared into the operating room, much care and attention was given to her by different people. None of them, however, was a person with any authority to whom I could cling while asking a heart-felt favor for Mother.

To make matters worse, from a certain point the surgery room became a restricted zone in which the family was not allowed. Just as I was unable to witness happenings in the operating room, there was no way under the sun that I could talk to a person in charge of the surgery. It wasn't clear to me whether the performing surgeon was permanently stationed in that operating arena or if another entrance was allocated for them alone. After Mother was sent to surgery, I lingered outside for quite some time. I hadn't seen any doctor, not to mention Dr. Hong, anywhere near the room. I felt terribly alone, fretting that I'd had no opportunity to meet Dr. Hong and talk with him even if only for a brief meeting before the surgery. When it came to a patient whose life was unconditionally left in the doctor's hands, such mutual trust was a must. Understanding and trust between two involved parties, I felt, were more crucial than a signature on a piece of paper, the consent for the operation.

In the midst of uncertainty concerning the outcome of her surgery, Mother appeared to be cheerful and stoic, even just before she was sent into that colossal arena. Her healthy emotional state consoled me a great deal. It was beyond me how Mother managed to stay incredulously calm and poised as she faced major surgery at her age. I suspected that Mother believed that the surgery she was about to undergo was the same as using *sangol* for her broken wrist. That was why, I concluded, she could be at peace. My brother was still a religion to Mother.

The huge operating room was shaped like an upside-down "L." The end of the room was used as either an entrance or exit. No one could peek through either door to determine what was going on inside the room. Countless family members of other patients waited nervously in the hall near the exit. I saw a young mother sobbing in her husband's arms as her small child was wheeled into the room. I also saw an aged mother chanting a Buddhist prayer, fingering her Buddhist rosary as her grown-up son was sent into the room. A nurse came outside every once in a while in an effort to lessen the anxieties of the families. She then wrote numbers on a patient's list that was taped on the wall. These numbers were the times that patients were moved to the recovery room after surgery. An hour after the patient was moved to the recovery room, it was a general practice for the patient to be wheeled outside. Whenever a patient appeared outside, regardless of whose relative, every family swarmed around the patient to make sure it was the one scheduled to appear and to assess his condition.

As the surgical suite door opened, the doctor came out. Only his shining eyes could be seen behind a huge mask. He slowly removed the string of the mask from his left ear, leaving the other side attached. He looked bone tired, yet a contented smile would ripple around his mouth. The smile would manifest success after a long, difficult task. He'd tell the family, "You can rest assured now, it was a successful surgery." Then that particular family would look at him in awe and show their gratitude by a deep, polite bow. They'd shed tears of emotion, mixed with a feeling of gratification and profound relief. However, I hadn't seen these moving scenes near the exit door. Through the entrance door patients were received while through the exit they were dismissed.

Family members only saw them on their way in and then met them once they were out.

In the list on the wall, there were columns for sex and age. Mother, eighty-six years old, was the oldest of them all. Next to Mother, the second oldest person was fifty-seven years old. Judging from the age gap, I was easily persuaded that Mother's surgery was indeed a ruthless adventure. Mother went inside the room at nine in the morning. After one o'clock in the afternoon, she was moved to the recovery room according to the list on the wall. After that, I was kept in absolute darkness about her. Whenever the exit door opened and a patient was wheeled outside, I frivolously jumped to my feet and rushed to see if it was Mother. I was nervous, fatigued, and hungry. My eyes became dim. Nevertheless, I continued my effort to crane my neck to peek inside the operating room for a good while.

"For crying out loud, Aunt, are you expecting Grandmother to come out as if she's had minor cosmetic surgery?" my nephew teased. I hated his sense of humor—*how dare he indulge in such a luxury at a time like this?* Nevertheless, I was comforted by my nephews' presence. They were like a pillar I could lean on.

Finally, Mother was pushed out on a gurney. She mumbled something upon recognizing us. Without dentures, she sounded feeble and uncertain. The single white hospital sheet failed to cover Mother's entire body. I glimpsed half of her bare shoulder. I couldn't stand this inexcusable oversight, so I pulled up the sheet and covered her right up to the neck. Because of several tubes for intravenous feedings and one for blood transfusions, it was impossible to keep the sheet undisturbed. Mother, naked under the sheet, was shivering violently.

"Are you cold?" I asked.

"No, not really. I just tremble for no reason," Mother said. The rest of the family rushed to Mother's bedside as if they were impressed by her talking. One by one, each tested Mother by asking a different question.

"Grandmother, do you know who I am?" my oldest nephew asked.

"You're Seok's dad. What did you think I was going to say?" she replied.

"Grandmother, grandmother! What about me?"

"You're Seok's mom."

"Who am I?" the younger nephew asked.

"Kyung-ah's dad."

Mother passed her family's test easily. She grinned proudly as she looked up at me. Mother had just come out of the operating room, and her smile somehow made me feel eerie again. Two men from the hospital staff, as tall and as big as lamp posts, pushed her bed. The family imprudently continued to shower her with questions as we followed hurriedly. We soon came out of the long hall and reached an elevator door. Mother was tested, so to speak, as we followed her between the hall and the lobby where the elevator was. All of us even more imprudently believed, based upon the test which she safely passed, that Mother's surgery was successful. Once we were in the elevator, we did not pay much attention to Mother.

"Ah, I'm drained! Tonight I'm going to sleep like a log," my older nephew commented.

"I have stomach cramps from hunger. The lunch I had was a drop in the bucket. Big brother, how was the beef soup in the cafeteria? Was it decent?" my younger nephew asked.

"Whose turn is it to spend the night at the hospital tonight?" someone asked.

"Hey, we don't need to worry about whose turn it is now," I said. "Your grandmother will have a rough night once the pain medication wears off, though she looks all right now. I'll stay with her tonight. You all go home and get a good rest."

"Oh, Aunt," my older nephew cried, "do you mean it? Thank you. I think it's best. We'll leave everything to you tonight. I'll send my wife the first thing in the morning to relieve you. Thank you."

"By the way," my younger nephew remarked, "we must respect our Grandmother's strong will, no matter what. For an old woman pushing her nineties, her mind is clear as a bell even after this serious surgery."

"You ungrateful ones!" I railed. "Would you be happy if she failed to wake up? Don't you remember how long she was held in the recovery room? I was worried sick, fearing something horrible had happened to her in that room. No one can defy one's age. Other patients came out after only an hour. Your grandmother spent three hours there before she woke up and was wheeled out."

"Oh, no, child." It was Mother talking. "I woke up right away. I screamed for someone to take me to my children as soon as I woke up. No one heeded me. I don't know what came over me. I was trembling. I tried my best to get their attention, but they simply remained deaf. I know I was totally free from the anesthetic, but something seemed to block my throat. No sound came out as I wanted. I dare say the people in that operating room are a heartless bunch."

Our babbling ceased as Mother interjected her lengthy remark. The eye contact we exchanged showed reassurance and a sense of wonder about a successful surgery for a woman who was nearly ninety. It also included a hint of amusement at her unwavering determination.

When Mother was settled in her hospital room, we again became gregarious. Mother tried to interject on every conversation. I became sick and tired of the strength of her mind and found myself beginning to rebuff her. I was exhausted trying to make out her obscure pronunciation without her dentures; it sounded as if she were talking in delirium. More than that, I was ashamed before my nephews and their wives. I wished Mother would pretend that she was lingering at the point of death after such a grave surgery. Unable to endure my self-imposed humiliation, I sent my nephews' family home right away.

"Why don't you all go home?" I asked as I shooed them on their way. "You look more exhausted than your grandmother. Eat something and go to bed. I think she will sleep well only after you leave. She believes all is well with her, and no one knows what'll happen to an old person like herself. Anyway, we have to pool our resources carefully to see her through this difficult time."

Mother chattered on non-stop after her grandchildren left. If I failed to pay attention to her words, she looked as if she were a cow chewing her cud. I became even more fretful and annoyed at her tireless energy.

That evening, along with interns and residents, Dr. Hong came to check on Mother. Judging from the hour, which was certainly not a usual time to be making rounds, they were checking only on patients who had undergone surgery that day. Nevertheless, they came in like a whirlwind and disappeared in a blink as they had during morning rounds. The stride and behavior of these doctors in the hall was like a breeze which never lingers long any place. They brushed by rapidly as does the wind, without any sign of human warmth.

I had been mentally prepared to pay Dr. Hong the most superlative compliment for what he had done for Mother. However, it stayed in my heart. The compliment I was ready to shower on him was respectful, considerate, and personal. Consequently, it would require time to convey it properly. Alas, an opportunity for me to carry out my intention passed. All I managed to do was to follow him to the hall in a flurry. I told him something complimentary, following the usual scenario expected after surgery. Then I asked about Mother's condition.

"The surgery was a success, you may rest assured, ma'am. As you know, she is very old, so I advise you to pay extra attention to nursing her." That was the longest conversation I had with Dr. Hong. I was so flattered that I couldn't bring myself to ask further. By the same token, I was unsatisfied with his stingy information.

Interns and a nurse came frequently to check on Mother and several tubes were hooked onto her. I was also instructed to record her condition during my vigil. Some of my responsibilities for Mother were to make sure that she often coughed up phlegm, to notify a nurse of her condition before the Ringer's solution dried up, to measure the quantity of the urine which she passed, and to let a nurse know when the vinyl bag receiving blood from her incision was full.

I tried to ask interns all the detailed questions that I failed to ask of Dr. Hong. The response I received from all the interns was an exact carbon copy. Mother showed a relatively normal condition after surgery, they said in unison. No intern forgot to add a footnote that Mother was an aged woman. Old age manifested neither disease nor abnormality; it was a mere footnote. Nothing more or less.

With a lack of energy as an excuse, Mother objected to being programmed to cough often. Whenever phlegm gathered around her windpipe, however, she suffered from a spasm in her neck and startled me. I told her numerous times that swallowing the phlegm could lead to pneumonia. My nagging was fruitless. Yet Mother kept mumbling something without pause. The voice didn't sound like that of a human, since she had lost all stamina. It sounded more like a trembling leaf set in motion by a gentle breeze.

"Please try to get some sleep," I urged, quite vexed by then. Mother looked at me, her eyes wide open as if saddened by my fretfulness. The way she looked at me was chilling.

"Would you like me to turn off the light?" I asked, trembling.

"No, no," Mother said as she shook her head.

"Shall I close your eyes? Please try to get some sleep. Don't worry about a thing, Mother." I held her hand and closed her eyes gently with the other hand. Mother pulled her hand from mine, not being able to remain still for a second.

"Are you hurting, Mother?" I asked. "If you can make it through tonight, I bet it will be a lot easier tomorrow. If you're hurting terribly, please tell me. I'll ask a nurse to give you an anodyne shot."

"Oh, no, I'm not hurting at all. It's just that I can't fall asleep."

"Would you like for me to ask for sleeping pills?"

When she didn't reply, I went to the nurse's station and let them know of Mother's problem. The head nurse acknowledged my request and advised me to return to Mother. Soon after, an intern came in with a tiny pill. He asked me to keep the room dark for her if possible. I offered the pill to Mother and then turned off the light. I left only one dim light on the wall right by the portable bed. This time Mother did not resist. A sense of relief resulting from my belief that the medicine would soon take effect caused a drowsiness to steal over me that I couldn't fight off. Intending to doze off for only a few minutes, I checked and found the Ringer bottle only a little over half full, the urinal and the feeding and transfusion tubes less than half full. After making these checks for which I had been made responsible, I collapsed onto the portable bed.

I must have plunged into deep slumber. I was awakened instantly by a stir in the air. The room was in silent commotion. I saw Mother's hands swaying to and fro. Her movement looked different from simply a meaningless, empty swaying. It had its own pattern as if her hands were being applied to some task in a diligent manner. As if I'd had a cold shower, I was instantly wide awake. I sprang up and turned on the light. Mother knitted her eyebrows at the sudden light but her hands kept swaying.

"What are you doing, Momma?" I asked in a child-like tone without realizing it.

"Can't you tell what I am doing? Once the laundry is done, you need to put a shirt on its stack just as you do with your underpants. What about the socks? They need to be put together, item by item, all in the same place. It's no good dumping everything together." Mother's voice rang out loud and clear.

"Laundry? What are you talking about?" I demanded. "Get some sleep."

"How can I sleep with all this mess around me? You ungrateful ones!" Mother spoke in a clanking, metallic voice. The blue hue of her eyes deepened even more, looking ghastly. Suddenly, I had an urgent desire to run away from her and seek help. Mother gestured with her hands busily in the void, sorting and folding clean laundry in her over-confident air. I could not believe her overflowing energy since she had eaten nothing since before the enema, anesthesia, and actual operation. Rather than marveling at this sudden development, I was so alarmed that I felt my legs trembling. At that moment, a nurse walked in.

"My mother is acting weird," I told her. "She is swaying her hands in the air for no reason at all. She must be seeing something in a vision."

"Some patients do that once the anesthesia loses its effect. I'm sure she'll be all right," the nurse replied nonchalantly. She then checked Mother's temperature and pulse, after which she left the room. I followed her, begging for something to make Mother fall asleep.

"I sent a nurse when you asked not long ago, didn't I? Didn't she give her medication?"

"It doesn't seem to be working. I think she's worse than before she took the pill. I know I'm right. She couldn't sleep then, but at least she wasn't having visions. What am I going to do?"

"I don't agree. Even if she is having some adverse reaction from the medicine, I don't think anything bad will happen to her. Try to take it easy, ma'am. She only took a tranquilizer. According to the results of clinical testing, the medicine she was given is widely acknowledged for having no side effect."

"Nothing is more serious than her present condition," I insisted. "She's not herself!"

"She'll be all right before you know it," the nurse said calmly.

"I suggest you give her either sleeping pills or a shot rather than that worthless nerve pill," I barked.

"I'm sorry, but I can't," the nurse said.

"What do you mean? I understood your hospital performed all kinds of surgeries, and now you're trying to tell me that a large hospital like this refuses to give proper medication to a patient suffering from insomnia? It's unacceptable!"

"We're doing the best we can for the patient. Family members should cooperate with us rather than being unreasonable. That is unacceptable," the nurse shot at me as she turned her back upon me sharply. I was embarrassed and furious at the same time. I returned to the room, vowing never again to beg for help from a mere nurse.

Mother must not have finished folding her laundry. She was still swaying her hands in a regular rhythm in the air. Suddenly she put her hands palms up toward me as if in a defensive posture. Her eyes, slightly bloodshot, widened in an expression of extreme fear. They were so large that they seemed about to pop out.

"What's wrong, Momma?" I ran to her, enveloped with fear too. Her arms wrapped around my neck, almost choking me. She possessed tremendous strength. I was trying to fend her off in order to gather my breath when she whispered in a frightened voice like a voice from Hell.

"That fellow came again. Good God, that fellow came again!" Mother was staring at the door with one hand still in a defensive position. I looked back to see if anyone had come into the room after me. I saw no one. I felt every hair on my head stand straight up.

"*Momma!*" I cried out. Drummed by my own fear, I freed myself from her. Mother, wearing the face of a devil, eyed the door as she trembled violently. Although no one was there, Mother was fighting with all her might with someone. At that very moment, I was overcome with the notion that a messenger from the other world had come to fetch her and stood there arms folded. Mother might be seeing that. I was so frightened that I felt every drop of my blood had frozen. I didn't dare take one step toward the door. Moreover, there was no way for me to ask for any help. It was quite natural for a messenger from the other world to covet an eighty-six year old patient. Mother might well be not only the oldest surgery patient that day but also might be the oldest in this mammoth university hospital. If the messenger from the other world had this much discretion, it would be a waste of time for me to ask an altered verdict as a favor to me. I was ready to hand Mother over to him.

Who would dare suggest that my eighty-six-year-old Mother had not lived a good, long, natural life? The only thing that distressed me was the messenger's move to drag Mother to the other world even before her blood dried up from the operation. On the other hand, is there any death that does not leave this magnitude of lingering regret to one's children?

"I'm ready to give her up, but I beg you not to show your presence to my mother, please! I know it's human nature not to want to die even if one has lived a hundred years. It's your duty and only mercy as the messenger from the other world not to show your presence even at the last breath of one's life. Please disappear swiftly, swiftly, I beg of you!"

I couldn't witness Mother's misery. I uttered my pleas silently, unable to look upon Mother's panic-stricken face. And then I was stricken with panic that I too might be able to see the messenger. Instead of having disappeared as I had asked, it seemed the messenger must be approaching Mother. I could tell by looking at her bulging eyes as they focused on an object that was apparently approaching her bed. Good heavens, it was I! I stood at Mother's death bed all alone.

"That fellow has come again. What are you doing? Hide your brother. Hurry!" Mother cried frantically.

"Mother, get hold of yourself. What are you talking about? How can I hide my brother when my brother is not here?"

"You mean that fellow has already taken your brother away?'

"Mother, please!"

Mother's hands groped in every direction. When her hand reached her bandaged leg, she whispered sharply: "My poor child, that is where you have hidden. Stay put there. I'll take care of everything."

Mother's trembling hands tried to embrace her bandaged leg. It had assumed for her the role of her son. Mother fiercely protected her leg with every part of her body as she glared at the enemy. Her visitor was not a messenger from the other world, as I had presumed.

"Officer comrade, honorable officer, only women folk live in my house," Mother said as her blue-hued eyes shifted sadly. A ripple of a servile smile formed around her mouth. At that moment I knew what she was hallucinating. Poor Mother! She would be a lot better off seeing a messenger from the other world.

Mother acted as if she were trying to hide her leg somewhere. However, her leg refused to budge an inch.

"Honorable officer, I tell you only we women live here. Don't waste your time any further, honorable officer!"

I was absolutely useless in facing a crisis with Mother when she failed to understand that imminent death was stalking. Her face was grotesquely twisted by a mixture of fear, servility, and a faint ray of hope. Beads of sweat dotted her forehead. Her hands that hugged her leg and her bare shoulders were quaking like an aspen tree in the north wind.

Poor Mother! Heaven have mercy upon her. Please let her die in peace. Why must heaven let Mother go through that horrible incident twice?

"Mother, please don't do this!" I pleaded. "Oh, Mother, get hold of yourself!" I cried bitterly, shaking her shoulders. I had no idea where she got the strength, but she shook me off as lightly as if I were a wisp of straw. Then she writhed violently.

"No you don't! No way, you scum. Are you a human being, you bastard!"

Mother pushed me to the wall. I was trembling violently as I was forced to watch her bizarre behavior. Except for her operated leg, her whole body rolled as if propelled by furious waves. Because of that, her leg looked ever more grotesque and wild, like an alien object not attached to her body. As if Mother's leg and her son had become one body, as if they were transferred to every cell in my system, I was frightened of Mother's leg.

Hurled words of thunder—"No, you can't, you wretched!"—and sugar-coated, flattering words—"Honorable officer, officer sir, officer comrade"—alternated as she writhed. In her violence, she jerked the needle from the IV tube. The needle was still in Mother's blood vessel and consequently blood was flowing backward. It soaked Mother's clothing and the bed sheet.

Mother saw the blood and her frenzied behavior reached its summit. "You stand right there, you scum bag! Why don't you kill me before you leave?"

Mother ground her teeth as tears flooded her face. She was merely pretending to grind her teeth as her dentures were missing. It was a heart-rending sight. I wondered if anyone else had ever witnessed such a pitiful scene. I hoped I was dreaming, that this was nothing but a nightmare. Mother grabbed her hair and pulled it out. She pulled at the tube that received her urine. The smell of blood made me stupefied, but soon I returned to my senses. Mother's yelling and screaming must have been heard outside, for as I was going out of the room to seek help, a nurse rushed in followed by a middle-aged head nurse.

To restore the tubes and equipment that had been attached to Mother, additional help was needed. Mother displayed the might of Hercules. While the head nurse, a young nurse and I were trying to press Mother to the bed, the nurse in charge of Mother restored everything to its original state. This time, to be sure, she inserted the needle of the IV solution on top of Mother's foot.

"How in the world could something like this possibly happen?" I said ruefully to the head nurse.

"Try not to worry so much. Although it's rather unusual, she is not the first diatheses patient we've encountered. I'm sure she'll be all right very soon," the head nurse said consolingly. Did she mean that Mother's nightmare had something to do with her diatheses, I wondered. In any event, who would dare interpret another's dream?

Mother's fight was tireless as if it were the final, desperate attempt in a "You kill me or I'll kill you" battle. The head nurse instructed the attending nurse to raise the rails on both sides of the bed and had her tie Mother's limbs to each rail tightly.

"I understand how you must be feeling as a daughter, but please try to ignore what's happening to your mother now. This is our last resort. Please try to get some sleep or you'll be sick. Everything will be all right. She'll be herself before you know it."

The head nurse thus tried again to comfort me before they walked out of the room. Mother was all tied up. I was worn to a frazzle by then and threw myself on the portable bed with my shoes on. Alas, soon after I collapsed on the bed, Mother, who had been roaring like an enraged wild beast, struck out with every ounce of her energy. The ropes that tied her began to break loose.

Once again Mother began to raise hell by kicking and spitting venom. I marveled at her strength. Her voice was a creepy tone concocted of rancor and poisonous venom. Wondrous stamina sprang up within me; I felt an acute pain, as if someone were slicing into my liver. Girded by this mysterious strength, I dashed to Mother. I made up my mind to handle Mother alone this time rather than asking for help. This was something to be resolved between mother and daughter without strangers interfering.

I pressed down on Mother hard, with every fiber of my body, riding myself on top of her. Rolls of agony entered like spasms into each cell of my being. At that moment I realized that I must be strong and decisive. Otherwise, I reasoned, Mother would overcome me by rolling on top of me. No matter how desperately I tried with all my might to confront Mother, I couldn't equal her strength. Whenever I felt threatened by her, I gently slapped her cheeks.

"Momma, please pull yourself together. Momma, please!" I pleaded.

I was stunned at my own immoral conduct. I slapped her even harder a second time. When I saw my own finger marks on her cheek, I pictured myself in Hell or having a nightmare. With this unrealistic sensation, I kept committing my immoral conduct without reservation. It wasn't Mother's strength that frightened me. Rather it was her facial expression. It didn't belong to Mother. My common sense dictated that I wasn't fighting with Mother but with my own self-induced fear.

I loved Mother very much. Needless to say, her face was among those I loved. Mother had aged gracefully and beautifully. It was truly a rare blessing. The credit was due to her faith in Buddhism, which she had converted to in the last chapter of her life. By believing in Buddha, Mother appeared to have nearly overcome a sense of mortification from the loss of her child under such extraordinary circumstances. Moreover, Mother had become more like Buddha as she grew older, a figure of benevolence, gentleness, and innocence. Although she lost her son, Mother loved her grandsons, who were the children of her son, her grandsons' wives, her grandsons' children, her daughter, and her daughter's children. Mother, however, kept a certain space between her and them, trying not to be too attached. In short, Mother aged more happily, peacefully, and gracefully than anybody else. When I saw Mother aging in this trance-like beauty, I was in awe, believing that she must indeed be a Buddhist saint.

People say that there is neither end nor limit in one's interior measure of life. Keeping this in mind, how in the world could I even begin to suspect that this passion was hidden underneath Mother's calm? It was neither goodness, peace, nor love hidden within Mother's interior. Instead, hate, profanity, and rancor were coming out. It was more than I could handle. Even if it is true that we human beings are nothing but wretched sinners, discovering Mother's real substance was beyond my reach.

Just like a confrontation of evil against evil, the merciless contest with Mother went on until she showed signs of defeat. Only then, did I rub my cheek against her swollen cheek, which showed clear marks of my fingers, and burst into a bitter wail.

It had been a riddle to me why Mother regarded our house on top of Hyunjo-dong as a refuge during the Korean War when we were able to escape from the tight grip of poverty. We had been living comfortably for some time like any other affluent family. The difficult situation that we faced was severely unjust and awkward. We could neither live nor die. Such difficult circumstances might have caused Mother—second only to her home town—to depend on this neighborhood where she had placed her first stake after moving to Seoul. Her trust and attachment in Hyunjo-dong might be related to the particular nature of our hardship.

The Korean War was raging. Our problem was as insignificant as a particle of dust when the entire country was bleeding heavily from a national tragedy. It was bound up in the respectable, middle-class neighborhood where we saw the true color of people—their treacherous and two-faced humanness. It was a classic case—my brother's joining the voluntary army. After Korea's liberation from Japanese colonial rule, he participated at one time in the left wing movement and converted to it. Because of that, my brother couldn't flee South. He was forced to stay behind in Seoul, and he was extremely fearful for his safety. When he was left alone, he suffered from an extreme degree of fear and uneasiness. My brother craved knowing what other converts in a similar situation were doing. According to information he managed to pick up in bits and pieces, it would be best for any convert to convert yet again if somehow the person could not flee South. My brother, who was not a communist, sank into a sea of renewed fright.

Trusting completely in our government's broadcast assurance that it would protect Seoul to the end, my brother missed the opportunity to flee the city. He closed his ears to the deafening roar of the cannons approaching from North Korea and remained in Seoul. He blamed his simple honesty and cursed the government officials who saved themselves by deceiving the people. Totally irresponsible and unfaithful to the reassurances they had given, our officials fled to South Korea under the protection of the retreating army. Nonetheless, he was not mean-spirited enough to save himself by converting back to the left wing, which had now become the political mainstream as our government and its protective army fled.

Although he converted to the right wing with a spirit of faith and courage, he had an unwavering sense of unethical displeasure at the use of the word "conversion" itself. If his first choice was obviously wrong, rather than correcting his mistake by "converting" he had simply returned to his initial faith; in taking this alternative, he was simply keeping faith with himself.

It was a manifestation of my brother's stalwart character that, like a true scholar, he would die for a cherished principle. Such was my scholar-like brother. With his high caliber of integrity, he could not endure the ideology of the left wing, which would do anything in order to achieve its goal. Caught in the whirlpool of conflict, his emotional torment was inevitable.

Right before the Korean War broke out, the demagogues who agitated strongly among the youth in order to implant the ideology of the left wing, exerted almost magical powers of persuasion. The reason I was able to stay aloof from that spell-binding movement was that I had before me the example of my brother who had gone through horrible experiences by conversion and later was disillusioned. The idea of converting only as a means of survival was extremely distasteful for him. The government, supposedly for the people and in which he believed, had apparently taken to deceiving the helpless people and had then left them under the control of the enemy as they fled to protect themselves. Preyed upon by feelings of injustice, distrust, and loneliness, his mental state became more fragile each day.

One day one of my neighbors complained to the authorities about my brother. In a surprise attack, he was arrested and dragged away. We stood helpless, watching but not knowing what to do. Later we received news, and it seemed our fears concerning my brother's life were without basis. We feared he had been handed over to the People's Court and either given a stiff sentence or executed on the spot. Judging by the news, he was instead the first to join the Volunteer Army during the People's Rally. After his action, numerous young men were moved to follow suit. Since we were kept, so to speak, in the dark, we had no way to verify this rumor. We merely heard it in passing. We had no idea what design Fate had chosen for my brother as it toyed with his life.

Actually Fate was being equally cavalier with all our lives. My neighbor, who had tipped the authorities off about my brother's political beliefs while actually not being at all aware of his inner turmoil, held great influence with our powerful enemy. The wind certainly changed for us out of the blue. Overnight we became our neighbor's protégés. In the beginning, my brother's action in joining the Volunteer Army seemed more or less unique. However, as the war progressed into its climax, men both young and older were snatched from nearly every household and forced to join.

I knew that having a brother who volunteered to join this army was not to be treated with elaborate fanfare, inasmuch as the communists were now in control of our destinies. Nevertheless, we were privileged to receive favored treatment from the authorities, including food rations. Only later did we find out that our influential neighbor, who stretched his powerful arms even to the neighborhood Peoples Committee, was responsible for our golden treatment. We no longer had the stamina either to adopt or reject his patronage. We did not have the luxury of refusing this special treatment because food was an absolute necessity if we were to survive and had nothing to do with freedom of choice. We were merely surviving in a whirlwind of loss and confusion.

Most people could not afford even a bowl of porridge, while we were devouring barley. Suddenly the notion seized us that we had sold a member of our family to obtain food. We never, however, questioned that we were eating fruit harvested from an unethical and unjust root.

"People say that hunger can make any decent person a common criminal. Heaven have mercy on me, how in the world can I so easily swallow food for which I exchanged my son's life! Oh, my son, my precious son! A son like him is truly one in a million." Mother thus lamented bitterly, suddenly laying her spoon on the table. She did not, however, worry about the consequences that would come later.

After three full months, the direction of the wind veered once again. We had to suffer severe persecution from the neighbors. We were notified by the authorities that we were the "Reds." A group of young men rushed to our house with clubs and handguns. They searched the house inside and out, up and down, destroying useful utensils and furniture in the process. With the tip of a stick, they poked my sister-in-law's stomach. Her baby was due any day. They conducted this search in a most rude and violent manner. People in the neighborhood came out to mirthfully observe their dreadful behavior, savoring every moment as if they were enjoying themselves at an exorcism. We were the target of revenge from the neighbors who had gone through hardship for three awful months while we enjoyed a plentiful food ration. We had no choice but to face obediently any mishap that befell us, no matter what suffering it caused.

"Look here! You tell me who ran away leaving the people in this inferno!" my mother wailed. "Even if I am put to death as a punishment for surviving through that living hell, I won't hold grudges. Let me just look into the face of the government heads who deserted us. I will be happy to die after I face those dreadful people with their crimes."

Her grumbling was not heard. All she received from our neighbors were nasty swearwords. They showered her with such detested names as "cold-blooded" or "Red."

All these malicious remarks or this vicious mockery was really not that hideous compared to being falsely accused of hiding a high-ranking communist who had used and protected us. In turn, Mother, my sister-in-law and I were summoned to the police station for questioning and stayed there for days. My nephew, who was taken to a relative's home while we were away answering the police summons, received mistreatment; this left a large and painful hole in our heart, not totally healed even to this day. Even an infant communist was someone to be hated and ill-treated.

In the meantime, the South suffered from setbacks which brought its retreat. First of all, Mother sent my fully pregnant sister-in-law and her little boy back to her folks. Needless to say, Mother's purpose in staying behind had everything to do with her hope of seeing her son return. Judging from the young men from our neighborhood who straggled home after joining the Volunteer Army, her hope was not entirely unfounded. Even if he failed to run away, Mother had a firm belief that her son would return to her as a soldier for the People's Army. The only thing that mattered to Mother was whether her son was alive or dead, not his status as to which side he was on—Red or not.

One day, like a nightmare rather than a miracle, my brother returned home. Mother, who had in all confidence awaited his return, dared not welcome him home. Hunger and cold, as well as severe insomnia, had transformed him into something hideous, as might be expected. The state of his emotions and his frame of mind had been destroyed. His eyes roved, flashing this way and that. He had lost much weight. Due to a delusion of persecution, the smallest sound startled him, and he was afraid of people. He didn't know how to show his affection to his own family. He apparently did not care about the absence of his wife and son. Mother and I could not find out what had happened to cause this drastic change in him. He locked himself up inside and pushed away everything outside, like a feeble-minded child who, gripped with fright, refuses to venture from home.

To make matters worse, the military situation continued to deteriorate for the South. People were forced to evacuate Seoul and head farther south. In order not to repeat its mistake of the summer, the government warned of a crisis far in advance. It also provided convenient means of taking flight. People showed their tragic resolution to leave the city in spite of the biting cold. With deadly decision, they chose to face death on the frozen roads rather than again succumbing to life under the enemy's control.

Even in his fragile state of mind and emotion, my brother was adamant in his desire to flee south. He was anxious to join the caravan of refugees. He was obsessed with the idea that he had to flee from the Reds, or communists, at any cost. This spiritual strength was the only thing he had left. I believed that it might have been virtually impossible for my brother to escape and break through the fierce battlefield alive in his unpresentable condition if he had not possessed this magnitude of will.

Alas, my brother had no citizen ID card. One could scarcely go outside without proper identification, not to mention fleeing the city. The restrictions became worse and worse. Spies for the Reds might well be traveling in disguise among the refugees. In order to apply for an ID card, one had to have two witnesses from neighbors on an application form. No one wanted to do this favor for my brother. No matter how poignantly Mother begged, they ignored her. Mother was advised to send my brother to the police station for direct questioning and go through the proper channel to receive his ID card. The neighbors said truthfully that he had no reason to be afraid of a legitimate process if he were not a Red. Even before he returned home, the rest of us—Mother, my sister-in-law and I—were summoned several times by the police before we finally received our respective ID cards, since no one in the neighborhood had agreed to place their signatures as witnesses on our applications.

In my brother's case, applying through the police was difficult. Hearing the words "police station," he instantly turned pale and began to tremble violently. He said he would be willing to stay behind or be happy to lock himself inside the house for the rest of his life if he could avoid walking into the police station voluntarily. And yet, contrary to these statements, my brother nagged Mother to take him south, pleading that he could not afford to be arrested again and suffer yet more hardships that he did not deserve. He repeated these phrases over and over as if he were talking in his sleep. He didn't know what to do with himself, fidgeting as if he were walking an emotional tightrope. Mother would tell him that she was willing to take the risk of traveling with him, for everyone was in the same shoes, not knowing what fate lay ahead for anyone. My brother would stare at Mother with his lackluster eyes as he yelled at her that she wished to see him shot to death because he would be accused of being a spy. My brother drove us into a dilemma, demanding that we help him get an ID card at any price.

"Mother, sell everything we have," he would yell. "Sell the house, furniture, everything. I bet I can get the card with that money. Why must you cling to all these meaningless things instead of selling them off?" He would shout such preposterous ideas at Mother, and she would be broken-hearted.

Then he would turn to me with his abuse. "Hey, you, why don't you lure some big fish to cough up the bribe for an ID card and save your own brother? What's the use of having a sister if she's not being useful, huh?"

This brash obstinacy, this unreasonable behavior was indeed indicative of his shattered mental condition. On the day of the retreat, when the government announced for the last time its abandonment of Seoul, the citizens were advised to leave their homes in an orderly manner. We—Mother, my brother, and I—left the house without any particular plan. Some neighbors who had been hoping for a last minute miracle left their homes at the same time we did, all of us carrying bundles hung on our backs or balanced on our heads. If our neighbors failed to see us join the flight, we were scared to death that we might be branded as Reds again in the future. Not only that, we were emotionally incapable of living under the communist thumb all over again. That prospect scared the daylights out of us. The crime of deserting from the Volunteer Army, unlike any other conversion from communism, carried a death penalty. My family's pattern was controlled solely by whether that action would brand us as being Reds.

Even though we joined the wave of refugees heading for the south, we ended up circling several times around the boundary of the city in order to deliberately avoid inspection at the various checkpoints. My brother had an extraordinary sense, like that of a hypersensitive insect, which enabled him to sense where such checkpoints were located. This was his only attribute. In all other aspects he was a ruined man, lacking either will or well-thought-out ideas. To me he seemed nothing but a burden. I tried to find an opportune time to separate myself from him and Mother, but at exactly that moment she came up with a suggestion.

"Children, let's go to Hyunjo-dong," she said.

At her mention of Hyunjo-dong, I became humble and docile, like the prodigal son who returned home after a long period of dissipation. Even my brother's eyes, empty and hollow except for an occasional flash of fear, lit momentarily with joy.

"That disorderly neighborhood, like the intestines of the city, would make an ideal place for us to hide," Mother said, her voice as calm as if she were safe and totally at ease. In spite of the derogatory adjectives she chose to describe that neighborhood, I sensed a feeling of affection for it springing up in my heart.

"I am sure the whole neighborhood is emptied out, just like all the others. Why don't we hide in just any house until our army returns? Only then can we go back to our own house. I have never in my entire life been afraid of people. Who am I to judge whose heart is wicked, theirs or mine? Anyway I don't think I'd be frightened even if we found one or two people still living there. The people of Hyunjo-dong are truly kind-hearted." Thus Mother summed up for us her feelings about the old neighborhood.

We had recently been deeply hurt and mocked by our snobbish neighbors as if we were nothing but worthless beings. In the slum area of Hyunjo-dong, on the outskirts of Seoul, we recalled spending our most financially trying times upon our long-ago arrival from the countryside where my father had died when I was very young. Yet we remembered people displaying unbiased goodwill despite the most pitiful human conditions. Our hearts became lighter and brighter as we thought of returning to where we had been surrounded by so much goodwill. I even felt rise within me a ray of hope that my brother's fragile emotional state might be cured also.

Just like returning home to a huge and loving bosom after a long absence, Mother and I found ourselves smiling at each other in silent ecstasy. The strenuous effort of climbing the hill to Hyunjo-dong seemed less tiring because of the hope that welled within us. Every alley looked familiar and friendly in our eyes, and we felt as though we were being embraced affectionately. Since it was the very last night of the strategic retreat, the entire neighborhood was absolutely deserted. Not even a trace of an ant was found. We looked from this hill into the downtown area of Seoul that was canopied by the gathering dusk, reminiscent of an empty tideland. Mother expelled a gentle sigh.

"I don't understand the Reds. They must be sorry people. How under the sun do they expect to rule a nation when they can't win the hearts of the people, not even the poor people who live in this neighborhood?" Mother whispered.

We went to a few houses with whose occupants Mother used to be friendly. Needless to say, they were empty. From among these houses we picked as a hideout one with a well. We unlatched the gate and walked inside. Since the house was of such shabby workmanship, entering it was a simple matter. We could have chosen a more comfortable house since every house was abandoned, but Mother deliberately selected one of these houses whose owner she knew. In this way, she could apologize later for our unlawful trespass. She also announced to us that she would pay for any damage that we might cause during our uninvited sojourn.

After taking refuge in our old neighborhood, we did not see even a shadow of a person for several days. Therefore, we had no means by which to keep posted concerning world affairs. We had about a month's supply of food with us. We found some grain, firewood, and kimchi (pickled cabbage) that would last for the winter months. The well would supply abundant water. My mother and I were content leading our lives in this fashion. Wasn't this the happy life my brother was dreaming while fleeing the Volunteer Army? I wondered. There might be a chance for his healing as we lived our quiet lives here. Now that he no longer had to fake his accent and mannerisms in order to prove his true self, I became hopeful of his cure. In fact, I thought I could see a signs of improvement here and there.

Once in a while, my brother now displayed his concern and interest in his older son and his wife, who had just given birth to a baby at her parents' home in the

South. He had never shown any such concern or interest since his arrival after leaving the Volunteer Army. I rejoiced in this possibility that a window of his mind had been cracked open first for his closest people.

Meanwhile we were grateful for our windfall in finding this ideally safe hiding place. However, we should have suspected there would be a pitfall. One day we were visited by a group of soldiers from the Peoples' Army. They were caped in white sheets. They told us that from the West Gate Prison compound where they were stationed that they could see smoke coming from a few houses every morning and evening when they looked up at the neighborhood on the hillside. They had explored every house whose chimney emitted smoke and found someone either old and dying or sick. Perhaps this is why they seemed surprised to see me when I opened the gate for them, and they glared at me with evident lust.

"Yes, only we women live here. You don't need to bother about looking further," Mother jabbered as she rushed out onto the courtyard. They pushed her aside and walked inside, ignoring her chatter, of which no one could make heads or tails.

"Comrade, are you a woman too?" the officer, who was walking ahead, asked my brother, smiling coldly. As if he had become speech impaired, my brother made only moaning sounds, entirely failing to form any sensible words of communication.

"He is not a woman, but he is handicapped. Less than a woman, since he can be of no help at all to us. I tell you, sir, a handicapped child is your life-long enemy." Mother's face was pitifully distorted by an expression of fear and servility. Even without Mother's over-emphasis on his condition, my brother definitely would not have appeared to be a whole person in anybody's eyes. It was even more evident if one compared him with these robust, tough-looking soldiers. My brother was thin and fragile, his eyes lackluster, and the words coming from his mouth were only incomprehensible clusters of sound. I hoped Mother would not overdo her "handicapped son" story.

From that day on, the soldiers made frequent visits to our house. This experience tried our patience to the utmost. A certain high-ranking officer from the Defense also made a visit. The officer must have sensed something about my brother. He would talk about his hometown, his wife and children in a natural manner. Then, out of a clear blue sky he would glare at my brother and demand in a coarse voice: "Comrade, did you somehow run away from the People's Army? Did you, perhaps?" Or "Comrade, didn't you straggle away from the South Korean Army?" Then all of us would be scared to death.

Whenever the soldiers came, my brother turned deadly pale and trembled. He still could not utter a single word. He was struck dumb as soon as he saw the uniform of the People's Army. The loss of speech made his handicap status more convincing, heightening Mother's claim. Her overacting was the problem. It was heart-rending to see him in this condition. I was very much afraid that he had passed beyond the point of ever being cured.

The officer was tenacious. He applied different strategies in order to find out about my brother, alternately using threats, appeasement, and pleading.

"Mother," he would say, "my heart aches when I see you with such a burden. What happened to your only son? He wasn't born that way, was he? Am I not right? If he were not born that way, I am sure he can be cured. North Korea boasts of the best medical skill in the world! Furthermore, we give top priority to the poor. Why don't you tell me the truth? If you do, I can send you the best-skilled doctor right away. Anyway, how long has he been like this?"

I don't remember exactly when the officer began to use the term "Mother" when addressing my mother in a mocking intimacy. She became even more nervous under this new mode of address, becoming so upset that her speech turned to jargon. Her nervousness kept me in a state of alarm, as I noticed her obvious trembling. Once the soldiers returned to their post, Mother winked at me and explained that her behavior was nothing but a deliberate act. She was really a great puzzle to me.

I had learned that the art of survival was something to be learned, polished, and if one were lucky, mastered. Meanwhile, each day seemed a perilous and hair-raising acrobatic performance—as if we were dancing with poisonous snakes.

Once again a cannon was fired near Seoul. Anxiety poured out of the bloodshot eyes of the men of the North Army. Mother, in both her waking and her sleeping hours, prayed that they would leave us in peace—*please don't let them harm my child, my poor son!*

Finally the officer came by, supposedly to say farewell. However, the way he bid us good-by was extremely peculiar.

"Do you think I'm deceived to the end by a sly group like you, Comrade?" he barked. "Confess everything right now! Won't you tell me the truth even now?" As he snapped questions, he pulled his pistol from its holster and aimed it at my brother.

"No, no way! Are you really human, you creep?" Mother cried, seizing his arm.

My brother moaned like a wounded animal, producing only a strange repetitive sound: "Uh, uh, uh."

"Aren't you going to tell me the truth even now?" he shouted. He fired, hitting my brother's leg. Still my brother produced only the sounds of an animal.

"All right then. You're not going to confess then?" He shot again for three more times and demanded that my brother confess. He then shot my brother each time when he failed to comply with the shooter. He kept shooting at the lower part of my brother's body in an attempt to prolong his life. It was a cruel and miserable act. My brother fainted, collapsing in a pool of blood. Mother, who had been thrown to the ground, brought forth a heart-rending screech before she fainted.

"I won't kill you now before you have a chance to tell the truth," the officer shouted as he turned to leave.

The officer did not return again. In just a few more days, once again the world showed a different face. The North Koreans were no longer in command.

Although his gun shot wounds were not immediately fatal, my brother died in a few days as a result of his severe loss of blood. Lack of proper medical attention contributed to his death as well. To his last breath, he did not recover the ability to speak. Can I or will I, between earth and heaven, ever forget the scene of that heartless blood bath and my pent-up rancor toward God? However, I could not bring myself to close the door to life altogether. I met a man and fell in love with him; I bore children and loved them while Mother raised and loved her grandchildren and devoted her life to the Buddha.

Due to the severity of Mother's disturbance as she relived this awful scene while still under the anesthetic, she was left in a condition of long and utter exhaustion. She was bed-ridden, giving the impression of a small, weightless bit of paper that could be blown away with a mere sigh. Occasionally relatives or friends would visit her bedside. They would shake their heads seriously as if they had not seen the smallest sign of recovery in Mother. Some even broached the subject of a funeral, as if Mother could no longer hear. They tried to console us by recalling Mother's long and well-lived life, as if they were already in a house of mourning. We were not offended, and we did not contradict them. Except when Mother swallowed her spoon-fed, liquid diet or was given an injection by needle, she showed not the slightest hint of consciousness.

One day a friend of mine came to see Mother.

"Have you prepared her shroud yet?" she asked flatly, glancing at Mother.

"Why, no! Why would I do such an awful thing so soon?"

"Look at her! What about her gravesite then?" she persisted.

"Gravesite? Do I have to do that in advance?" I cried.

"Good Lord! Are you saying that you haven't done either one? Why, you're just too much!" my friend cried.

"What are you talking about?"

"Don't you see that you're a classic example of being a fake?'"

"'Daughter of nylon?'" I echoed blankly.

"You said it! You're pathetically inconsiderate. How can you be so nonchalant, especially since your mother has no son to look after such things for her? You're neglecting your duties."

I didn't mind my friend's accusations that I was a fake or a sham; still I pondered the truth, feeling a new sense of shame as I reviewed my efforts in Mother's behalf.

"We have a gravesite in our home town," I said apologetically.

"Where is that?" she asked.

"How can you ask? It's Gaepoong, near Gaesung."

"What good will it do you there? That's simply ridiculous. It's like trying to get a loan using as collateral a piece of land you left behind in North Korea." My friend continued to lash me with sharp words.

"But an ancestral burial ground carries with it a kind of tacit understanding. Mother would never be able to return there in her lifetime, but I'm sure she'd want to be buried there. Even though she hasn't expressed her wish openly, I just know it. It's a matter of family tradition. How could I then, knowing Mother's dying wish so well, buy a gravesite elsewhere? If she dies, then perhaps I'll feel differently. It won't be too late to buy a gravesite then. A grave, after all, is a house for the dead!"

As soon as I finished talking, I saw Mother open her eyes. Suddenly her face, which had been white as paper, was lit by her eyes. They were full of life and shining. My friend gave a faint scream and clutched my sleeve.

"Ho-sook's mother, I want to talk to you." Mother's voice was strong as she summoned me.

"Yes, Mother." I neared her bed cautiously. She took my hand in hers, which felt warm and strong. Not only did this unexpected touch astound me, but it also saddened me, although I was not sure why.

"Please don't buy a gravesite for me," Mother said. Her voice was as stern and poised as when she stated her commands to me as always in my childhood.

"You overheard us, Mother?" I asked nervously.

"I certainly did and I'm glad that I did. By the way, I meant to tell you this before. I'm going to tell you now, and I want what I tell you now to have the power of a final will. Please listen to my last testament carefully and honor my wishes accordingly. After I die, please do the same thing we did for your brother, no matter who might oppose it. Don't pay any attention to anyone no matter how hard they may try to sway you. I'm asking you to do this for me since you're the only one who can do it."

"As was done to brother?" I asked dumbly.

"Yes. Just like that. You haven't forgotten, have you?"

"Forgotten? How in the world could I?"

The pressure from Mother's hand was as firm as before when she was healthy. Furthermore, it made me feel her strong will and stark stubbornness just as when she dragged me over Dresser Rock Pass when she had taken me against my will from the countryside near Gaepong to Seoul.

The body of my brother was buried in a shallow grave at the head of the vegetable patch in the open field over Mooakjae Hill. It was a temporary burial without a proper ceremony, as if intended for a person who had fallen sick and died on a journey. It was the best Mother and I could do for him in the midst of the deserted city over which a state of near anarchy loomed. Within our limited power, that burial was the best alternative for him.

Seoul recovered its status as a capital city. As soon as the policy of cremation was imposed, Mother consulted us concerning cremation for my brother. My sister-in-law, who had rejoined Mother and me by then, insisted upon transferring her husband's body to the public cemetery. She wanted to have a grave by which her two fatherless sons could remember their father.

Mother had become quite dispirited after my brother's death as if she had been the major architect of his murder. Consequently, Mother tried in most instances to please her young, widowed daughter-in-law. However, this time Mother showed no sign of conceding to her daughter-in-law's tenacious insistence. My sister-in-law could not be at her husband's side when he died, and now faced a confrontation with her mother-in-law who was determined to have her son cremated, doing away with plans for a tomb. My sister-in-law may have been bitter and resentful of Mother's cold-hearted, arbitrary decision. However, she dared not contradict Mother and so yielded with quiet and tragic dignity to Mother's desire for cremation.

My brother's flesh was transformed into streaks of smoke and his bones into a fistful of powder. With Mother leading the way, we went to the bus station where we could obtain transportation to Kangwha Island. My sister-in-law and I followed in silence. We got off at the terminal on Kangwha Island. Mother kept asking passers-by until she found a place by the seashore where we could glimpse a tip of the land that leads to Gaepoong, the location of our ancestral burial site. Facing in the direction of the town, which was seen but could not be reached, Mother let a fistful of powder scatter in the wind. I did not see Mother as a weak woman, hiding her resentment in her heart and remaining stoic as she yielded to her fate. Rather, I saw her as brave soldier, girding herself for the challenge of the battlefield.

Mother attempted to confront a battle of enormous consequences with a mere fistful of dust and a puff of wind. To her, a fistful of dust and a puff of wind were not insignificant by any means. They were the only tools by which Mother could express her total disbelief in the existence of that abominable monster that had taken everything away from her after trampling her down: the separation between two Koreas, North and South. This was something Mother couldn't comprehend, let alone accept, not even in a thousand years.

Mother was asking me to do with her body as she had done with her son—the same thing and at the same place. She expected me to do it so she coul also become dust and wind.

Although more than thirty years had passed since then, was that really the only way to nullify the existence of the monster?

"I'm sorry, but I'm earnestly asking you to honor my last wish," Mother said, with her face distorted sadly, as if she were truly sorry that this final wish was the last legacy she could hand me.

Alas, I realized that I was left with no choice but to comply with her wish.

Mother is still bed-ridden.

MOMMA'S STAKE

PART THREE

Mother lived seven years after the accident. It was a quiet and grim seven years. At her advanced age—she was in her eighties—a fractured bone could very well have been fatal. To make matters worse, the fractured bone was her pelvis. In the last of several surgeries, a long, metal rod, like a knitting needle, was inserted to connect her pelvis to her thigh bone. The rod was instrumental in allowing her to walk to some slight extent, but her leg appeared to be three and a half inches shorter than before. After recovering from the surgery, Mother limped terribly, and due to the angle of the metal rod, it was impossible for her to sit on the floor, as is the Korean custom. She now had to sit in a chair, and she had no alternative but to sleep in a bed. Getting onto the bed was no easy process. She had to sit on the edge of the bed and then twist her upper torso backward and sideways in order to lift her legs to the bed. We were fortunate that by this time every household had flush toilets, so we didn't have to take care of linen odorous with urine and feces. If she'd had this accident at an earlier time, she would have had no choice but to go through the humiliation of wearing diapers. Her mind remained quite clear, so she would have been keenly aware of this humiliation.

"It could have been a lot worse," was the first remark Mother made upon returning to her oldest grandson's house following a lengthy hospitalization. We sensed that her remark wasn't, in any measure, merely an expression of gratitude because she'd survived, but a feeling of relief that she didn't need to impose upon others the chore of cleaning her soiled linen. Mother impressed me as being as fragile as a bit of discolored white paper that could be blown away by a single breath. I couldn't believe for a moment that enough warm blood was left within her to engender any really deep or galvanizing emotion.

Her grandchildren accepted her physical condition as something to be expected, conceding that she'd gone through several gravely significant surgeries at a very old age. They seemed to be convinced that she'd get her usual strength back before long, once her health was improved by tonics and nutritious food.

I was different. I was the only witness to Mother's awesome strength. I alone clearly remembered the almost superhuman intensity of her disorderly behavior, which I had to face with my own maximum strength, not unlike in a living hell. She was still under the influence of the anesthesia, and if I hadn't been a witness to it, I wouldn't have believed that she could possibly have acted the way she did. Her behavior was an expression of her thoughts, acted out with all her remaining might, in what she thought were the last moments of her life. Poor Mother had used up all her energy then and now was left only an empty shell, a shell in which I failed to find the Mother I knew.

After consulting with my nephews, we agreed to take turns caring for Mother. This seemed to be what my nephews desired. In spite of her effort to be not even as much of a burden to her family as a bit of white paper, Mother's mere existence became a burden indeed. I prepared nutritious foods laboriously and took them, along with invigorating tonics for the recovery of strength, to Mother when she stayed with my nephews. Although they cared for her as much as I did, I doubted that my young nephews and their wives would indeed offer food or medicine to Mother at the right time.

When Mother stayed with me, my oldest nephew brought Chinese medicine. He said that he'd paid a bonus to have it prepared at a pharmacy that specialized in Chinese medicine. He asked me over and over to pay undivided attention to giving it to Mother twice a day without skipping. I presumed from his concern that he must have wondered about me as I worried about my nephews. He was the second closest relative to Mother. I was the first. How dared he think that I'd be less devoted? While displeased by his lack of understanding, I admired him. Still I failed to administer the broth as directed. With a faint smile, which again reminded me of faded white paper, Mother refused to take this tonic, which was packed conveniently in the correct amount for each single dose. Mother said she'd take antacid for indigestion or anti-febrile for a common cold, but she wouldn't take anything simply because it was said to be beneficial to her body. Without attempting to argue, I yielded to Mother. She'd take proper medication for definite symptoms but refused any tonic for her body. I could understand her determination. I couldn't discuss this determination with her, but I was sure it was the same determination that helped me fathom her emotions. I couldn't ask her what she did with all those tonics we bought for her. Getting rid of the tonics my nephews sent overburdened me. By word of mouth, I'd found an old person who needed these tonics, and I sent them to this person and lied to my nephews, saying Mother took them all.

Mother ate the least possible quantity of food for her meals. Without bothering to ask her, I presumed that this slight consumption of food was adequate for her to keep the energy necessary to use the bathroom. I failed to tempt Mother, either with the nutritional value or the flavor of her food, to cross over the line she'd drawn for her daily consumption. Mother, however, was faithful to her exercise program every single day, twice a day, in the morning and in the evening, without being told. Mainly, she walked. While she stayed with me, Mother walked along the verandah, back and forth ten times at a slow pace. Except for her limping, Mother walked fairly well without the aid of her cane. Like her arrogance, her straight posture was intact.

From my verandah, we could see the senior citizens' pavilion. It would be time for the neighboring senior citizens to gather in the pavilion when Mother was ready to take her morning walk, and when she was taking her evening walk they would be ready to leave. Among these old folks, I saw a few who walked a lot worse than Mother. Among the elderly women who came to the pavilion each morning and went home in the evening, I saw a few with their upper bodies stooped over and their legs as big as the size of a normal, healthy person's waist. I couldn't tell whether their legs were swollen or their normal size. At times, Mother would gaze at them absent-mindedly as she stopped walking. *Was she being consoled? Or was she feeling sorry for the old ladies?* More than anything else, I hoped the old ladies who seemed to be worse off than Mother would encourage her to make an attempt to go outside.

One fine spring day, I got up the courage to ask Mother if she would like to go to the pavilion.

"Are you mad? Me? So that I can play *hwatu* with those old folks?"

Mother's passionless rage was as inhuman as a crisp white paper shivering violently in the wind. Although her tone of voice was as calm, the "are you mad" was so challenging and lingering that I felt as if a vise were squeezing my consciousness. An emotional reaction became impossible. I would never say such words aloud, but in my heart I was crying and exclaiming, "Ah, I can't stand the sight of you. Please go away. Go either to Seok's or Kyung-ah's house this instant!" Mother's effort to maintain a regular regime of exercise paralleled her self-imposed determination to consume a given portion of food at each meal. This was her way of maintaining enough motor skills and stamina to use the bathroom.

"Don't skip your walking exercise at home. At your age, if you skip even a few days, you won't be able to use your hamstring and that won't allow you to walk to the bathroom. Do you understand?" When Mother was ready to be discharged from her long hospitalization, the doctor in charge had emphasized this.

Mother applied herself to following her doctor's instructions to the very best of her ability. At the same time, she refused to consider going above or beyond his requirement. My patience was wearing thin at Mother's doggedness. I suppose no one could calmly accept having someone in the family whose sole purpose in life was to use the bathroom, even though that person carried no more bulk than a bit of white paper.

For seven years Mother never planted her feet to the ground except the times when, over a period of months, she traveled from her daughter's to her oldest grandson's home, and then on to her younger grandson's. Mother was incapable of bending her hip more than the slight angle of the bent rod which held her body together. Fortunately, my two nephews and I had cars that were able to transport her safely. This was not, however, an outing but a mere shifting from one locale to another. At the homes of her grandsons, who lived in single homes, Mother had never, not even as an empty gesture, put her foot outside the main gate. *We must recognize, once and for all, Grandmother's high self-esteem.* My nephews were astounded at Mother in this respect. Her grandsons seemed to think that their grandmother, who refused stoutly to show her limping leg to strangers, was toughing it out purely because of stubborn determination. My assumption was different from theirs. Mother had no curiosity whatsoever about the outside world. If I concluded that Mother no longer had a sense of determination, would I be considered a heartless daughter?

Mother understood clearly that connecting the pelvis and the thigh bone with a metal rod was intended to enable easy walking without a walker. My nephews and I were told by her doctor that Mother would have to learn to live with a certain degree of difficulty for the rest of her life, whatever its duration. She would experience some degree of discomfort, even though the surgery had been successful. We were exhausted by the distasteful task of cleaning her soiled linen during her long hospitalization, so the possibility of her walking again seemed like a miracle.

The fact that she could no longer squat on the floor seemed so insignificant to us as to be laughable. Each of her three caretakers lived either in an apartment or a western-style two-story house. The kitchens had dining tables, living rooms had sofas, and each bathroom had a commode. None of us saw any problem in buying an extra bed for Mother. Moreover, if she lived, how long could her life continue? Thinking of the short span of her remaining life made us generous. In the present pattern of our changing society, people regard taking care of their parents as nothing but a reluctant favor. How could we not be affected by this public sentiment? Therefore, Mother's sense of defeat in realizing the lack of freedom caused by the foreign agent inserted in her leg brought a poignant loneliness to her.

"How in the world? It seems like my plan to visit Mrs. Yee on Kangwha Island is totally destroyed." It was a soft lament from Mother, who'd become as helpless as a piece of wet paper, causing an acute sense of dejection and frustration. Her grandsons heard her, and their mouths twitched in an effort to suppress laughter. *Gee whiz, is that all she's worried about? Is her only concern that she can't visit the Yee's?* Her grandsons seemed to think that their grandmother was slowly becoming senile. Mrs. Yee was Mother's second cousin's daughter and from the same hometown as Mother. She'd married into the Yee family and was living now on Kangwha Island.

During the January 4th retreat from the attack of the North Korean Army, a number of people from Gaesung and Gaepoong sought refuge near the sea on Kangwha Island and had been living there ever since. People who were closely related to one another had built the village and lived there together. Whenever there were congratulations or condolences, they shared the news with one another, maintaining contact because they believed it was each family's duty to keep communication lines open between relatives. However, it was only those relatives on the island who strictly ful-filled this duty. The Seoul relatives made excuses, not only because of their hectic lifestyle, but also because their long-established relationships were either job or school related. These relationships were too varied and consuming for them to miss their rel-atives living in the countryside, even on special occasions. Such was the attitude of the city folk. Mother, in the middle, always paid extra attention to those on the island so that we might not offend them, since they, too, were our relatives.

If she had a reason beyond her control for not being able to attend either a wed-ding or a funeral service, Mother never failed to have her grandsons send a cash gift to the appropriate relative. If we showed our displeasure, Mother expressed herself with obvious vexation. "Please put up with it while I'm alive. After I die, they'll all be strangers to you. You wait and see!" Despite these ties, Mrs. Yee's family was the one for which Mother would leave Seoul like the wind for an outing. She'd spend a day or two there even if it was only an ordinary day—not necessarily a day of celebration or of mourning. In contrast, she'd never dropped in uninvited on me, her one and only daughter, and had never spent even one night with me, although we both lived in Seoul.

Such was Mother. She made a distinction between herself and a married daughter, considering me no better than a stranger. She kept a prudent, respectful distance between her daughter's families and herself. Mother didn't seem to mind a bit visiting her second cousin's married daughter, who was barely able to make ends meet finan-cially. Mrs. Yee had many mouths to feed, and farming got them by only by the skin of their teeth; consequently, she had to make floral-decorated straw mats all year round to supplement their meager livelihood. It was my understanding that, fortu-nately, the Yee couple were good-natured, simple, honest people and made Mother feel comfortable in their home. Whenever she returned from the Yee's, Mother praised them to the hilt. However, the closer she became in this relationship, the more she tried not to be indebted to them. She was well aware of this aspect of their rela-tionship. I could tell this from the gifts she bought to take to them when she visited, which were above and beyond Mother's means.

The Yee family lived in a village called Yangsan-myun on the northernmost coast of Kangwha Island. To enter the village, which was on the front line, you had to go through a checkpoint, informing the guards in detail of the household you were visit-ing and what kind of business you had with them. Then you would leave your regis-tration card at the post. Behind the house, there was a low hill, which was understood to belong to the Yee family. From the top, one had a panoramic view of the sea. On the horizon, the tip of North Korean territory came into sight.

Since the span of the sea between the land and the island appeared to be no more than the width of a river, it gave one a sense of the limited distance between himself and the opposite side, across the Han River. When I realized that across this short stretch of water, only a beckoning away, where we were not allowed to set foot, lay Gaepoong-kun, my home town, I'd be covered with goosebumps. But the distance appeared to be boundless when I thought of that place as the site of my brother's grave and Mother's pain. I sensed that Mother was trying to abstain from visiting the Yee's too often; yet, she visited there at least two or three times a year. The sole purpose of her visits, I found, was to reminisce by the sea and gaze from the hill behind the house over the horizon to the land which lay beyond.

Mother used to mutter in a low tone of voice, "You heartless ones, you unflinching ones!" as if she were totally defeated. It was unclear to exactly whom she was address ing these remarks. Everyone may have seemed hardhearted to her. Even her great-grandchildren looked at Mother with quizzical eyes whenever she mumbled this phrase.

Even though it had been more than three decades since my brother's ashes were scattered over that sea, Mother continued to visit the island. It gave pleasure to her unbending spirit to practice this ritual visit to her son's grave. We'd all become weary of Mother's piteous ritual. We wanted to be free from it. After she realized the limitations imposed by her injured leg, her biggest shock was in coming to grips with the fact that she could no longer visit the island and carry out this ritual. The Yee family lived in a conventional farmhouse, and needless to say the outhouse was located in the middle of the field outside the front gate. Every room had a chamber pot.

Suddenly one day, Mother could no longer come and go to the bathroom. After that day, she slowly died in one month. I was told about Mother's behavior while she was staying with her oldest grandson's family.

"Aunt, Grandmother is acting strangely. She no longer goes to the bathroom."

"What? She does her business without using the bathroom?"

Indeed, I sensed the seriousness of the matter. Mother was frighteningly fanatic about keeping herself clean. It might not be an exaggeration for me to say that keeping herself clean had become the purpose of her life. I rushed to see Mother and found her sleeping soundly. Just in case, I bought toddler's diapers and took them with me; fortunately, the largest size was a perfect fit for her. As I was fitting a diaper, I thought how gracefully her body had become thin. Her skin was light, clean, and her body was weightless. Even if she lacked control of her urine and feces for some time, I thought I might not have to worry about her getting bedsores since I saw no unnecessary flesh. Her body seemed to consist of skin and bones. Mother awoke from her heavy, death-like sleep and smiled weakly as soon as she saw me.

"My dear, am I dead or alive?" she asked.

At her preposterous question, I pinched slightly on the upper part of her hand as I answered that she was alive.

"Still?" Mother closed her eyes as she made a faint sound which was neither joy nor disappointment. However, she wasn't sleeping. Mother swallowed some juice and porridge, using a straw. I shook her and had her open her eyes and asked her who I was. Again, she smiled weakly and called me by my correct name. Her grandsons and granddaughters-in-law, who watched Mother in this state, seemed to have come to the cold conclusion that she might not die quickly. They decided among themselves that only one person at a time was under obligation to stay by Mother's bedside and watch over her. Being free of any ties, I was left out of the rotation they'd set up for this duty-bound task. I had a feeling they took it for granted that I'd tend to Mother at all times.

Mother wandered the borderland between sleeping and being half-awake all the time. The main job of caring for her was to offer, when she wasn't asleep, her liquid diet, taken through a straw, and to change her diaper in a timely manner. However, every once in a while, her eyes and expression would become shiny and bright in the twinkling of an eye, just as a sunray may suddenly shine through a tiny opening in the clouds. When such moments occurred, she'd not only recognize each member of the family who surrounded her bedside, but she'd also ask for any member not present. At times, she'd seem to see beyond reality, and this became a problem for us all. She'd look down at her own feet to an imaginary person and say, "Ho-bang, it's been a long time now," or she'd say, "Oh, you also came along! Who are you carrying on your back? Why don't you put the baby down and make yourself comfortable?" Sometimes, she'd make an annoyed face, complaining of a group of children running around her. My nephews and their families disliked this and even felt scared of Mother, who'd talk so innocently to empty space where no one stood.

Of the many names Mother mentioned, I was able to recognize only a few. For instance, Ho-bang, whom Mother often saw in hallucination, was only a hobo in my childhood who used to pass like the wind through our village in the countryside. The reason I still remembered his name was that I used to follow him with a group of urchins my own age. We'd tease him, calling him silly names, accusing him of having lice in his shirt and feces in his pants, and other things of an equally silly nature. These rude remarks were the only reason I could remember Ho-bang. He had no special ties to my family in any shape or form. Basing my assumption on this, I felt that the other people who appeared in Mother's illusions had also played only insignificant roles in the midst of her life's main story, where she'd been the major performer. They'd slipped by only on the periphery of her life. If that was the case, her memories of them seemed grossly odd, especially only now in the time of her decline.

In the whirlpool of her clouded consciousness, why, for pity's sake, when there were so many others in the main cast, did these mere "extras" pop into her head? Why now, when the curtain of a long life was about to be drawn down and each remaining hour was as precious as gold? I felt nothing either splendid or mysterious about the mystery of a human's consciousness. I was embarrassed to admit that I regarded one's consciousness as only a crude fabrication. Not only for Mother, but for the human race in general, Mother might now be acting her life's last and greatest performance. Mother might be performing these acts of trifles in an effort to carefully hide something that was preserved in the innermost chamber of her consciousness.

Indeed, the sense of anxiety I was experiencing had everything to do with my own tenacious consciousness, which held something steadfastly at the center of my being. *After I die, please do the same thing for me that I did for your brother. You're the only one capable of complying with my wish, ignoring any remarks to the contrary by anyone.* How could I possibly forget Mother's heart-rending request? It was not only her last testament, but also her expression of faith in me. After she made this request, Mother lived seven more years. However, she'd never repeated it to me again.

I pined for Mother to say something reasonably sensible, something not totally gibberish, before it was too late. Seven years ago when I told my nephews about Mother's wish, they didn't appear to be particularly attentive. They couldn't possibly have remembered it through all these years. My nephews were classic contemporary men whose largest concern and the source of their pride was to be as busy as bees. They had pathetic memories. Unless Mother repeated her request, or at least gave us a meaningful hint of her last wish, I had no confidence that I could uphold her faith in me.

However, Mother's condition, wandering between reality and dreams, deepened even more. To make matters worse, if and when she did say something, it became increasingly difficult to make any sense of it due to her stiff tongue and sheer exhaustion. The only thing I could barely make out, mainly from pure guessing, was either, "Am I alive?" or "Am I dead?" This inquiry stirred ripples such as are caused by skipping a stone across the water. In this solemn atmosphere where imminent death lingered, I was sorry to admit that they were pleasant ripples. Family members cackled as our emotional intensity loosened somewhat at Mother's nonsensical talk.

"Aunt, who in the world is Ho-bang?" my oldest nephew asked as he controlled his laughter. Although Mother had not mentioned Ho-bang's name for a few days now, my nephew asked about him abruptly.

"He was a hobo who wandered to our village when we used to live in the countryside. My word, I can't understand the old woman's senility. Why must she see Ho-bang out of the blue? It's beyond me!"

"Then Grandmother must be young, too," he said.

"Of course. That was more than a half-century ago. An ancient time!"

"Was Ho-bang handsome?" he asked.

"Handsome?"

Even before I could fathom what my nephew wanted to talk about, involuntary laughter slipped out. It may well have been the urchins' exaggerated teasing of him for having lice or dung. Nevertheless, his unshaped features were those of a beggar; and he was slow-witted. However, a sense of honesty had marked his character. He earned his keep by working hard, and that seemed to spare him from being treated like a beggar.

"In those days, I wonder if our grandmother had something going on with that guy Ho-bang!" My nephew was wily, and he grinned from ear to ear. If it were a joke, it was imprudent and made in the wrong place at the wrong time. Since his remark was based on such an irrational conjecture, it would be incongruent to take him down too offensively. Keeping that in mind, I was going to brush him off by discouraging such silly remarks. Surprisingly, my nephew was tenacious.

"I'm not talking nonsense, Aunt. Don't you find it rather strange? How many of our family have died before Grandmother so far? It isn't just her family I bet. Nearly all her close relatives or friends, I'm sure, have already passed away."

"So? What about it? If you live a long life, it's an inescapable fate. It's not Grandmother's fault!"

"Who said it's Grandmother's fault? I just said it's odd. That's all. Why must you be so high-strung, Auntie?"

"What is so 'odd' to you?" I asked.

"Don't you find it odd then? Why do you think Ho-bang, rather than any other close relatives or friends, comes from the other world to greet Grandmother?"

I was so flabbergasted at his remark that I was forced to burst at once into a repressed laugh. Does my nephew believe that Ho-bang has actually come to her as a messenger from the other world? I rejected my nephew's statement as I explained that Mother's gibberish was nothing but that—just gibberish!

Among the countless dreams that one dreams, it's extremely rare for anyone to dream something which really comes true. Moreover, that dream which we call prophetic may not be so. In our numerous dreams, we see either an acquaintance or a total stranger rather than a friend or someone we miss very much. As a result, a dream is meaningless and the subconscious cannot be trusted. Therefore, gibberish is no different than a meaningless dream. This I told my nephew.

"Aunt, I'm relieved to know that you don't interpret Grandmother's talk as more than gibberish," my nephew said as he finally returned to a serious state. Then and there he made it crystal clear that he'd regard Grandmother's wish, which had been uttered after her first surgery and had created a great fuss seven years before, as nothing but gibberish. At that moment, I realized that I'd been tricked by my nephew's roundabout reasoning. However, he was so stern and adamant that my spirit was dampened.

"That wasn't gibberish in any shape or form, don't you see!" I said feebly.

"I can't do anything about it even if it was her wish. I don't want to do as she said, and it's up to me!"

"Will you just listen to what you're saying? How can you possibly consider it a difficult task?"

"I didn't say it was difficult; I just said I don't want to do it," my nephew replied. "Are you telling me I ought to cremate Grandmother and scatter her ashes over the sea that washes ashore at my home town as she did for Father? Aunt, please don't even think about making this fuss ever again. What I don't like is that you and Grandmother are planning to repeat a ritual expressing indescribable rancor and a deep grudge which is inappropriate in this day and age. In Father's time, I suppose it was the only way and I concede that it must have been rather tragic. But if we carry out Grandmother's wish now, it will be nothing but a show. I also want to give her a normal funeral service as others do. I have to think about my social standing, and I must also act, as I always strive to do, with integrity. Also you must admit, I'm in charge of the mourning party."

"Yes, dear. Are you insinuating that I don't belong to this family because I'm married? Even if I'm the only child left who was born to Grandmother, you're going to completely ignore me. That's what you're saying, isn't it?"

Although I whined and carried on, even shedding a few tears, deep inside I felt light and cheery as if an aching tooth had been extracted. This sensation was completely unexpected on my part. I, too, didn't want to repeat that ritual again.

"Aunt, are you upset? Who would dare to ignore you, Aunt? Please don't be angry. I'll leave picking out a gravesite completely up to you."

"Is picking out a gravesite as commonplace as choosing a sweater? Can anyone select it?" I barked. Yet I didn't dislike my nephew's suggestion. The gravesite had, more or less, been decided. My nephew said that he had already investigated several sites in the cemeteries in the outskirts of Seoul where the transportation was convenient. He told me these places were already beyond full capacity and nothing could be found there.

"I think it's better to find a place where a relative is buried."

"You mean the cemetery called New World where your mother's grave is?"

The New World cemetery is a memorial park. Mother's daughter-in-law, who died before our uncommonly long-lived mother, was buried there. It was an impeccably ideal place, within a reasonable distance and accessible by good means of transportation. However, after having developed the hillock into gravesites and sold them to customers, the company had gone bankrupt and the president of the company had disappeared. Since this scandal, numerous presidents had come and gone. Due to this, the park suffered from poor management. As a result, the place had become a somewhat wild and ruined area.

"I'm not particularly crazy about the place," my nephew admitted, "but I have no other choice. The location should be convenient for the living. It's a difficult task to take care of a grave during the national holidays. What shall I do if Mother's and Grandmother's graves are in different locations? If that's the case, I'm afraid there's a possibility that one of the two might be left unattended."

"Will you listen to yourself? You've just insisted upon your right as the oldest descendant and now you're openly threatening," I said, glaring at him. Yet I admitted to myself that my nephew had said nothing that was incorrect from any angle. The only thing left for me to do then was to finalize our talk.

Although we discussed this matter for a long time right by Mother's bedside, nothing that resembled a miracle—such as Mother opening her eyes and insisting upon her own wishes—happened again.

My nephew had already phoned the head bookkeeper of the New World Cemetery Company, Inc. and made an appointment for us to meet him at the location. The New World Cemetery was located close to Il-Young off the suburban railway station. The office had only one lukewarm stove, heated by coal instead of petroleum, making its space bleak and cold. The cafeteria, which adjoined the office, was manifestly even more dreary and chilly. Dust-covered tables were pushed carelessly against the wall and chairs tumbled over in neglect here and there on the uneven cement floor. After my nephew and I opened the stove door wide, hoping for a little heat, we moved to the window and gazed blankly at the boundless, spread out graves along a stretch of hillocks which reminded me of variously sized billowing waves. Humanity's eternal sense of avoiding danger yet realizing its own inescapable fate—these philosophical thoughts wandered through my mind as I indulged in dismal fancies.

"Just looking at this wretched cafeteria, I can tell no gravesite is left to sell," my nephew commented after he opened the cap of the stove with an iron pick. Judging from his dire longing to show off his competence, it was safe to assume that a lot had already been sold to us, even if the transaction had been made only over the telephone. A short, middle-aged man in a gray duck-down jacket walked in, a biting wind blowing in at his back. My nephew pulled out his business card and introduced me to the man who presented himself as Manager Song. He offered no business card. He emphasized the fact that not even one lot was available which could be officially sold; however, he felt we had some connection because of my nephew's mother being buried there.

"I'm not sure whether you've visited other cemeteries, but I can assure you that no cemetery as good as this one can be found in any location nearby. After the first announcement of a public cemetery park system, we developed this area. As a result, wealthy people could buy a large space and decorate their graves with a fancy tapestry of lush landscapes and monuments. It's an excellent spot in terms of transportation and topography, facing Nojuk Ridge. So you see, this place compares to the place for graves for residents of the richest residential district, Apkujung-dong!" Manager Song explained.

Oh, my word! This place is like the cemetery for Apkujung-dong! Judging from everything about Manager Song, I conceded it would be useless for me to contradict him, and yet I couldn't help thinking that he was expressing himself too irrationally and thoughtlessly. I was disgusted that we had no choice but to buy a lot from a character like him. I thought Mother was right after all.

I didn't want to carry out Mother's wish, yet the sense of duty that I ought to comply with her wish still lingered obstinately at the bottom of my heart. I feared that I would never be free from this sense of obligation although I could avoid actually fulfilling her request. Perhaps this feeling had something to do with a sentimental attachment. Although I was afraid to carry out Mother's wish, there was a certain form of tragic beauty in complying with it. The attachment I felt to this tragic beauty caused me to blush in front of my nephew, who handled matters realistically and in a timely manner.

The stove was much warmer than when we had come in, but my nephew didn't give Manager Song time to warm himself in front of it. Instead, he hurried Manager Song to act.

"Well, let's go up there," my nephew urged. "We must make a quick decision."

"You brought your car, didn't you?" Manager Song asked. Without waiting for an answer, he walked quickly ahead of us toward my nephew's silver LeMans. The hilly road to which Manager Song directed us was extremely steep.

"Is there any place lower than this?" my nephew asked.

"Beggars can't be choosers; and if you are, let's not even bother to go! I had to whine and cry to the president for the lot I saved for you, mind you." Manager Song became unyielding. My nephew drove in silence. As we turned a curve that encompassed a hillock, a sweeping area was cleared and a flat parking lot came into view.

"Another parking lot here!" my nephew said, softening the gloomy expression on his face. He seemed to be greatly pleased to see the extra parking space there. Manager Song said the burial site was a short distance away as he pointed with his chin and suggested we walk from the parking lot. He pointed to a trail which was easy to walk but was too narrow for a car. "People have to carry the coffin from the parking lot!" my nephew murmured to himself. I was aggravated by his thorough practicality.

Before we walked far, the gravesite to which Manager Song was pointing came into view. However, it was situated near a cliff and I had no idea how we could use it as a gravesite.

"Good God!" my nephew cried. At this initial unkind reaction from my nephew, Manager Song beamed at him and then jumped down in a flash from the layered terrace. The place where he landed, needless to say, was someone else's gravesite. Manager Song took out a wooden measuring stick from his pocket and swung it in the air as he emphasized that if an embankment were built directly from the other side and the same were done from the back, encroaching on the roadbeds, at least six or seven *pyung* of flat space would be gained. "There are thousands of graves right here that were made possible by cutting down the slope and building embankments. Have you never seen a mountain destined to be a public cemetery?" Doctor Song's explanation had a greatly persuasive power. My nephew's expression softened.

"So be it! But don't you feel it's not quite right to encroach on part of the roadway?" My nephew omitted a phrase "in a moral sense" when he said this. All things considered, in my opinion it would be sheer comedy to talk to Manager Song about anything to do with a moral issue.

"Ah, that's our problem, not yours, sir. To be honest with you, this road right here, sir, its life is limited. We're going to sell every bit of it sooner or later piece by piece. You just wait and see!"

"Do away with the roadbeds?"

"Roadbeds? Doesn't it really belong to the president? Well, it's up to the owner of the property. Don't you think it's enough to have a main thoroughfare? What good will an extra road do anyway? Every space between graves is a pathway. To put it more bluntly, if I may, who'll complain even if one crosses over a grave? It's the living who talk a lot, not the dead!"

Manager Song spoke with deep emotion, and my nephew seemed to conclude the matter right then and there. He asked how long it would take for them to complete a grave about 8 *pyung* in size. Manager Song said it would take a fortnight, mentioning the difficulty of finding labor, but my nephew warned him sternly to cancel the project altogether if he could not complete it in five days.

"Judging from your remark, the person who's to be buried here must be fighting for life now. Anyway, if you feel that strongly, I have no choice but to put you first on the list."

Manager Song, who had thus hastily concluded, brought up Nojuk Ridge again, fearing that we might, because of some whim, change our mind. With his finger he pointed out the crest which faced us directly in the distance and reminded us that it was Nojuk Ridge. He then said over-confidently that the vicinity of this gravesite was the only spot in this cemetery which faced the crest directly. In haste, we decided to purchase the site before he reminded us once again about the rich, which would make us feel embarrassed.

As we walked back to the car my nephew informed me that he bought 8 *pyung*, paying 100,000 *won* per *pyung*. He added that he wanted to buy more space but was told they had a regulation which limited a private grave to no larger than 8 *pyung*. I knew it was unnecessary to mention the issue, but I figured that he'd said it deliberately so that Manager Song would hear him. I was also greatly doubtful that they could possibly find 8 *pyung* at the site we were purchasing. My greatest doubt, however, was whether I had any need to find a grave for Mother. The breadth of the sea between Kangwha Island and Gaepoong-*kun* is as narrow as that of the Han River. Mother's pain itself became a warm yearning which flowed through my body. I slowly closed my eyes. My nephew rejected the idea of participating in my desire to dissolve Mother's rancor, and I yielded to him. Was it right for me to concede, to yield to him?

When we returned to the office, another problem sprang up. Manager Song emphasized repeatedly that 800,000 *won* covered solely the eight *pyung* gravesite, including no part of the expense of the gravestone, the burial fee, or any landscaping such as sod. After he received the payment from my nephew, Manager Song gave him a receipt for only 500,000 *won*. We turned pale, but Manager Song didn't blink an eye. In his calm voice, Manager Song explained that 100,000 *won* per *pyung* was quoted by present market value. He said it had been different when the site lay where the sale of lots had already been completed quite some time ago. However, under the present circumstances, when a person who is in charge and a person whose family member is to be buried have reached an agreement and the person in charge manages to find a spot for a gravesite by a stroke of luck, the profit should be shared equally between the owner of the property and the person in charge. He added that this was a customary practice. He was so sly that we were speechless as we stood there.

"Are you with me?" Manager Song asked rather impatiently as if he were bored stiff.

On the way back home, my nephew seemed terribly deflated. His fallen countenance mirrored his dejection.

"In a way I'm glad you didn't argue with him since we had no other choice. Anyway, why were we so naive? I think you could have bargained a little!" I said with extreme caution, trying to show my support.

"Why, Aunt, you said it a long time ago! It's not right to bargain when it comes to the price of a gravesite or a shroud." My nephew's tone was decidedly blunt and disrespectful.

"Oh, my word, listen to you! I know it's said that people blame their ancestors for their own mistakes. So, you're blaming me, aren't you? Since when did you listen to your aunt so well?"

"Forget it, Aunt. I'm sorry." As he drove along looking straight ahead, his stiff face reluctantly softened a bit. I sensed that he feared more harsh words might come out of my mouth if he didn't apologize, so I favored him with a slight, reluctant smile.

Every day my nephew prodded Manager Song over the phone about the speedy completion of a gravesite. His pressure on the matter sounded to me as if he were hastening Mother's death, and it vexed me. However, I was stoic about it, fearing that I might be blamed for something again.

My nephew was right again.

It took ten days for Manager Song to give us his pompous call inviting us to inspect the completion of an ample 8-*pyung* gravesite and then buy him a drink. As if Mother had waited for the right moment, she passed away then. Strangely, I couldn't shed any tears. There's an old saying that a daughter's wailing reaches the other world, so I should have cried. Since I didn't, there was no wailing at the home of the bereaved family. Everyone who came to pay last homage to the dead made the remark that it was a propitious mourning, thus saving face for the non-wailing family.

On the contrary, most of Mother's relatives from Kangwha Island arrived late, but wailing appropriately. Especially Mrs. Yee wailed most poignantly. At her lamenting, the entire family gazed at her austerely. I tried to comfort her, but ended up crying with her. It was the first time I cried after Mother died. We sobbed together, locked in each other's arms. I felt as though true emotion, deeply-felt sorrow for the loss of the person behind the folding screen, bound our two separate bodies into one.

There was an eighty-year-old person among the relatives from Kangwha Island who came to pay respects to Mother. According to Korean reckoning of the clan, his forty-year-old grandson, who accompanied him, was like a great-grandson to me. When I thought of the fact that this middle-aged man was like a great-grandson to me by Korean concepts of descent, I couldn't help but laugh. I was reminded of an old saying that an undesirable relative always seems to belong to a higher generation of the clan.

The old man made a short wail by custom and was received at the wine table immediately thereafter; he then called for the head of the mourning group and asked where he had arranged the burial ground for Mother. My nephew replied that Mother would be buried at the New World Cemetery. At that, the old man cupped my nephew's hand passionately and said, "Thank you, thank you very much. What do you know of our clan? A very prominent family! We had tens of thousands of *pyung* of fertile rice paddies and vegetable fields at Poongduk. We even held a mountain area of tens of *jeongbo* [approx. 2.5 acres]. When all the family congregated during a memorial service to the ancestors during each season of the year, nearly the entire town of Poongduk went through a large commotion. Yes, our family was blessed and prosperous. Such a family fled to the South during the war and faced some hardship, and some relatives made this an excuse to cremate. The number has increased considerably and I am very annoyed. Now that you, my dear younger brother, tell me that you are not following suit, I am so grateful!"

The old man lamented as he recalled this and that family in Seoul who had cremated their parents. The old man, who had only a few remaining teeth, pronounced *wha-jang* [cremation] as with an extra syllable so it wouldn't sound like *whan-jang* [crazy].

"Country folks like us may be poor, but we are not *whan-jang*. So please rest assured," the old man's grandson said nervously, unable to continue listening to the old man. Then he explained bluntly that his grandfather was senile. The grandson must have known that it wasn't true that our family was uncommonly wealthy in our hometown. Our family lived like scholars, but most of them led modest lives. Among our clan, there were quite a few families who were poverty-stricken. Later, Mrs. Yee told me that after he was struck with senility, the old man would habitually climb the hill behind the house and gaze at the sea. He would then tell people haughtily that all the land which the hill overlooked belonged to him.

The village where my own family used to live was located inland, but the Poongduk village of the old man, my nephew by descent, could be seen from Kangwha Island. The grandson who mingled with the young people later made the harsh remark that all the old men like his grandfather must die if unification were to be realized. My old-est nephew didn't dare to agree openly with the grandson; however, he grinned as he exchanged meaningful glances with him. I interpreted my nephew's expression as say-ing, "Yes, you're absolutely right. An old man spouting hot air like that must surely die before we can accomplish anything!" This sign of agreement was offensive to my eyes, and in my mind I said, "All right then, have it your way. The generation of ran-cor is dying one by one now, and you can go ahead and take care of everything!" However, I showed no sign of these inner thoughts.

It was warm on the day of Mother's funeral, but I was concerned about the traffic due to heavy snow the previous night. I knew it wouldn't be that difficult driving through the major streets or highways as the sun rose and its finger touched the snow. However, when I thought of those steep slopes leading to the gravesite it made me dizzy. When I remembered how mother dislked snow, I even entertained the idle thought that the heavy snow of the night before might be an expression of Mother's strong will not to be buried in the mountains. This unpleasant thought drove me to an anxiety attack.

I couldn't change anything at this juncture. Regardless of my uneasiness, every pro-cedure was going smoothly at the appointed time, and there was no one who showed any sign of nervousness or anyone who expressed a single word of the concern that I was experiencing. The snow seemed to brighten the memorial service which usually conjures up an atmosphere of solemnity and sadness. *You really know nothing, children. You really don't! I hope nothing will happen for your sakes.* I talked silently to myself. I couldn't tell whether I was hoping something disastrous would happen or was just overly worried. I was tormented by this continuous emotional roller coaster.

Fortunately, it was a weekend and the hearse snaked through downtown streets at a fast speed. As we came out to the suburbs, the panoramic view of field and moun-tain was covered with a much cleaner and warmer snow than that of the city, creat-ing an image of a totally different world. I saw no problem ahead for this caravan of cars driving on a snowy road. I worried that the hearse and the cars behind it were driving a little faster than I would have liked; nevertheless, traffic flowed smoothly.

Our family made a temporary stop in front of the office; women unloaded pre-cooked food they had brought with them and put it in the dining room. They also left special instructions for the lunch and agreed for three young women to stay there. Friends of the chief mourner went to the office to make sure that there was no prob-lem in the preparations for the burial. After that, we resumed our journey.

The hearse struggled along up a steep slope when it panted and then made a sud-den stop and went into reverse involuntarily. I heard a sharp shriek from it. It was a scream of concern for the safety of sedans following the hearse. An imaginary article in the newspaper flashed through my head: a dead woman was responsible for killing several people in a deadly accident on the way to the burial site.

Fortunately, since the hearse was going up at a snail's pace, leaving a considerable space between it and the next car, it was able to make a stop without any particular incident. The driver, however, came out and told us that it would be dangerous to drive up further. Young men came outside and tried to clear the snowy trail with a shovel, but the driver seemed unimpressed by their effort. My heart pounded as I was gripped with this omen that something awful would surely happen then and there. I closed my eyes, locked my hands, and began to pacify Mother. *Mother, please try to let go of your rancor now. What does it matter where your flesh and bones are buried? You know, I really wanted to comply with your wishes at any cost, but what was I supposed to do when the young people didn't want to carry out your desire? I had to go along with them. I hadn't sufficient talent to win them over. In reality, who knows but that they may be right?* I prayed tearfully in silence with a child-like heart—that of the little girl who used to cling to the hem of her mother's long skirt.

The hearse started to move again. I heard people murmuring in the car and realized that it was not my prayer that caused the hearse to move but bribery. At first my two nephews didn't fully understand the driver, so they had their friends clear the snow enough for the cars to move on. However, one of their experienced friends tipped my nephew off that it wasn't the hearse that was giving the driver a problem. He wanted money, the friend said. So the driver got the money. After that, the driver continuously asked for more money, and after much bribery Mother was safely buried. My nephew and their friends were skilled wheeler-dealers.

I visited Mother's grave three days later and saw by her grave a stake bearing her name. I was told that the permanent gravestone would be ready in about a month. As if drawn by a magnet, I was pulled to the stake where her name was written in Chinese characters. It was the first time I'd read her name thoughtfully, giving meaning to each of the characters. It was a mysterious thing. I felt as though Mother, with soft and gentle whispering, was soothing away the self-blame that still lingered in the deepest chambers of my heart. *Daughter, it's all right. It's okay. What difference does it make where my earthly body is laid? Any place is all right. Don't you see? Whatever place you and my grandsons prepared for me is my sleeping bed!*

During her lifetime Mother was an aloof person, although she stressed being clean and tidy. She'd never been warm or friendly, but her name, given to her so long ago, now became a comfort to me.

In Chinese characters, Mother's first name was "*Ki*" meaning "body," and her middle name was "*sook*" meaning "sleeping."

Since my childhood I'd believed her that the Chinese characters for her name were the same as the more common characters for the word "clean."

ABOUT THE AUTHOR

Wan-suh Park was born in 1931 in Gaepoong-kun, Kyunggi-do Province, North Korea. She spent her early childhood in the countryside, and attended Seoul National University until the outbreak of the Korean War.

In 1970 her novel, *The Naked Tree,* won the annual literary contest sponsored by the newspaper *Dong-ah Daily.* Since her debut in the literary world, Ms. Park has written numerous novels, short stories, essays, and children's stories, many of which have received the acclaim of literary critics.

In 1980, Ms. Park received the highly coveted Korean Literary Writers Award for her novella, *During Three Days of Autumn.* She was a recipient of the Fifth Yee Sang Literary Award in 1981. Ms. Park has traveled throughout Europe, the United States, and India under the sponsorship of the Korean government.

In 1990, Ms. Park again received an award from the Korean People's Literary Association, sponsored by the Korean Culture and Arts Foundation. The book for which she won this award was *The Unforgettable.*

Ms. Park anow lives and writes in Seoul and lectures extensively worldwide.

ABOUT THE TRANSLATOR

Hyun-jae Yee Sallee was a recipient of the 1989 Translation Award sponsored by the Korean Culture and Arts Foundation (KCAF) in Seoul, Korea. Her translations have appeared throughout the United States, Canada, England, Australia, and Korea. White Pine Press previously published *The Snowy Road,* a collection of stories translated by Ms. Sallee. Her most recent translation was published by Cornell University Press. She was a 1995 recipient of a grant from the Daesan Foundation of Seoul, Korea and a 1999 recipient of a grant from KCAF..

Ms. Sallee is presently employed at Walt Disney World in Orlando, Florida.